COMET Dust

An Apocalyptic Chiller
Based on Real Propehcy

3rd Edition

*It will be a punishment greater than the
deluge, such as one will never have seen
before. Fire will fall from the sky and will
wipe out a great part of humanity, the
good as well as the bad, sparing neither
priests nor faithful. The survivors will find
themselves so desolate that they will envy
the dead.*

*Apparition of Our Lady
Akita Japan (1973)*

Misty Moon Media

Comet Dust

3rd Edition © Copyright 2018 by C. D. Verhoff

Published by Misty Moon Media

ISBN: 9781720193760

1st Edition © Copyright 2016 by C. D. Verhoff
2nd Edition © Copyright 2017 by C. D. Verhoff

For additional information about this book or the author visit the World of C.D. Verhoff website:

http://cdverhoff.blogspot.com

The main category of the book—Christian Fantasy & Science Fiction. Other categories—Apocalyptic, Catholic Eschatology, Coming of Age, Dystopian, Paranormal, Suspense.

Misty Moon Media is the private imprint of C.D. Verhoff

For sparking my interest in the mysteries beyond the veil, I dedicate this book to you, Mom.

Other Novels By C. D. Verhoff

The Wish Thief

Resist the Machine: Avant Nation, Book 1)

Escape the Machine: Avant Nation, Book 2)

Red, The First

Emerge: The Galatia Series, Book 1

Seeker: The Galatia Series, Book 2

The comet arrived a year-and-a-half ago, breaking apart upon hitting the atmosphere. One piece struck Asia, triggering earthquakes, setting off firestorms, sending a plume of debris up into the air. The other chunk landed in the Arctic Ocean, flooding the coastal regions with massive tsunamis. North America was spared a direct hit, but no place was left untouched. Due to the dust blanketing the planet, and the subsequent reduction of sunlight, drought and famine are spreading around the globe. The experts are scrambling to come up with a fix, but a growing consensus believes that humanity is doomed.

Chapter 1

I'm Gina Applegate, a 21-year-old business major with a job at the mall. In my spare time I vlog about what it's like to come of age during a time of escalating violence, political upheaval, and natural disasters. Though most of my videos are just me and my friends goofing around between classes, or catching a college baseball game like we are today, I'm always on the lookout for something deeper I can share with my small band of internet followers. Overhead, the setting sun and rising moon share the sky, but their combined efforts aren't enough to clear away the dusty gloom. The baseball diamond, the campus grounds surrounding it, and the sprawling city beyond resemble a sepia photograph in shades of brown. Kylie Huang, my roommate, has joined me on the fourth row of metal bleachers. We huddle together beneath a fleece blanket, cheering on the home team as if everything is perfectly peachy.

I take out my phone, aim it at an attractive young woman with hazel eyes and fringed golden brown hair—me—and talk into the camera. "Dear Followers, there was the Baby Boomers, Generation X, the Millennials, and then there's us—the Generation of Fading Light. In the wake of Comet Yomogi, crops are failing all over the world, but we continue to play ball and plan for the future as if we still have one.

1

Sometimes I think it would be easier to drop out of school, like so many others already have, and wait for the end to come. So, why don't I? I'm not sure, but maybe it has to do with my belief that hope is our greatest natural resource …"

A tug on my sleeve interrupts my profound insights, which I'm sure Gandhi himself would have envied, if only he had thought of them. My dainty, yet freakishly strong, roommate grabs at my camera phone.

"Stop that, Kylie," I complain. "You're making the video go all wiggly."

"Why don't you film something more interesting than your face for a change?" she suggests. "Point it over there." She tries to guide the lens toward the baseball diamond. I resist her efforts and pan out so she appears on the screen seated next to me. Kylie is willowy, darkly beautiful, and generous with her opinions. She gives the viewers her customary wave and greeting. "Hey, y'all. Hi, y'all. How y'all doing?"

My followers, all 252 of them, are already well-acquainted with the irreverent Kylie. She needs no further introduction. On her insistence, I turn the lens back toward the baseball field. The grass hasn't greened-up this spring. Instead, a sea of brown weeds and mud spreads out before us. Zooming in, I capture slivers of dead grass and loose candy wrappers wildly circling the pitcher's mound.

"Lookie here, folks," I address my followers. "We got ourselves a dust devil."

After it calms down, I angle the camera over to first base. "That hot stud with the broad shoulders and goatee is my boyfriend, Jerome Miller." I shift the camera over to home plate where the batter is doing a couple of warm-up swings, then back to first where the runner is boldly inching toward second. The pitcher doesn't appear to know what's going on, or so it seems, until he hurls the ball toward first. Jerome snags it out of the air and sweeps it down, but the referee says, "Safe!"

I yawn and stop recording to watch what I've captured so far. As I'm reviewing my video blog, I add a title and a few captions, preparing to download it to my JustSharing account. If a channel like Dogs Eating Gross Things can clear over 5 million dollars a year, why not my vlog? So far I've earned a whopping $1.51 on all my videos combined. A girl's gotta start somewhere, I suppose.

Unfortunately, due to a solar flare, the web has been down for the last 24 hours. This better not be a repeat of the last flare. Communication systems across the planet were out for a whole week. I lost ten followers. It was horrible.

As I return the phone to its sequined clutch, a frenzied cawing turns my attention to a murder of crows circling above the stands. Six of them land in the pea gravel around the bleachers. They're pecking and clawing at each other over a dead bird—another crow—raising a ruckus. The biggest crow drives the others off. The smaller ones hungrily eye the prize from a safe distance. The victor pulls off pieces of sinew and shamelessly gulps them down.

"That's nasty," Kylie comments, watching a huge flock of them continue to fly in from the east. "I hate crows."

My eyes roam back to Jerome. He's an arrogant ass who would sell his soul to make it to the major leagues, but he's generous when he wants to be, and handsome even when he's acting like a dickhead. We've been an item since the campus Christmas party. I was four or five drinks in, feeling good, when he showed up strutting around. Our relationship sprouted from a mutual appreciation of beer, sex, and baseball.

To be honest, I only pretend to like the baseball. There's a lot of dead space between the action, and the metal seats are uncomfortable. I tolerate the boring games because the team's after-parties are a blast.

A group of five or six students are sitting one level down from us. The guy smack in front of me was in my cost accounting class last year, and he's in my business ethics course this semester, but I can't think of his name. His looks and deep voice remind me of the big guy who plays the brother on that old sitcom, *Everybody Loves Raymond*. He goes out of his way to talk to me in class, but it always feels awkward. Despite my wildest hope that I'll escape his detection, he turns around as his face lights up in recognition.

"Well, hello there, Gina," he says with a goofy grin. "I didn't see you back there." He offers me a metal thermos. "Would you like a cup of hot cocoa?" Proudly holding up a sandwich bag full of little white puffs in his

3

other hand, he gives it a shake. "Marshmallows are harder to score than crack these days, but I'm happy to share."

"That's very nice of you, Robert, but no thank you."

"The name's Zach—Zachary Lombardi."

"Oh, sorry." I feel my cheeks flush with embarrassment. "That's what I meant to say, Zach."

"No need to apologize." He waves his hand over his face. "It's a forgettable mug."

He turns back around to watch the game, making me feel like a jerk.

"What a dork," Kylie whispers and rolls her eyes at the back of Zach's head. She is shivering beside me, holding a paper cup, pretty much complaining about everything as she always does. "This coffee tastes like dirt, and it's friggin' cold out here." She sets the cup down on the bench beside her to snuggle deeper into the blanket. "Why do I always let you drag me to these stupid games? I should be studying for my discrete math test or finishing my paper on the future of biochemical nanocomputing."

"I'm glad I'm a business major," I reply. "Just hearing you talk about your classes makes my head want to explode."

"Are you finally admitting I'm your academic superior?"

Kylie makes like she's kidding, but I have seen her intellectual swagger in action. She thinks her brain is a gift to the engineering world and that business degrees are for dummies. Knowing how to push my roommate's buttons, I tease her back.

"A degree only means you know stuff," I explain. "Superiority is when you control the people who know said stuff."

"That makes absolutely no sense."

"It will in a few years when you're pecking away on a keyboard like a chicken, or whatever it is that you computer engineers do, and I'm up in my plush office deciding whether to finance or cut your latest project." Kylie snorts with incredulous laughter, but I continue to share my little fantasy. "In the real world, the scientists work for the business majors. That makes me your superior."

"Dream on."

In the space of my sigh, the playful mood downshifts. Hearing our big plans aloud, knowing my head is full of stars that will probably never shine, I've gone and depressed myself. When will I learn it's best not to look too far ahead?

Kylie reaches into her winter coat and pulls out an item she usually keeps hidden. It's her switchblade with the yellow paisley handle. I send her a look of disapproval. If a girl is going to risk incarceration for carrying a weapon, might as well make it a gun. I don't understand women who refuse to arm themselves properly in this age of record crime rates. As for me, I'm always packing.

"Oops," she says, returning the blade to the inside of her coat. "Wrong item." She fishes around in her pocket to trade it for a matching paisley flask. Kylie untwists the cap and pours the clear contents into her cup. Wordlessly, she hands it over to me. I tilt the flask back and swig deeply. The burn spreads down my throat, sending warmth through my body. Continuing to tilt my head back, I find myself longing for the blue horizons I enjoyed as a child. Sadly, the sky hasn't looked that way for a decade. Even before Yomogi's arrival, back when I was in elementary school, due to a fast and furious world war that began when Syria dropped a nuke on Israel, the earth began to take on a darker shade. We thought the world would end, but luckily the war was short-lived. Some nations fell completely out of existence, but most of them limped on.

During my high school years, the environment began to make a comeback. Employment was on the rise. Hope was in the air after graduation. Then the comet came. They're saying there won't be a summer this year. We're not going to bounce back this time. My eyes wander to the town beyond the campus, falling on the church steeple in the distance, specifically the golden cross at the top. When I was younger, I never questioned the goodness of God. The endless string of catastrophes has made me a lot more cynical.

Kylie comes from a family of atheists. Living with her and hearing her scoff whenever the topic of religion comes up has increased my doubts. With all the different beliefs out there, and people swearing their own religion is the only one with the correct answers, it's hard to sort the truth from the lies. I was raised a Catholic until age thirteen. After my father died and my mom remarried, we switched to my stepfather's religion, New Apostolic Third Assembly. Under either set of beliefs, all I saw was a mountain of unanswered prayers, so I decided to skip organized religion all together. Don't get me wrong, I'm a fan of Jesus. If everybody followed His teachings the world would be a better place. Love God and love each other. Easy as toast.

Unfortunately, organized religion has convinced people that getting into heaven is so complicated that they'll never figure it out on their own. The fear of worshipping Him wrong is what keeps them showing up for church to fill the collection baskets. That, and it's a safe place to make business and social connections. Not that I'm judging anyone. If others draw comfort from all the arbitrary rules, or look at church like a country club, that's their prerogative. Speaking for myself, the rules get in the way of my relationship with God, so I prefer to go it alone.

"The haze is light today," Kylie says absent-mindedly, her eyes scanning the horizon. "It's weird to see the moon out this time of day." I turn around and glance upward, noting the two celestial orbs glowing white through the ever-present brown film in the atmosphere. It's rare to see the sun and the moon in the sky together, so I capture the event with my camera. Before I can comment on the event for my followers, Kylie proceeds to point across the horizon at a distant skyscraper. "I can actually see the America Tower."

"Professor Langley says the haze symbolizes the clouding of America's collective intellect," I reply as the batter swings and misses. "Social reform has been moving backwards at the speed of light for the last nine years."

"At least we're not France," she says. "The way its government is trying to revert back to a monarchy is just crazy. Somehow we got on the subject of politics and religion during my circuits class. Dr. Jenkins was saying the comet was the final nail in the coffin of scientific advancement. He's upset about the way young people are turning to old superstitions for solutions, dropping out of college and life in general, when they should be looking to the sciences."

"Isn't he the prof who passed out donuts to celebrate the beheading of the pope by the Neuists?"

"That was Professor Kirchner," Kylie replies. "She was merely observing the symbolic decapitation of Christianity."

"Whatever her intentions were, passing out donuts was an insult to the Christians in your class."

"I say, let them be insulted. More people have been murdered in the name of religion than for any other cause."

"And we all know the benevolent Neuists would never hurt a fly," I reply sarcastically.

"Don't get on your soapbox, Gina."

Too late. My mind is already sifting through the data. Basically, the Neuists are an offshoot of Communism. In theory, the goal of Neuism is to create a peaceful society where nobody has more than anyone else. All material goods and services are shared equally. In order to achieve this kind of harmony, everyone must share a common morality. Under Neuism, morality is determined by a committee of twenty-four men and women from a variety of academic disciplines. Citizens are required to hand over everything they own to the government. This includes land, income, and homes. In turn, the government divvies it back out to the people so that everyone receives an equal portion. It's nice in theory. Of course, that's not what actually happens. Those in power take the best of everything for themselves, leaving only scraps for the common people. Making matters worse, according to the Neuist philosophy, the populace must be taught that the government is the final authority on all matters. Therefore, anyone who believes in a power higher than the government becomes an enemy of the state.

It's difficult to comprehend why anyone would vote such a group into power. Then again, it's not. After the Muslim extremists caused so much trouble in Europe, and started World War III, Neuism's ban on all religion looked like the only logical solution. Despite the pope's warning the ideology was an affront against human dignity that would lead to tyranny on an unprecedented scale, Christianity had already fallen by the wayside in Europe, so only a handful were listening. Most of the people considered themselves non-religious. Therefore, they wrongly assumed the ban wouldn't affect them and didn't see the more sinister implications.

The Neuists began to sweep the elections. As soon as they took control of the government, their "zero tolerance of religion" policy was put into effect. Inevitably, this led to zero tolerance of any behavior or thinking the government saw as a threat. Now it has gotten to the point that men are afraid to gather together for a game of poker for fear they will be accused of plotting against the government.

I did a research paper on the rise of Neuism back during my freshman year, so I'm practically an expert. It's one of the few subjects I'm more knowledgeable about than Kylie, and she knows it. That's why she doesn't want me to get on my *soapbox*.

"The Neuists have stolen Europe from underneath its citizens," I pontificate as the batter knocks the ball way out to right field. The outfielder looks like he has it, but the ball bounces out of his mitt. Turning my attention back to Kylie, I continue the conversation. "The Neuists have taken control over the banks, the businesses and schools. Children are being indoctrinated with the party rhetoric. They're taught the government is God and not to be questioned."

"You're clearly confused," Kylie retorts. "Neu is a political group, not a religion."

"Don't kid yourself. It's the old religion of Communism packaged under a new name."

"Communism is not a religion either," she points out.

"My sociology professor defines religion as the set of beliefs that guides a person's thoughts and actions. Therefore, it's impossible NOT to have a religion. Neuism is just another organized religion with the motto *convert or die*. As for me, no man-made institution is going to tell me who I can or cannot worship."

"About that. Who do you worship exactly?" Kylie inquires. "You've never been clear on that."

"I believe in an Intelligent Designer."

"Like in Jesus?"

"Possibly."

"I see. Did the Designer make a heaven and a hell?"

"Of course."

"How does the *Designer* determine who goes where?"

"A person would have to be really bad to go to Hell—like a murderer, child molester, or a country music fan," I say, repeating something I read on a T-shirt a few years back. "It doesn't really matter what name you call god here on Earth because as long as you try to be a good person, you'll learn the Designer's true name when you get to heaven."

"That doesn't sound right to me."

"You're an atheist. What do you know about God?"

"Truth is my God," Kylie retorts with her usual superior tone.

"What's that supposed to mean?"

"It means that God is a formula like $E = mc^2$. You can't alter the formula on a whim and expect to find the correct solution," Kylie says in her condescending way. "If the Buddhist follow the Truth, you're not going to get to heaven by following the teachings of Islam. If Islam is the Truth, you're not going to get to heaven by following the teachings of Christ. Personally, I think the Truth is unknowable."

"I thought Truth was your God."

"Hence, the reason I'm an atheist." Feeling one of Kylie's anti-religion rants coming on, I roll my eyes in annoyance, but that doesn't stop her. "Since the time human beings first became cognizant of their own mortality, people have been coming up with elaborate lies to ease their fears of death. Overtime, these lies became known as *religion*."

"Not this again."

"Take the Catholic Church, for example. It's based on a faulty formula that a god became a man, died, rose from the dead, ascended into heaven, and now the pope rules on Earth in his place. It's hard to imagine that anyone in this day and age can still believe in such nonsense, but the world will always have mindless sheep willing to follow anyone with a shepherd hook."

"Screw you," I say, not hiding my offense. "I used to be Catholic, but was never a mindless sheep."

"I didn't mean *you*, obviously—because you were smart enough to leave."

"Most of my family is Catholic—are you calling them stupid?"

"You're twisting my words. That's not what I meant."

9

A crack of the bat is a welcome diversion from our heated discussion. The ball pops straight up, making it an easy play for the catcher. He tears off his mask and catches it on the way down.

"Out!" shouts the ump.

I dutifully clap. Kylie stands up, saying she needs a refill of 'liquid dirt'. I see through her excuse to exit the uncomfortable conversation. Good. It will give both of us a chance to cool down.

The two of us are like sisters. We argue, borrow each other's crap without asking, and then promptly forgive each other. The subjects of religion, politics and Phillip West—a douche bag we unknowingly dated at the same time last year—are sore spots. I need to be more mindful about avoiding them.

Glancing up at the scoreboard, I see it's—2:58 p.m. It's only the first out of the third inning. I hate wasting the day playing the role of a dutiful girlfriend supporting her man. With Kylie gone, and nothing else to distract me, I return my attention the game. The batter hits a ball straight toward Jerome. He catches it in his mitt, then quickly throws it to the catcher, who outs the guy sliding into home plate.

Somewhere in the distance, a church bell bongs. People stand and cheer. The bleachers begin to vibrate. At first I assume it's caused by the applause, but when the clapping stops, the shaking intensifies. A sixth sense tells me that this is no ordinary tremor. Something dreadful is coming from the distance.

Other people are noticing it, too. The spectators watching the game and the players themselves are anxiously glancing around, trying to figure out where the low rumbling is coming from. It doesn't take long for the players to start pointing at us on the bleachers. Wait, no—they're pointing to something above us. I turn around with my camera phone in hand to see the moon. Red veins are growing from its center outward, slowly turning the surface to the color of blood.

Chapter 2

The sky deepens to shades of gray, then to black, in the space of a minute. For a moment, I think a storm has rolled in. But then I realize the red moon and the stars are shining through. The game has stopped. Players and spectators are gathering together in fear. Narrating into my phone for my followers, I say, "I've lived through a nuclear war and a comet impact. Yet the onslaught of sudden darkness fills me with more trepidation than the other two combined."

The rumbling turns to shaking, forcing me to steady myself with one hand on the bleachers. Behind me, past the ball field, a sound like earth ripping apart rends the air. I turn my camera in that direction. A jagged fault line is cutting a path toward the campus at the speed of a bullet train. About twenty yards to my right, it races past me, growing wider, the people and cars caught in its path drop out of sight into the bowels of the earth. Screams surround me. The moon begins to pulsate. Meteors streak across the heavens. The sky is crying stars. Teardrops of light explode like bombs, pounding the earth beneath. People flee in every direction, as if they can escape the descending firmament. Knowing death is inevitable, in my confusion and escalating fear, the phone slips from my fingers.

Has the world fallen off its axis? The explanation doesn't make any sense, but it's all I've got. The sun seems to be falling toward the earth. The ball of brightness is getting bigger, bigger, filling up the sky. This can't be happening. I'm too young to die. Realizing only a miracle can save me, I want to cry out, *Jesus! Mary! I love you!* But fear has sucked the breath from my lungs. The words will not come.

"You cannot say what you don't mean," a dry voice penetrates me, "for God knows the truth in every man's heart."

The sun slams into the earth, shattering everything.

The journey between this world and the next happens in a blink. I find myself standing on a giant black and blue checkerboard, floating in the middle of gray nothingness. Billowing walls, the color of turtle dove wings, surround me on every side. I cannot see God, but there is no doubt that He can see me, every wretched inch. I have never felt so bare and exposed. His Presence is beyond my ability to fathom. Overwhelming. Terrifying. Judging. I do not see my specific sins, but I'm suddenly aware of the mess they have left behind. Each one of them has made a mark on my soul, like creosote buildup on glass. Whereas I should be shining like a brilliant star, only a few pinholes of light show through. I stand defiled before the Holy of Holies, wanting to hide myself under a rock, but there is nowhere to go. *I'm basically a good person,* I try to say, wanting to make excuses for myself. *Give me a chance to explain why I said those things, did those things, against my brothers and sisters, and I'm sure You will understand.*

Regrettably, that's not how it works in this place. I don't get to plead my case with clever words. There is no explaining. No convincing. No more time. I exited my life as a prideful, greedy liar. However, this isn't what condemns me. It's the fact that I do not love God. In this space between heaven and earth, the voice is silenced, the soul laid bare, and truth is all that remains. An awful knowing passes through me. I belong in Hell. The sentence has been passed. There is no changing it. My fate is locked in stone.

As I struggle to come to grips with the verdict, the tile beneath my feet opens like a trap door, sending me plunging into the abyss below. Down I go. The light in my soul has gone out forever, replaced by black rot. Everything good has been ripped out of my flesh. *Oh, the misery! My God, my God, forgive me!* But it's too late. He has turned His head away. The separation is complete. *Oh, the emptiness! Who can save me? No one! No one!* Despair devours my every pore, my every thought, as I fall deeper into the darkness.

Instead of heat, I feel cold as the moans of the damned rise up to meet me. Glancing down through a netting of black rock below, illuminated by an eerie red glow, I see an endless landscape of writing and charred human shapes. Flecks of red embers glow through the cracks of their skin as if they're burning from the inside out. Millions of intertwined bodies rise and fall *en masse* like battered waves on an endless ocean. *No, please, no! Don't let that be my fate!* I'm flailing my arms madly, in a vain attempt to change course. But my path is set. Closing my eyes against the madness, my body crashes through the ceiling of Hell, into the death of hope, to meet my eternal doom.

Chapter 3

A church bell tolls, slowly bringing me back to a conscious state. My eyes flutter open. Fully expecting to find myself in Hell, burning in a fire that gives no light, relief floods through me to find myself at the baseball diamond. However, I am lying in pebbles beneath the bleachers. I crawl out of the shade and back into the anemic daylight. The sky is still the same dirty-mustard color, but it is a far sight better than Hell. Everyone at the game seems to have blacked out as well.

Many of them are lying on the ground, or on the bleachers, in the outfield, infield, and dugout—all in various stages of waking. What in the literal Hell is going on? I turn my gaze to the west. The various buildings on the campus are all in place. So are the cars. There is no crack running down the parking lot. But to the east, I can hardly believe my eyes. There's a cross taller than a skyscraper made entirely of white light, hovering in midair. I glance around to see if other people are seeing what I'm seeing. All eyes are turning toward the amazing sight. The cross is accompanied by an eerie hum, like a blast of a thousand trumpets. All at once, the image goes supernova. Thinking I'm going to be incinerated, I fall to my knees, instinctively shielding my face.

When nothing happens, I slowly stand.

The sky is clear—well, I shouldn't say clear. It's the usual dusty shade of beige. The clock on the scoreboard says 3:01. The storm and the judgment, and the vision of the cross, happened in the space of a dong or two. How can that be?

My mind is racing a mile a minute. I'm mad at myself for not thinking to video the cross before it disappeared. I reach for my phone in my pocket to find it empty. Glancing around, I spy it on the ground near my feet. Sweeping it up with a hand, I begin to vlog the aftermath.

"Dear Followers," I say, centering the lens on myself. "Excuse the quality of this video, but my hands are still trembling. Something most extraordinary just happened. I don't know how to explain it. I'm just going to film and shut up while I gather my thoughts."

The other spectators and players are stirring and looking as confused as I feel. Pivoting my camera toward the concession stand, I look for Kylie. Her nose is pointed to the sky. Tears are streaming down her face. Oddly enough, she's smiling. Before I can make a move toward my friend, a matronly-looking woman in reading glasses grips me by the shoulder.

"Do you know what's going on?" the older woman asks me. I keep my camera rolling. "I just had the strangest experience."

"What kind of experience?" I cautiously test the waters.

"I-I'm not sure, but I think I met God." My heart skips a beat. So, it wasn't just me. "And He led me through a mansion. Some of the rooms were lovely. But others were in disarray, cobwebs and filth everywhere." The older woman is facing me as we're talking, but her eyes aren't focused. They seem to be gazing inward as she reflects on her experience. "I came to understand that the mansion was mine. Company was coming, but the house wasn't ready. I was so ashamed." Her eyes come into focus. She asks in earnest. "Is that what you saw too, dear?"

"Uh, something like that."

The woman wanders off, leaving me alone. The place where I saw Kylie standing a minute ago is now empty. Pivoting my head left to right, right to left, I don't see my friend anywhere. At least I know she's okay. Maybe I should check on Jerome. I head away from the bleachers to the chain link fence, peering out toward first base. He's not there. Scanning the area with my eyes, as well as my camera phone, I see him far in the distance, walking way out past the outfield with a couple of other guys. I notice that he didn't bother to see if his sort-of-a-girlfriend was okay. I wonder what that says about our relationship.

The coach of our school's baseball team is sitting on the warm-up bench, head in his hands, sobbing his heart out. I can't tell if they're tears of sadness or joy. It finally occurs to me this is too intimate a moment to share with the world. I shut off my phone and continue to look around.

Some of the players are wandering off the field in a daze. Others are gathering together, talking in hushed tones. Several guys are kneeling in a huddle, hands folded, saying the Our Father. It's pretty much the same scenario for the spectators. Some are heading to the parking lot or back to the dorms. A woman begins to belt out a hymn: "Then sings my soul, my Savior, God to Thee, how great Thou art!" Voices join in, but I don't know the words. Even if I did, the last thing I feel like doing is singing "His" praises.

I have always found the relationship between God, Jesus, and the Holy Spirit confusing. All I know is that Jesus is the Son in this unique arrangement and the easiest of the Three to relate to. I picture Him as a soft-spoken, kindhearted, effeminate, hippie kind of fellow. If my experience was truly from Jesus, He's not at all what I imagined. The Presence that I encountered was demanding, scary, and judgmental. When I didn't live up to His expectations, I was cut off like dead weight. Could that have really been the God I learned about back in elementary school? There has to be another explanation. Perhaps the city has suffered a chemical attack, or there's been an explosion at a pharmaceutical factory, causing a group hallucination.

Hoping to catch a news bulletin about the situation, I check my phone to see if the internet has come back up. Nope.

My eyes go to Zach. He's sitting on the lowest bleacher, holding himself, rocking back and forth, seeming lost in another dimension. "I've always tried to do right by people," he cries out. "I don't understand." The muscles in his neck visibly strain when he lets out a frustrated bellow. "Where did I go wrong, Lord?"

I totally understand his frustration. Sure, I have my faults. But I'm basically a good person. Why did God turn against me? Even now, the pain still stings. Feeling forsaken, I hug myself, wondering if I'm hopelessly damned.

Chapter 4

A hush has fallen over the world. There are no annoying car horns blaring, no wailing sirens, not even the dull hum of traffic. In the distance, cars and semis have pulled off alongside of the highway. As I move down the main street that runs through the center of campus, it seems nearly everyone is standing around in a daze. Some are sobbing hysterically. One man is being restrained by a friend as he attempts to claw out his eyes. There is a tension in the air that drives me to move faster until I reach my room on the fourth floor of the Rausch Building. I pass my reflection in the oval mirror by the front door. I look pale, disheveled, and shell-shocked, like everyone else I passed on the way here. The clock on the wall says 3:45 p.m.

The dorm room I share with Kylie is formed of concrete blocks slathered in white paint. It's not exactly posh, but after what I've been through its simple familiarity helps to calm my frayed nerves. The bunk bed is pushed up against the only window to conserve space. It's a fire hazard, but the arrangement allows us to squeeze in a loveseat, two desks, a mini-fridge, and a wall-mounted television. A private bathroom makes up for the room's many deficits, and it's better than living with my mom and stepfather.

I don't care for Kylie's sci-fi posters. She hates my butterfly obsession. In my book, that makes us even. Perhaps I would have outgrown the butterfly thing if the comet hadn't robbed the sky of them. My collection compensates with bright sun catchers, a mobile of fluttering flowers, my rainbow butterfly bedspread, and 3-D artwork on the walls. No matter how long I gaze at the beautiful butterflies, though, I can't seem to block the dark vision of Hell out of my mind.

The coat Kylie wore to the game is normally tossed over her desk chair if she's home. Not there. I regret having lost track of her whereabouts in the confusion. Jerome, too. The door to the bathroom is open. I can see from here that the ceramic throne is vacant. I call her name just to be sure.

"Kylie—you here?"

No reply. I check my phone one more time, hoping to find a message. Service is still down. Damn.

Desperate for news, I power on the television, knowing it's probably useless. Yep. All I get are rainbow screens. A message repeats every few minutes, "Please stand by, the station is experiencing technical difficulties." Yesterday's solar flare couldn't have come at a worse time.

It suddenly occurs to me that there's a landline pay phone down in the lobby. If I hurry, maybe I'll beat anyone else who gets the same bright idea. When I get there, a guy about my own age is already tying up the phone. Sucking in a breath of frustration, I get in line behind him, impatiently tapping my foot. He keeps on talking, not caring that he's hogging the line.

While I'm waiting, I read the notices tacked to the public bulletin board. They're mostly homemade ads done by students looking for roommates and vacant apartments for rent. There's a bulletin for an upcoming financial planning seminar. Also, the Brazilian jiu-jitsu class I'm already enrolled in is advertising a complimentary *gi* for anyone who joins. I frown at the Neuist advertisement: *A happier and safer world begins with you! Call a NEU Eden Center near you and we will show you how!* I pull the paper down, give it a crumple, then let it drop to the floor. My attention returns to the ads done by enterprising students who are offering services such as computer repair, tutoring, transportation and childcare. The line of people waiting to use the phone continues to grow. On a more somber note, there are posters with the faces and descriptions of people who have gone missing from the university.

My former political science professor, the man who molded my anti-Neuist stance more than anyone, is among the missing. His disappearance is old news, but I'm saddened by the reminder. There are two other professors on the list, an administrative assistant, a guidance counselor, and twenty-one students in all. Six of the missing are wearing crucifixes in their photos. That seems like an unusually high number for a secular institution of higher learning. Rumor has it that most of them have dropped out of society of their own accord, running off to some Christian doomsday cult.

As I study the faces and the names of the missing, the people waiting to use the phone are starting to complain. A young man at the back is hollering for the phone hog to hurry it up. The phone hog holds up his middle finger without turning around and keeps on talking. What a jerk. People get angry and start shoving. I've been told that I have one of those voices that carry. Experience tells me that's true. I decide to put it to good use and take over crowd management.

"All righty, folks!" The crowd, eager for a fair way of handling the situation, seems happy to have someone take charge. "This is how it's going to go. We each get the phone for five minutes. No more, no less. Anyone who gets pushy, or interrupts the person on the phone before their five minutes are up, goes to the back of the line. If someone goes over the five, I can't help them. They're at the crowd's mercy. How does that sound?"

"Like a good plan," a young woman says.

"Cool," a guy agrees.

I tap the phone hog's shoulder. "You have sixty seconds to wrap things up."

He turns around to glare, sees the growing crowd glaring back, and decides not to argue.

As soon as he hangs up, I rush in to dial my mother's house in Arizona. Her husband, Ray Cook, answers. As stepfathers go, if Ray wasn't so domineering, he'd be almost tolerable. The way he made my mom agree to join his fly-by-night religion, the New Apostolic Third Assembly, before he would marry her, has never set well with me. If Ray truly loved my mother, why did she have to change her beliefs for him to keep on loving her? I don't know why I let it bother me so much. Over the years, I've come to understand that my mother views religion like a designer handbag. She switches it out according to the color of the outfit—i.e., the man she's interested in at the time. When it goes out of

19

style, she has no qualms about tossing it aside. If Ray should die, she'd embrace whatever religion matched the next relationship. Despite her quirks, and maybe because of them, I love my mother. So does Ray. For her sake, we try to get along.

"Hello?" A man's voice comes over the line. It's Ray, sounding pretty much like he always does—tired and slightly grumpy. Not knowing how to address the issue at hand, I hesitate. "Who is this?" he asks, sounding even grumpier.

"Hi Ray, it's me, Gina. Um, how are you doing?"

"Not happy. The compressor broke on the fridge. That's going to cost an arm and a leg."

"That's too bad." If that's his biggest concern right now, he obviously didn't just go through what I did. "Is my mom home?"

"Yeah, hold on." I hear him yell across the house, "Laura, Gina's on the phone!"

The muffled sound of them conversing back and forth comes over the phone, but I can't make out what they're saying.

"Hold on," Ray finally explains. "She'll be out of the bathroom in a jiffy."

"Okay." Feeling the clock tick away, I try to make small talk about the family. My mom is still on good terms with my deceased father's parents. She and Ray visit my paternal grandparents from time to time, so I start with them. "Are you going up for your annual visit with Grammy and Grandpa Applegate in May?"

"Probably."

"Isn't that great about Grammy? I knew she'd beat this thing."

"The numbers are looking good," Ray points out. "But it's not in full remission."

"I know."

The conversation hits a lull, but mom isn't done in the bathroom. Running out of time, I decide to get straight to the point with Ray. "Is there anything strange going on where you live?"

"Television, internet service, and cell phones have been down since yesterday."

"Here, too. But I'm not talking about that. I mean have you had any unusual, uh … meteorological events?"

"A snowflake or two."

"Are you sure?"

"Positive."

"Well," I blurt out, "over here, we just had a Chicken Little, the sky is falling kind of event. Then I fell into Hell, but woke up to find myself back at the baseball diamond, where a huge cross floated over the entire city, and …"

"Gina," Ray interrupts, voice tinged with concern of the wrong kind. "Have you been dropping acid again?"

"That was a one-time thing back in high school." Ray has never let me live that down. "Is Mom almost finished?"

"Laura! How much longer are you gonna be?"

"Can't you just bring her the phone, Ray?"

"It's on a cord—so, no."

"Oh, yeah. I forgot." Someone in the line calls out that I have two minutes left. "Tell Mom I'll call her back later." There's a long pause as I wait for him to reply. "Ray—can you do that for me?"

"Hello?" Ray says. He sounds out of breath as if he's been running. There's a quiver in his voice and a great deal of confusion. "Hello? Who is this?"

"It's still Gina," I reply, thinking there's a blip in the connection. "Is mom out of the bathroom, yet?"

"Gina—is that you?"

"No, it's the Easter Bunny. Of course, it's me."

"It was the craziest damn thing." He's practically giddy. "Have you been holding all this time?"

"Yes, yes. For one whole minute. What's the matter with you?"

"You're never going to believe what just happened. I was caught up in a firestorm, and whisked away by the angels to stand before the Lord. The heavens opened. I saw the Earth below, covered in darkness. It was a warning about where the world is headed if we don't change our ways." He interrupts himself to holler at my mother. "Calm down, Laura. I can't understand what you're saying." He returns his attention to me. "Your mother's upset. I'll have her call you back later."

"Wait, no. I want to hear more …"

"Sorry, gotta go. Bye."

"At least let me talk to my mom."

He hangs up just when the conversation had gotten more interesting. Figures.

"Time!" someone tells me from the back of the line. "Move along."

With a flustered *humph*, I return the phone to its holder. The clock on the wall says 4:01, which means the storm in Ray's time zone arrived at 3 o-clock, just as it did here. I step aside for the next person to turn around and survey the lobby. Several young women sitting on comfy chairs are bawling. Grown men are pacing anxiously back-and-forth.

While people are continuing to struggle to make sense of what happened, a husky sandy-haired young man in a Chicago Bears jacket comes into the lobby claiming to have the answers.

"If you want a better understanding of today's event," he says, effortlessly projecting his voice over the excited crowd, "there will be a meeting at Walb Memorial at 11 p.m. tonight. This could be a life-changer, so don't miss it!" People rush at him. He can barely keep up with the demand for his fliers. I push my way through the other students to get one. "Everyone is welcome," he says. "Tell your friends."

The flyer doesn't offer any useful information beyond the place and the time:

MEETING TONIGHT
WALB GYMNASIUM, 11 PM

If you want to make sense of the illumination you experienced today, and how it might apply to your future, plan to attend.

✟ ✟ ✟

PUBLIC WELCOME

I return to my room. There's still no sign of Kylie. I stick the flyer to our board with a square black-and-white magnet. The message printed on it says: *If God exists, he better have a good excuse.*

Ha. The irony is not lost on me. I climb into the top bunk, unable to shake the devastating feeling of being rejected by God. I'm not perfect— I cuss and party too much. Admittedly, the no-sex-before-marriage thing has been a struggle, but everybody does it. I'm sure God isn't going to send us all to Hell for slipping up here and there. Compared to most people, I think I'm pretty damn good. I have never murdered anyone. Well, there was that homeless guy outside of the Circle K. He tried to strangle the life out of me for a warm hoagie and my coat. I had no choice but to blow his guts out. I haven't looted or stolen anything. I'm big on recycling and very accepting of everyone—regardless of their race, sexual orientation, economic status, religious preference, or lack thereof. How can someone as nice as me end up in Hell?

On the off chance that the weird experience was from God, then I'm not sure if I want anything to do with the Big Cosmic Meanie. My version of Jesus just doesn't match up with the one I met today. There has to be a science-based explanation for the vision.

Looking to the door, I hope Kylie hurries up and gets here. She was raised to believe reason is the highest virtue. I'm sure she'll come back with a logical explanation—chemical warfare, an industrial accident, whatever. Until then, I'm going to push it out of my mind. Cocooning my body in my colorful butterfly quilt, stitched together by the loving hands of my grandmother, I feel safe again as I snuggle in for the night.

Chapter 5

"Gina," a voice says from somewhere faraway, trying to pull me out of a deep slumber.

I flip my face toward the window, only to be annoyed by something wet in my ear. I realize it's Kylie's slobber-coated index finger and slap her hand away. Turning around, I see her standing on the desk chair to peer over the top bunk. She's holding the flyer in her hand. Curious as to how an atheist like her is dealing with the phenomenon, I immediately perk up.

"How are you doing?" I ask.

"Never better."

"Where have you been all night?"

"Visiting a church."

I wait for the punch line. It doesn't come, so I have to ask, "Did hell freeze over?"

"Nooo." She rolls her eyes. Holding up the flyer, Kylie points to the place where it says 11 p.m., Walb Memorial Gymnasium. "I'm going— are you?""

"Wouldn't miss it."

I grab my coat off the loveseat. We head out into the cool starless night across the campus toward the gymnasium. The stream of students heading in the same direction is heavy. There's even a few professors in the mix. Up front, there's a podium and a large projection on the wall in large type:

The Warning
(Illumination of Conscience)

The young man in the Chicago Bears jacket who passed out the fliers earlier is up front, talking to an older lady at the laptop projector. Kylie and I squeeze into the middle of the crowd, awaiting the explanation, as hundreds of conversations go on around us. I take out my camera and begin to vlog.

"Dear Followers: I'm at a meeting that is supposed to enlighten us as to the strange happenings of the day. Speaking of strange," I turn the camera to Kylie. "You are all familiar with my lovely roommate, her firmly held belief that God doesn't exist and that all religions are bad. Well, sources say that this Warning, Illumination of Conscience thingy, or whatever they're calling it, has put a crack in her skepticism. But you don't have to take my word for it, let's get the dope straight from the source." I pan in closer for a headshot. She waves and says, "Hey, y'all. Hi, y'all. How y'all doing?"

"Hey, girlfriend, is it true that you spent the afternoon in a church?"

"Yes," she nods. "Totally true."

"Would you care to explain why an avowed atheist like yourself would do such a thing?"

"Because I'm no longer an avowed atheist. I was trying to figure out how to pray. Like, am I supposed to use specific words, or should I just talk to Him like I am doing right now?"

"Him—as in Jesus Christ," I'm still waiting for the punch line, "Who was conceived by the Holy Spirit and born of the Virgin Mary?"

"None other."

"All righty, then." My eyes widen. Unsure where to go with the vlog, all I can do is tease her a little bit. "Falling into Hell scared you straight, eh?"

Kylie tilts her head, giving me a puzzled expression. She's about to respond, but a middle-aged man in an oversized tweed suit has walked up to stand next to the podium. He nods to the young man in the Chicago Bears jacket, who comes over to take the microphone. The young guy clears his throat, but it does little to calm the chattering crowd. He tries again, this time tapping the mic a few times as well. Conversations slowly die off. When the room is completely silent, I turn my camera in his direction as he begins to speak.

"Considering the late hour, we didn't expect such a large crowd. I'm glad you all could make it. My name is Miguel Cruz. I'm a graduate student here at the university and a volunteer with *Shelter Me* over at St. Faustina's in Burlington, a program that helps the unemployed with all aspects of home repair." He gestures toward the older man in the tweed suit. "This is Felix Mott, Esquire. He's a husband, father of four, the owner of Felix J. Mott Professional Corporation, and a third order Carmelite from Sioux City, Iowa." I whisper into my phone for my followers: *Never trust a lawyer in a cheap suit.* "He has written numerous books on Eschatology. For those of you not familiar with the term, it refers to the branch of theology concerned with End Times Christian prophecy." Yesterday, the topic would have caused most of the crowd to walk away. Today people are much more receptive. Still, groans go up from sections of the crowd. Miguel ignores the naysayers and continues his introduction. "Mr. Mott was giving a talk on Carmelite spirituality at St. Faustina's when the sky appeared to descend. Tonight's meeting obviously wasn't planned but, in a way, Mr. Mott has been preparing for it over the last thirty years. I thank him for coming to the university on such short notice. Without further ado, I'll hand the mic over to him."

"Thank you, Miguel." Mr. Mott's voice is hoarse, but he seems undeterred. Giving a nod to the woman running the laptop projector, a portrait of a nun, with Jesus standing behind her all aglow, materializes on the white wall to his left. "This is my fourth presentation today, and I'm starting to lose my voice," he explains, "so let's get right to it. The frightful experience we just lived through has been called different names by mystics throughout the ages. The Warning, the Illumination of Conscience, and the Mini-Judgment all refer to the same event. People use the labels interchangeably, so don't get confused."

The projection on the wall fades to quotes written in plain black font. He reads straight from the page:

> "I pronounce a great day, not wherein any temporal potentate should minister, but wherein the Terrible Judge, should **reveal all men's consciences** and try every man of each kind of religion. This is the day of change."
>
> ~St. Edmond Campion (1540–1581)

"A great purification will come upon the world **preceded** by an **Illumination of Conscience** in which everyone will see themselves as God sees them."
~*Blessed Anna Maria Taigi (1769–1837)*

"There are dozens of credible prophecies related to the Mini-Judgment we underwent today. For the sake of brevity, I will only be mentioning a few. If you would like to see more of them, after the presentation you may checkout my website: *Mott's List of Private Revelation Related to the End Times.*

"Now, let's get back to the fundamental question: what is the Illumination of Conscience? It has been described as a punishment for the just and the wicked alike. For the just, it will bring them closer to God. For the wicked, it's an alarm bell, warning them that time is running out."

"Who is Saint Faustina?" a young man asks from the crowd.

"Saint Faustina Kawalska was a Polish nun. Jesus and Mary spoke to her in a series of apparitions. During one of these heavenly encounters, St. Faustina described The Warning with these words: *Once I was summoned to the judgment of God. I stood alone before the Lord. Jesus appeared such as we know Him during His Passion. After a moment, His wounds disappeared, except for five, those in His hands, His feet, and His side. Suddenly I saw the complete condition of my soul as God sees it. I could clearly see all that is displeasing to God. I did not know that even the smallest transgressions, will have to be accounted for.*

"That, my friends, is what we went through today in a nutshell, each of us forced to look at ourselves with the blinders off. A shocking experience, to say the least. According to my sources, this phenomenon has occurred across the globe, affecting each and every person regardless of belief or social standing, precisely at 3 p.m. in their respective time zones."

A young man shouts out, "If this so-called *Illumination* was spoken of by the prophets, why is it that nobody has ever heard of it before?"

"I have heard of it," Mr. Mott says. "My family and friends have heard of it. If you ask around, I am sure there are those among us who have been aware of the prophecies for a very long time."

"I'm a Bible-believing Christian." A gray-haired woman holds up a Bible. "If it's not in here, then it just isn't so."

"The purpose of private revelations such as these isn't to add or take away from the Deposit of Faith. It's given to deepen our understanding of what is already there." Ignoring the grumbles, Mott goes straight into his spiel. "In the Book of Revelation, the Apostle John had a vision of a scroll with seven seals, each representing a different punishment. Jesus took the scroll and broke the seals one-by-one."

"The punishments may take years, or even centuries, to fully manifest. The next seal may be broken before the previous one completes its course. Inevitably, some will overlap. But make no mistake about it, we are living deep in the days of the broken seals. In fact, the seventh one was broken open when most of you were children. Due to the overlap I just mentioned, what we experienced a few hours ago, the Illumination of Conscience, also known as The Warning, was the final culmination of the sixth."

"There are Bible scholars who are of the camp that St. John's vision wasn't a warning of future events. They argue it wasn't even a vision, but a text written in code, to protect the early Christians in case it should fall into the hands of the Romans. On the other hand, other scholars believe that the Book of Revelation strictly pertains to the End Times. Personally, I believe it is both, God weaving the past and the present together in a single vision."

"Jesus said," a woman in the crowd shouts, "'Because you have seen, you have believed; blessed are those who have not seen and yet believe.'"

"I've seen a lot today," a man responds. "But nothing proving the Illumination was an act of God. There has to be another explanation."

"Amen," I grumble to Kylie, expecting her to side with science. "You know I believe in a higher power. But the God I know likes to keep things on the down low. He's never so obvious. Scaring the crap out of people, and throwing them into Hell, just isn't his modus operandi."

"Shhh," she says. "I'm trying to listen."

"The more things change, the more they stay the same." A man with an English accent speaks into a second microphone at the back of the gymnasium. "The ancient Greeks didn't understand why the sun moved across the sky, so they invented the God of Helios and his chariot of fire." I turn around to the source—a man about the same age as Mott, in blue jeans and a blazer, with spiky blonde hair. Aha, John Langley, my Business Ethics professor, has joined the debate. How he manages to seem larger than everyone else in the room, despite his small stature has always mystified me. "Today, pseudo-intellectuals like Mr. Mott here, invent fictional stories instead of doing the hard work of gathering data and analyzing the facts. I am confident there is a more logical explanation for today's mass hallucination than God."

Langley hands his mic over to a young man who has been eagerly grabbing for it since the professor arrived. "I'm a med student. From my observation, the so-called visions were a mass hallucination brought on by chemical agents released into the air." I'm nodding in agreement, thinking this med student is going to make a great doctor someday. "At this stage, we don't know if it was intentional or by accident, but I'm sure time will prove me correct."

"Finally, the voice of reason." I look over to see who's talking. It's the pitcher, Jay Gupta, of our baseball team. Jerome is there beside him, giving a smirk of approval. "Anyone who buys into this 'seven seal' crap is a superstitious idiot. Science and the government are the only things that have kept us alive this long. As per usual, God is nowhere to be found."

"For those with faith, no explanation is needed," Mr. Mott counters. "For those without it, no explanation is possible."

Evan Moore, a basketball player who is known for being a partier and a womanizer, speaks up. I don't expect him to side with the God hypothesis, but this has been a day of surprises. "We have ignored Jesus Christ for the last century in favor of the scientists and the politicians. And what has it gotten us?" Evan asks, and proceeds to answer his own question. "A nuclear war, failing crops, and people killing each other in the streets over a bag of Kit Kats. Where are the scientists with their fancy explanation as to why we all saw the same cross in the sky after we woke up? As long as I can remember, we have been told to be patient, hold on a little while longer while the experts figure out what to do. Look around you, people. The world keeps getting worse and worse. Today we get yet another excuse from our self-proclaimed saviors—a solar flare knocked out delicate communication systems, please stand by for answers that won't fix anything. So excuse me if I no longer trust the scientists to save us. I'm putting my hope in a higher power than you." The basketball player is backed by a smattering of enthusiastic applause.

"You can't blame the scientists or government for the comet hitting the earth," a young woman shouts angrily.

"But you can certainly blame them for the nuclear war," counters another woman.

Pockets of arguments are breaking out all over the gymnasium.

"Those prophets up on the screen aren't Christian," an older woman I recognize from the registrar's office says with disdain. "They're all Catholic—idolaters, every single one of them."

"Non-Catholics have had similar visions." Mr. Mott struggles to be heard over the din. The crowd begins to settle down. "However, the Catholic Church has a detailed process for weeding out the con artists and the mentally unstable. That makes the prophecies it backs more reliable. So I chose quotes that are supported by years of investigation. By the way, Catholics are not idolaters, but that is a topic for another day."

"The Warning," he continues, "isn't the beginning or the end of these troubled times. However, it does signal the coming of another unusual event called The Miracle. Not much is known about The Miracle except that God will leave a permanent sign on Earth as proof of His existence. Even then, many will refuse to believe in Him, and the persecution of the believers will intensify.

"In response, God will send a punishment that will make the darkness that swept across Egypt in the days of Moses look like a warm up." A different quote materializes on the screen, another one by Blessed Anna Maria Taigi, which Mr. Mott reads aloud:

> There shall come over the whole earth an intense darkness lasting three days and three nights. Nothing can be seen, and the air will be laden with pestilence which will claim mainly, but not only, the enemies of religion.
>
> It will be impossible to use any man-made lighting during this darkness, except blessed candles. He, who out of curiosity, opens his window to look out, or leaves his home, will fall dead on the spot.
>
> During these three days, people should remain in their homes, pray the Rosary and beg God for mercy. All the enemies of the Church, whether known or unknown, will perish over the whole earth during that universal darkness, with the exception of a few whom God will soon convert. The air shall be infected by demons who will appear under all sorts of hideous forms.

"The darkness will last three days, one for each agonizing hour Jesus hung on the cross. Instead of the angel of death targeting firstborn males, God will open the gates of Hell, allowing the demons to kill the wicked, but not even the righteous will be spared if they are caught outdoors. When the darkness finally lifts, the few who survive will know without a doubt that Jesus Christ is Lord."

"What about the tribulation, the antichrist, and the final judgment?" an old man asks from the front of the room. "Where does today's event fit into the timeline?"

"By my estimation, we are midway through the Tribulation. However, in God's time, a thousand years is but a blink of the eye. Seals have been broken, but the Generation of Fading Light will not see the rise of the last antichrist or the Final Judgment. The Three Days of Darkness and the subsequent Era of Peace must come first."

"I'm trying to understand," a woman says, shaking her head with a bewildered expression, "are you saying the world isn't going to end?"

"It's going to end. God has promised it, but ..."

Without warning, a small blur of white streaks over the crowd and strikes Mr. Mott square in the forehead. The poor man falls backwards, knocking over folding chairs with a clatter. For a moment, the entire room is frozen still. Then Miguel rushes to the professor's aid, followed

31

by the med student and a few other audience members. The rest of the crowd erupts in a yelling match.

"What happened?" Kylie stands on her tiptoes, trying to get a better view, as the crowd shifts and ebbs around us. "Did you see what hit him? Was he shot?"

"No, but whatever hit him was spherical, almost like—"

I cut myself off and start scanning in the direction the object seemed to have been thrown from, spotting Jerome and his teammates. including Jay Gupta, the pitcher. Then it clicks. *It was a baseball.* Most of them are pushing back at the crowd while a few of them laugh and yell towards the podium. I can't make out what they are saying, but by their amused expressions and blatant lack of concern, I can guess how little they think of Mr. Mott.

While I try to convince myself that Jerome and his friends wouldn't openly assault someone with a baseball, things go from bad to worse. Angry yells turn into flat out screaming matches. A folding chair is tossed out of the crowd towards the podium. It falls short, but those trying to protect Mr. Mott take the opportunity to start throwing chairs haphazardly back into the audience. Shouts of pain mix into the screams of protest and those in the middle start to flee towards the doors. The surging crowd turns into a tidal wave that sweeps up Kylie and me. We're carried along by the momentum while what had once been a peaceful discussion turns into an open riot.

Chapter 6

Afraid of my phone getting crushed, I slide it into my coat pocket. It's a struggle to stay upright as the crowd pushes us about. Despite a few stumbles, I'm able to remain on my feet. Kylie isn't as lucky and is swept under. She huddles into a protective ball to shield her head as much as she can. I plant myself behind her like a mighty oak, trying to force the river of bodies to flow around her. My roots aren't very deep though. Before I'm taken down as well, Zach appears from out of nowhere to help us out. His large frame makes for a better barrier, forcing the people to flow around us as I help Kylie regain her footing. But even Zach cannot hold back the tide indefinitely. Eventually he's overwhelmed and swept one way. Kylie and I are swept the other.

Caught in a logjam of bodies fighting their way to the doors, the pressure squeezes the air out of my lungs, making me feel faint. Just when I can't take a second more of this, the double doors swing open. People pour through like ketchup exploding out of a squeeze bottle, releasing the pressure, and letting me take in a deep, refreshing breath of air.

Finally free of the stampede, Kylie and I run out of Walb Memorial, spreading out across the campus along with hundreds of other people. We pass police in riot gear on their way to the gymnasium. Seeing them makes me pick up the pace. The right of citizens to bear arms was revoked several years ago. Generally, you just get a slap on the wrist for having one, but the American justice system isn't what it used to be. People arrested even for minor infractions can be trapped in jail for years, waiting to for trial in our overwhelmed courts. I'd hate for that to happen to me, so I run even faster.

By the time we reach the dorm and make it to our room on the fourth floor, I'm soaked with sweat. Kylie looks like she just stepped out of the salon. Every dark strand of hair in place. She's a cross country runner, in top physical shape, so that's to be expected. Other than my weekly jiu-jitsu class, lifting my hand to shove food into my mouth is the only exercise I get, but right now eating is the last thing on my mind. What I'm hungry for is information.

After Kylie and I confirm with each other that neither of us are badly hurt, just scraped and bruised from all the jostling, we obsessively check our phones to see if communication has been restored. Nope. Same goes for the television. After we give up on accessing the news, exhaustion settles in. Both of us retire to our respective bunks and go to sleep.

I awake to the beep of my phone. It's my 8:00 a.m. alarm, which I forgot to turn off before passing out the night before. Kylie groans in the bunk below, mumbling for me to shut it off. With everything that's happening, I can imagine that classes have been canceled. I roll over to grab my phone from the windowsill, but my hand misses. Through bleary eyes, I finally snatch it and poke around for the off button. Glancing outside, I see students on the sidewalks and in the parking lot, carrying backpacks and laptops. A layer of pale taupe dust coats everything like morning dew. It seems to be a regular Monday like any other. In this day and age, one little riot isn't going to make people put their lives on hold for more than a second, but I thought The Warning might. Apparently, not even an alleged act of God can slow us down.

A short while later, I'm huffing it across campus. Foot traffic is thinner than usual, which is to be expected after yesterday's crazy.

I plop down in the middle row of my Business Ethics class. The number of students has dropped by about half since the last time we met. Normally, I don't pay much attention to where Zach sits. After he came to the rescue last night, I'm immediately drawn to him in the last row. As our eyes meet, I wave to him. He glances around as if he assumes I was gesturing to someone else.

"Zach," I raise my voice, not caring if it annoys people. "Thanks for last night."

Heads go up at my comment. A couple of guys make snide remarks. Zach's ears instantly turn red. Kylie's right—he's a dork, but is that really such a bad thing?

Professor Langley arrives right on time. Since he was at Walb last night, I'm hoping he will address the incident. Unfortunately, he goes straight into his lecture. Aiming his remote at the classroom laptop, a list of titles appears on the white board at the front of the room:

- Tom Beauchamp and Norman Bowie, *Ethical Theory and Business*

- Thomas Donaldson and Patricia Werhane, *Ethical Issues in Business: A Philosophical Approach*

- Vincent Barry, *Moral Issues in Business*

"Now," he begins. "Young lady with the butterflies." That's me. I'm wearing a small crystal butterfly barrette. Plus, my laptop is covered with butterfly stickers. Langley rarely bothers with names, so he addresses his students by their clothing and accessories. "Can you tell me what these all have in common?"

"They were written in the same year—1979." I boldly try to change the subject. "But I was hoping we could talk about yesterday."

"Please, Professor Langley." Another girl backs me up. "I'd like to hear your perspective on the odd things we saw."

"What was the deal with the police raid at Walb last night?" a male students asks.

"I heard it was a drug bust," another guy chimes in.

"That's not what happened," a girl volunteers. "There was a meeting last night about The Warning. Things got ugly. People were taken out on stretchers."

Professor Langley sucks in a deep breath, as if the discussion at hand is a terrible inconvenience, but surprisingly he relents. "All right, class. I might as well tell you, moratoriums have been placed on both subjects. As an employee of the university, I am not permitted to discuss the mass hallucination or the related violence that took place on school property because of it."

"So that's what they're calling it—a mass hallucination?" a girl inquires.

"That's what reasonable people are calling it, yes."

"Does that mean they've discovered the cause?" she persists.

"I'm not at liberty to say."

"It was Jesus," says a female student. "Why is that so hard for some of you to accept?"

"Because some of us aren't stuck in the Middle Ages," a male student in the seat next to mine says with a sneer. "It was chemically induced. Anybody with half a brain can figure that much out."

"Chemically induced, my ass," Zach pipes up from the back of the room, his voice edged in irritation. "It was a warning from God, just like the lawyer was saying before some evil bastard lobbed a baseball at his head."

"It was not a warning from God!" Professsor Langley blows up, walking over to stand in front of Zach, shaking a finger in his face. "End of discussion."

"You are a bully, Professor," Zach says, his voice flat with a hint of fire behind it.

"And you are a Christian fool."

"You better get that finger out of my face, little man." Zach's eyes narrow.

Langley folds his arms over his chest and stands his ground. The room holds its breath when Zach stands to tower over the professor like he isn't going to take any shit. Langley automatically steps backwards, stumbling over a chair, causing a loud clunk. Zach frowns in disgust and walks out of the room, leaving the professor's dignity spilled on the floor.

Professor Langley straightens his tie and tosses his nose in the air as if he's won the battle of wills. "Anyone else care to leave?" he challenges the classroom.

A woman and another young man gather their things and make for the door. As a defender of the underdog and a hater of bullies, part of me wants to join Zach and the others. But Langley is right. It had to be a hallucination out there on the baseball field.

"Good. Get out of here." Langley throws a stack of papers at the exiting students, which harmlessly float down. "Go join your doomsday cult, or head off to your prayer meeting, whatever it is that you silly people do."

Some of the students begin to clap, cheering their departure, hurling insults.

"I bet they're all virgins," a male student quips.

The room erupts into laughter.

"The internet is back up!" someone exclaims.

Postures tense as if the students are ready to spring from their seats.

"Okay," says the professor. "Let's call it a day. I just hope the rest of you can return with rational minds on Wednesday so we don't have to endure any more of this religious nonsense."

Chapter 7

Professor Langley tucks his electronic notepad under his arm and is the first out the door. I file out of the classroom, following a stream of other students. My phone rings as I'm headed down the hallway. Checking the number, I can't help but smile. It's my grandmother—the most wonderful person this side of the Mississippi.

"Hi, Grammy."

"It's so nice to hear your voice, butterfly girl. How are you?"

"Fine. And yourself?"

"Okay, considering everything that's going on. Are you still planning on coming over on the eighth?" That's the anniversary of my sister's death. My father passed away two days later. Every year around those dates, my grandmother and I get together to visit their graves, and share our special memories of them. "The flowers are ready."

"I'll be there," I say softly.

"Wonderful. We have a lot to talk about."

"I can't wait to see you."

"Will you be bringing Geronimo?"

"Who?"

"Your new boyfriend."

"You mean Jerome. No, I don't think so."

"Oh, dear. I don't like it when you travel alone."

"I'll be all right, Grammy. Tell Grandpa hello."

"I will. God bless and tootles."

"Love you, Grammy. Bye."

I put away the phone to resume my trek toward the lobby. It's an airy space, hosting a lounge area filled with chairs and sofas, surrounded by huge picture windows, giving a sweeping view of the sickly oak forest out in the distance, but all eyes are focused on the big screen up on the wall.

I arrive in the middle of the story. The anchor woman is a ginger with artificially plumped lips and breasts, in a low-cut top.

"Meanwhile, researchers across the globe are working hard to get to the bottom of the event the religious are calling The Warning or the Illumination of Conscience. An alternative explanation that has been gaining momentum in the scientific community has come from, of all places, astronomy." A picture of an observatory on a hilltop appears on the screen, followed by an image of a giant flame shooting from the surface of the sun. "The solar flare that knocked out dozens of communication satellites over the weekend emitted a series of intense infrasonic waves, triggering mass hallucinations. An infrasonic wave is a low frequency vibration, undetectable by the human ear, but readily measured by scientific instrumentation." The report switches over to an earlier interview with a scientist in a white lab coat. The captioning beneath him reads: Dr. Greenway, Director of the Neurological Unit of the Joan Hawkins Institute. He goes on to explain for the camera, "When infrasonic waves stimulate the vestibular system, they are capable of producing feelings of awe or fear in human beings. Although not consciously perceived, test subjects exposed to these waves often feel as if a supernatural event is taking place."

"Hey, good-looking." A familiar voice whispers in my ear as two strong arms wrap around my waist from behind. Jerome. Remembering how he laughed after Mr. Mott was struck in the head, his touch makes my skin crawl. "How about you and me raise a little hell?"

"Not now, Jerome. I want to hear this."

I lean my head away as he plants frisky little kisses along the nape of my neck. After the report ends, I pull myself out of his arms and turn to face him. "Were you at Walb Memorial last night?"

"No." He lies to my face, making him seem guiltier than ever. "I was out at the baseball diamond—drinking with my chums. Why do you want to know—did the police come ask you about me?"

"No—should I expect them to?"

"I have four buddies who will confirm we weren't anywhere near Walb Memorial. We were together the whole night."

"I'm sure you were." I agree, even though I have video that proves otherwise. "I heard that the guest speaker got hit in the head with a baseball and died." I do a little lying myself, just to test his reaction. I honestly don't know if Mr. Mott died or not. "Isn't that horrible?"

Jerome takes a sharp intake of breath, holds it a moment, then slowly lets it out before asking.

"Dead—are you sure?"

"That's what I heard. I wonder if the security cameras were running in Walb. With all the budget cuts, it's hard to say."

"Oh, shit," Jerome says, glancing down at his phone. "I'm going to be late to my Finite Exam. Can we get together later?"

"I suppose." I suddenly long for a boyfriend who is more to me than just a good time. Someone who doesn't laugh when people get hurt or tell lies. "Call me whenever."

Chapter 8

In between classes, I call my mother just to make sure she's okay. As much as I want to know what she saw during the event, I avoid asking for fear that she will inquire about my own experience. After a few moments of trivial banter, she cuts to the chase.

"I'm dying to know if your warning was as awesome as mine. Tell me, Gina, what was it like for you?"

"It was terrifying, mom."

"Of course it was terrifying," she says, excitedly as if waiting for more. "And then what happened?"

"It became even more terrifying."

"What do you mean?"

"Does it matter? It was just infrasonic waves messing with our heads. The experience was meaningless."

"I don't care if you think it was caused by supersonic waves or whatever, I just want to know what you saw."

"Infrasonic waves, mom—not supersonic."

"My mistake," she says dismissively. "Go on, sweetie. Did you see Riley, too?"

My breath catches in my chest. Riley. My little sister who died of cancer. I was 13-years-old at the time and in no way prepared to lose my best friend. I'd give my left leg to see her again.

"Riley," my voice is husky with emotion. "Yeah, sure." I go along with my mother's vision because it's easier than telling her I went to Hell. "Oh, shoot. I'm late for class, mom. We'll talk later. Okay?"

"Wait, Gina, I just want to ask you about ..."

"Love you. Bye."

After my last class of the day, I head over to the cafeteria. It's where me and my friends often meet between classes. However, Kylie and I run in different circles that rarely intersect. She prefers the company of science geeks. Most of my friends are business, education, or communication majors.

Carrying a tray of watery instant potatoes and Sloppy Joe on a bun, I join four of my friends, including Jerome, who are already seated at a round table by the big fern. They're already deep in the middle of a lively debate and barely acknowledge my arrival.

"Immigrants infected with violent religious indoctrination were mindlessly welcomed into Europe," says Julie, a leggy blonde marketing major.

I've known Julie since high school. She has grown more beautiful and more liberal with age. She's debating Aaron, an accounting major with jet black hair and a conservative mindset. He's set to graduate this semester. I'll be sorry to see him go because where the Neuists are concerned we see eye-to-eye. He's a better debater than me, so I usually just leave it to him to take on Julie.

"Inevitably," Aaron reminds Julie, "it didn't take long for the Muslims, through immigration and their high birth rates, to gain half the vote. The democratic process, passionately divided by opposing ideologies, lost its ability to function. It seemed like nothing could be done to stop the violence."

"Enter the Neuists," I say, adding a ominous riff just to be funny. "Bum, da, da, da."

"That's right," Julie continues enthusiastically, seeming to miss my sarcasm. "Bringing common sense back into politics. Synagogues, temples, churches, and mosques were rightly branded as hate factories. The Neuists stripped the fanatics of the right to own property and took over the education of their children, preventing the religious infection from spreading to the next generation. Outside of the Muslim community, the majority of Europeans no longer indentified with any particular religion, so Neuism had a lot of appeal."

"You think you're refuting me, Julie." Aaron's voice is calm, yet rimmed with anger. "But you're only proving my point about how the

Neuist rise to power has many similarities to the Nazi takeover during World War Two."

"Here we go again." Julie rolls her eyes in annoyance. "Every time we have this conversation, we end up talking about the Jewish holocaust. I'm sorry about your ancestors dying at Treblinka and all, but what's happening across the pond today is nothing like that. The Neuists would never put people in concentration camps."

"They don't have to," Aaron contends through gritted teeth. Julie's chest is visibly heaving. The tension between them hovers like a storm cloud. "The Neuists no longer bother to hide their murderous deeds. They kill their enemies out in public, on live television no less, and nobody cares. In a way, Europe has gotten what it deserves for not listening to the religious leaders around the world who tried to warn them that the Neu ideology was an affront to human dignity. When the Neuists began to sweep the elections, their zero-tolerance-of-religion policy was gradually put into effect. In essence, anyone who believed they were answerable to a power higher than the government became an enemy of the State. Neuism is a disease that needs to be eradicated before it spreads over here. Just as the pope predicted, the Neuists didn't stop after they killed off the religious. Next, they targeted the elderly, the sick and anyone who spoke out against Neuist policies."

"You're wrong," Julie says. "It's your narrow-minded thinking that needs to be eradicated."

"How about that funky Illumination?" Jerome says jovially, indicating that it's time for them to change the topic. "Who wants to go to Heaven anyway? All that harp-playing would get on my last nerve."

"If Hell is where all the loose women go," says Brad Shank, Julie's live-in boyfriend, "sign me up." It's strange to hear that coming from him. He's normally the classy type—quiet, reserved, and into poetry.

That prompts Julie to punch Brad on the arm. "Hey," she says, acting offended in a playful way. "I heard that."

Jerome snorts, causing soda to shoot out his nose, making the rest of us roar with laughter. It feels good to make light of our visions of impending doom, but my stomach has turned itself into an anxious knot.

My boyfriend looks up at the clock on the wall—6:15 p.m. He immediately wraps an arm around my neck in a light headlock, giving my head a knuckle rub. Normally, I enjoy the way he likes to goof around. Today it's just annoying. If only I knew for sure if he had anything to do with throwing that baseball.

"It's getting to be about that time, babe," he reminds me. "Are you ready for some ass-whooping?"

"Yeah—are you?" I say, patting my duffle bag and trying to act natural around him. "My gi is washed and ready to go."

"Remember, the next Fraternity of Dionysus meeting is tomorrow night," Julie says to Jerome as we make to leave for jiu-jitsu. "If you want to be promoted to my level someday, don't forget to bring the beer."

I have been told that in the past fraternities had to justify their existence by supporting worthy causes. Apparently, like the rest of society, standards have grown lax. The mission statement of the Fraternity of Dionysus is: *Party On!* Instead of naming their organization with a combination of Greek letters as do most fraternities, they adopted the name of the Greek god of wine and fertility. When someone points out that Dionysus is also the god of ritual madness and religious ecstasy, they just laugh it off.

"I won't forget," Jerome assures Julie. He lifts a hand to give our friends a sloppy goodbye. "Hang with ya later, dudes."

Chapter 9

Our weekly Brazilian jiu-jitsu session is held way across campus, taking us thirty minutes to get there on foot. Jerome is a brown belt. I'm just a blue. Only four students show up for class today, which is about a third of the usual number. The instructor has us work on arm bars and the one-step front snap-kick for most of the two-hour session. By the time we bow off of the mat, I'm tired, sore, and in desperate need of a shower.

It's getting late, so Jerome insists on escorting me back to the dorm. He can be so protective at times. It's hard to imagine him purposely hurting anyone. I push aside the memory of him laughing at the expense of the injured lawyer and just concentrate on the moment. For most of the walk, he's complaining about a good friend of his who has given up drinking, cussing, sexual intercourse, and every fun thing outside of baseball, all because of The Warning.

"When Chevy handed me a prayer book, telling me I needed Jesus in my life, it took every ounce of willpower not to tell him to fuck off. Who does he think he is, trying to tell me what I need and don't need?"

"I know what you mean. Kylie came home late last night—not because she was out gaming down at the club; but because—get this ..." I lower my voice as if I'm revealing a terrible secret. "She went to MacDougal Chapel to pray."

"You're shitting me."

"As if that's not enough, all she wanted to talk about was Jesus, Jesus, Jesus."

"Kylie, a Jesus Freak?" Jerome's brow raises in surprise. "No. Way."

"It's totally true, but don't worry. It's just a phase. I'm sure our friends will snap out of it sooner or later."

"Let's hope it's sooner. Chevy is talking about dropping out of school to live in the desert like John the Baptist."

"Here's my stop," I say as we approach the patio area leading to the back entrance of the dormitory. "Thanks for walking me home."

"Would you like me to come up with you?" I know what that means—he's in the mood.

"No, thanks. I have a big test in the morning."

"C'mon, I won't stay long."

"You never do," I say sarcastically, irritated that he's pressing the issue. "In and out in one minute—it's hardly worth it."

"Whoa. What's with the crappy attitude?"

"I'm not the one with the crappy attitude," I snap back. "You are. I saw what your friends did at the meeting last night." His face pales for a moment. When his eyes turn into dangerous slits, I know that I have stepped over an invisible boundary. I quickly backtrack. "I mean, I saw you guys laughing after Mr. Mott went down. But I didn't see who threw it."

Without warning, Jerome pushes me up against the building. He presses his forearm against my chest, pinning me to the wall. His actions take me totally off guard. He slides a hand down the front of my sweat pants.

"Not tonight," I say, still reeling from the way he just threatened me. It's so unlike him, I don't know how far he will take it. "I really need to study."

"What's the point of studying for tomorrow?" he says, his breaths getting heavier in my ear as he loosens his own sweat pants. "All we got is today. I'm going to let you have it, Gina. I'm going to let you have it real good."

"Ow!" I try to push him away. "You're hurting me!"

"If you mess with the devil," he says with a thrust and a grunt. "You'll get him horny."

"I'm serious, Jerome. I don't want to do this. Let me go."

We struggle. I'm getting more scared and Jerome seems to be getting off on it. He gets so into it that he doesn't notice when I cup the back of his neck with my palm, sliding my other arm around his armpit to grasp his shoulder. Caught in my lock, a move I learned in jui-jitzu, I snap our bodies around 360 degrees.

Jerome is helpless to do anything except go along for the ride until the top of his head slams into the brick wall. With a thud, he collapses to the ground on his stomach. Rolling onto his back, holding the top of his head, he groans in confusion, "What the hell, Gina, I thought you liked it rough."

"What ever gave you that idea?"

"It's not like we haven't done it before. Why are you being such a prude?"

"I don't know, maybe it's because you're being such a prick," I say, on the verge of tears, frantically trying to pull my sweats back up. "What has gotten into you?"

"Reality," he says as he pulls himself to his feet, glaring at me the whole time. "We're wasting our time."

"For once, I think we agree," I sputter angrily. "This relationship is over."

"That's not what I meant."

"Well, that's what you got."

"You're overreacting. I was only trying to point out that life is short and then we die. We are wasting our time, playing it safe, following the rules." He's on his feet now, approaching me fast with eyes full of lust. "Come on, Gina. Let's live our lives to the fullest."

I reach into my coat pocket, wrapping my fingers around a cold familiar presence and pull out my demure Ruger with the butterfly handle. "Don't come any closer."

"Holy shit," Jerome says, his voice turning soprano. "It was just a case of me misreading your signals—I swear." He points to the ground near my feet. His phone is face down there in the asphalt. "Can I please get my cell?"

I kick it over to him, scraping it along the cement. He's lucky that I don't take my foot and smash it to pieces.

He picks it up, brushes off the screen. "Dammit, Gina. You scratched it."

"When you mess with the devil, you get a scratched screen."

His glare is like boiling lava. I keep my gun pointed at him. He snorts and tosses his head in the air like a fearless cock.

"I don't need this kind of drama," he snarls. "We are through."

"Hallelujah."

He grumbles and saunters off.

I don't lower my gun until he fades into the darkness.

When I get to the room, my hands are still shaking, while I try to sort through the incident. Did Jerome truly misread my signals and make an honest mistake? Was my reaction over-the-top, as he claimed? I wish Kylie was here to listen to the recap and lend me her perspective. I'd call Julie, but she is tight with Jerome. She'd side with him, I think.

Fishing a beer out of the mini-fridge, I contemplate our relationship. We've broken up twice in the four short months we've been dating. Once for him cheating. Once for me almost cheating. I cried each time, not ready for it to be over. This time feels different. He's never forced himself on me before. Plus, seeing him laugh when that poor lawyer was struck in the head has changed the way I look at him. I'm left to wonder if I mistook cold indifference for what I thought was happy-go-lucky.

If history repeats itself, Jerome will show up in a couple of days, bearing gifts of chocolate, begging for forgiveness. Sitting here with a beer in my hand, I feel strangely at peace about letting him go for good this time. Giving a tired yawn, I set the beer down, trying to forget the ugly incident between us. Instead, I focus on my schedule. I have a big economics exam in the morning and later I have to work the late shift at Fashionable Young Things. Instead of drinking alcohol, I should be drinking something caffeinated so I can stay up late to study but, not wanting to be wasteful, I finish the beer.

Chapter 10

My eyes flutter open to the sound of faint whispering. My electronic notepad has slipped out of my grip and is lying on the floor. The lights are down low. I must have dozed off on the loveseat.

Six feet away next to the bottom bunk, Kylie is a silhouette on her knees. Seeing my friend humble herself, praying to her newfound God, ought to fill my heart with wonder, but all I feel is revulsion. Since I remain open to the belief in a higher power and accept Christianity as a valid life choice, my negative reaction doesn't make sense, but I'm too tired to analyze it.

"Can you babble quieter over there?" I grumble. "I'm trying to sleep."

"Sorry, Gina. Realizing Jesus died for me after all this time thinking He was just a myth makes me want to shout His Name to the rooftops. You know what I mean?"

"All I know is that I have to get up in four hours."

"A quick question first. Could you recommend a prayer for a newbie believer?"

"Start with the Our Father." My eyelids are heavy. The yawns are coming in rapid succession. "Also known as The Lord's Prayer."

"It sounds familiar. Why that particular one?"

"One day, the people asked Jesus to teach them how to pray. That's the prayer He taught them."

"Cool. What language did He teach it to them in?"

"Who cares?" Knowing Kylie, she wants to pray it in the original language. "G'night."

There's a rustling sound as she crawls into the bottom bunk. Feeling too lazy to move, I think I'll stay parked here right on the sofa. My thoughts are already drifting off again when she calls over to me.

"You have been cranky ever since The Warning. I'm getting the sense that yours was a lot different than mine. Do you want to compare notes?"

"No."

"Do you want to hear about mine?"

"Some other time."

"All righty then." I hear the disappointment in her sigh. After less than twenty seconds of silence, she blurts out, "Jesus showed me how He carried my sins in His wounds. I fell down on my knees and wept with shame. I explained that I didn't understand how I had been hurting Him. Jesus said He already knew that. It's why more mercy was extended to me than to believers. He was so beautiful and loving, Gina. My life will never be the same."

"Well, good for you, because that's not what happened to me. I didn't see my dead sister. I didn't see angels. I didn't see Jesus. And I certainly didn't feel the love. What I saw was my filthy soul and the knowledge that it didn't belong in Heaven. I fell into the deepest darkest void of nothing that you can imagine and it was as far from beautiful as you can get. I went to Hell, Kylie. How is that for a comparison?" I'm glad she can't see the tear sliding down my cheek, because as much as I try to deny it, The Warning shook me up quite badly. It's easier to hide behind the infrasonic theory than face the possibility that what I saw was true. A long silence fills the room. I call over to her in exasperation, "Now that I actually want to talk, you've suddenly gone quiet. Don't even pretend to be asleep."

"I wasn't pretending, Gina. It's just that I was still pondering your Illumination."

"And your conclusion?"

"Scary friggin' stuff."

"Thanks for that brilliant analysis, Einstein."

"I'm sorry. Religion isn't exactly my field of expertise. Maybe you should talk to a nun or a monk or someone."

50

The impromptu conversation has my nerves buzzing. I'm never going to fall asleep now.

The next morning, feeling both mentally and physically exhausted, I barely get up in time to make it to my ethics exam. I hustle in, happy to find Zach sitting in the back of the room. I wave at him and whisper, "Good luck."

Part of me had been worried that the kerfuffle with Langley would drive Zach out. In these times, I've seen more than my fair share of classmates drop out for lesser reasons. Hope is a rare commodity on campus, or anywhere else for that matter.

I'm one of the first to finish. Normally I would head straight over to the cafeteria to eat with the gang. My stomach growls in anticipation but, not wanting to see Jerome, I think about all of the spare change lying on the floor of my vehicle. I can probably dig up enough for a taco or two from the food court at the mall. Instead of hanging around school, I decide to leave for work an hour early, mouth watering in anticipation of a warm meal.

Once outside, I walk past the university's sprawling library, corner around the Technology Center, and then cut across a couple of parking lots. As per usual, a thin layer of comet dust coats the cars that have sat dormant overnight. As I weave through them toward my own dusty ride, I'm feeling optimistic about the exam and my social life as well. With Jerome out of the picture, Zach is certainly starting to catch my eye. Maybe an 'A' and a date with a cute dork are in my future. Of course, my good mood can't last for very long.

Halfway across the parking lot, I get a text from Jerome.

I deeply regret last night's misunderstanding. I think you gave me a concussion. I forgive you. Can you find it in your heart to forgive me, too?

The way he's trying to spread the blame is pathetic. My eyes roll at his refusal to own up to his bad behavior, while my finger hovers over the delete button. The older I get, the more I've come to recognize that the strong image I strive to project to the world isn't entirely accurate. In the past, I have hung onto men longer than they deserve, just because I'm afraid to be alone. Anyway, that's my self-diagnosis as to why I must always have a boyfriend. Thank you, Psychology 101. My finger continues to hesitate. Should I or shouldn't I? Finally, my finger goes down. *Cord cut,* I tell myself. *That wasn't so hard.*

Chapter 11

My car is a battered 12-year-old SUV. The driver's side door is mangled because last winter a tree jumped out at me from nowhere. Okay, okay, I was talking on my phone, not paying attention, and slid into it. Not having the money for repairs, the driver side no longer opens. This means that I need to enter through the passenger-side door, contorting my body at weird angles to maneuver over the gear shift. Once I'm settled in, I set my purse on the floor of the passenger side, and press the ignition button. It takes three tries before the engine rumbles to life. The wipers automatically swish across the dusty windshield. It's a dry layer this morning, so it clears away into the breeze without smearing my window. Heading out, I pray that my jalopy will last long enough to get me through college.

Money is so tight, even with a part-time job, there's never enough. I worry that Fashionable Young Things, like so many other retail outlets, won't survive the economic crisis. Inventory at work has been alarmingly low—a bad sign.

I pull into Hillsboro Mall, thinking about work and the gnawing sensation at the pit of my stomach. Like the rest of the city, the mall parking lot and the stores are coated in fine dust from Comet Yomogi. Trash rolls across the asphalt whenever there's a breeze. Only about a sixteenth of the parking spaces are full, which is typical for a Tuesday afternoon. What is not quite so typical is the stream of terrified people exploding out the exits.

"Oh, balls," I exclaim. "What now?"

My mind races back to my own experience at the mall with an ax-wielding maniac, but it could be a bomb threat, an actual explosion, or a gunman. Sirens are already going off in the distance. I was really looking forward to a taco, dammit. Worse yet, I'm going to lose eight hours off of my already skimpy paycheck.

Familiar with emergency procedures, I know that the exits to and from the mall are going to be blocked off. Nobody will be allowed in or out as soon as the first responders arrive. Not wanting to be forced to hang around, I weave past the people fleeing the store, and hit the gas. As I pass police cars and ambulances heading toward the mall, heart set on a taco, my mind goes down the list of nearby Mexican places.

Suddenly aware of my thought process, I pause to reflect on my screwed up priorities. It seems sociopathic to focus on food when people could be dying a block away. In my defense, I lost an aunt, an uncle, and four cousins when the bomb went off in New York City. Cancer is way up across the nation, especially in children. My sister died of neuroblastoma a couple of years ago, possibly from the radiation carried by the wind after the attack. Half the classmates I went to kindergarten with are dead, taken by diseases, earthquakes, floods, and random acts of violence.

The way I figure, people spend enough time mourning the victims they personally know. If the world stopped every time a stranger became a statistic, nobody would get anything done. Some people would call my attitude cold, but it's the only way to cope with an overwhelming amount of bad shit.

I spot a sign outside Taco Cabana. It's a two-for-one Tuesday. Olé! While I'm waiting my turn, I text my coworkers, hoping for insider information on the happenings at the mall. A few minutes later I leave with my tacos. No word yet from my coworkers.

The next morning, I wake to twenty new texts and eleven voice messages—all but four are from Jerome. Doug and Margaret from work have texted me back. There was a shooting at the mall. Two Fashionable Young Things employees were injured. I fully intend to get more information, but first I go through the rest of my messages.

Despite Jerome's numerous text and voice apologies, it's clear from the same repeated drivel that he hasn't owned up to his actions the other night. He keeps mentioning how he forgives me, too, which pisses me off because I'm not in need of it. A guy that tries to force himself on a girl deserves to get his head smashed into a wall. However, I no longer want to put any more energy into our relationship. I try to make sure he understands that things are over between us by reiterating it in a text:

> The problems between us started before "the incident." I forgive you, but you were right. We shouldn't waste any more time trying to fix something that isn't meant to be. It's best that we end things now before we get too serious.

He texts me back almost immediately:

> **I couldn't be any more serious about you if I tried. Whatever is broken is fixable.**

From there, our conversation goes back and forth, starting with my reply back:

> Don't make this any harder than it has to be, Jerome. We shouldn't see each other anymore.

> > **We run in the same circles. Let's keep open minds about this. Maybe we can just be friends with benefits.**

> Maybe you can screw yourself. Pig.

> > **Okay, I had that coming. Let's just be friends then … no benefits other than the pleasure of each other's company.**

> I don't trust you anymore.

> > **I apologized a thousand times. I care about you so much, Gina. I swear on my life that I would never do anything to hurt you.**

> I'll talk to you when we're among friends, but I don't want to be alone with you. And no more phone calls or texts.

> > **How am I going to earn back your trust if we're never alone together?**

> I'll see you around. Good luck with the baseball.

Will you come to my game on Saturday?

I have to work.

**We're all going to the Blue Moon Club
afterwards. You can join us after your shift.**

The boy doesn't know when to give-up, forcing me to take drastic measures. I block his number.

Later, in the day, wanting to avoid an uncomfortable situation, I go to the cafeteria for lunch at an off time, knowing he won't be there because it's the same time as baseball practice.

While I'm eating, I call my coworker, Doug, to get more details on what happened at the mall yesterday. According to him, the eating joint across the hall from Fashionable Young Things shorted the wrong guy a couple of chicken wings. The manager refused to make it right. Wrong Guy flew into a rampage, shooting the employees, and random customers.

Nance, our Fashionable Young Things assistant manager, was shot in the back. She is expected to live, but might never walk again. When I was new, Nance was my trainer. I have never forgotten how she went out of her way to make me look stupid. In hindsight, she saw me as a threat to the pecking order because of my schooling. I think she was hoping to make me cave under the pressure. Obviously, it didn't work. Although I feel bad about what happened, I can't help to be glad that it happened to her instead of me. Does that make me an evil person? Probably a little.

The other injured employee is Austin—a single father of two young children. He fell when he was running to safety and broke an arm. I don't know him very well, but he has always been a good worker. Austin was really shaken-up at the idea of leaving his children orphans. He is considering quitting the store altogether.

As tragic as the incident was, from my perspective there's a silver lining here. Since lightning rarely strikes in the same place twice, the odds of me getting caught in another random workplace shooting have gone way down. At least that's what I like to tell myself when I get nervous at the prospect of returning to Fashionable Young Things.

After my accounting class, I find Jerome leaning against the wall near the door, waiting for me with a single white rose, eyes downcast. It takes him a few seconds to work up the nerve to make eye contact. He reminds me of a whipped dog, seeking reconciliation with a cruel master. It takes every ounce of discipline not to give him a consoling hug. Steeling myself, I return only a passing glance and continue on my way. Regrettably, he decides to follow me across campus to my next class, pleading for another chance the entire way.

"We have something good here, babe." He trails behind with flower in hand. "Let's work it out."

"Quit following me. You're making me uncomfortable."

"And you're breaking my heart. Don't you understand what you mean to me?"

Not knowing what else to do, I pretend like he's not there, and continue walking. When I go inside the Business and Education building, he continues to be a nuisance. I finally stop to plead with him to leave me alone. He grabs me by the shoulders and gives me a shake.

"Don't do this to us over one stupid mistake!"

"It's not just that. After your buddies nailed that lawyer in the head with a baseball, I saw you laughing and haven't felt the same about you since."

I hadn't meant to ever bring that up again, but his annoying behavior made me lose my cool. The expression on Jerome's face changes from wounded puppy to that of a tiger pushed into a corner. Danger signals go off in my head. He grips me tighter and opens his mouth to yell, when a couple of women professors appear out of nowhere. They step between me and Jerome, sandwiching him between themselves. I'm relieved when they escort my ex away to give him a thorough scolding.

"Jerome," I hear one of them say his name. Maybe he's one of her students. "What were you doing to that poor girl?"

"That's no poor girl—she's my girlfriend."

"It looked like you were threatening her."

"I would never hurt Gina. I love her, but if she won't even talk to me, how am I supposed to win her back?" His voice breaks with emotion.

Holy crap, he's crying. The women look back at me with disapproving frowns. Oh, I get it now. His tears are a ploy to gain their sympathy, making me look like the bad guy. I don't know what else the women say to him as they move out of earshot, but for the rest of the day, he leaves me alone.

Chapter 12

As the days roll into weeks, I see Jerome only in passing. If I'm already with our circle of friends at the cafeteria, he sits somewhere else. If he beats me to the circle, I take my tray elsewhere. He occasionally gives me a nod, or a tip of his baseball hat, but that's the extent of it.

Lately, I've been seeing him with another girl—a pretty blonde freshman. I'm surprised by how jealous I'm not. I can't remember the last time I was without a boyfriend for a whole month. And I'm doing okay. In fact, it's kind of liberating to attend social functions without having to worry about him getting drunk, insulting someone, or acting like an adolescent, making us both look bad. I could get used to being single, but I wish Zach would make a move. I've dropped him hints that I'm interested, like smiling whenever we make eye contact in class, and that time I picked a piece of imaginary lint out of his hair. Either he's totally clueless, too scared to ask me out, or possibly gay.

People are talking less and less about The Warning. Not Kylie though. She spends all her spare time researching the related prophecies and the history of Christianity in general. Her efforts to clean up her life and not talk smack about anyone is a drag, but I suppose it doesn't matter. Between school and work, there isn't much time for socializing.

Since the injured employees decided not to come back, I've been offered the assistant manager position. The store manager, Dora, has agreed that I can still take my scheduled vacation and don't have to go full-time until the week after finals. Needing the money, and knowing the experience will look good on a resume, I take the promotion. Look at me, I'm moving up in the world.

Chapter 13

On a cold day in early May, I pull into the last row of the mall parking lot for the early shift, snowflakes lightly drifting down. The first thing I notice is that the huge front windows of Anchor & Bales department store appear to have been smashed out. Trucks and workers are already on the scene preparing to install new ones.

The digital display high above on the mall's overhead billboard shows 8:50 a.m. as it flits through various advertisements. There's a big linen sale at Home Scapes. Barclay's Jewelry is offering a special on wedding rings. In an attempt to attract the ever-growing polyamorous market, the discount applies to matching sets of up to four. The ad goes on to mention that rings can be altered to accommodate spouses with paws, or even hooves, but additional charges may apply. For the life of me, I don't understand why anyone would want to marry a cat or a horse, but who am I to judge?

Taking my spiffy new name tag out of my purse, I glide my fingers admiringly over the words: *Gina A., Asst. Manager.* It's one of those nice magnetic name tags, the kind that don't leave pinholes in your top. This is my third week as second-in-command. The district manager came in to observe the store for a day. We immediately hit it off. She says I'm a natural organizer. Despite the low inventories I have managed to make the store look full through creative zoning, and she likes my professional attitude toward the customers. The district manager shook my hand and asked me to consider making a career with FYT. That was a moment of affirmation for me. I know that someday all my efforts at school are going to pay off. Even though the idea of working retail for the rest of my life makes me want to jump headfirst from the nearest building, I'm not writing it off. With businesses folding left and right, I may have to take whatever I can get until the economy picks up again.

Purse strap over my left shoulder, I climb over the gear shift in my skirt and stylish navy captain's jacket, making an awkward exit out the passenger side door. My breath turns to fog upon contact with the cool air outside. In a pair of two-inch pumps, I make my way over the trash-strewn asphalt, a caffeinated cup of Jo Jo Java heavy on my mind. I can't afford coffee made from actual coffee beans (few students can), but Jo Jo's secret blend tastes close to the real thing.

As I'm walking across the lot, toward the side entrance, I spot a middle-aged man dressed in a tattered business suit. He's staggering around like a flakka junkie and talking to himself. Thinking it might make an interesting vlog for my internet channel, I take out my phone.

"Dear Followers: The number of homeless people are increasing all over the city. I look at them under the fading light and wonder what they used to be. Notice his grimy Armani suit—could he have been an accountant, a salesman, a lawyer? What led to his downfall? Does he have anyone left in the world who cares about him? But the most worrisome question is—*could whatever happened to him, happen to me?*"

When he starts moving in my direction, my free hand reaches toward the Ruger LC9 tucked away in my handbag. The closer he gets, the tighter my hand wraps around its handle. Strings of glistening green mucus hang from each nostril. His pale skin is dotted with purple scabs. Oh, balls. I hope he doesn't have the pox or something. He's almost bald, but the ring of hair he has left looks like a twiggy bird nest going every which way. The most disturbing thing is his eyes, an unnatural shade between gold and orange, glinting with gleeful malevolence. His expression is that of an insider on a cruel joke that's about to unfold. Upon spotting me, an angry fountain of obscenities bubbles out of him.

"Ignorant, dirty beasts. They do not listen. Do not see. Do not know what is coming. We are the Fade." So full of malice, his voice is like a snarling wildcat, making me wish the doors to the mall were a helluva lot closer. "The days of darkness are at hand."

Tattered Man is about ten feet away, still staggering around. I arc my path away from him, hoping he will pass me by without incident. Me, being me, I'm trying to avoid staring at him directly, while keeping him square in my camera lens. He stops at the shrub bed built into the parking lot filled with dead azalea bushes, tilting his head as if to listen to the dirt. A second later, with a gleeful shriek he begins to dig under the azaleas with his bare hands, emerging with a fat juicy earthworm. He proceeds to slurp it into his mouth like a strand of spaghetti. After I finish gagging, I whisper to the camera. "I can't believe it. He. Ate. The. Worm." I'm like a bystander who comes upon a gruesome collision. I know it's wrong to get off on tragedy, but morbid curiosity holds me fast to the scene. My internet followers are going to love the Tattered Man footage.

He's still chewing when the sun peeks out of the clouds for a moment. The haze is still everywhere, but the world brightens from grays and browns to lighter grays and mustard colors. Tattered man shields his face as if the light is a knife stabbing at his eyes. Shaking his other fist at the rising sun, he cries out in a voice that sounds noticeably different than the wildcat sound he made earlier. It's deep like a big kettle drum. "The music will be blotted out with crying and gnashing of teeth. The Fade will feast on the flesh of man."

Living in the city, I've seen my share of mental cases roaming the streets, and have learned to take it in stride. However, there's an extra scoop of crazy on this dude. I decide to move on. Head slightly down, I keep my gaze on the mall doors. Risking a glance back, I'm relieved to see he's not following me. By the time my foot steps onto the sidewalk, he's fifty yards away. The danger has passed and my muscles begin to relax. I let go of the gun in my purse. Feeling home free, I'm going for the door handle, when Tattered Man's reflection appears in the glass like a ghostly specter right behind me.

Chapter 14

Heart thundering, I accidently drop my phone. My other hand dives for the Ruger in my purse. They teach you in jiu-jitsu never to turn your back to your opponent, so I spin around to face Tattered Man.

"Do you smell that taint?" He sniffs the air like a bloodhound. "She's one of ours. Let's take the whore now."

"Back off." I lift the gun out of my handbag, pointing it at his face. "Or I'll waste ya."

The laughter that follows sounds like it's coming out of five or six distinct individuals, including a woman or two in the mix, giving me the heebie-jeebies.

"Metal cannot stop the princes of the air," he replies in an old, raspy voice this time. "The chains are loosening."

"We will drink her dry." The man says, but this time his voice sounds like the Wicked Witch of the West, complete with the maniacal laughter. "Wait, brothers." A Tinker Bell voice comes out of him this time. "The girl is sealed. Touch her before it's time, and the guardians will rush to her aid."

"I see the rotting edges," says yet another voice, impossibly deep. "Ripe fruit for the Fade, yet bearing the seal. How can this be?"

"The prayers of an intercessor protect her," cackles the man's inner witch, "but it won't be enough when the darkness comes."

The swirling of lights from the mall's security golf carts are a welcome sight. Two carts, each carrying two guards, pull up in front of the sidewalk. The guards get out to stand about ten feet away. I know they have seen my gun. A lot of mall employees carry them. None of the guards has ever reported us, because even though they're only supposed to carry non-lethal weapons themselves, they carry guns, too.

"Is this man bothering you, ma'am?" asks one of the guards.

"Yes, definitely."

"Lies. Lies." Spittle flies from the crazy man's mouth. I blink in the deluge. "We pledge our allegiance to the Father of Lies."

"Step away," the guards order him. "Or we will forcibly remove you from the premises."

"Toil, boil, mortal coil." He turns toward the guards, laughing like a lunatic. "You cannot hurt the Fade." All the different voices seem to come out of him at the same time as he falls to his knees, raking his nails down his own face, leaving a trail of blood. "When the world walks in the night, the living will envy the dead."

"The crazies are coming out of the woodwork this morning," one of the guards says to the others as they charge up their tasers. "Call the paddy wagon. Tell 'em we're bagging another one."

Seeing my chance while Tattered Man is distracted, I snatch up my phone, yank open the mall doors and slink inside. I hold onto the door handle, just in case he tries to come in. Feeling safe once again, I aim my camera through the glass to catch Tattered Man charging at security. One of the guards tases him. His body goes epileptic as he falls to the sidewalk. After thirty or forty seconds of violent twitching, his body goes still. Lying there on the sidewalk, Tattered Man goes straight into a rant, "Come the darkness, cursed children of Adam and Eve, the Fade will suck you dry!"

"Yeah, yeah," says one of the guards. "Suck you, too, buddy."

When the guards try to cuff him, he writhes and calls them names. "Do not touch us, mortal bags of excrement!" Which earns him some whacks from a shiny black nightstick. A police van rolls up just in time to miss the action. A door slides open and they carry him over to shove him inside without ceremony.

"Wow, that homeless man was something else." I turn the camera to myself. "Rounding up vagrants is a normal part of the mall security gig. If you ask me, they're not paid nearly enough." I show my hands, how they're trembling with adrenaline. "I was lucky the mall cops showed up when they did. *Toil, boil, mortal coil* is going to be running through my head for the rest of the day. Wild stuff."

Excited to have caught the incident on video, I start prepping it to upload to my JustSharing channel as I'm walking toward Jo Jo Java's.

The main part of the mall where customers shop is airy and cheerful. Just below the murmur of numerous conversations taking place along the corridors are the tropical strums of ukuleles, accompanied by the hollow clang of metal drums. This time of year the owners always pipe in the scent of coconut and mango. It's supposed to get shoppers in the mood for backyard barbeques, lounging outside by the pool, and the new apparel to go along with it. Didn't the owners get the bulletin that summer has been cancelled?

After I complete the upload, I video myself once again, talking about random things.

"Dear Followers: The retirees are already coming in for their morning exercise. They're so cute and friendly. I hope the world is around long enough for me to reach the age where I care more about comfort than style.

"On to the next topic. In case you don't know how this JS thing works, it goes something like this. The more views my vlogs get, the more I earn. The more subscribers to my channel, the more I earn per view. As of today, I have 450 followers." I wave to the camera. "Thank you, loyal viewers. I'm hoping to reel in even more of you with my Tattered Man video. If you find it entertaining, please spread the word.

"As for me, it's back to the grindstone. Wait a second. What the heck is a grindstone? People are always going to it, but where is it, and what does it do? I picture a huge cogwheel made of stone. Slaves turn the grindstone on its axis, sweating and huffing day and night. By the end of their miserable lives, they've walked a million miles, without ever having gone anywhere. I wonder if FYT is my grindstone. If you have a grindstone, or an ax to grind, please tell me about it in the comment section."

Okay, enough of that. Powering off the video, I suck in a few breaths, steeling myself to face the day. Stores are already beginning to open for business. The metallic rumble of their gates rolling up to let the customers in gets me moving faster toward Jo Jo Java. Along the way, I pass lots of stores whose gates no longer open. I'd estimate half the mall has gone out of business. That doesn't mean the closed stores are actually empty. I have rarely laid eyes on the squatters, but I hear them from behind the walls on occasion. At night, after the lights go down low, if you listen carefully, you can hear the voices of the homeless people who have taken up residence in the vacant stores. I've been told that the mall attracts the more upscale homeless—educated couples with children. They aren't above fighting for their turf, though. It took the mall owners a while to realize this is a good thing. The homeless families keep the gangs and prostitutes away for free. Regardless, it's unnerving to know they're lurking about unseen like rats in dark corners.

According to the guards, after the late-shifters all go home, it's like the ghouls and goblins have left the graveyard. Hundreds of vagrants roam the employee passageways. They let their kids play on the climbing sculptures in the Commons. As long as they don't cause trouble or try to steal anything, security no longer tries to keep them out, but sometimes they turn up dead from starvation or unknown causes, in the employee hallways. It's a sad way to go, if you ask me.

Requiem From A Dream begins to play from my coat pocket.

A GIF of me and Kylie fills up the screen. It's from about a year ago when we went up to Lake Michigan on spring break. On the beach with the sand dunes of Michigan behind us, Kylie and I braved the cool weather in skimpy bikinis, raising our beer bottles, on the road to Totally Sloshed Town. In the GIF, we're toasting to long life and prosperity, in an endless loop.

"Hi Kylie," I answer. "What's up?"

"Just calling to see how you are doing."

"You must have watched my Crazy Tattered Man vlog."

"Not yet, but I got the link. I'm calling because I had that nightmare again. We were lost in a black fog. Demons everywhere. Just when I thought we were going to die, a church appeared in the distance, like a lighthouse guiding us to safety. I think it's a message about The Three Days of Darkness."

"Have you been studying eschatology before bed again?"

"What if I have?" She says defensively. "The prophets were right about the Illumination. The signs are rolling out just like they predicted. Only the brain-dead can ignore them. Do you remember that article I had you read about the signs?"

"Which one? You made me read a million of 'em."

"Don't exaggerate—it was two or three at the most. I'm talking the list of things that are supposed to happen right before the darkness arrives."

"Something about the lights not working."

"That's right. Just before the darkness arrives, the temperature will drop, lightning will strike, ushering in a storm of Biblical proportions." I roll my eyes, wishing I had let the phone go to voicemail. "All artificial sources of energy will fail right before the gates of Hell are opened to the Earth. Promise me, if any of these things start to happen, you will come home immediately."

"You know I don't believe in all this apocalypse crap—at least not in the Biblical sense of the word. And, considering you're a science major, neither should you."

"My parents are going to be leaving in August for Antarctica," Kylie reminds me. "It's a three year project. Three years! Despite my pleas for them to heed The Warning, they just won't listen. You are all I have, Gina. Please, don't make me go through this alone."

"You are upsetting yourself over nothing."

"I called just to make sure you were okay." I can tell she's mad. "And you are. So, bye."

"Uh, bye."

Pressing END, I think about how college was supposed to have been a time to get away from the religious superstitions of my family. Living with Kylie is giving me flashbacks. I'd rather hear my grandmother's stories of the angels and saints than this gloomy tribulation stuff.

I remember Grammy's account of how a dove flew out of St. Joan of Arc's mouth as she was being burned at the stake as a heretic. Her heart was discovered perfectly preserved in the ash. Thinking about that "oh, shit" moment, when the English realized they had murdered a saint, tickles the imagination. However, my favorite story was about a solider named Peregrine. He had a cancer that was eating away at his leg. The night before it was to be amputated, he went into a trance and saw Jesus reach down from the cross to touch him. The next morning—no more cancer. Naturally, when my little sister got sick, this story gave me great hope. I asked God to do for Riley what He had for St. Peregrine. Grammy and I would sit on the porch swing for hours, praying the rosary, asking for St. Peregrine's intercession, expecting a miracle. A miracle that would never come.

The morning after Riley died, I woke up wondering if everything I knew about God was wrong. I cried out to Jesus for a sign that He was there and truly cared about our suffering down here on Earth. His reply—my father's death a couple of days later. Trying to make sense of it all, friends and family said Dad had been blinded by tears of grief, causing his car to accidentally swerve into a guard rail. The word *suicide* was tossed around in hushed tones at the funeral. Not knowing what to believe, all I knew for certain was that nothing would ever be the same.

When I arrive at Jo Jo Java's, the gate is still down. That's odd. They usually open a half an hour early for the morning-shifters. A couple of other mall employees are waiting around for their daily fix when a security guard happens by.

"Sorry, folks," she says. "Jo Jo didn't renew the lease."

The woman next to me asks, "What does that mean exactly?"

"Another one bites the dust," I explain.

"Son-of-a-gun," says an older gentleman who runs the tuxedo rental shop down the hall. "Jo Jo's was the last place in the mall to buy a civilized cup of joe. Now what am I supposed to do?"

"Bring a thermos," the security guard suggests.

If the others are thinking what I'm thinking, they're wondering if their place of employment is next on the chopping block. My mother already sends me more money than she can afford. If I lose this job, I'll be totally reliant on the school's meal ticket system, and I'll lose my car. Telling myself that there is no point in fretting over it, I pull myself away.

Chapter 15

Not worrying about my employer going bankrupt is easier said than done. My stomach knots up in the ninety seconds it takes to walk from Jo Jo Java to Fashionable Young Things. Since the store isn't opened for business yet, I have to enter through the Employees Only access hallway to unlock it from the back.

The door to the restricted area opens to a long corridor made of gray cement block. Fluorescent tube lights buzz overhead. The floor is gray concrete polished with a shiny coating, littered with wadded up toilet paper, empty snack sized potato chip bags, used needles, and a couple of torn condom wrappers. I think about how the homeless roam these halls at night when all the customers are gone, how they're here right now, hiding in the shadows, and it causes my fingers to grow twitchy for the gun in my purse. Down the hall the old gentleman I saw at Jo Jo Java's has arrived to unlock the back door of the tuxedo shop. I wave. He doesn't notice, but it's good to know other employees are nearby while I open the store. Now that I'm an assistant manager, locking and unlocking the store, depending on what shift I'm working, is part of my new responsibilities.

After I press in the key code, the door opens right into the stock room, which doubles as the employee break room. It's a narrow area— about twenty-five feet long and fifteen feet wide with a long folding table against the wall. Dora, the store manager, has her desk back here as well. The computer terminal, which interfaces with the home office in Cincinnati, sits off to the side. Whoever opens the store has to log into the computer system to power on the registers and read any memos coming from the home office. Flicking on the switch, I wait for the computer to boot up, and then I open the store's email. Nothing of interest today, just the usual updates about how they are dealing with the supply shortage and shipping interruptions due to the poor policing of our nation's highways. The number of jacked supply trucks seems to go up every day. The home office wants every FYT employee to send a letter to our state representative to address the issue. It's already been worded. All I have to do is print out a stack of them and hand them out to the employees for their signatures.

By the time I'm finished, it's the top of the hour. I go to the front of the store to unlock the metal gates and slide them away out of sight. This is the day our biggest shipment of the week comes in. Fingers crossed it's not a repeat of last week. Less than half our orders were filled and inventory is dangerously low.

A petite woman in her thirties, with bleached blonde hair and a peppy walk, wearing a black leather mini-skirt, and a faux rabbit fur jacket, comes strolling in with a scowl etched into her face.

"Good morning, Margaret," I tell her.

"I'm so pissed," she hisses. "I can't believe Jo Jo Java's went out of business."

"It's a real shame," I agree. "A lot of people are going to miss it."

I'm about to reply, when in comes Doug, a twenty-year-old sales associate, dressed in black from head to toe. This is a departure from the Thor, God of Thunder, look he sported all last month, which included brown leather trousers, a white tunic with draw strings, blonde hair pulled back in a ponytail. Today his hair is short, spiky and also black. His blue eyes are rimmed with thick black eyeliner.

"What's with the cape?" Margaret asks him.

"Hello, ladies," he says, his voice unnaturally smooth and deep. "I am no longer Doug. From this day forth, I shall be known as *The Shadow.*"

Margaret and I exchange amused expressions. Now I get it. He's pretending to be Shadow, a brooding vampire who fights the bad guys, while battling his own thirst for blood. This is typical behavior for Doug. He's really into superhero movies. His dream is to turn the heroic look into a fashion empire. Doug's desire to be called by the superhero's name takes his obsession to a worrisome new level.

"My cousins had a German Shepherd named Shadow," I inform him. "All it wanted to do was eat, sleep, and lick its balls. Because I like you, we are going to continue to call you Doug at Fashionable Young Things. Okay?"

He just laughs and heads to the storeroom to put away his coat—er, cape.

As I'm powering on the front register, I get a call. The truck driver has arrived and is unloading our shipment onto the dock at the back of the mall. I tell Doug and Margaret to go out to meet him. After all, an assistant manager shouldn't be doing the grunt work. It takes them about thirty minutes to return with the first load on a dolly. By then, I've helped a couple of customers and rung them up with a friendly smile.

Margaret comes out of the stockroom. "It's a big ass shipment," she says, talking loud enough for the customers to hear every word. "I mean it's small, but bigger than the last couple of shipments. It's going to take at least three trips to bring it all here."

Sidling up to Margaret I remind her in quiet tones, "Our store is all about promoting a *young* attitude—hip and carefree—for people of all ages. We want them to picture themselves having fun in our stylish new clothing. So let's not spoil the image by burdening them with our shipping problems."

After I send Doug over to help the customer, I go back with Margaret to the stockroom, leaving Doug to monitor the sales floor. The first box I open holds the shirts that have been on backorder for three months.

"Dora told me this vendor is impossible to work with," I explain to Margaret, hoping she'll see I deserve to be the assistant manager. "She said I was wasting my time by calling them, but more power to me if I wanted to give it a try." I hold up a lightly sequined top, perfect for a night on the town. "Look, they even sent us extras. Am I good or am I good?" Ignoring my co-worker's eye rolls, I calmly delegate. "Margaret, please call the customers who were waiting for these. Be sure to apologize profusely for the delay and offer them a ten percent off voucher on their next purchase."

"Will do, boss."

As we dig through the merchandise, we find three boxes of jeans in the new inventory, a rare item during the cotton shortage. I couldn't afford denim if it wasn't for the steep employee discount. As is, I buy most of my clothes at Loved Again, a second hand store for those on a limited budget.

I fish around through the clutter, grumbling about the disorganization of the backroom, until I find the 'JEANS in stock! Come on in!' sign. Taking it in hand, I head out to the sales floor, telling Doug to "zone for abundance." That's store lingo for pulling the merchandize forward, spreading it out to make the racks look full. It sounded so corny to me when I first started working here, I could barely gag the words out of my mouth. Now the lingo flows out of me without a second thought. Uttering more corny store lingo, I add, "Let shoppers come into our store to find an oasis of fun and good taste."

"Amen, sister." Doug bows his head and folds his hands in prayer, mocking me. "Let there be peace at FYT and let it begin with me."

Margaret rolls her eyes at both of us. A couple of women walk into the store with young children in tow. I send Margaret and Doug back into the storeroom to finish inventory, while I say hello to the customers. They seem to want to browse without me hovering over their shoulders, so I back off, telling them I'll be nearby if they need anything.

"Ewww!" Margaret's terrified screech reaches from the storeroom to the selling floor, causing the customers and me to turn toward the storage room. "What is it?" she cries out.

"How the hell should I know?" Doug replies.

"Kill it!"

"I'm not touching that thing. You kill it!"

I flash an apologetic look to the customers as I take a step towards the storeroom. "Excuse me a moment." My fists curl into balls as I prepare to murder my unprofessional underlings.

Chapter 16

Entering the storage room, I see Doug poking at something under the sorting table with the long pole we use for hanging banner ads. Margaret is pressed against the far wall with apprehension written all over her face. Another rat must have snuck in with the shipment.

"The customers can hear you out on the sales floor," I chastise them. "Just catch the stupid rat and be quiet about it."

"That's no rat," Margaret says, her voice going up a notch. "It hissed at me and flew around the room."

"Hissed and flew?" I raise my brow in my best questioning expression. "What could it be?"

"Either an insect from outer space," Doug quips, "or a new breed of cockroach straight from New York."

In my opinion, it's far too soon to be making jokes about the destruction of New York City. I lost relatives in the blast, my sister from the aftereffects of the drifting radiation, and, if the truth were known, it's probably the cause of my grandmother's cancer as well. Pushing Doug aside, I take the flashlight off the shelf to take a look for myself. The thing I see in the beam is unlike any creature I've ever encountered.

It reminds me of a tiny winged monkey, but it has long bristly legs and a brown exoskeleton. There's a curled stinger for a tail, like a scorpion's barb. It scurries across the beam of light. I cringe when I finally get a good look at its head. Unlike the rest of its body, the face is pale in color, with two large front-facing black eyes rimmed in gold, giving it an intelligent, almost human expression. Three golden horns sweep back from the top of its head like a crown.

"Give me the pole," I order Doug. "We'll use an empty box to trap it. When I sweep it out, you pounce on it. "

Margaret hands Doug a box and returns to her spot against the wall. As soon as the end of the pole makes contact with it, the insect-like thing opens its slit of a mouth, revealing a zigzag of white teeth, and it hisses. In my freaked-out state, I don't back off fast enough for the thing's liking. It leaps right at me.

In stereotypical girlie fashion, I drop the pole and scream. Margaret and Doug scream, too. The beating of its wings sounds like tiny horse hooves galloping over a metal race track. I wildly flail my arms as it circles around my head, buzzing through the room, diving at Margaret, then circling back to land on the wall. Margaret runs out of the storage room, waving her arms. My eyes follow her in longing. Unfortunately, I'm the one in charge today. It's up to me to handle the situation.

Unsure what to do, Doug and I stare at the thing, waiting for it to make the next move. The creepiest part is the way it seems to be studying us back with those creepy calculating eyes. Doug takes hold of an old sign, intending to smash it dead. The insect is so big, it's going to be filled with a lot of gunk, making a ghastly stain on the wall.

"Wait," I say, backing up toward the storage cabinet. "Let's try the insect killer first."

A can is nearby, in the same room, so it doesn't take me but a minute to find it. Part of me thinks Doug should do the honors, since he is a guy. I'm the one in charge though. The duty falls on me. Taking a breath for courage, I point the nozzle and spray. That just pisses it off.

The bug hisses and dives at me. Doug swats at it with the sign but misses. It gets past the sign and, seemingly angered by the attack, lands on Doug's cheek. Its scorpion-like tail uncurls and jabs him right under his left eye. Doug spins in a circle, frantically brushing the bug away. It doubles back to land on his face again. This time it stings him on the right cheek. In a panic, I douse Doug, the insect, and myself with the insecticide, creating a cloud that chokes me and Doug, though the bug seems to be just fine.

"Smash the son-of-bitch!" Doug begs. "Smash it dead!"

"I'm trying to, but you keep moving!" Grabbing one of the new boots that came in with the shipment, I yell at Doug, "Hold still!"

It finally lets go of his face to drop on the ground. I crunch the bug between the floor and the boot heel. The wings continue to flutter. I lift the boot and smash it down again, sending its icky green guts splattering around the room. I bet I hit it six times before it goes completely still.

Meanwhile, Doug is groaning in pain. The stings have left behind two vicious red welts. "My face is on fire!" Doug cries out. He clenches onto the fabric on the front of my shirt, taking me by surprise. "You gotta help me."

"I will. I will." I yell out the door for Margaret, trying to ease him down to the nearest chair. "Call for an ambulance and get security here on the double—tell them to bring their first aid kit—anything they might have to stave off an allergic reaction."

Margaret runs for the phone. He lets go of my shirt to slide to the floor, where he holds his face, writhing and screaming in agony. I straighten my legs, heart thumping wildly, unsure how to help him. Oh, balls. Why did I have to be the boss today? *A good leader takes charge in a crisis,* I coach myself. *Stay calm and help your employee.*

Margaret reappears in the doorway. "An ambulance is on the way," she announces. "People are starting to come in to see what all the yelling is about. A lady says she's a nurse, asked if there was anything she can do, but I told her customers aren't allowed in the storeroom."

I turn sharply, "You better not have told her to go away."

"But we could get fired for letting people into the employees only area."

I brush past Margaret. Running onto the sales floor, I see a rotund woman leaving the store. "Hold on!" I chase her down. "Are you a nurse?"

"Yes," she slows and turns around. "I am."

"Thank, God. We really need your help."

I usher the nurse into the back room. I swear Doug's face has swollen huge in the thirty seconds I was gone."

"When did this happen?" The nurse inquires.

"About three minutes ago."

"Oh, my goodness." The nurse's eyes widen. Her voice is cool and collected though. "Have you called 9-1-1?"

"An ambulance is on the way."

"Are you having difficulty breathing?" she asks Doug.

"Who cares, lady?" He yells impetuously. "Give me some damn pain killers!"

"As you can hear," I say, shaking my head, "his breathing is fine."

"Let's keep it that way," the nurse replies. "I don't like how fast it's swelling. We need some ice right away."

There's a soft pretzel place with an ice machine down the hall. I sprint out of FYT and through the mall, cutting in line in front of other customers.

"I need two cups of ice," I tell the woman behind the counter. "The largest you got, and hurry!"

"Wait your turn," she tells me with an indignant frown.

"I'm sorry," I try to make her understand. "This is a medical emergency."

"Cups of ice aren't free, you know. They're $4.50 each."

"Did I mention this is an emergency?"

"Did I mention, I don't care? No pay, no ice."

I leap over the counter, pushing her aside with my hip to grab a couple of supersize cups.

"You better be planning on paying for this."

"Bill me later, bitch," I snarl, ignoring her protests. While I have them under the ice dispenser, she's cussing at me and dialing security. They'll take my side when they get a look at Doug's grotesque face, so I'm not the least bit worried.

I return as fast as I can with the ice. The nurse wraps it in a new shirt to hold it against Doug's increasingly puffy wounds. The paramedics arrive about ten minutes later to take over.

"It looks like a royal hisser sting," says the first paramedic.

"That makes three attacks in two weeks," replies his partner.

"I've never heard of a royal hisser," I admit, while the nurse and I hover behind them in the background.

"They're not from around here," the first paramedic explains. "They're a recently discovered species native to Siberia. But with the weather being all screwed up, the world is their oyster.

"We thought the first attack was a fluke," says the other paramedic. "In light of two new cases, maybe not."

"Someone else was bitten?" Doug groans weakly through a swollen cheek. His eye is completely closed up now.

"A high school soccer team was attacked last week during practice."

"Are they okay now?"

"Nope," says the first paramedic. "Dead as doornails, the whole lot of 'em."

Doug's eyes widen. His mouth let's out a hoarse whimper. My stomach sinks. What am I going to tell his family? Just as a wave of panic is about to sweep me off of my feet, the paramedic slugs Doug on the arm.

"I'm just messing with you, kid. Other than a little scarring, the girls made a full recovery. But you're in for one helluva painful night."

"You're a fucktard," Doug tells the paramedic.

Both paramedics bust out laughing.

It is kind of funny, but I agree with Doug. What a fucktard.

Chapter 17

Just before dawn a few days later, crows cawing outside the dorm window wake me from dark slumber. The clock says 3:58 am. Knowing my phone alarm is set to go off in two minutes, I stretch to hit the off button. The crack of space below the bathroom door lets in a sliver of light. I peek below the top bunk to see that Kylie's bed is empty. She knew I was getting up extra early to head to my grandparents' home in Valparaiso. Why is she up, invading my bathroom time?

While I'm waiting, I check my JustSharing account. The Crazy Tattered Man vlog has more than doubled my number of followers. As of today, I have 1,011. Whoohoo! My thoughts drift to poor Doug.

Dora, our manager, wasn't happy when I called her about the hisser incident in the storage room. The last thing she wants is a lawsuit on her hands. She and I went to the hospital the day after he was stung. Never knowing what to do in these situations, I brought him some flowers and a dozen balloons. Crap a coot, he looked awful. Pale and shaky. Where the venom went in there are cesspools of black goo encircled with crusty red skin. Doug described the pain from the stings like acid eating through his face and sinking down into his bones. Even with pain medication, he spent the night screaming for death. By the next day, he was feeling a lot better. The swelling went down. He kept itching at the scabs while we were visiting. The nurses told him if he didn't stop, they were going to leave awful scars. Doug told us he wouldn't mind a scar or two because all the best superheroes have them. That boy is so weird. Doug thought he would be able to return to work in a day or two.

On the way out of the hospital, Dora complained that we can't have him on the sales floor looking like that. Not my problem though. Next week is finals. I'm taking seven vacation days to study. However, I'm planning on devoting the first three days to my grandparents. That is, if Kylie ever gets out of the bathroom.

"How long are you going to be?" I yell through the door.

"Just a few. Hope you don't mind if I tag along for the trip."

"Uh," I stammer. "My grandparents are only expecting one. You know how old people get set in their ways. I don't want to upset them."

"No worries," Kylie smirks. "Your grandmother invited me."

"Say what?"

"You heard me."

"When did you talk to my Grammy?"

"She called to make sure you weren't going to drive up there alone."

"How'd she get your number?"

"I dunno, but we ended up talking for two hours."

"What did you possibly have to talk about for two hours?"

"The Warning, cheeseburger casserole, End Times, gas prices, stuff like that. I see why you love her so much. She's a really neat lady. Since the roads are so dangerous, she feels better knowing I'm going up with you."

"You don't have to do that. I'll be studying for finals, listening to my class notes, all the way up there. It's probably going to annoy you."

"Nah. I'll just pop in my ear buds and listen to whatever."

"Oh." I'm not enjoying the idea of sharing my Grammy-time, but it's a six hour drive to her house. Having a travel buddy isn't the worst idea ever. "I suppose having you along might be fun."

"Damn straight," she says. "Oh, shit. I meant to say *dang* straight."

I snort with laughter. Kylie's efforts to stop cussing have been a source of amusement. It's so engrained in her vocabulary, she doesn't notice when she's doing it. I'll give her credit for trying though.

Kylie and I are on the road by 5 a.m. About an hour in, I stop to fill up the tank. It's turning out to be a sunny day. Well, there's still the dust blowing around in the atmosphere, creating a hazy brown shield around the Earth, but there are no clouds. The air is warm, mid-forties. It's supposed to reach the upper fifties later in the day. Summer might just show up after all.

Kylie offers to pay for the gas, which totals more than I make in a week, and heads into the Gas & Goodie Mart. My resentment at having her along is rapidly dwindling. After she returns with an armload of candy, chips, and soda, which surely cost a small fortune, my petty reasons for not wanting her here melt away. Off we go again, with me behind the wheel, munching on corn puffs while Kylie sucks on a jawbreaker in the passenger seat, working out a math problem on her electronic notepad.

"I can't read when I'm in the car," I say. "It gives me a migraine."

"Doz nit boer me abert."

It takes me a few moments to figure out what she is saying with that big ball of candy in her mouth—*doesn't bother me a bit,* I think.

The two of us fall quiet as I concentrate on my supervision notes recited by the computer voice coming out of the car speaker. Twenty or thirty minutes later, my focus begins to stray. I'm noticing how half the trees along the highway look dead, not a single bud on their branches. The other half have buds, which seems abnormal for May. If memory serves, they should be mostly leafed out by now. Damn Yomogi has screwed up everything, including Mother Nature. In springs gone by, this road used to be full of wildflowers in every shade of blue. There are still flowers here and there, but yellow and brown brush cover most of the land in either direction. There is no denying that Earth is seriously ill. If the planet cannot recover, what will become of us? I know the answer, but I like to pretend it's an open-ended question.

Further down the road, we enter an area known as Dead Man's Stretch. The jagged outline of darkened skyscrapers, abandoned after a series of dirty bomb attacks, stands forlornly in the distance. The exits to the crumbling city are plastered with *Do Not Enter* and *High Radiation* signs. Its perimeter has become a dumping ground for junk and rusty old vehicles, but the highwaymen call it home. This is a bad place to have a breakdown.

"Remind me to vlog about this on the way back," I tell Kylie.

"Isn't this where your friends got carjacked last year?"

"Yep, Julie and Brad. They were traveling late one night, when they came to a semi parked across the road. As soon as they stopped, the highwaymen came out. Luckily, they only wanted the car and their belongings. It could have been a lot worse."

"If you're stupid enough to travel after dark, you're pretty much asking for trouble," Kylie replies. "Speaking of stupid people—what's going on with Jerome?"

"Don't know. Don't care."

"That's the spirit, girlfriend." Not having seen the old snarky Kylie surface since The Warning, I laugh. It's nice to know she is still in there somewhere underneath all the Christian claptrap. "Running off your boyfriend with a gun, after he tried to rape you, ought to qualify for some kind of bad breakup award."

We're driving through a small town when a call comes in from Grandpa Applegate. I put him on the speaker, so I can concentrate on my driving.

"Have you left, yet?" He yells through the speaker, making Kylie practically jump out of her seat.

"He's hard of hearing," I whisper to her as I turn down the volume. "I hope you don't mind a lot of yelling back and forth." Then I shout into the speaker. "We've been on the road since five or six, Grandpa."

"Hah! Hear that, woman? You owe me a coffee cake." That's him talking to Grammy. It always makes me smile to hear Grandpa and Grammy playfully tease each other. "And you said she would still be in bed. Where are you now, Gina?"

"In a town called Van Wert."

"Good. You haven't hit Fort Wayne yet. There's a riot there today. Don't know what it's about. They say the downtown is on fire. People are getting pulled from their cars and killed right there on the street. So you're going to have to find a way to skirt around."

"We were planning to anyway," I say. "But thanks for the warning."

"The devils are running amok," Grandpa says. "Be careful out there, girls. Does your little friend play chess?"

"Her little friend does," Kylie says with a smirk.

"What rating are you?" he wants to know.

"I can hold my own."

81

Gripping Kylie's arm, I shake my head, trying to warn her not to engage my grandfather on the subject of chess. "She's exaggerating," I tell him. "My little friend doesn't know a rook from a bishop."

"Yes, I do." She furrows her brow in my direction like she thinks I've lost my mind. "I was third in my district in high school. I haven't played for a while, but at the top of my game, I rated a 1500."

"That's good enough for me," I hear grandpa say. "I'll get my board ready."

He hangs up.

"You are an idiot," I say. "Didn't you see me shaking my head?"

"Yeah, so?"

"My grandfather lives for the game, but most of the people he used to play against are dead. Now that he knows you have a little skill, he'll be after you to play for the entire visit."

Kylie shrugs like I'm worried about nothing, but she will see what I mean all too soon.

Chapter 18

We arrive at my grandparent's house just outside of Valparaiso, Indiana around noon. They live in a long yellow ranch with slate brick accents. The lawn used to be immaculately kept, lined with flowerbeds full of vibrant blooms and boxwoods trimmed into rectangles. The only color I see today are ten different shades of brown. The sickly boxwoods have been left to return to their natural shapes. No matter, I'm happy to be here. I pull up into the driveway. It's been a while since I've said hi to my followers, so I take out my phone to get a quick vlog before heading inside.

"Dear Followers: When my little sister Riley was sick, my parents had to spend weeks—no, make that months at a time–at the children's hospital, while I stayed with my grandparents. They enrolled me in school here in Valparaiso, which was fine by me. Grammy and Grandpa always made me feel special. Protected. Loved. This house has always been my oasis.

"Now, whenever I look back on my childhood, this is the place my heart goes to." I pause to wipe a tear from my eye. Glancing up, I see Grandpa coming out of the front door, which is weird because usually it's Grammy. "As all of you are well aware, there's been an epidemic of cancer since the war. It seems like no family has been spared. My little sister Riley died from neuroblastoma when she was only eight years old. My grandmother was diagnosed with ovarian last year, but thankfully she's beat it back into remission."

Grandpa comes to the driver's side door and tries to open it. It won't budge, of course. He circles around to open the passenger side instead.

"Good to see you, kiddo," is all he says to me before turning his attention to Kylie. He takes her hand in both of his, giving a warm handshake. He's always had a thing for pretty dark-eyed girls and chess players. Kylie is both, so I think he is going to be smitten. "Got my chessboard ready. I was the third runner up in high school, too. Let's bring your things in, grab some food, and then we can get started."

She glances over at me questioningly. I return a grimace that says *I-told-you-so*. Grandpa takes Kylie's bag and leaves me to carry my own. As I trail up the drive behind him and Kylie, I ask in concern, "Where's Grammy? She always comes out to welcome me."

"She wanted to take a nap so she'd be fresh for your visit to the cemetery. You know, she hasn't been doing well with this new chemo."

My feet stop on the front stoop.

"Wait a second. I thought she was through with chemotherapy."

"She was. This is round two."

"I don't understand. Are you saying the cancer is growing back?"

"Well, yeah. Nobody told you?"

"No," I say testily, feeling like someone has sucker-punched me in the gut. "This is the first I've heard about it."

"Uh-oh," Grandpa says nonchalantly, without even breaking his stride, seeming clueless to the fact that he has just shattered my world. Kylie turns around. Her eyes are sympathetic, while Grandpa keeps talking. "Your grandmother must not have wanted you to know, yet. Oh, well. Guess the cat's out of the bag."

"Frickin' cat," my voice chokes with emotion. "Sorry, Followers, I gotta go."

As soon as we enter the foyer, the familiar scents of bread, vanilla and laundry soap tickle my nose. I always look forward to that smell. Today it makes me queasy. The living room is to the right. The outdated floral furniture is covered in clear plastic, as if it's fine art in need of protection. I used to be embarrassed to have my friends see it. Now I'm upset to think it might not be there someday. On the right is the dining room. As a kid, the way the chandelier's teardrop crystals send rainbows cascading along the walls, I thought it was an enchanted object worthy of a fairytale castle. Today the magic is gone. All I can think about is how my Grammy is dying.

"You two can get yourselves settled into the guest room," Grandpa says. "While I go check on my famous Teriyaki chicken."

Used to the cheapest crud the university cafeteria can scrape off the food truck, this will be a nice change of pace, but it's not enough to lift my sagging spirits. Poor Grammy.

The guest room looks just like I remember it. Two twin beds with patchwork quilts done in pastel pink, yellow, and green. There's a nightstand between them. On top is a lamp with a base shaped like an boat anchor. A wooden crucifix hangs next to the door. On the wall above the bed Kylie has chosen, there's a picture of two young children crossing over a rickety wooden foot bridge. A raging stream runs beneath it. The children look scared, unaware of the ethereal angel following behind them, guarding their every step. As a child, when I stayed with my grandparents, I'd look at that picture every night, and think of my own guardian angel.

"I've been trying to learn everything about Christianity, but some of it can be confusing," Kylie says, studying the picture. "Are angels real beings or are they simply symbols of God's will?"

"They're real beings, I'm pretty sure."

"The angel in the picture looks so gentle and loving, which is a whole lot different than how they are described in the Old Testament. They were real badasses back then."

"I was taught that we each have our very own angel to look out for us." I head into the attached bathroom to take care of my business, but leave the door open so we can keep talking. "There are special prayers to invoke their protection. I still remember one of them: *Angel of God, my Guardian dear, to whom God's love commits me here, ever this day be at my side, to light and guard, to rule and guide. Amen.*"

"Nice."

"A word to the wise, you probably shouldn't call angels badasses." I pause to flush and wait for the gurgle to subside before I finish talking. "It's not very respectful."

"I meant it in the most complimentary of ways—like angels are strong, angels are cool, angels are warriors—you shouldn't get on their bad side."

"Hence, the reason you should be careful what you say about them."

"Point taken."

"Did you know that Satan and the demons used to be angels?"

"What?" Her voice is incredulous. "Are you sure?"

"Of course. Before the creation of the world, God put all the angels through some kind of big final exam. A third of them flunked. As a result, they were kicked out of Heaven and turned into demons."

"And here I thought that losing financial aid was the worst thing that could happen to you for flunking out. Wow."

A knock on the bedroom door cuts the conversation short. "Lunch will be ready in five."

"Okay, thanks, Grandpa."

Kylie slides into the bathroom, while I head out to the kitchen. In the hallway, I run into Grammy coming out of her bedroom.

"Butterfly girl," she exclaims. "Come give your Grammy some sugar."

My God, she looks so thin and frail. Her skin is as fragile as tissue paper. In an attempt to stifle a sob, my hand shoots to my mouth, but it's too late. Grammy sees the grief all over my face.

"Your grandfather is a big blabbermouth. He told you about my cancer coming back, didn't he?"

Unable to speak, I nod.

"I wanted us to have a good time, so I was going to wait to tell you at the end of your visit." Grammy rolls her eyes toward the ceiling in vexation, while wrapping an arm around my shoulder. "I ought to wring his neck. Do try to enjoy lunch. Your grandfather worked hard on it. Then we'll head out to the cemetery and talk. How does that sound?"

All I can do is sniffle and follow her out to the kitchen. I've lost my appetite, but my grandfather is so eager for us to enjoy his food, I force it down. After lunch, Kylie and I volunteer to do the dishes. When we're through, Grandpa takes Kylie by the elbow, leading her to his den. Even though I don't follow them in, I am more than familiar with the room. It's done in dark cherry woods. The bookshelves are filled with leather bound books. There's a stocked humidor in the corner. His chessboard is set out—an expensive set with onyx and ivory game pieces.

My grandfather studied philosophy and canon law back in the seminary. He was only six months from ordination when he met my grandmother. Then it was bye-bye priesthood, hello married life. Somehow he ended up selling fleet trucks for a living. Did quite well for himself. Yet he's never lost his zeal for the faith or intellectual pursuits.

In hindsight, he might be exactly the right person for Kylie to hang out with for a couple of days. With her incessant questions about Christianity, and Grandpa's love of sharing what he knows, this has the potential to be a match made in Heaven. Meanwhile, I get Grammy all to myself.

She tells me to leave my SUV in the driveway. We'll take their twenty-year-old sedan. It's been painstakingly maintained inside and out. Still runs like a dream. My grandpa's pride and joy. I pull out of the driveway with extra care, wondering if he would disown me if I wreck it. Nah, Grammy wouldn't let him. Even so, I'm nervous all the way to the cemetery as if it's my first time behind the wheel.

Chapter 19

I guide the car along a thin ribbon of asphalt winding through the cemetery. Up ahead to the left there's an oxidized statue of the weeping Virgin Mary holding the dead body of Jesus in her arms. Inching off of the lane, I pull onto the grass. Two tombstone rows in, stands a mighty oak tree. Against the odds, it has grown a glorious canopy of green leaves. Bravo, oak tree. Beneath its protective limbs, my sister and father await the resurrection, their gray tombstones glittering under the dim sunlight.

Grammy stays in the car while I retrieve her things from the trunk—two folding lawn chairs, a large wicker beach bag with a couple of blankets folded up inside, and her silk flower arrangements. I bring everything over to the graves and return to help Grammy get out of the car. She holds onto my arm for balance as we amble over the bumpy grass to make our annual pilgrimage. I help Grammy ease herself into the chair. It's not very cold, about fifty degrees, but she asks for a blanket. I tug the black linen one out of the wicker basket.

"That one is for later. The red plaid please."

I shove it back in and hand her the red plaid one as requested.

Following Grammy's commands, I kneel down to remove the old flowers from the vases flanking the tombstones to replace them with the bright new bouquets. Riley's is interspersed with pink bows. Dad's are blue. Grammy is fussy about the placement of every single flower. If it was anyone else, I'd tell them to bugger off or do it themselves. But it's Grammy. She has a way of bringing out my patient side.

"Is that good?" I ask.

"It will do. Thank you, butterfly."

I go to my chair beside hers. She holds up a necklace made of silvery string. Carefully spaced knots serve in place of the beads. Dangling from a line of knots is a cross, made of the same string, tightly coiled together. Ahh, a rosary. I take it from my grandmother's outstretched hands for our yearly ritual.

On the anniversary of my father's death, Grammy and I say a rosary for the repose of his soul. Since Riley died so young, Grammy says she went straight to Heaven. We pray for her anyway—just in case. I go along with it, but I have trouble believing that prayers help the living, let alone the dead. They certainly can't hurt though. Since it gives Grammy so much peace, I enjoy doing it.

"I made this rosary myself," Grammy explains. "Having something to do with my hands helps me pass the time during chemo."

"It's beautiful."

"Shall we begin?"

"Whenever you're ready, Grammy."

Since I'm out of practice, and have forgotten the order of the Mysteries, each commemorating a scene from Jesus' life, my grandmother takes the lead. Clutching the crucifix and the bottom of our rosary, she begins, "In the name of the Father, the Son and the Holy Spirit. I believe in God, the Father Almighty, Creator of Heaven and Earth …"

A few minutes into the prayers, my eyes begin to roam. I notice the new gravestones off to the side of my father's. It has my grandparents' names and birth dates etched into the stone. There's a blank spot left for the dates of their deaths, like it's a sure thing. Of course, it *is* a sure thing, but seeing it in print has a way of deepening the reality. By the time we finish the rosary, I'm weeping.

"What's the matter, butterfly girl?"

"I don't want you to die!"

I can't hold in my sobs. They're coming rapidly now. Grammy opens her arms to offer me a consoling hug. I kneel in front of her chair, laying my head in her lap.

"There, there, now." She strokes the back of my head. "None of us get to stay here forever and, frankly, I don't want to. If I have my way,

I'll go onto my reward soon, before the Three Days of Darkness gets here. I'm a chicken that way."

"Please, don't talk like you're going to die," I whine. "I need you here."

"What you need is prayer. I should think mine will be stronger when I say them before the throne of God."

"I don't want you to go to Heaven. I need you on Earth with me."

"Think of us as caterpillars. You're still young and green. I'm old and faded. Feeling the change coming on, I know it's time to build a cocoon." She pulls the blanket tighter around in imitation. "I'm not dying, sweetie. Think of it as a transformation. Because after the long winter, I'll wake fully transformed into a beautiful butterfly." Her analogy is only making me sadder. I'm crying even harder. "I'll always be with you, my dear granddaughter."

"I don't want to hear this anymore."

"Well, you need to. And I'm not done. Your eternal fate has been heavy on my mind since The Warning. I had a vision of standing at the top of a gray cliff covered with clouds." Her eyes get misty. "Down below, souls were falling into Hell like dry autumn leaves. Mother Mary made me to understand that if only they had had someone to pray for them, many could have been saved. It made me aware of how neglectful I had been, worrying more about my creature comforts than the salvation of souls. I wept in the Virgin's arms for a very long time."

"Prayer," I humph. "What good is it? I prayed for Riley until my knees bled and it didn't do her any good. My prayers didn't help Dad either."

"How do you know?"

I sweep a hand toward the gravestones with their names on them. *Duh*, I want to say, but it's Grammy, so I withhold my sarcasm.

"I didn't mean good in the physical sense," Grammy replies. "I'm talking about the good prayer does for the spirit."

"Maybe that's what you are talking about now, but back when Riley was sick, I recall both of us praying for her body to be healed."

"The radiation took so many children," Grammy sighs heavily. "It was wrong of me to assure you that God would cure her cancer. What I should have said was that from tragedy God can bring forth a greater good. Through pain, unexpected gifts. From death, new life. Trust in the Divine Will."

"So you're telling me it's wrong to pray for physical healing?"

"Not at all. I am saying if God answered every prayer, everybody would be billionaires. Nobody would ever get old. Or die. Which means nobody would get to Heaven. And I would be married to Sean Connery—the handsomest of all the James Bonds. You see, life here on earth can be full of wonderful things, but if we stayed here forever, we'd be missing out on something much, much greater.

"What I'm trying to say, Gina, is I used to approach God as if He was a magic genie and my every wish was His command. If I didn't get my way, I'd pout like a spoiled child threatening to runaway. Now that I'm older, I've come to understand that God never tires of us asking Him for things, but He also wants us to believe in His Goodness even when He tells us no."

I'm stuck on the thing she said about Sean Connery and can't stop chuckling.

"What's so funny, Gina—don't you understand? I saw you burning in the fires of Hell, the flesh melting off your bones." She pulls a tissue from the pocket of her baby blue coat and dabs her eyes. She's so upset and serious, my laughter evaporates into guilt. "It was horrible to see you suffering like that. Just horrible."

"I'm sorry, Grammy. Please, don't cry."

"During The Warning, I asked if there was any hope for you." Ignoring my attempts to comfort her, she continues talking. "Mother Mary replied by giving me the cloak from her head and telling me these words: *My mantle is a shield in the battle for souls. In the days of darkness, anyone who wears it will be invisible to the wicked spirits and their earthly agents of evil.*"

Grammy gestures toward the beach bag. I hand it to her. She sets it in her lap and pulls out the black blanket, holding it up to the light. Although it's linen, it has a bit of heft. The reverse side is a beautiful sapphire blue. There's a slight sheen to the material, but it doesn't look like anything extraordinary.

"This was a gift from heaven—Mary's mantle." My grandmother places it in my hands. Curious, I take a closer look. It's a nice blanket, but there's nothing special about it that I can see. "I want you to keep it."

Even though I'm sure The Warning was caused by infrasonic waves, and that she only *thinks* the blanket is Mary's mantle, I'm deeply touched.

"Thank you, Grammy. I will cherish it forever."

"When things start to go south, wrap yourself in Mary's mantle, and you'll be well protected. More importantly, you need to return to the sacraments. Let Holy Communion be your strength."

"You know how I feel about organized religion."

"Yes, I do. But I'm unclear on whether or not you still consider yourself a Christian."

All I can do is shrug.

"Why do you agree to pray with me if you don't believe?"

"I believe," I admit. "I just don't know in what exactly."

"Well, figure it out, Gina." My grandmother's voice is calm, but there's an urgency in it I haven't heard before. "We are soldiers. This is war. There is no middle ground anymore. When a person refuses to stand up for good, they have chosen evil. Now go on to your chair and together we, the Church Militant, in communion with the Church Suffering and the Church Triumphant, will pray for your conversion.."

I crawl back into the lawn chair, trying to hide my sulking expression. She makes the sign of the cross. Her lips begin to move, but the only sound is the wind rustling through dry grass. This long stretch of silence is also part of our yearly ritual.

While she's praying, I pour myself a cup of coffee from the thermos and settle in, trying to meditate like my grandmother. However, it feels like a waste of time. If only I could be more like Grammy. Even in the worst of times, her faith has never wavered. She believes that Riley's guardian angel carried her straight to Heaven when she died. My father wasn't so lucky. His faith was shaken by the suffering in the world and even more so by the scandalous behaviors of high-ranking members of the clergy. For giving into despair, he was going to have a long layover in Purgatory. My understanding is that Purgatory is a place where sinners are cleansed of their sins beneath a great cosmic showerhead that sprays sparks instead of water. The worse your sins, the hotter they burn, but since heaven is one hundred percent guaranteed, there is joy beneath all the pain. Grammy also believes that when we pray for the poor souls in Purgatory, their time under the showerhead is shortened. That's how it was explained it to me shortly after my father died. Already soured on religion, I didn't quite believe it.

Nonetheless, just in case I'm wrong, I quietly utter more prayers for my sister and father, asking God to let perpetual light shine upon them— lofty stuff like that. However, over the course of the next hour my thoughts drift away from spiritual things. Glancing over at Grammy, I see that her chin is resting against her chest, and she's snoring a little. I think she has fallen asleep. Nonetheless, I don't want her to see me on my cell phone. I slide it out of my coat pocket to hold it next to my thigh, on the side opposite of her.

There's a message from work. They want me to return early. Screw that. I ignore it and bring up a text from Julie. She's inviting me to an off-campus party. I text her back asking if Jerome will be there with that bimbo girl he's been seeing. When she says yes, an unexpected twinge of jealousy goes through me. Maybe I'm not as over him as I thought. I text her back that I'm visiting my grandparents and probably won't be home in time to go.

As I'm texting, I feel something crawl over my foot. I look down to see a winged creature with three horns like a golden crown. A royal hisser! Jumping to my feet, I let out a "Whah!"

It leaps off of my foot and begins to buzz around. Instead of swatting at it this time, I hold perfectly still, praying that it won't land on me or Grammy. It circles around my head a few times, totally ignoring my grandmother, then flies off. Breathing a sigh of relief, I look over at Grammy. She's half-awake now with a confused look on her face. Wanting to get her to safety, I gently nudge her shoulder.

"It's getting late, Grammy. Time to go."

The next morning, back at my grandparents' house, I'm pulled out of my dreams by an overbearing female voice on the other side of the bedroom door.

"Wakie, wakie, girls." It's my Aunt Vivian. I can recognize her grating voice anywhere. "We're going on a ride!"

Opening one eye, I note that it's still dark outside. The clock says 5:17 am. My Aunt Viv lives close to my grandparents—about a ten minute drive. That doesn't explain her being here at this ungodly hour.

Kylie is sitting on the edge of the bed, opening up her switchblade, only partially awake. "What's happening?"

"Nothing, Kylie. Put that away. Everything is okay. It's …"

"Get the lead out, girls!" Aunt Vivian, my father's only sibling, barges in and flips on the ceiling light.

Kylie startles and drops her knife.

My aunt is nearly six feet tall, weighs at least two hundred pounds, with a muscular build. In her younger days she was a power lifter. Won a few prizes, which she never hesitates to mention in passing. Could have taken it to the professional level, but she opted to be a police officer instead. That's how she met Uncle Tyrese. She's a homicide detective now, while my uncle remains a beat cop. They are both loud and bossy, but it's comforting to know they're always around to look out for my grandparents.

"Let's hit the road, Jackies!" In an effort to get us moving to a faster rhythm, she rapidly claps her hands. "Move, move, move! Everybody's waiting!"

"Who's waiting?" Kylie groans. "And what are they waiting for?"

"You must be the chess player." She walks over to shake Kylie's hand. "I'm Vivian—Gina's favorite Aunt."

"Because she's my *only* aunt," I chime in. "Which also makes her my *least* favorite aunt. Especially, this morning."

Aunt Viv smirks and keeps shaking Kylie's hand.

"Dad says you're a tough opponent and he's excited about finishing the game, but this trip sprang up out of the blue."

"What trip?" I inquire groggily. "Where are we going?"

"Something amazing is happening in Rome City and we don't want to miss it."

Chapter 20

"What could possibly be happening in Rome that I'd give a flying fig about?" I ask in annoyance. "It's uninhabitable and across the ocean. Remember?"

"Not *the* Rome, silly. Rome City, Indiana."

"Oh." I collapse back onto the pillow, already bored at the prospect. "You guys go. I'm sleeping in."

"Get dressed." Aunt Viv throws my travel bag at me. "You can sleep on the bus."

"Bus?" I whine. "Tell me it ain't so."

Aunt Viv laughs and leaves the room, while Kylie and I bump into each other like pinballs, trying to put ourselves together in a hurry. When we get outside, the St. Michael's church bus is waiting in the street.. Uncle Tyrese is in the driver's seat.

"Yo, Gina-Bo-Bina." He's way too cheerful for this time in the morning. "Welcome aboard the Soul Train."

"Back atcha, Uncle Tyrese Bo-Beese."

Surveying the other passengers, looks like we will be traveling with forty or fifty other people. Grammy and Grandpa are sitting toward the front in separate seats. She's seated with a clump of old ladies, so busy gabbing she doesn't even notice me until I tap her on the shoulder as I brush past her seat. She smiles and says good morning, then returns to her conversation with her friends. Grandpa is sitting across the aisle from Grammy with the old guys, laughing about something. He nods at me as Kylie and I shuffle to the back half of the bus. After we settle in, I notice a woman with short blonde hair seated in front of us with a couple of young boys. I tap her on the shoulder. She turns around with a question mark on her face.

"Excuse me," I say. It's a struggle to act friendly this early in the morning, but I manage a weak smile. "Can you tell me why we're going to Rome City?"

"To see Sylvan Springs."

"Never heard of it."

"Neither did I until last night," the woman confesses. "I'm Linda, by the way. You're not Gina Applegate, are you?"

"As a matter of fact I am."

"I thought so," she says. "Your Aunt Viv used to be my babysitter. I remember when you were just a little tot."

"Oh, yeah?" My brow raises in interest. "Aunt Viv forced us out of bed to come here. Can you fill us in on what's got everyone in such an uproar?"

"Well, I'm only just learning about it myself, but I'll tell you what I know. Back in 1956, the Virgin Mary appeared to a nun who was working at the sanitarium on the grounds of Sylvan Springs in Rome City. Mary told the nun that parents should strive to make their homes holy places where all activity was centered on the love of Jesus. After the nun was transferred to a different city, Mary continued to pay her visits under the title *Our Lady of America*. The sanitarium in Sylvan Springs eventually closed. The grounds were neglected for years. There's a winery there now and a barn that's used for wedding receptions. The apparition in Rome City has been all but forgotten, but I have a feeling that's about to change."

"Why—what happened?" Kylie jumps into the conversation.

"A heavenly light appeared there on the grounds around 8:30 last night. A woman from our parish was there when it happened. She swears that when she gazed upon the lights, she was cured of the shingles, a condition she has been suffering with for twenty years."

"The light cured her shingles?" Kylie asks.

"That's what they're saying."

"Oh," I reply, not bothering to hide my disappointment. "I see."

97

"I know it will probably turn out to be hoax." Linda sounds apologetic for giving the healing power of the lights any consideration. "But some people think it's the promised Miracle to follow the Illumination of Conscience. Since Rome City is only an hour and a half away, I thought it wouldn't hurt to check it out."

"You would be nuts not to." Kylie's practically bouncing out of her seat now, eyes alight with optimism. "What else do you know about it—The Miracle, I mean?"

"Nothing," Linda says. "I was trying to brush up on the specifics, but my phone ran out of charge a few minutes ago. I read something about a Permanent Sign being left at the sight of The Miracle. It's supposed to remain there until the end of the world."

"That's right," Kylie replies. "The seers haven't given many details about The Miracle, but they say you'll be able to photograph it. Your hands will pass through it like smoke. I'm confused about the mysterious Permanent Sign though. Is it the same thing as The Miracle or something different?"

"I'm not sure," Linda says. "But I do know that The Miracle will happen simultaneously in holy places all around the world."

"Are you sure about that?" Kylie says, thoughtfully tilting her head. "I've heard it's only supposed to occur in one or two spots."

"Maybe I'm remembering wrong," Linda says, tapping her temple. "My mind isn't what it used to be."

"Let me do a search to see if the lights have been seen anywhere else." Kylie fumbles with her phone. She shows me a website all about The Miracle. I'm too tired to drum up much interest. "Here's something about healing lights in Knock. Where's Knock?"

"Ireland," the lady says excitedly. "Kids, switch places with the nice lady, so she can sit up here with me."

Kylie gets up. The woman's two boys, maybe four or five years of age, slide past Kylie to sit with me. Kylie plops down next to Linda, gabbing on with her about the lights.

One of the boys lays his head across my lap and goes to sleep. Great. Just great. He better not be a drooler. I plug in my ear buds and doze off to a love song from my new favorite indie rock band, which touts itself as *Pink Floyd Wannabees.* I've never heard of the original artist, but I like the sound.

About two hours later, I sense the bus slowing down. Opening my eyes, I see dawn breaking over a field of high sprouts. Not having seen anything growing so vigorously in a while, my eyes widen as we continue past. There's only a few farmhouses in sight, but the traffic is thick. Cars are parked on either side of a narrow rural route. Uncle Tyrese is having trouble finding a big enough spot to park the bus. He finally settles on a meadow that's rapidly filling with vehicles.

Up ahead lies a sprawling three-story building of reddish-brown brick. That must be the sanitarium Linda was telling us about. A barn made from the same color of brick, with a steep green roof and dormers, sits off in the distance. There is a white silo and several smaller buildings sitting atop a hill not too far away.

Uncle Tyrese finally finds a space long enough to park. People on the bus are oohing and ahhing, pointing out the windows at something in the distance. All I see is what you'd expect to see in farm country—dirt, buildings and foliage. As soon as the bus comes to a complete stop, the people can't seem to get out the doors fast enough. The boy asleep on my legs pops his head up to rabbit after his mother, without so much as a thank you for being his pillow.

I file out of the bus behind Kylie and step onto matted grass. The place is like a zoo. Hundreds, no, thousands of people are streaming in hopes of seeing a miracle. It's peculiar how most of the visitors seem to automatically know where they're going.

Uncle Tyrese is pushing Grammy in a wheelchair, but it's hard moving through the grass. A couple of men come out of the crowd to lift the entire chair, helping my family carry her up the hill. Just ahead, food and craft booths like you might see at a county fair are set up and opened for business.

It occurs to me that I should be videoing this for my JustSharing channel. Using the field of parked cars as a backdrop, with the excited people rushing out of them toward the unseen wonder over the next hill, I pull out my phone and do a selfie.

"Dear Followers: I am in Rome City, Indiana, where an alleged miracle of lights began late last evening. I am here with my family and my roommate Kylie, against my will."

I pan over to Kylie. "Hey, y'all. Hi, y'all. How y'all doing?" She waves.

Then I pan over to the vendors. "Entrepreneurs, looking to cash in on The Miracle, are already setup to hawk their wares to the hungry pilgrims." I walk through the booths, vlogging along the way. "In addition to hotdogs and lemonade, they are selling cheap religious trinkets like plastic statues of the saints, angel blankets, and chocolates with Bible verses printed on them." I zoom in for my viewers, letting them watch as I buy a colorful candy rosary. I pop the entire yellow cross into my mouth. "Mmmm," I say in mocking fashion. "Who would have guessed the crucifixion tastes like lemons?"

Still sucking on the candy, I work my away through the booths zooming in on the tackiest items I can find. There are soaps that look like Jesus, packaged with the logo, *Cleanse Me of My Sins, O Jesus!* I leaf through a book called, *Where in the World is the Pope?* Illustrated in the spirit of *Where's Waldo?*, it capitalizes on the fact that the real pope is missing. Each colorful page is busy with characters and activity. The object of the book is to find the pope among the hubbub.

The first page depicts the storming of the Vatican. Tanks, helicopters, and Neu soldiers are everywhere. Grenades are going off. Bullets are flying. Nuns and monks in their habits, priests with their black and white collars are running back and forth with comically frightened expressions. I scan the page for the pope in his white cassock and beanie, but I can't find him, so I begin to leaf through the book for an easier page.

"Are you planning on reading the entire book?" the vendor says impatiently. "Or are you actually going to buy it?"

"Oh, sorry." Embarrassed, I quickly set it down.

As we walk, the land gently rises up until we come to a building made to look like a rustic log cabin. The sign says 'Winery'. I do a close-up.

"Civilization—at last." I say into my camera phone. "Hey, look." I tug on Kylie's sleeve. She has been patiently following me around, while the others have gotten far ahead of us. "Maybe this trip won't be a total waste after all."

"Whoa!" Kylie gushes. "It's beautiful!"

Chapter 21

For a moment, I think Kylie's excitement is directed toward the winery, but she's not even looking at it. Like so many of the visitors arriving in Sylvan Springs, she is gazing up the hillside. Gotta say, I can't figure out what they think is so damn interesting.

Rain begins to fall, making the open doors of the winery all the more enticing. Peering through the entrance, I spy a shelf full of assorted cheeses. A middle-aged man in an apron comes out the door and makes eye contact with me. He reminds me of Luigi from the old Mario Brothers games.

"Early Bird Special," he calls out from somewhere beneath his mustache. "Get half off the regular tour price! The first five customers of the day leave with a free cheese ball!"

"A free cheese ball!" I try to drag Kylie with me into the winery, but she resists. "Come on!"

"Don't you want to get a closer look at the lights?" She asks, tilting her head as if my behavior is a puzzle to be solved.

"What lights? I don't see any lights."

"If you want to miss The Miracle, it's your choice." She yanks her arm out of my grip. "But, I'm climbing the hill."

"Fine," I say testily. "I'm going to eat and drink and be merry."

"Good luck with that."

I enter the winery alone.

"How can I help you?" Luigi asks.

"Am I one of the first five?"

"My number one." The man is favoring me with a wide grin. "Did you just come downhill or are you going up?"

"Neither. I'm staying right here."

"Ahh," he nods his head knowingly. "You don't see it either, do you?"

"See what?"

"A pillar of fire. The tourists claim it's the very one that led the Israelites to the Promised Land. Ezekiel's Wheel of Fire is also popular with the crowd. Others call it the Burning Bush of Indiana."

"And what do you call it?"

"Good for business."

It's my turn to smile. "How much is the tour?"

"Fifty dollars a head."

"That's out of my league. What do you have for five bucks?"

His friendly demeanor melts away. He scowls and points to the door.

"Jackass," I mutter under my breath to my followers. "Fifty dollars a head—what fantasy is he living in?"

The rest of the group is out of sight now. The stream of people coming up and down the hill seems endless. Merging into the line, braving the drizzle, I start to climb, passing by those who have already been to the top, and who are now leaving. Many of them are crying. Not sad tears. More like what you might see at a wedding. Or from someone who has won the lottery.

"Praise the Lord!" A young man is saying, holding up a pair of crutches. "Praise the Lord!"

"*Te veo!*" An old woman comes by, ushered by her large brood of a family. They're crying up to the clouds and praising God. "*Te veo!*"

"This is getting interesting," I tell my followers. Two skinny adolescent girls are walking ahead of me with their parents, stringy hair dampened by the light sprinkle of rain. I video the back of their heads and capture their conversation.

"It's so pretty," the shorter of the two says. "What is it?"

"It's God, dummy," the taller girl replies.

I halt in my tracks. Straining to see what the girls are seeing. Dusty pale skies above. A couple of birds flying overhead. That's it.

As we approach the hilltop, a gorgeous perfume wafts through the air.

"Does anyone else smell flowers?" the woman behind me asks.

That's when the raindrops transform into white rose petals. People are oohing and ahhing again. I pluck a petal as it floats down, roll it up in my hands to make sure it's not fallout. Nope.

"Soft and supple," I tell my followers as I zoom in on it in my palm. "Definitely a flower petal." I scan the sky, expecting to see an airplane that might have dropped its cargo by accident. Trying to come up with an explanation, I speculate on camera. "Maybe a storm tore through a greenhouse. If the wind picked up the petals, it goes to reason that it would have to let go of them somewhere. Sylvan Springs is as good a place as any, I suppose."

"Take off your shoes!" A man is walking down the line of people from the top of the hill. "This is holy ground. Take off your shoes."

Everybody is taking off their shoes. Those who can't do it themselves are assisted by their companions.

"This is ridiculous," I mutter to my followers. "My feet will get muddy. I'll ruin my shoes when I put them back on."

A woman is coming down the line now. "Remove your shoes!" She insists, looking me sternly in the eye, pointing down at my feet.

"Who does she think she is?" I whisper to my followers. "The Shoe Police?"

I act like I'm complying, but when she's out of sight, I leave them on and continue walking. At the top of the hill, I look down the other side to see a meadow with a garden of yellow rose bushes in full bloom. Thousands of people of all ages are kneeling, bowing, lying prostrate on the ground all around it. Some are raising their hands to the heavens. Seeing healthy flowers is a beautiful and unexpected sight, but disappointing as far as miracles go.

"Somebody hide the Kool Aid," I say to my followers. "This is getting weird."

"Are you seeing what I'm seeing?" the woman behind me cries out to her friend.

"The bushes are in flames," the other woman shouts, "but they're not consumed."

"The flame is so pure!" Cries a man up ahead. "It's not of this world."

I pan over the excited crowd, then turn the video back to myself, wearing a surly frown.

"It's insanity out here in Rome City, Indiana. Then again, maybe it's divinity. All around me people are claiming to see flames rising up from the rose bushes. Personally, all I see are a bunch of wackadoodles standing around in a field." Glancing up at the bright spot in the sky called the sun, I think aloud, "I bet you anything we'll find out later there's been a chemical leak in the area."

I pan around to shoot the roses again. Instead, I catch sight of a teenage boy jumping for joy. "I was born blind, but now I see!"

I turn the video to myself. "This is too much."

"There you are." A hand grips my shoulder. Turning around, I see Aunt Viv. She asks, "What do you think of all this?"

"I have to be honest, I don't get it."

"Whew," she replies. "I thought maybe it was just me. Everybody, including your little friend, seems to be having the religious good time of their lives. My husband says it's a golden sphere spinning above the roses like a top. Dad swears it's Ezekiel's wheels. Mom is having visions of cherubim."

Aunt Viv and I stand on the hilltop, sighing in unison, staring at the garden of yellow roses below. We commiserate like birds of a cynical feather. After several minutes of staring, perhaps it's only the power of suggestion, but I too am beginning to see the light. I attempt to blink it away, to no avail.

"Glory Be, Aunt Viv," I gasp as a transparent golden oval as big as a house materializes over the roses. "I see something!"

"Great," Aunt Viv says with an even heavier sigh. "Am I going to be the only one who comes back without witnessing The Miracle?"

"Don't give up, Aunt Viv. If you look hard enough, I'm sure you'll see something."

"We promised to have the bus back to the church by noon, so I'm out of time. How about making yourself useful, kiddo, and helping me round up the passengers?"

"Will do."

Aunt Viv leaves, but I linger to point my camera over the roses, narrating in the background.

"Dear Followers, I'm seeing a golden aura, at least thirty feet high, shimmering and pulsing like a dancing candle flame, but it's so faint, I can't be sure if it's a trick of the sunlight or of supernatural origin."

I squint all the harder, but within a minute, the aura completely fades away, leaving me doubting if it was there at all. Those around me still seem to be seeing it though. Stopping the video, I proceed view it on screen. In a few places, I can see the aura. How about that? It's interesting, but I'm clearly not seeing anything as grand as the others, making it easy to talk myself out of it being from God. I'm sure there's a scientific explanation behind the phenomenon. If not infrasonic waves messing with our heads again, perhaps it's light bouncing off the moisture in the air, making people see what they want to see.

On a whim I decide to add a poll, asking my viewers to indicate what they see. Eager to be the first to upload the event on JustSharing, I immediately add it to my channel without any editing. Fingers crossed, it will earn me more followers.

To keep myself distracted from constantly checking my numbers, I start to help Aunt Viv look for the other passengers. It takes me about ten minutes of milling through the crowd just to find a familiar face. Linda is with her two boys, holding the hand of a man I presume to be her husband. He must have been sitting elsewhere on the bus. I tell her that we are getting ready to head back.

A couple of minutes later, I find Kylie walking up the back side of the hill with a couple of young men, talking and laughing as if they're the best of friends. The men both have sandy brown hair, brown eyes, and similar square jaws. The one in the Notre Dame hat is tall and thin. The other is only a few inches taller than me with a stocky build. He's wearing a Chicago Bears jacket and seems vaguely familiar.

Kylie drapes an arm around my shoulders to introduce me to her new buddies. "This is my roommate and best friend, Gina. We were lucky enough to be visiting her grandparents in Valparaiso when The Miracle started."

The taller of the two offers a hand. We shake as he introduces himself.

"I'm Logan Vargas. And this bum over here is my cousin, Miguel Cruz. Nice to meet you."

"Mutual." I turn the Miguel. It suddenly dawns on me how I know him. He was the one who introduced the speaker in the gymnasium right after The Warning. Having always wondered about the fate of the lawyer who got hit in the head with a baseball, I blurt out. "Kylie and I were there during the riot in Walb. I've been wondering how Mr. Mott is doing."

"Last I heard, not great." Miguel says, shaking his head. "Struggling to recover from a traumatic brain injury."

"We should bring him here," Kylie suggests. "Maybe Mr. Mott will get a miracle."

"I don't know him very well," Miguel confesses. "But I do feel partially responsible for what happened at the university. I'll try to contact his family in Sioux City and offer to bring him out here if they wish."

"If you need help," Kylie says. "Maybe we can go with you."

"That's very kind of you to offer. If it works out, I might just take you up on that."

"How did you get to Rome City so fast, Miguel?" I inquire.

"I was already in the area, visiting my cousins in South Bend." He nods his head to Logan. "As soon as we heard about the lights, we drove over to check them out."

I ask the little group, "So, what do you think—is this The Miracle the Christians were waiting for?"

"Possibly," Logan says. "On the other hand, it could be a diabolical deception meant to mislead the faithful. I'm trying to suspend judgment on its authenticity until the church can conduct an investigation."

"Diabolical, my ass," the words tumble out of Kylie's mouth. "This is definitely of God." The young men exchange perplexed expressions as if they weren't expecting Kylie to swear. "Please excuse my language," she apologizes. "Bad habits are hard to kill. I'm new to this religion stuff."

"That's right. She didn't get aboard the Crazy Train until after The Warning." The silence that follows lets me know that I've taken my skepticism a little too far. Realizing how insulting I just sounded, I awkwardly clear my throat. "Well, it was nice meeting you, but our bus is getting ready to leave."

"I'll be there in a sec," Kylie says.

She continues talking to both of them, while I excuse myself to help Aunt Viv find more of the missing passengers. After everyone is rounded up, we reload the bus, and trek back to my grandparents' home. Not wanting to share my lackluster vision of the lights with those around me, I nap the whole way.

Chapter 22

Early the next morning, I wake Kylie up early to head back to school. I want to get going so we can avoid getting caught on the highway after dark, but Grammy has other plans. She has a full breakfast of fried bacon, scrambled eggs, and sliced melon spread out on the table. All that food must have cost her a fortune, which makes it impossible for us to skip out before getting our fill. While we eat, Grammy flits about the kitchen with more energy than I've seen in her since we arrived. I allow a little hope to settle into my stomach with the food. By the time we're rubbing our full bellies, two additional hours have passed. She sends us off with hugs, kisses, and two huge sack lunches for the road.

Grateful for the breakfast, but not wanting to lose anymore time, we hurry out and toss our suitcases into the trunk. Using the side of my hand, I clear away a swath of dust from the driver's side window. Then I wipe my skin clean on my blue jeans. Kylie gets into the passenger seat first and slides over behind the wheel to drive us back. I drape my new blanket—er, Mary's mantle—over the passenger seat, just in case I get cold, and slide in. Grandpa comes over to the driver's side window to talk to Kylie some more. She rolls it down halfway, which is as far as it will go since I banged in the door awhile ago.

"Hold onto that phone number, young lady. Father Kramer is a great resource right there in your own diocese. If he doesn't work out for whatever reason, give me a call. I'll hook you up with a different instructor, but for goodness sakes, don't go to just any old priest. These days it's hard to know which ones are loyal to the true pope and which ones are Neuist wolves hiding in sheep's clothing. I'd hate for you to be misled out of the gate. If you have anymore questions, or just want to talk, don't hesitate to call me."

"I won't, Mr. Applegate. Thank you for everything."

"Kylie is a good girl," he says to me. "You could use more friends like her."

If only he knew how she used to be, he might not be singing her praises.

"Okay, Grandpa. Love you."

Kylie begins to back down the driveway.

"Be safe, girls!" Grammy follows the car, waving goodbye. "Take shelter in Mary's mantle, Gina!"

About a mile down the road, Kylie begins to gush, "I wasn't expecting my visit with your grandparents to be so enlightening. It was like a spiritual retreat or something. You are so lucky to have such a nice family."

"Yeah, I am." Engrossed in my phone, I'm barely paying attention to the conversation. "They'd be about perfect if it wasn't for all the religion."

"Try growing up in a family of staunch atheists. They're intellectual snobs and the most miserable bunch of people you ever want to meet."

"What are you talking about? You're parents are great…" I'm about to say more, but when I see my JustSharing stats, I choke on my own spit. It has grown a hundred thousand followers since the last night. Kylie reaches over to pat my back.

"Are you okay?"

"My 'Miracle or Hoax in Indiana?' vlog has gone viral! It already has two million hits!"

So much for studying. I spend the next hour or so reading the thousands of comments left by viewers, explaining the elaborate images they see in the video, ranging from holy fires, to heavenly angels, and God himself—as if that were possible. Others claim it's a demonic deception. There's a lot of jokesters making comments about seeing pink elephants, Elvis Presley, and hot celebrities in compromising poses. Plus, of course, the Christian-haters have come out in droves. The poll I attached to it is getting a lot of activity.

What do you see above the bushes?

40% - Nothing unusual.

10% - I see something unusual, but I think it's a trick of the light.

11% - I see something unusual. I'm leaning toward it being of supernatural origins, but I'm going to take the wait-n-see approach.

24% - I see something unusual. I'm certain it's of heaven. Nobody can convince me otherwise.

6% - No matter how you look at it, the origins are diabolical.

9% - Other

I find it interesting that so many people can look at the same scene and come away with an entirely different image. Is it the power of suggestion or something supernatural? If only I knew for sure. Either way, the video is going to fluff up my bank account.

Up until now, I haven't paid much attention to the specifics of how the JustSharing payouts are set up. Doing a quick skim of their procedures, I realize I won't get paid for at least three months. The way it works is that whenever someone watches my video, it shows up in real time as a view. However, it won't show up on my private dashboard as a sale until three months later. Furthering the delay, JustSharing sends out payments on a quarterly basis. Doing the math, the earliest I'll see a penny from my *Miracle or Hoax in Indiana?* video is late September. That sucks. Still, I've gained a hundred thousand new followers overnight! A slow *cha-ching* is better than no *cha-ching* at all.

Happy that I'm finally going to get a piece of the pie, I plug the phone into the car charger and pop in my ear buds, leaning back to listen to my class notes. In trying to commit them to memory, I frequently pause and repeat them back to myself out loud. I'm sure it's annoying the bleep out of Kylie. After a couple of hours of listening to me, she's beginning to grit her teeth. I tried to warn her that this was how it was going to be when she insisted on coming along. Finally, I take a break to create another vlog.

"Dear Followers, it's just me and my *sister from a different mister*, on the road." I aim the camera at Kylie. She waves and gives her customary greeting. "Let's see what the Grammy has packed for us," I say, digging through my sack lunch, giving the play-by-play. "Ham sandwiches, sliced oranges, homemade cookies—peanut butter. Yum. Snack pack of fruit cocktail with cherries." My eyes go big as I take out a small plastic gift card. "Sweet zombie guts on toast—it's a six hundred dollar gasoline card!" In an effort to keep prices low, the United States has swung its oil reserves wide open. It seemed to help at first, but the cost of everything is rapidly rising. I'll be lucky to get two tanks of gas out of the card, but I'm very grateful. Plunging my hand even deeper into the sack, I discover a roll of cash. I count the bills. There's a thousand dollars here. I burst into tears. "I can't believe my grandparents would do this for me." Kylie hands me a tissue. I cry some more and blow my nose.

"Edit out the part with the gas card and cash," Kylie tells me as I get a reign on my emotions. "We don't want anyone breaking into our room to steal it."

"That goes without saying."

"What's in the sack with my name on it?" Kylie eagerly inquires.

Digging in, besides a sandwich and some cookies, I find a crystal rosary, a couple of small prayer books, and a necklace with a round golden religious pendant in a plastic box. I take out the pendant to study it. One side has a cross covered with letters molded into it. The other side is of a man in a robe. One hand is holding up a book. The other a crucifix. Going around the circular edge of the pendant are the words: EVIS IN OBITVNRO PRE ✞ SENTIA MVNIAMVR. I'm not up on my Latin, so I have no idea what it means. In the bottom of the box there's a folded piece of paper with instructions. Taking it out, I begin to read.

"It's a St. Benedict medal. There's a handwritten note from my Grandpa—says he got it blessed."

"What's a St. Benedict medal?"

I read straight from the pamphlet, zooming in so my followers can read along. "The purpose of using the medal in any of the above ways is to call down God's blessing and protection upon us, wherever we are, and upon our homes and possessions, especially through the intercession of St. Benedict. There's a long grocery list of things it's supposed to do."

"Yeah, go on."

"I was hoping you would tell me to skip it."

"No way."

"Okay. You asked for it. One, it wards off from both the soul and the body all dangers arising from the devil. Two, the medal is powerful in obtaining for sinners the grace of conversion. Three, it obtains protection and aid for persons tormented by the evil spirit, and in temptations against holy purity. Four, it procures assistance in the hour of death." Instead of reading the rest of the benefits, I sum it up. "The medal is also supposed to help with the safe delivery of babies, ward off contagious diseases in both people and animals, protect against storms, leap tall buildings in a single bound, and whitens teeth in one application. Can I stop now?"

"If you must, smartass." Kylie flickers her finger at the bag. "Cookie me."

I open my sandwich bag with the peanut butter cookies and hand her one before setting them on the console between us.

"Dead Man's Stretch ahead," Kylie announces.

"Keep your eyes and ears open," I tell her, aiming my camera toward the abandoned city in the distance. "Dear Followers: We have just entered the notorious length of highway known as Dead Man's Stretch. A couple of friends of mine ..."

"Uh-oh." Kylie interrupts my narration, pointing to a barely perceptible metal strip going across the entire road. "What is that?"

It takes me two second to realize I've seen something similar on the television series, *Good Cop Gone Bad*. It's a remote control spike strip.

"Brake!" I scream as long metal spikes pop out of the strip.

Kylie slams on the brakes, but we are going too fast. There's a horrendous sound of tires screeching, tires blowing, then the two of us screaming as the SUV spins out of control. The vehicle comes to a stop at a 180 degree angle in the wrong lane. Crap a coot, the thing that we should never let happen along Dead Man's Stretch has happened. We have stalled out.

Chapter 23

Trying to get my bearings, I glance about to see four scraggly men in dusty fatigues emerging from behind the abandoned vehicles along the side of the road. They are carrying knives and big guns. My heart is racing hard, wondering if they are carjackers, robbers, rapists, murderers, or all of the above.

Two of the highway men are approaching my side of the car on foot. Another pair of them walk up to the driver's side.

"This can't be happening," Kylie says, starting to lose it. "No, no, no."

"Drive."

"Our tires are gone," she protests.

"Drive on the rims."

"The accelerator isn't working."

"It's stalled, dummy. Press the start button."

Her trembling hands manage to press the button. Nothing happens. I reach over and do it for her—rapidly pressing again and again until the engine finally sparks to life. One of the men smashes in the driver's side window with a metal rod. Glass shatters all over us as he reaches in to grab hold of her. I repeatedly kick him in the face like I'm peddling a bicycle, until he lets go and falls onto the road.

Kylie accelerates. Bullets ping all around us. As our rims grind into the pavement, the sound of a million fingernails running down a blackboard slices down my spine. The back window breaks, sending my heart into fibrillations. After traveling a couple of miles down the road, the gunfire quiets. A semi approaches to the left, honking as it passes us by. Terrified that the next vehicle to catch up with us will belong to the highway men, I'm ready to pee myself.

It isn't long before smoke begins to billow out from beneath. At first we ignore it, but it's getting worse, and we are starting to smell a mix of oil and gasoline. Worried about the tank exploding, Kylie finally pulls over. I grab my dropped cell phone from the floor, shove my grandparents gifts into my pockets, and as an afterthought, I sling Mary's mantle around my neck like an oversized scarf. Kylie is still inside the car as flames come up over the hood.

"Hurry up, Kylie!"

She shimmies out the passenger door with her travel bag, St. Benedict medal dangling between her teeth, while the flames lick up over the windshield. She's not out more then ten seconds before the whole thing is engulfed.

"I can't afford another effin' car!" I stomp my feet and feel like crying, but cuss a little instead, "Damn my rotten luck!"

The only positive is my camera has been running the entire time. It was on the floor during most of our escape. There's probably some salvageable footage.

"Our suitcases are still in the trunk," Kylie says with a despondent sigh, while she's dialing emergency services. "Can you believe this crap? All I'm getting is a stupid recording." She puts it on speaker so I can hear. "*All of our dispatchers are busy right now, please hold.*"

We both glance anxiously down the road in the direction we came, hoping the men have decided not to pursue. Kylie continues to wait for a live person to answer, while we anxiously debate about what to do.

"Maybe I should forget emergency and just call a taxi."

"Where's a cloudburst when you need one?" I complain, looking up at the overcast sky. It looks dreary, but not dark enough for storm clouds. Even if it decides to pour, it's too late to save my SUV. As I'm feeling the pain of its loss, a strange low cloud all by its lonesome in the east catches my attention. It's undulating like a rolling wave.

"I'm sorry about your car," Kylie says. "Did you catch its untimely death on video?"

"Yep."

"Those guys might still be looking for us. We probably shouldn't be standing out in the open like …" Her sentence drops off when she gets an eyeful of that strange cloud. Her brow furrows in puzzlement. "What the heck is that?"

As she's speaking, a Humvee slows down to a stop right in front of us. For a brief moment, I think they're good Samaritans. Then I see the same dirty faces exit the vehicle as four pairs of dirty fatigues and boots touch the ground.

"Oh, shit," Kylie says, echoing my exact sentiments. "Run."

Kylie and I take off down the embankment. A weedy field stretches out before us. No trees, bushes, housing, or anywhere to hide. Four of the men are chasing after us, but we have a big head start. Kylie is a well-conditioned cross country runner, so she at least has a chance. As for me, I'm probably screwed.

"St. Benedict, pray for us!" Kylie yells. Her medal is clutched tightly in a fist. "Jesus deliver us from our enemies!"

The two older men cannot keep up, but the other two are young and bridging the distance. I guess Kylie is more of an endurance runner than a sprinter. She might be in trouble, too. My mind goes to Mary's mantle still slung over my shoulder. Wasn't it supposed to protect the wearer against earthly agents of evil? Not that I ever really believed it, but now my doubts are confirmed.

"Girlies, wanna have fun?" One of the highwaymen calls out. The others hoot and make cat-calls.

"Uncle Joss wants to give you a wild ride on his big pony!" says another. "It'll be swell, I promise." I can't see who is saying what. I really don't care. Escape is all that matters. "Don't be scared, beautifuls."

"We just want to have you over for supper!"

"Over a grill pit, that is! Johnny's eating fine tonight!"

Cannibals. My sense of panic bursts to a new level. The distance between Kylie and myself is increasing, while the men are getting closer. My foot catches a rock. I stumble to the ground. Kylie turns back to help me. She isn't even breathing hard. Obviously, she has been holding back just so she doesn't leave me behind. Now that she has me back on my feet, we start running again.

"Don't wait for me," I tell her. "Save yourself."

"Do you still have the gun?"

"It's no match against that kind of firepower."

"Listen." She cocks her ear to the wind, glancing back at the rolling cloud which is about to overtake us. "It sounds like spoons hitting a metal roof."

A flying brown insect as long as my forearm drops down in the field in front of us. Three golden horns poke out of its head like a crown. Kylie swats at it. It lets out an angry hiss like a snake cornered in the garden.

"A royal hisser!" I scream, noticing it's even bigger and scarier than the ones I've seen in previous encounters. "Watch out for its tail!"

Kylie's eyes widen. She looks more afraid of the bug than the men. A second hisser flutters around my head. Then another. Then another. There's suddenly so many of them, I dart this way and that, nearly forgetting about the men in my efforts not to get stung. One of the men tackles me from behind. My phone goes flying as I hit the dirt. The air is knocked from my lungs. I try to wiggle free from his crushing weight, but he manages to turn me onto my back, pinning my arms to the ground.

"Hold still, bitch!"

As we struggle, more hissers arrive with a deafening clatter of wings. The highwayman looks at the swarming insects in confusion, but doesn't seem very concerned. A hisser lands on his hand. Its stinger uncurls and lances his wrist.

"Yowch!" the bandit yowls.

Using a jiu-jitsu move, I bump up my hips. It forces his head forward so that he has to catch himself with his hands. Rolling him over, he's now on the bottom and I'm on the top. In his pain, he knocks me aside to rise to his feet, no longer interested in anything except escaping the swarm. The hissers are landing all over his hands, neck and face.

A short distance away, his buddies are running in circles, bouncing against each other, trying to escape the stinging hissers.

"Back to the car!" one of them yells.

"There's too many of them!" hollers another.

"My skin is on fire!"

"They're killing me! Help!"

Kylie appears by my side, without a single hisser attached to her body, offering me a hand up. Not wanting to lose my phone, I run back to where I dropped it. The camera is still running when I swoop it up. I aim it at the highwaymen, who are wildly flailing about, running in circles, or writhing in pain on the ground.

"Quit worrying about your dumbass vlog," Kylie yells at me, forgetting her no-swearing policy under the pressure. "Let's go!!"

One of the highwaymen begins shooting at the insects, bullets flying everywhere. His buddies, Kylie, and I all dive to the ground. A stray bullet hits one of the men. His head shatters like a cantaloupe hit with a hammer. Blood and gray matter splatters, droplets hitting my muddy clothes.

Kylie seems to be the only one thinking clearly. Losing her patience, she starts pushing me along, away from the highwaymen and across the field. Coming to my senses, I forget about making a video and start to run.

Chapter 24

After five to ten minutes on the run, my chest feels like it's going to explode. I beg Kylie to slow down. The men are no longer in our sights. She reduces her pace to a jog and eventually lowers it to a brisk walk. Oddly enough, even though the hissers have been with us every step of the way, they haven't stung. Not even once. They're quite the nuisance though, buzzing around our faces, hissing in our ears, making us really nervous. Strands of long black hair are matted to Kylie's blood splattered face. Hissers swirl all around her head. She looks disheveled, but impressively composed while dialing her phone.

"I'm sending an S.O.S. with our GPS coordinates to everyone in my directory," she explains. "Hopefully, somebody will be nice enough to come get us."

We trek ahead for three or four more minutes before she gets a text message.

"It's Miguel," she informs me. "He was on his way back to the university from South Bend when he got my S.O.S. He's only a few miles from here. Said he'll meet us alongside Route 119 in ten minutes."

"Talk about great timing."

"I call it Divine Providence."

She is still holding the phone, reading the screen as we traverse the clumpy field.

"Are you texting Miguel again?"

"No. I downloaded his phone coordinates to my tracking app. It's showing that he's twelve miles due east and heading this way."

"What do you know about Miguel?" I inquire. "I mean, what does he do outside of religious stuff?"

"He's an architect. Well, he was until his firm closed. Nobody is building right now, so he decided this was a good time to get his masters."

"Is he going to ask you out?"

"How would I know?" she replies, swatting away a bug.

Talking about mundane things helps keep me calm, but I can't help to wonder aloud, "Why aren't we getting stung?"

She holds up the St. Benedict medal.

"That doesn't explain why I didn't get stung by the hisser in the storeroom at work. Come to think of it, neither did my co-worker, Margaret. Just Doug."

"Maybe the hissers don't like men."

"Hmm." Her idea has merit. "Could it be that male pheromones make them aggressive?"

"Possibly, but I rather like the idea of Divine Providence."

Confident that my scientific explanation has won the debate, I walk alongside Kylie, feeling proud of myself as she continues to track Miguel with her app. We come to an embankment. At the top, we find a nearly deserted two-lane highway, a red four-door truck parked alongside it with its headlights on. The driver side door opens at our approach. Out comes a stocky sandy-haired man in a Chicago Bears jacket. He's smiling and looking calm despite the flying monstrosities buzzing around him. Apparently, he's not getting stung either. Too bad. He's blown my male pheromone theory right out of the water.

"Miguel." Kylie takes off to meet him. "I can't believe you came." She hugs him in greeting and then pulls away to look at the swarm. "Isn't this insane?"

"And how," he replies. "I'm curious as to how you both ended up here. It wouldn't have anything to do with the SUV I saw smoldering along the interstate?"

"Yes," I say crisply. "That was mine."

"Jenny," he says, as if noticing me for the first time. "Hi."

"It's Gina," I correct. "Can we please leave, now?"

He opens the back door behind the driver's side just wide enough for one of us to climb in.

It seems like Kylie has already called dibs on Miguel, so I take the back, leaving her to join him in the front. Hissers are scurrying over the outside windows. The air is a fog of wings. The highway itself is carpeted. Miguel puts the car in drive, taking it slow. The hissers sound like breaking glass as we roll over them for mile upon mile.

While Kylie tells Miguel all about our experience with the highwaymen, I use the opportunity to check my JustSharing stats. My heart does flip-flops when I see the numbers. "I have over three hundred thousand new followers," I tell Miguel and Kylie excitedly. "My 'Miracle or Hoax' vlog has over twenty million views."

"After what we just went through—how can you be thinking about your internet channel?" Kylie turns around to give me a frown.

"Keeping your eyes on the goal, no matter how wild the ride gets, is what separates the winners from the losers," I say, not bothering to look up from my screen. "Just wait until I download my next set of videos: 'Car On Fire,' 'Attack of the Cannibals,' and 'Hissers Versus Highwaymen'—*cha-ching*. I mean, if you don't mind me sharing it."

"I never cared before." Kylie shrugs. "Go ahead."

"Great."

Before I do though, I'll have to edit out a few things—like the part where we talk about the gas card and, of course, the mention of me having a gun. I don't want to land in prison over a careless comment. Running my hand along Miguel's leather seats, I think how nice it would be to have a truck with a full-sized back seat and an open bed to haul my stuff around when the dorm closes in the summertime. With JustSharing numbers like I'm seeing today, and the cash it's going to bring in, it could happen.

"I like your truck," I tell Miguel.

He doesn't respond. He's so busy talking to Kylie, and vise versa, I think they have both forgotten I'm here. "Guess I'm the third wheel," I grumble under my breath. Leaning back in the seat, I watch today's road trip from the small screen, fast forwarding to just before our encounter with the highwaymen. When the SUV is spinning out of control, I dropped my phone. Everything is a blur. Kylie and I are screaming. This is going to be some of the most intense footage ever. I can practically feel my purse growing fatter.

Twenty minutes later into the drive, we enter the city, noting that it seems to have developed a rash of shiny brown bumps flecked with shards of gold. Streets, signs, lamp posts, parked cars and buildings are crawling with hissers. I take out my camera to share it with my followers.

"The fifth trumpet," Kylie says out of the blue. "The seventh seal."

"You know about that?" Miguel turns to her in surprise. "The Book of Revelation is heavy reading for a new convert."

"Since The Warning, I've become fascinated with the Bible and anything to do with eschatology."

"Fascinated isn't the word I'd use," I pipe up from the backseat. "Try obsessed."

"I'm fascinated with eschatology, too." Miguel is so focused on Kylie, I don't think he heard my little jab. "Father Kramer over in Burlington has a class on the tribulation you might enjoy."

"You mean the priest at St. Faustina's of the Divine Mercy?" Kylie inquires.

"Yes—do you know him?"

"Not yet, but I will. He's the priest Gina's grandfather recommended to me for religious instruction. This can't be a coincidence. Sign me up."

"Excuse me." I lean forward between the seats. "What is this fifth trumpet thingy?"

"St. John wrote about it in the Book of Revelation," Kylie explains. "Chapter Nine, if I recall correctly."

"Very good," Miguel sounds impressed.

"'*And the fifth angel blew his trumpet*'," Kylie begins, "'*and I saw a star fall from heaven unto the earth: and to him was given the key of the bottomless pit. And he opened the bottomless pit; and there arose a smoke out of the pit, as the smoke of a great furnace; and the sun and the air were darkened by reason of the smoke of the pit. And there came out of the smoke locusts upon the earth: and unto them was given power, as the scorpions of the earth have power. And it was commanded them that they should not hurt the grass of the earth, neither any green thing, neither any tree; but only those men which have not the seal of God in their foreheads. And to them it was given that they should not kill them, but that they should be tormented five months: and their torment was as the torment of a scorpion strike."*

"It's edifying to find a brand new Christian who knows the Bible so well," Miguel comments.

"Kylie can remember anything," I inform him. "It has nothing to do with how religious she is—if that's what you're thinking."

"I have a pretty good memory myself," Miguel says, winking over at Kylie. "*'And in those days men shall seek death, and shall not find it; and shall desire to die, and death shall flee from them. And the shapes of the locusts were like unto horses prepared unto battle; and on their heads were as it were crowns like gold, and their faces were as the faces of men. And they had hair as the hair of women, and their teeth were as the teeth of lions. And they had breastplates, as it were breastplates of iron; and the sound of their wings was as the sound of chariots of many horses running to battle ...'"*

"Enough already," I complain from the backseat. "This is like the weirdest flirt fest I've ever had the misfortune of hearing. How about bonding over something less morbid than the end of the world? I suggest pizza and a movie like normal people."

"Never mind her," Kylie says. "Gina has a bad attitude, but so did I back before The Warning. Be patient, God is still working on her."

"On all of us," Miguel says as if he's not only wise, but humble. "In His good time."

Spare me. My eyes roll in annoyance. He catches my expression in the review mirror. Our gazes lock a moment. Slightly mortified, I look away and fold my arms, vowing not to open my mouth for the rest of the trip.

While we head down the highway, I bide my time fretting over my SUV. I'm still paying off the loan. With finals coming up, money shortages, an ill Grammy, and the hissers taking over, I have more stress than I can handle. Hopefully, summer break will offer reprieve, but I'm not holding my breath.

Chapter 25

Finals have been delayed until the authorities get a handle on the royal hisser problem. The insects are attracted to the hum of engines. They like to congregate under the hoods of cars and other large machinery. A dozen plane crashes have been blamed on them. Millions of people have gotten stung, but there have been very few deaths. The government has released broadcasts on the subject, stating that unless you're allergic to bees or wasps, a hisser sting is not a life-threatening emergency. Don't go to the hospital. Treat yourself with ice, Benadryl, and extra rest.

According to the news, the royal hissers have made themselves at home on every major continent. The only positives about the insects is that they have an aversion to children and don't eat plants. So far, there is no record of a sting to anyone under the age of ten. Christians are feeling vindicated, pointing out how well this latest scourge seems to fit into their prophecy about the fifth trumpet. Science, of course, has its own logical explanation.

A look at the hissers' biology and habitat provides clues as to why they have suddenly come upon the scene in such prolific numbers. First, they share attributes with the lowly earthworm. They absorb nutrients from the soil and are prone to sun scald. Therefore, they spend their days burrowing underground and are drawn to cool temperatures. They come out strictly for mating purposes. The fading of the sun has thoroughly confused the hisser's natural rhythmic cycles. Having no natural enemies, they have been breeding in record numbers. One thing that both the scientists and the Bible agree on is that the swarm will not be able to sustain itself indefinitely.

That seems to be holding true because the hissers have only been here a week, and their numbers have already lessened. Don't get me wrong, there are still a helluva lot of them. A person can't go three steps without crushing one on the sidewalk, but for me the insects are just an inconvenience. For those who have suffered a sting, the sight of a hisser can induce terror. Kylie and Miguel believe that those who remain sting-free have an invisible mystical seal placed on their foreheads, giving them special protection. However, the CDC has a different explanation. Similar to the way mosquitoes are more attracted to someone who eats a lot of bananas because of the potassium, the hissers are attracted to or repelled by a specific mix of chemicals in a person's blood. Basically, whether you get stung or not, depends on your diet. The CDC hasn't been able to narrow down the specific combination. They're advising everyone to stay indoors. For those who have to go outside, the best solution is to cover up. Duh.

Halfway into the finals reprieve, I join Brad in the cafeteria for a study session. We're in the same statistics class and thought the extra time quizzing each other would help. Brad's forehead has a three-day old sting on it. The swelling is gone, leaving behind a black crusty spot the size of a quarter, which is hard not to stare at because it's so gross. Julie has tagged along for the hell of it. Although we're pals, I know she'll just get in the way. I feel like telling her to scram, but I'll be renting a room from her in the summer, so I don't want to irk her off. She was stung on the ass a couple of days ago, explaining the inflatable cushion between her and the seat.

Other than a group of four young women over in the corner, laughing about something, and a guy sitting alone at his laptop, we have the cafeteria to ourselves. Apparently, we're the only ones brave enough to risk the swarm.

"Garlic is a natural repellent," Brad says over a bowl of gray potatoes. "I've been popping bulbs like Tic Tacs and the hissers aren't bothering me anymore."

"It certainly repels people," Julie says, holding her nose and making a face.

As we're sitting there talking, the television is running an interview with an elderly man sporting a wispy gray beard. The words at the bottom of the screen identify him as Bishop Crowley, the leader of this diocese. He's reassuring the public that the swarm is not related to the tribulation. "The Book of Revelation is symbolic," he says, "a teaching tool written in code to protect the early Christians from the Roman empire, not a prophecy about today."

"Thank you, bishop," the reporter says. "Before we go, I'd like to switch gears a little. Many are saying the mass of healings happening around the world, including in our own backyard at Rome City, is The Miracle prophesized by the saints of old. Those who claim to be in-the-know predict that events will unfold in a specific order: the Illumination of Conscience, followed by The Miracle, and then the dreaded Three Days of Darkness. What advice would you give to the believers among us who want to prepare for the next event?"

"For starters, don't listen to those who claims to be in-the-know and don't waste your time chasing after miracles." Bishop Crowley speaks sternly into the camera, shaking a finger as if scolding his flock through the screen. "Stay home and read the bible. Accept that Jesus Christ has already saved you. Love your neighbor and do good works. Nothing else is required."

"What do you have to say to those who have claimed to be healed by the apparition in Rome City?"

"It's your faith that's healed you. That's the true miracle."

More generic rhetoric from our religious leaders. Is that all they can offer us in these troubled times? My friends and I quickly lose interest in the interview. Our conversation returns to speculation about finals and our hope that the school will permanently cancel them. As we're sitting there, a text comes over our phones, all at the same time. Basically it says, hissers or not, finals will resume next week.

"Well, there you have it," I say. "It's business as usual."

"Yep," Julie agrees. "The world has it's problems, but life always goes on."

"Are you sure about that?" Brad asks, shaking his head. "Some morning we could all wake up to find everything we have worked for is gone. And then we'll look back on today and realize none of it was worth the effort."

Julie replies, "Could you be anymore morbid, love?"

"Glorious it was when the universe began with a bang," he says. "Tragic it is as the world dies with a whimper."

"I guess that's a yes," I joke. Glancing at the clock, I realize I need to leave for work. "Oh, crap. I'm going to be late for my shift." Gathering my things, I wish my friends good luck on their next week's exams, and depart with Brad's gloomy comments hanging over me like a storm cloud.

The next week, students and faculty alike don sunglasses and wrap themselves in heavy quilts with only their eyes peeking out, to trek out for finals. Even though I don't need to, I wrap myself up to avoid the stares and the nasty comments of the envious. The non-believers accuse those who walk outside unprotected of Christian arrogance. Can I help it that the hissers decided to ignore me?

Kylie and Miguel, who stroll around like lovebirds in only their regular street attire, have had to endure their share of insults around the campus. Yesterday, while I wisely covered up and walked with them to the convenience store on campus, I got to experience the persecution firsthand.

"See how they strut around like they're the elite or something," said a group of guys about Kylie and Miguel. "Don't you feel like knocking them down a peg or two?" Kylie and Miguel ignored them and kept on going. A few yards down the sidewalk, three women decided to hassle them as well. "If you Christians knew what was in store for you, you wouldn't be smiling like a couple of dipshits." Feeling the hatred, I told myself it was finals week. Between the bugs, and the hard testing, people are extra stressed out. It's just talk. I hope.

Most of my exams go off without a hitch. However, in the middle of my applied statistical analysis final I'm startled by a tremendous clang. I turn around to see that Brad has heaved his desk chair at the wall. The other students and professor look up in surprise.

"Screw this," Brad yells. "We are all going to starve to death anyway, so what's the damn point?"

A smartass male student sitting behind him sing-songs, "Somebody didn't study."

Brad dives at him, catching the bewildered student in a bear hug that takes them both to the floor. While everyone is frozen in shock, Brad manages to wrestle himself on top of the other student, laying into him with heavy-handed punches. A few of the other students shake off their surprise to grab him by the arms and drag him off of the smartass. The smartass gets up, blood gushing out his nose, calling Brad every bad name under the sun..

Brad tries to break free from the grip of the students but they hold him fast. He begins to snarl like a wild animal. "When the darkness falls, I'll have your flesh!" It's hard to believe that this is the same quiet guy I've known for years. "And the darkness shall rule!"

"Brad," I gasp, thinking a friend like me might help him calm down. "What has gotten into you?"

"Don't talk to me, you blood bag," he says. "You're not one of us. You're not one of them. You're a shadow without substance."

Taken aback by the odd reply, I stand there with mouth agape, unsure how to respond. School security appears in the doorway. The professor quickly lets them in. The uniformed trio drags Brad out of the classroom, with him cursing and screaming the whole way. The injured student, with the assistance of a couple of his friends, walks out after them with a wadded up T-shirt held to his bleeding nose.

Our professor tries to lighten the situation by making a lame joke about how some people just can't handle finals week. People laugh, but it's a nervous laughter because, if we're honest, we ask ourselves that same question every single day—*what's the damn point?* Maybe Brad's just more honest with himself than the rest of us.

If the injured student decides to press charges against Brad or the school, the cops will probably come by to ask questions. In the meanwhile, the exam resumes. In these days, violence is an everyday part of life, so even after the bloody brawl in the middle of our classroom, we carry on as usual. When I finish, I go outside immediately to call Julie.

This is the first that she's heard about the incident with Brad. She is stunned and deeply concerned. Nearly in a panic, she hangs up to try to get to the bottom of his breakdown.

On the way out of the building, Zach stops me just outside the doors to wish me a happy summer break. I'm too distracted by the incident with Brad to be much of a conversationalist, but I tell Zach I hope to see him when he returns in the fall.

"I'm taking a semester off," he informs me.

"I've heard that line too many times to count," I say, unable to hide the bitter accusation in my voice. "You're dropping out to await the end of the world—aren't you?"

"Nooo." Zach tilts his head like my reaction puzzles him. "I'm helping my parents on a big project back home. Provided civilization doesn't collapse, I have every intention of returning to school."

"You better," I say, narrowing my eyes. "Or I'll hunt you down to kick your ass."

"Promises, promises."

We share a chuckle, then go our own separate ways. I watch him until he turns the corner, thinking it's the last I'll ever see of Zachary Lombardi.

Later that evening, partially out of concern, and partially to start moving my stuff into my summer digs, I head to Julie's apartment. She has already given me a key, so I let myself in to find her curled up in a ball on the living room floor, sobbing her heart out. According to Julie, Brad has taken his things and left school for good. He sent her a single text message: *It's been nice knowing you. Have a nice life.* Beyond that, he never bothered to say goodbye or give a reason. His parents and siblings haven't heard from him either and are frantic with worry.

What a selfish bastard to do that to Julie, especially during finals week.

Now that I'm going to be her roomie, it falls on me to console her, but I really don't know what to say. I do my best, but feel woefully inadequate. Yet Julie somehow manages to forge on.

A week later, the incident with Brad aside, finals went well for me. With my high GPA, I can see myself landing a well-paying job in upper management, but when I'm alone in my bed at night, Brad's words continue to gong in my head. *What's the damn point?*

Americans for Change

The NEU Eden

Choose Reason, Not Religion
Preach Science, Not Hatred
Embrace Progress, Not War

Call: 1-555-NEU-4YOU

Chapter 26

After the finals madness ebbs, I shift into a lower gear. I'm signed up for two summer classes, one per session, but the dorm has closed its doors for regular maintenance. Kylie has gone home and won't be back until the fall semester. Julie has urged me to rent out a vacant bedroom in her apartment, and with the discount she's offering, I'd be a fool not to take it. The beige room isn't anything special, but it will do. A red beret hangs on the black iron bedpost. There's an ugly Neuist poster on the wall over the headboard. It pictures a black tree made of human hands. A red star with a green eye in the middle looks out from the branches. It's message is printed out in bold black letters:

Choose Reason, Not Religion
Preach Science, Not Hatred
Embrace Progress, Not War

At the bottom is a phone number for anyone interested in learning more about the Neuist movement. It's hard to fathom the idea of Americans ever embracing Neuist ideology, especially with all the violence that happened over in Europe during the takeover, but some people only learn the hard way. After Brad's disappearance, Julie fell into a deep depression, so instead of making a fuss about the distasteful poster, I offer her a shoulder to cry on.

I try to be there for Julie as much as I can. She seems glad for the company. We spend a lot of time together, simply hanging out on the sofa, drinking wine coolers and streaming movies. Whenever she brings up Neuism, I'm quick to steer away from the topic, explaining that I'm working 50-60 hours a week at the store, on top of being enrolled in an accelerated summer course. Talking politics stresses me out and I just want to unwind. I suspect the thought of scaring me off is the only thing keeping her from pressing the issue. She says that having me around is helping her get through this. In turn, I've come to rely on Julie as well. Since I don't have a vehicle, when the bus route doesn't mesh with my work schedule, she has been giving me rides. However, as the summer wears on, whenever I ask for a lift, her mouth turns into a disgruntled line of reluctance. Yesterday she took it to a new level, telling me to take the bus, she's not my chauffer.

I was hoping to put off buying a vehicle until September, when my JustSharing money comes in. Apparently, if I want to keep our friendship intact, I need to speed up my plans. I already know the exact specimen I want. It's a turquoise, 4-door pickup truck at the dealership down the road from the mall, only five years old. Regrettably, I still owe a wad on my old SUV. Plus the rent, book fees, cell phone service, and the skyrocketing cost of food, money is going to be an issue. Heart set on the truck, I decide it's time to get creative.

On my lunch hour at work, I walk over to Anne Davis Auto where *my* truck is waiting for me to drive it home. The young salesman recognizes me on the spot.

"Hey," he exclaims. "You're the girl from the Dear Followers videos."

He's so enthusiastic, it makes me feel like a celebrity, which is totally awesome, but I manage to play it cool, like I'm used to the attention. I offer a hand and we shake. "Yes, I am. Nice to meet you."

"My wife is never going to believe this. Do you think I could get a picture with you as proof?"

"I can't say no to a fan."

He stands beside me to hold out his camera phone. I give my most demure smile. Customers and staff alike turn around to gawk with curiosity. A couple of customers seem to recognize me as well and come up to ask for a picture. Fancying myself a savvy business woman, as well as an internet sensation, I smell blood in the water. If my grandfather has taught me anything from his years as a salesman, it's to ask for more than you expect to get, and make the other party negotiate on your terms.

"I would like to see the manager, please."

"Sure thing, Gina. Have a seat," the salesman says, pointing to a vinyl chair in the lobby. "I will see if she's available. Would you like a soda or a coffee while you wait?"

"No, thank you."

A few minutes later, an older woman with blond hair stacked high on her head, walks out in a short gray skirt and black heels. I immediately recognize her from the commercials as the owner of the dealership. She offers her hand, which I take firmly in my own.

"I'm Anne Davis," she says with a well-practiced smile. "Welcome to my store. How can I help you?"

What a stroke of luck. I hope.

"I am short on time," I say. "So I will get straight to business. If you give me that turquoise truck out on the lot for say . . . one dollar, I'll do a JustSharing video of me shopping for a car at your fine establishment."

Her eyes widen like she thinks I'm crazy. "We don't do business that way here," Anne replies, acting miffed by my request.

Undeterred, I give her my well-practiced spiel. "In this economy, it pays to think outside the box. I'm offering you a unique opportunity that has the potential to bring you customers that are difficult to reach through conventional mediums."

"I'm sorry, but I don't know who you are."

"I'm the owner of the FadingLight channel on JustSharing. Last month alone, my channel had over twelve million hits. Since May, an average of fifteen thousand new followers have signed up every single day. Imagine millions of customers hearing the name Anne Davis Auto rolling off the tongue of a sophisticated, yet down-to-earth, young woman they think of as a trusted friend. They'll see me shaking your hand and smiling, then driving away in one of your vehicles as a happy and satisfied customer."

"An interesting proposal." She didn't say no. That's a good sign. "Let me think about it."

"I'm on my lunch break, so don't take too long."

"Let me go to my office to discuss this with a couple of my associates."

While I'm waiting, the salesman offers me a coffee again. This time I'm glad to accept. He also throws in a cookie, which I gobble down in four bites. Thirty minutes later the owner emerges, looking like a cat who swallowed a couple of tasty morsels.

"I checked out your channel." Anne is smiling large, like she has gained an appreciation for what it is I'm offering. "I watched some of your vlogs, including the one where your SUV went up in flames, so I understand now why you're in the market for a new one. Come into my office. Let's talk."

As expected, the deal ends up costing me a good deal more than a dollar, but I'm not complaining. I got half off the sticker price. All I have to do is video myself buying the truck with a handshake and mention how Anne Davis Auto is a dealership with integrity. In addition, I will be required to sign a contract agreeing not to remove the Anne Davis Auto sticker from the dashboard or tailgate for as long as I own the vehicle. Also, the truck must be featured in a minimum of fifteen videos within the next twelve months. Anne is a shrewd business woman. She knows my followers will see her logo every time I video from inside my car. Potentially, it's an advertising campaign that could last for years.

I insist on adding an exclusion. If the truck is rendered inoperable through vandalism, theft, accident, or act of God—I'm released of my obligation. I finally signed and we shake on it.

Two days later, I return to Anne Davis Auto with my phone camera at the ready. Anne has her own camera crew on sight to film the exchange. We shake hands in front of the Anne Davis sign.

"If you want a fast and hassle free experience, come see my good friends at Anne Davis." I smile into the camera. "They're the dealership with integrity." After spending two hours out on the lot, getting everything exactly the way Anne wants it for her commercial, I drive away as the proud new owner of a gently used truck.

Chapter 27

The summer doesn't leave me much time to enjoy my new used truck. Mostly, I just drive it back and forth to work. Due to the mall's reduced hours of operations, changing from 9:30 a.m. to 9:30 p.m., to 11 a.m. to 6 p.m., Fashionable Young Things has had to reduce its hours as well. The change has to do with a combination of slow sales, the city's bus routes being slashed, and increasing violence around the area. It's like a war zone out here at night. Mall security is on patrol 24/7. Last week one of our guards was found shot dead in the parking lot..

I'm working the late shift tonight. Since we've been told to cut hours, I send the other employees home an hour early. The lights dim at 6 p.m., leaving me to close the store alone. As per procedure, I call the security office to let them know I am still here and will be needing an escort to my vehicle in approximately forty minutes.

After I run the sales totals for the day and close the registers, I drag a trash bag of paper stuffing out the back door to the employee hallways. I notice the door to the vacant store next to FYT is standing wide open. My breath catches in my windpipe at the sound of voices—a man's and a woman's coming from inside.

I'm ready to run back into my store and slam the door, but the sound of a whimpering little girl catches my attention. If it was an adult, I'd leave her to fend for herself, but it's a child. I can be a little selfish at times, but I'm not heartless.

Pressing myself against the wall, I edge my way to the door and peer inside. The vacant storeroom is strewn with crumbs. A dirty mattress is set out on the floor. There's an electric burner on a cart with a pot steaming on top of it. Ramen noodle packages are stacked beside it, along with a two liter bottle of soda, and a glass jar full of what looks like

136

ketchup or mustard packages. A girl, maybe thirteen years old or so, is squeezing ketchup packages into the steaming pot. I think she's trying to make tomato soup or something. She doesn't look distressed or upset. Maybe I imagined the whimpering.

Then, I see her—a painfully thin girl of about eight or nine—lying on the mattress. Her skin has an unhealthy blue pallor. She's calling out for her mommy. A woman comes from the vacant store's front into the storage area with a blanket. "Mommy's here, Ashley," she says. "Would you like me to sing you a song?"

The little girl, Ashley, nods. Her mommy sits down on the mattress next to her, proceeding to cover her up with the blanket. The mommy lovingly strokes her little girl's matted brown hair, and begins to sing with a voice like an angel. "Speed bonnie boat like a bird on the wing, Onward, the sailors cry."

I about jump out of my skin when the door fills up with a large bearded man in an army jacket, the barrel of a shotgun inches from my face.

"Whoa." I put my hands up in the air. "Don't shoot."

"What are you doing here?" he asks menacingly from inside the doorway. "This is our turf."

"I-I-I'm just taking out the trash."

"Put that down, Eric," the woman tending the girl snaps. "Look at her nice outfit. I don't think she is after our turf."

"That's what they want you to think, Claire," says Eric. "They use a pretty girl in clean clothes to get you to lower your guard and then boom."

"Daddy," the youngest girl says, softly whimpering. "I'm so thirsty. Can you get me some cold water?"

"She's burning up," says the mommy, Claire. "Did you have any luck finding Tylenol?"

"All of the stores are locked up tight."

The little girl on the mattress is crying pitifully. Thinking I can defuse the situation, maybe save my own butt, I say, "I can get you Tylenol."

"Sure you can," Eric says incredulously. "And then you'll go straight to your gang and bring them back here."

"I don't have a gang. I'm the assistant manager of the store next door."

"That's even worse. You'll go straight to security and tell them I have a gun. Next thing we know, I'm in prison, and my girls are all alone, left to fend for themselves back on the streets."

"I swear, I won't turn you in. If you're worried, just follow me into the store while I get it."

"Go with her," says Claire. "For Ashley."

He looks back at his daughter. Sweat is pouring off of her, while her teeth chatter. The older girl continues to squeeze ketchup packages into the pot. Eric pushes me on the shoulder with the gun barrel, motioning for me to turn around and head down the hallway. It's a short walk to the FYT's storeroom.

"You must think I'm an awful person," he says. "A criminal."

"Well, you are pointing a gun at my back."

"Two years ago I was an engineer at Brog Industries. I had a nice house. My kids went to a private school. Claire was a preschool teacher." His voice is bitter. "Now, look at us."

"Times are hard. I'm sorry."

"You don't know how lucky you are to still have a job."

"The Tylenol is in there." I point to the locker where I store my purse. He takes a shooting stance and orders me to open it. Keeping my movements slow, I explain. "I'm taking a key out of my pocket so I can unlock it. Is that okay?"

"Go ahead. But if you try anything, you'll force my hand."

My back is to him as I reach for my purse. Fear brings the worst case scenario to my mind. What's to stop this man from killing me and taking whatever he wants? He's certainly large enough to be able to do it even without the gun. A quick blow to my head with the butt of his shotgun would end me, and his family would be none the wiser. I can't take that chance. In a split second decision, I pick up my whole purse with the gun inside it and spin around, catching the man's gun with the bag.

It flies from his hands, clunking across the floor.

At the same time, I sweep a foot into his ankles. He goes down and I jump on his back, pressing a knee into his spine. Taking out my own gun, I aim it at the back of his head, my adrenaline pumping hot.

"I'm tired of people like you ruining the world for the rest of us." All my frustrations come pouring out of me. "Give me one good reason why I shouldn't blow you away."

"Don't hurt my daddy!"

A little voice has come from the storeroom door. I turn around to see Ashley clutching a pink lamb. The mother, Claire, shows up behind her with a frantic tone. "I turned my back for only a second, but when she gets delirious like this, she tends to wander off. It's all I can do to …" Her voice trails off as soon as she gets a load of me on top of her husband, threatening his life. Mother and daughter's eyes go wide in fear, making me feel like a bully.

"Don't look at me like I'm the bad guy. He started it." Unsure what else to do, I slowly ease off and let the man get up, but only to his knees, while keeping my gun at his head. I order his wife, "Pick up my purse." She complies, her hands trembling the whole time. "Open it. There's a full bottle of Tylenol inside. It's yours to keep. And, just because I'm such a good person, take the 40 dollars in the side pocket as well."

"You don't know what this means to us," Claire says, retrieving the items as ordered. Tears are streaming down her cheeks. "Thank you. Thank you so much."

"Don't thank her," Eric snarls. "As soon as she gets the chance, she's going to security. And then what are we going to do?"

"Isn't there family you can lean on?" I ask.

"You're looking at what's left of it."

"What about the shelters?"

"They were the first place we turned to for help when we lost our home, but they were already full."

"Surely, the children's hospital will find room for a sick child."

"Surely, they won't," Eric mocks my apparent ignorance. "There are so many sick kids these days, they're only taking the ones who can pay, and even then they have to turn half of them away."

"There has to be some kind of safety net for a family with a sick child."

"Don't you get it, lady? There's no room in the inn or even the stable for people like us. Nothing in this world is free. If my family needs something, I have to steal it, or take it by force."

"Okay, okay. I get it."

"Do you?"

"For what it's worth, I'm not going to turn you into security. But as soon as she gets better, you have to go."

"Our daughter has neuroblastoma," Claire whispers as if it was a terrible secret that only gets mentioned in the darkest corners of Hell.

I flinch at the sound of the offending word—neuroblastoma. That's what Riley died from. My hand holding the gun sinks. I look at the sick girl and painful memories flood back. My eyes begin to well.. "I lost a sister ..." I bite my lip before I finish because I don't want to scare Ashley. "I'm so sorry. Can I get her some ice?"

When Eric speaks again, his defensive tone has become more civil. "Ice would be nice," he replies. "Thank you."

I let Eric and his family return to the store next door, while I go down the main corridors of the mall to the soft pretzel place, grab four cups, fill them to the rim, and return, knocking lightly on the door with my foot.

There is no answer. A family can't be too cautious, I guess.

"Your order from FYT is here," I say, trying to sound like I'm just doing my job, should anyone else overhear.

"Leave it in front of the door," Eric calls from the other side.

I set it on the ground and step back, pausing to watch the door open. A hand slips out to retrieve the cups of ice one by one. Satisfied they got them, I return to work to finish the payroll.

It's hard to concentrate knowing the suffering that's happening on the other side of that wall. To think it's been going on for weeks, perhaps months, without my knowledge, leaves me feeling guilty. I long for the return of my previous ignorance, but all I can think about is Ashley. If only there was something more I could do.

The next afternoon, I have to report to work again. Before I go, I stop at the taco place, and get a bargain 12-pack of chicken burritos. I work the sales floor with Doug most of the afternoon. Around 5 o'clock, I send Doug home and wait until the coast is clear. Then I take the box of burritos from the mini-fridge in the storage room and head out into the employee only hallway. When I'm sure there's nobody else is around, I set the box on the floor and knock, calling out, "Special delivery from FYT."

I lurk nearby to make sure the box disappears, in case an employee from another store happens to walk by. Thirty seconds later a hairy hand reaches out and snatches up the box. A good feeling awakens that has been asleep for a very long time. I can't put a label on it, but there's a spring in my step when I return to the sales floor.

Over the next three days, I leave gifts of fast food for the family. I haven't laid eyes on them, or heard any noise coming from next door, but I know they're there because the food vanishes like magic. By the fourth day, I wise up and plan ahead.

Instead of stopping at fast food places on the way to work, I shop at STAPLES FOR LESS the night before, filling a sack with items that won't go bad quickly. Not only is it more bang for the buck, but I can buy imperishable items. That way, on my days off, the family still has plenty to eat. With me working full-time this summer, and the absence of a social life, I think I can pull off the additional expenses.

Over the weeks to follow, I fall into a routine of dodging hissers, attending classes, going to work, sneaking food into the mall for the family, and coming back home to catch some sleep. I don't know what's going to happen to Eric and his girls when I go back to being a part-time employee in the fall, and that's a worry.

I've nearly given up on prayer, but I see the silver string rosary my grandmother made hanging on my bed post. With nowhere else to turn, I take it in my hands, figuring it cannot hurt to ask. I make the sign of the cross and pray: *Dear God, I know I'm among the damned, but please, if there is anything more I can do to help Eric's family, show me the way. Amen.*

Simple and to the point. I don't expect Him to answer, but at least I tried.

Chapter 28

On a fifty degree day in June, I head out from the apartment in my trusty used truck for classes. On the way into the building, I scope out the forest beyond the campus grounds. The way many of the branches failed to sprout has resulted in a Swiss Cheese effect, leaving the canopy of the trees full of holes. As long as there are some leaves, I tell myself there's hope that life will go on.

I'm almost to the building when I get a text from Aunt Viv:

> Mom's numbers are completely normal. The cancer is gone. The family is crediting it to The Miracle. All I can say is ... ALLELUIA!

Did I read that correctly?

I do a double-take. Blink several times. Read it again—it still says the same thing. Yet I'm not ready to believe it without hearing it for myself. I immediately dial my grandmother's number. She answers on the second ring.

"Grammy," I say breathlessly. "Is it true—are you really cancer-free?"

"The doctor wants to run a few more tests to verify. But things are looking good."

"That new round of chemotherapy really did the trick!"

"The doctor said the drug has never worked so rapidly in a patient, especially someone in stage four. I give the glory to God. He healed me at Rome City, but I don't understand why."

"Who cares why?" I explode with happiness. "Just be glad."

"I don't understand why I was cured and others were not." Her voice is subdued. Considering the circumstances, she doesn't sound as

143

excited as I would expect. "Do you remember Linda from the trip—the woman with the two small boys who sat in front of you?"

"Oh, yeah. Sure."

"She died last week."

"How?" I ask in surprise.

"From a brain tumor."

"She never mentioned being sick."

"Linda wouldn't. She always put on a cheerful face in front of her boys, but three years ago she had surgery to remove it. They thought they got it all. Last Christmas it returned to wrap itself around the brain stem. The surgeons said there was nothing they could do. To think of Linda being taken so young, leaving those little boys behind, I just don't get how God works sometimes. His will be done, I suppose."

"That's why I have a hard time with prayer. If His will is going to be done anyway, why bother?"

"Oh, Gina." Grammy begins to cry, making me feel like an insensitive schmuck. "I didn't ask to be cured of cancer in Rome City. I was there to beg the Lord for your conversion. It is my most ardent hope that you will return to the bosom of Holy Mother Church. Promise me you will start going again."

"I'm helping a homeless family. That has to count for something."

"Good works without faith are empty."

"Can't you just be happy about beating the cancer?"

"Not when I know you are lost and running out of time. When was the last time you went to confession?"

"Well, um …"

"At this point, I'd be relieved to know you went to any church at all. I can't get the image of you burning in Hell out of my mind. At least when I had the cancer, I was able to offer up all that suffering for your salvation. Now what am I supposed to do?"

"Drats, my phone is running out of charge," I lie. "If we happen to get cut off …"

Pressing END CALL, I sever the connection. Hanging up on my own grandmother. Is it any wonder why I'm Hell bait?

Later that night, while I'm lying in bed on the verge of sleep, I can't stop thinking about my grandmother. If only I could believe God stepped in to cure her from cancer, it would change my entire outlook. Making the sign of the cross, I toss out a quick prayer: *Dear God, I'm not sure who or what to credit for the healing of Grammy. If it was You, thank you. I'm sorry my faith is so weak, but I don't know how to fix it. Please help me be a better person. Amen.*

"Leap," a male voice fills up the room, "And trust Me to catch you."

Sitting up with a startled gasp, I flip on the light fully expecting to find a man standing by my bed, but there's nobody here except me. It must have been my imagination, but part of me wonders if it was Jesus. I make the sign of the cross again: *If that was You, Lord. I'm dropping a note into the suggestion box. Your message to leap and trust was rather vague. Try to be more specific in the future. Amen.*

The next day, I find myself standing in front of the homeless family's door, trying to prove that I'm a good person.

"Your package from FYT is here." This time when the door opens, instead of stepping away, I push my way through. Eric puts me in a headlock, but lets go as soon as he realizes it's just me. His older daughter has a broom in her hand. She pauses at my entrance. Ashley is propped up in the corner next to her mother, looking thinner than ever. Her eyes are sunk in as if she's on her way to becoming a corpse. Claire, her mother, is holding a paperback copy of *The Magic School Bus*.

Hand wrapped tightly around my truck's key fob, I'm having second thoughts about my plan. However, the word 'leap' has been flashing in my head like a blinky light since last night. If I don't act, I have the feeling it will never stop. So instead of doing a song and dance around the issue at hand, I get straight to the point.

"Miracles of healing have been happening in Rome City, Indiana. My grandmother went there with stage four cancer. Now she's cancer-free. Are you interested in checking it out for yourselves?"

"I don't believe in miracles," Eric replies.

"Well, I do," the oldest daughter cries out from across the room, a hint of desperation in her voice. "If there's even the slightest chance of saving Ashley, we have to try."

"We don't have any way to get there," Eric growls. "No car, no money, nothing."

"Now, you do." I offer him the keys to my truck. "If you leave now, you can be there before dark."

"You're just going to hand me the keys to your truck?" Eric's voice is incredulous. "What's the catch?"

"No catch, but let's be clear. I'm not giving you my truck, it's just for you to borrow for a few days."

"And you don't want anything in return?"

"Actually, I have a channel on JustSharing. If you wouldn't mind me taking a video of you going off to Rome City …"

"And there's the catch," he says. "You want to look charitable for your adoring fans."

"If the lady helps us out," the oldest daughter says, "why shouldn't she get something out of it too?"

The girl has made a good point, so I shut up while Eric considers the deal.

"What do you think, Claire?" Eric finally asks his wife.

"I don't know. It's a long drive and Ashley's not doing very well. What if we get there and find out it's a hoax?"

"Haven't you heard the other families talking about The Miracle?" the eldest daughter replies. "It's been in the news. Healings taking place all over the world. I think we should go for it."

"I can't pay for gas," Eric says.

"Taken care of." I show him my gas card. "There's 300 dollars on it."

"Aren't you worried about us driving away and stealing your truck?" Eric asks, still not completely sold.

"Yes, I am."

"So why are you doing this?"

"To be honest," I shrug, "I'm not sure. Can I video you or not?"

"All right," Eric slowly replies. "I guess it's okay."

About ten minutes later, the family and I pause at the doors leading to the mall parking lot. The parents and the eldest daughter wrap themselves in blankets to avoid hisser stings. The mother tries to cover Ashley, but the little girl refuses.

"Mommy," she says so sweetly, "I want to feel the wind on my face."

Since hissers don't bother children, Claire relents. I've never been stung, so I don't bother covering myself, either. The family follows me outside to my truck. I open the back door for them. Claire climbs inside and Eric hands Ashley off to her mother. He gets in the driver's seat, while the eldest girl climbs into the front passenger side. I video them driving away, wondering if I just made a huge mistake.

"Dear Followers," I say, doing a selfie. "I know what you're thinking—*Gina has lost her friggin' mind. She's never going to see that truck again.* Well, here's the thing. I talked to my Grammy yesterday. She told me God healed her in Rome City. Like a putz, I couldn't accept it. I attributed it to the chemotherapy. That made Grammy cry because she's worried about my lack of faith. She thinks I'm not right with God and, as much as I've tried to convince myself otherwise, deep down I know my Grammy's right.

"Maybe that's why I handed my keys over to a homeless family and sent them in search of a miracle. It's not so much that I'm looking for brownie points from the Big Designer upstairs. It's because, if that little girl comes back cancer-free, I will know without a doubt that God is still with us, The Warning was the work of His hands, and the coming Three Days of Darkness needs to be taken seriously.

"That might sound like a ridiculous jump in reasoning, but hear me out. Since The Warning and The Three Days of Darkness were often lumped together by the prophets, it goes to reason that if one event comes to pass, then they all will. A used pickup truck is a small thing to wager for that kind of assurance." I pause to gaze anxiously in the direction my truck drove off in. "Oh, balls. What have I done?"

Chapter 29

My recently adopted phrase is *no good deed goes unpunished.* Forty-five days ago I let a homeless family drive off in my truck and they haven't been seen since. *Reckless Generosity,* I've labeled the video of me giving the truck away on my internet channel. The police laughed at me when I told them what happened. I suppose that's what I deserve for being a trusting tart monkey. There was no clause in the contract with Anne Davis Auto about me giving the truck away. What's going to happen when they find out I can't live up to my end of the deal? Just thinking about how foolish I was makes me sick to my stomach, but I'm trying to move past it to focus on the positive. At least I don't have to pay for insurance, gas, or its upkeep.

Despite the fact that we've had a string of 60-degree days, it's hard to maintain the positive attitude. Over the summer, the city has made drastic cuts to its bus routes. It only stops at the mall three times a day now: 11 a.m., 2 p.m., and 6 p.m. That might work okay for customers, but not for employees. When I'm the scheduled closer, my shift doesn't end when the store shuts its doors. I'm usually there at least another hour after the last bus leaves. If I can't find a ride with a friend, I'm screwed.

Even when the bus schedule works out, I detest public transportation. Different versions of Tattered Man have accosted me while I'm waiting for the bus and sometimes even while I'm on it. It's eerie how they all say similar things, calling me a dirty beast, saying the darkness is at hand, and they'll feast on our flesh. While it makes awesome material for my JustSharing channel, it's scary while it's going on.

Now that the fall semester is starting up, Kylie and I will be roommates once again. I don't imagine she will give me grief over asking for the occasional lift to and from work, unlike the few friends that lived around campus over the summer months who have grown tired of me asking them for rides. In order to keep my job, I had to reach down to the bottom of the barrel. That's how Jerome came back into the picture.

Kylie isn't going to be happy. Even before The Warning, she didn't care much for him. Unless he was drunk or partying, she said Jerome always acted bored, like he had someplace better to be. In other words, he was rude. After he tried to force himself on me, the man sunk even lower in her eyes. If I know Kylie, she's going to demand an explanation as to why I let him back into my life. I have my excuse all worked out—it's Julie's fault.

In my mind, that's the truth. *You see, I will explain. I had to close the store one night. Julie was supposed to pick me up at 7 p.m. I left her several messages to make sure she hadn't forgotten. By 8 p.m., I was still waiting. The security guards were growing impatient. Out in the parking lot, the loonies were beginning their nightly stroll through the city. There were like five or six Tattered Men and Women, bumping off of each other in the parking lot, ranting about the coming darkness. Feeling like I was out of options, I called one of the few people brave enough to venture out into the city at night, Jerome.*

I doubt that will appease Kylie, but what choice did I have when Julie repeatedly failed to show up? Over the course of the summer, calling Jerome got easier and easier. He has behaved like a perfect gentleman—well, mostly. He doesn't make it a secret that his goal is to win me back. I told him I'm not interested in anything more than friendship. However, I don't know if that's true. He has a boyish charm about him that's hard to resist.

Summer was far from perfect, especially that nasty letter I got from Anne Davis on Thursday, but the weather has been nice and warm. Temperatures have hit the seventy-degree mark five or six times. Now that it's August, the hissers have been quickly dying off. Being able to walk around outside in shorts without them buzzing around my head gives me hope that the world might be recovering. It's supposed to reach

74 degrees this afternoon. I couldn't have picked a nicer day for moving out of Julie's apartment and into student housing.

With the help of a few friends, it takes me less than four hours to move everything in. Kylie is going to flip out when she sees how spacious and pretty our living space is. About a decade ago, this building was built for the wealthy students. There's no longer enough rich students around to fill it up. Hell, the school is running low on poor students as well. Whoever is in charge decided to consolidate. Only the best buildings remain open, but our rent remains the same. For once something has worked to my advantage. It's like the Ritz of dorm rooms. There are two separate bedrooms, each with a built-in desk. A huge common room with a full-sized kitchenette and refrigerator/freezer. The countertops are chocolate quartz. The bathroom includes a spacious walk-in shower and double sinks.

As I finish unpacking my last box of clothes, I have the news channel playing on the big screen. The journalist is saying that the temperatures will hit the 70s all week long. Heat wave. There will be a harvest this year. Hoorah! But yield will be poor. As I'm worrying about the prospect of skyrocketing food prices, a text comes over the phone. It's Kylie:

> I'm 5 minutes away. Can you help me carry in my stuff?

I text her back that I'll meet her out in the parking lot. Our assigned spots are side-by-side, only a couple of rows from the front door of the building. As I wait, I swat away a couple of hissers. Then I power on my phone to vlog.

"Dear Followers: Today is Saturday. I'm out in the lot at school, waiting for Kylie to help her move in. Fall semester starts Monday. This means I'm going back to part-time at FYT. When I think about the loss of all that income, I have to admit it's tempting to say to hell with school.

"Well, enough of that pity party and onto the next one," I continue to narrate, moving to the empty spot where my truck used to sit. "You've been leaving comments, asking me if I've had any contact from the homeless family that borrowed my truck, and I'm sad to report the answer remains a big, fat, no. However, I have been contacted by the courts." I hold up the legal document for all the viewers to see. "On Thursday, I received this letter via registered mail: *Anne Davis Auto versus Regina M. Applegate*. I'm being sued for breech of contract. There was a stipulation that, over the course of a year, the company logo had to appear in my videos a certain number of times.

"I do recall reading that. However, I'm taking the stance that the end of the year isn't up. There is hope that little Ashley has found her miracle and the return of my truck is imminent. Until then, you can kiss my ass, Anne Davis. Plus, there was the stipulation that if the vehicle was stolen, I would be released of my obligations. I've been reading up on my legal rights. The fact that I willingly handed over the keys shouldn't make a difference because ..." As I'm vlogging, a familiar sports car pulls up. The back seat is packed full of boxes and clothes. "Kylie!" Behind her car comes a familiar red truck. Also full of stuff. "Miguel." I video him getting out of the truck. "I didn't expect to see Kylie's boyfriend today." I turn the camera to show my irritated expression. "Don't get me wrong, Miguel's a good guy, but I think he's adding fuel to the fire when it comes to my roommate's recently acquired religious obsession. Don't you?

"Miguel, for those of you who don't already know, has a bachelor's in architecture and a couple of years of experience under his belt. There's not any demand for new buildings right now, so he was let go by his firm. Now he's a bartender—one of the few occupations still in demand. He's decided this is a good time to attend graduate school, so lucky me. I'm sure he'll be hanging around."

When Kylie exits her vehicle, she looks thinner than I remember and a little sad. I give her an enthusiastic hug. Holding up my camera in front of her face, I exclaim, "Welcome back, roomie!"

"Hey, y'all. Hi, y'all. How y'all doing?" she gives her customary greeting.

"Tell us about your summer, Kylie—how did it go?"

"Getting baptized and confirmed was great. Other than that, it was a terrible summer." Her brow furrows and her mouth turns into a pout. "When my parents found out I had become a Christian, they blew up.

Said I was an embarrassment. Foolish. A disappointment. After that vitriol was out of their system, they resorted to the silent treatment. I thought they would get over it before they left for their research study in the Antarctic, but they didn't."

"Oh." I'm not sure how to respond. Afraid of making things worse, I keep it simple. "I'm so sorry, Kylie."

"On the bright side, I won't have to deal with them again for a few years," she says, bravely trying to make light of it. "They didn't cut off my funds. And it doesn't suck to be back among friends." She aims her key fob and pops open the trunk. "How about giving me a hand, bestie?"

Her last comment makes me smile. I grab a laundry basket of foul smelling clothes and a desk lamp from the trunk. Miguel loads himself up with Kylie's computer equipment. Both Kylie and Miguel pause to stare forlornly at the dormitories that have closed down over the summer and never opened back up. A few windows have already been broken out.

"It's weird how unoccupied buildings fall apart so quickly." I muse aloud. "It's like they grow lonely and just give up and die."

"There's nothing weird about it," Miguel says. "It's all about maintenance. Empty buildings hold up quite well if they're attended to properly."

"I know that." My eyes roll in annoyance. "I'm being philosophical for my followers."

We enter our building and climb the steps to the second story. Along the way we pass several other students moving in with boxes. Kylie is excited to see how nice our new place is. With the three of us working, it only takes a couple of hours to get her moved in.

In celebration, I open a condensed can of vegetable beef soup. For the side, I baste bread with olive oil, sprinkle it with garlic salt and broil it. We sit around, sipping soup, chewing on bread, talking about nothing and everything. For dessert, I tear open a bag of chocolate chip cookies.

"There is a rumor going around that the state and federal coffers are empty," Miguel says with a mouth full of cookie. "If that's true, the university is going to run out of money. We won't be able to pay our military or law enforcement. It's going to be anarchy."

"It's just talk," I reply. "If the school was out of money, we wouldn't be here."

"I suppose we should just be grateful to live in the United States," Miguel adds. "At least our women aren't being raped in the middle of the street in broad daylight. Nor do Christians have to worry about being labeled enemies of the state and executed for showing up at church."

"Neuism does not see the individual as good or rational," I continue the conversation, though Kylie remains quiet. She used to support Neuism. I wonder if her Christian values have made her view it in an unflattering new light. "They see the masses as a product to be controlled and manipulated. It's always about what the individual can do to further the interests of the nation—never what the nation can do to help the individual."

"Maybe so," Kylie says. "But nobody can dispute that the Neuists have helped restore order in the countries they have taken over. The cops here are being killed like ducks in a shooting gallery."

"That's terrible," Miguel replies, "but over there, it's the police doing the indiscriminate killing. When you live under a Neuist regime, there is no freedom of assembly or due process of law. Worshipping God, or having a couple of friends over for a backyard barbeque, can get you shot as a terrorist. People are afraid to leave their homes."

"I can't believe that France is trying to restore its monarchy," Kylie says, trying to shift to a slightly different topic. "It makes no sense."

"It's the only way to avoid being taken over by the Neuists," I suggest.

"That's right," Miguel agrees. "Crowning a king is France's way of fighting fire with fire." Huzzah. It's cool having Miguel on my side for a change, because in all honesty, I could never hold my own against Kylie. I'm happy to listen as he continues. "A monarchy gets to bypass all the bullshit red tape of a democracy, without the politicians, lawyers and special interest groups getting in the way. Like the Neuist dictatorship, a king isn't answerable to anyone, which allows him to act fast."

"I can't imagine going from being a politically active citizen," Kylie says, "to the voiceless subject of a king. Why would anyone willingly give up the right to vote?"

"Maybe because the French realize their vote counts for nothing under the Neuists," I counter. "Just like under communism, the people have no say in how things are done, despite claims to the contrary. At least with a monarchy, they're up front about it."

"I'm not saying Neuism is the answer." Kylie said, making me hopeful that she's finally coming around to my way of thinking. "Restoring the throne isn't a solution either. It's like going back to the Dark Ages."

"Hold that thought," Miguel says.

He dismisses himself to go outside. A few minutes later, he returns with a bottle of blackberry wine. As we continue the discussion, he fills our coffee mugs and raises a glass to toast.

"To a successful new semester," he says.

"To friendships old and new," Kylie says, raising a mug.

"To the Generation of Fading Light," I say. "May our tomorrow be brighter than today."

The three of us clink our glasses together, saying, "Here, here." And we talk about the state of the world late into the night.

Chapter 30

Around the end of September, after the new semester is in full swing, the reign of the royal hissers comes to an end. They saved my life once, but I'm not going to mourn their passing. Mounds of dried-up insect carcasses have brought crows out in record numbers. Cawing echoes across campus day and night. Even during class, I hear them screeching through the windows.

Kylie isn't around as much as she was last year. She and Miguel have become quite serious. Come to find out, Miguel was her sponsor when she got baptized and confirmed into the church last summer. The two of them are volunteers at St. Faustina of the Divine Mercy over in Burlington, an hour away. There are closer churches, but for some reason they're both attached to that one. Kylie helps with the Job Seekers program, teaching computer application courses at the church. Miguel is using his architect skills to help Father Kramer build a second homeless shelter on the edge of town. The infrequent occasions when Kylie and I hang out, she goes on and on about how dire the homeless situation is and keeps bugging me to help out. My constant response is that I lent my truck to a homeless family and they friggin' stole it. As far as I'm concerned, I've done my good deed for the century.

Come the end of the month, I begin to obsessively check my bank account for a deposit from JustSharing. So far, not a penny. Worried that I'm getting screwed, I go to the JustSharing online forum to look for an explanation. There's a message from the company. They apologize for the delay but, rest assured, payments are forthcoming.

The online JustSharing community is very concerned. Banks and financial institutions, both online and physical stores, have been folding every day. What if our money is simply gone?

The thought keeps me frugal. Besides using my meal tickets for the school cafeteria, I'm living on peanut butter and jelly crackers. If it wasn't for Jerome taking me out to eat now and then, I'd never have a nutritious meal. I don't want to give him the wrong idea, and promise to pay him back, making sure he understands that our time together is just as friends. He often just brushes off my concerns and tells me not to worry about it. Not worry about it? If only I could. The problem is that my internal worry machine seems to have gotten stuck in the ON position. Whether it's over misleading Jerome, ending up homeless, or the fate of my eternal soul, it's getting harder to convince myself that everything is going to be okay. It feels like civilization is gasping its final breaths and I can't stop myself from feeling anxious.

Chapter 31

On a rainy Saturday morning in October, I'm sitting on the city bus, enduring the scent of dirty armpits and sour barf. The driver is waiting at a red light to turn left into the Hillsboro Mall parking lot. Vivaldi's *Spring* begins to play over my phone. A photo of my Grammy's sweet face comes over the screen.

"Hello, Grammy," I say brightly.

"Hi, butterfly. Is this a good time to talk?"

"I'm on the bus, heading to work. I've got a few minutes."

"Does this mean your truck hasn't come back?"

"You know about that?"

"Oh, yes. I watch all your videos." Grammy has always been intimidated by computers. I'm surprised she's even heard of JustSharing. The realization that she endured "all that electronic gadgetry" to subscribe to my channel fills me with warmth. "I especially liked it when you told Anne Davis Auto to kiss your ass. But you really need to watch your language, sweetie."

"Uh, okay," I reply, trying to hold in my laughter. Hearing "kiss your ass" coming out of her mouth strikes me as hilarious, even though she's only repeating what I said. "How are you feeling today?"

"Blessed. That's part of the reason I'm calling. The church is throwing a party for those who were healed at Rome City. You and Kylie are invited."

"Awesome. When is it?"

"Next Sunday at five. They're having a hog roast. Did I mention that your mom and Ray will be there?"

"Mom is coming?" My voice goes out in longing. We haven't seen each other since last Christmas. "Is that for sure?"

"You know she comes up every year on Riley's birthday. It's the same weekend."

"Oh, yeah. Sounds great. It's just that I'm scheduled to work. I'll talk to Dora to see if she will switch with me."

"Try to get Kylie's new boyfriend to come along. Or yours—if you're seeing anyone." There's a pause like she's hoping I'll fill in the empty space with an answer. I don't. She continues. "I'd feel better knowing you girls had a man along for the ride. I watched your video with those awful highwaymen. Thankfully, the Lord sent those hissers after them." *Oh, no,* I think. *Here it comes.* "Speaking of the Lord—have you been to church lately?"

"Um, no."

"That's too bad." Her voice is heavy with disapproval. "I wish my healing had been enough to convince you of the goodness of God. Why is it so hard for you to accept a miracle?"

"It might have been the new chemo drug."

"Others were healed that day as well."

"I don't know any of them. They could be mental cases, or just looking for attention, or mistaken about how sick they were in the first place. I can't just take someone else's word for it. I have to see for myself."

"St. Thomas didn't believe Jesus rose from the dead. Once he saw Jesus with His own eyes, touched the wounds with his own hands, he finally believed and went on to become a great saint. So I'm not writing you off, Gina. If you will open your heart to the truth, I know you will go on to do great things."

"I don't know about that, but I've always admired St. Thomas for his skepticism."

"In your JustSharing video you said if the little homeless girl, Ashley, was healed in Rome City, you would accept Jesus as the Lord and Savior."

"That's not what I said."

"I'm paraphrasing, honey. You said you would go back to church though, correct?"

"In so many words, yes."

"Did you mean it?"

"I meant it at the time, but that was five months ago. Hate to say it, but the odds are the girl is dead."

"You are probably right, but promise me this—if you find Ashley is alive and well, you will keep your promise."

"Yeah, sure."

"That's not good enough."

"What do you want me to say?"

"Promise me you will pour your heart out to Jesus, make a sincere confession, and throw yourself into the arms of Holy Mother Church." Reluctant to do it, I sigh in exasperation. Grammy can be so pushy. The elderly black woman in the next seat is giving me a stern stare. Averting my gaze, I wonder if all old ladies belong to a secret club where they teach each other how to make a person feel guilty in a single glance. "I'm waiting," Grammy says testily.

"Okay, okay," I give in just to keep the peace. "If I find out that Ashley was healed, I will pour my heart out to Jesus, go to confession, and throw myself into the arms of the Church. Happy now?"

"Ditch the sarcastic attitude, young lady. Your salvation is heavy on my heart."

"I'm sorry, Grammy. You know faith doesn't come easily to me."

"It's good you recognize that much. When it finally comes, you won't take it for granted." Much to my relief, she changes the subject. "How is school?"

"Challenging. Just the way I like it."

"I'm proud of you, Gina. You work so hard in school and at the store. These are trying times, but you're good at taking care of yourself. Just don't forget that taking care of your soul comes first."

The bus is rolling to a stop in front of the mall. The brakes let out a hiss of air.

"I'm at my stop," I'm relieved to announce. "I'll get back to you when I know if I can make it or not. I love you."

159

"I love you too, butterfly. Be safe out there."

I leave the stale smells of the bus and step off into the mostly empty parking lot, noting the three crazies in the distance, digging around for worms in the dead flowerbed. They're far enough away not to be a threat, but I don't take my eyes off of them until I'm safely inside the mall. As I head toward Fashionable Young Things, my feet feel like anvils at the thought of asking my manager to switch weekends with me. When I broach the subject, hard-nosed Dora responds with her standard reply, "The schedule is the schedule for a reason. If you have better places to be, I'm sure I can find someone who would love to be here in your place."

Her response is no surprise, but nonetheless humiliating. A couple of hours later at break, I call Grammy on the verge of tears, letting her know I couldn't get the time off. She assures me everything will be okay. Not to worry about it. Everybody knows I'd come if I could.

My mother calls back shortly thereafter to express her disappointment. At first I'm annoyed that Grammy felt the need to share the bad news before I got the chance, but the feeling quickly turns into gladness. My mother and Ray have talked it over. After the party at the church, come Monday, they are going to make a special trip to the university to see me. It will be only her fourth visit since I've started attending, so I'm super excited.

The downside is that the rest of the week drags on. If I could, I would kick Monday, Tuesday, and Wednesday to the curb. By Thursday, I'm feeling stoked and beginning to prep for the visit. Dusting is part of my daily routine because of the comet debris always manages to find its way inside, but I go the extra mile today, sweeping beneath furniture, cleaning out the fridge, removing dead gnats from the ceiling lights, rearranging pillows. I even put out the fancy soaps shaped like butterflies that I've been saving for a special occasion. On Friday, I plan the menu and type out the itinerary of all the places I plan to show them around town, including the mall where I work. Saturday requires an expensive trip to the grocery for all the ingredients.

Sunday afternoon around 5 p.m., I get a call from Mom and Ray as they're heading out to the party at St. Michael's. They're kind of in a rush,

160

so we don't talk long, but they expect to be at my place late afternoon tomorrow. As soon as we hang up, I continue with the preparations. Just like a kid on Christmas Eve who welcomes Santa to her home with sweets, I make a chocolate cake in anticipation of their arrival. It's from a box, but since I have to add my own eggs and oil, I can call it homemade without lying. Mom and Ray will be so impressed.

Early Monday I get up to make the icing from real butter and melted chocolate chips. Then I frost the cake, making artsy swirls on the top with a spoon. And that's not all. Feeling like the famous Homespun Chef from JustSharing, I get out the crock-pot to prepare my specialty, a heavy stew I call White Chick Chili. I drop in northern beans, chickpeas, onions, and chopped green peppers into chicken broth, sprinkling it with salt, pepper, and cilantro like a master foodie. Between the cake and the chili, I've blown my emergency budget. My mother is totally worth every penny. She has scrimped to help me get through college. It's the least I can do.

Around 1:15 p.m., about ten minutes into my last class of the day, I get a text from Kylie:

Some people are here to see you. Come right away.

My mom and my stepdad must have arrived early. Hoorah! I gather my things in the middle of class and dash across campus. As soon as my feet touch the hall on the second floor, the hearty scent of White Chick Chili hits my nose. I hope my guests like it. In my exuberance, I swing open the door and yell, "Mom! I'm so glad you ..." My excitement droops at the sight of two strangers in casual business attire and a police officer sitting on my sofa. My brow furrows in puzzlement.

The strangers stand up at the sight of me. Kylie is lingering in the background with Miguel, Julie, and Jerome. My friends are hanging back, looking unsure of themselves and shaken up. Something bad has happened. I can feel it deep down.

"What's going on?" I address my friends, ignoring the strangers standing in front of the sofa and the blonde middle-aged woman coming toward me with a look of sympathy. "Why are the police here?"

"Hello, Gina," says the blonde woman. She's wearing a pink button-down cardigan over a plain white blouse and gray pants. A thick silvery crucifix hangs around her neck. She wraps an arm around my shoulders, leading me toward the sofa. "I'm Pastor Bianca Mouflon, a counselor here at the university. Please, have a seat."

The space in front of the sofa clears as she tries to force me to sit down, but I'll have none of it. "I don't want to take a seat." I shove well-meaning hands away, glaring at everyone in the room. Anger is already rising inside me, and I don't know why. "No song and dance. Just tell me the truth—is my mother okay?"

"I'm afraid not, dear," the pastor replies with so much empathy, I want to rip her throat out. "There was an incident."

Kylie bursts into tears, flinging herself into Miguel's arms. I glance over at Julie. She averts her eyes. Jerome mumbles something and disappears into the bathroom.

"Was it a car accident? A jacking?" I barely know what I'm saying. "Is Ray okay? What hospital were they taken to?"

"Gina," the pastor says softly. "It wasn't a car accident. There was an attack at St. Michael's church last evening. In the basement, during a party, thirty people were injured. Eighteen were killed—including your mother, grandparents, and uncle."

Hands reach out to comfort me but, realizing there is been a terrible mix-up, that my family cannot be dead, I push them away. "That's not possible. My mother and Ray will be walking through the door any minute. Then you're all going to feel really foolish." I point over to the crock pot on the counter. "See. I made it especially for them—I call it White Chick Chili."

"Gina, honey," Pastor Mouflon insists. "Your mother is dead."

"Liar!" The pastor is still talking, when I give her a hard shove onto the sofa. The policeman pulls me off her before I can do any damage. Kylie is trying to tell me something, but I can barely hear her over all the noise. Some rude woman is screaming shrilly in the background as I struggle to break free from the officer's grip.

"Gina, I'm so terribly sorry," I think Kylie is saying, but the annoying screaming is making her difficult to understand. "What can I do to help you?"

"Let her go," Pastor Mouflon orders the police officer.

When he does, my anger toward Mouflon is redirected toward the screamer. All I want to do is find the annoying idiot making all the noise and sock her in the mouth. "Shut up!" I fall to my knees on the ground to protect my ears. "For the love of God, just shut the hell up!"

The oval clock on the wall smears to the floor like a Salvador Dali painting. The people in the room contort into impossible angles. My brain melts down my spinal cord. I continue to cover my ears to block out that woman's horrible screams. Then I realize it's me. I'm the one screaming.

Chapter 32

Four days later, I'm standing on a familiar patch of ground at the cemetery in Valparaiso. I remember only fragments of the trip here. Miguel and Kylie drove. They offered to let me sit in the front, but I declined. Jerome joined me in the back seat, although I didn't invite him to come along. I guess he's trying to prove he cares about me or something. Offered his flask of JD to help me sleep. Didn't work. The rest of the drive was a blur.

A cool breeze rustles through the dry grass as the minister reads a passage from the Bible. My mind is fogged with sorrow. His words might as well be the braying of a donkey for the little I comprehend. My mother is being buried between my father and sister. Grammy and Grandpa are a few sad steps away. Uncle Tyrese's place of interment is just across the lane. The coffins hover over the freshly dug pits, waiting to descend. I can't believe I will never see their faces again. The sadness I ought to be feeling is a chunk of ice in my chest, creating a choking sensation that refuses to let up.

The service ends and the mourners dribble away. I tell my friends I need to be alone with my dead loved ones before they're put into the ground. Kylie, Miguel, and Jerome give me space. I glance across the lane where Aunt Viv remains by her husband's casket with my two cousins standing at her side. She sets a red rose atop Uncle Tyrese's coffin. Their son, 16-year old Jackson, has his arm in a sling. He took a bullet to the shoulder that night. The doctors said if it had hit a few inches lower we would be burying him too. His face is twisted with anger as the tears roll down. His 14-year-old sister, Macie, wears a haunted expression. As hard as it was for me to lose my father when I was her age, at least he wasn't murdered by a senseless act of rage.

The death toll is still climbing. My stepfather might not make it. He's in the hospital, on a ventilator, fighting for his life. Ray's adult children from his first marriage are up there with him right now. I heard he flung his body over my mother's when the shooting first started. It didn't do any good, but that was heroic of him. I hope he pulls through.

The shooter, as it turned out, was a well-liked member of St. Michael's parish, Carl Howe. He was on the bus with us on the way to Rome City, but I honestly don't remember him. Linda, the woman Kylie befriended, was his wife. She was the one Grammy was telling me about who died from a brain tumor. Her husband Carl, outraged by the way God had skipped over his wife when passing out the miracles, came to the party seeking vengeance. Covered in Kevlar body armor, armed with automatic weapons, he stormed into the parish hall. My family had the misfortune of being seated at a table close to the door.

From the accounts I have heard, my Aunt Viv and Uncle Tyrese were off socializing at a different table when the attack began. It's the only reason they had time to form a defense. Even so, the shooter was nearly impossible to take down, due to the body armor. Out of options, Uncle Tyrese threw himself on top of Carl and took him to the floor. In the struggle, my uncle was shot in the stomach, but he refused to let go, giving Aunt Viv a chance to step in. Sliding her revolver beneath the gunman's chin strap, she gave him what he deserved. If it hadn't been for my uncle's sacrifice, the casualties would have been a lot higher.

Uncle Tyrese was always so upbeat and cracking jokes. It's hard to believe he's gone. This whole thing sucks so bad. What am I going to do without my mother and grandparents? They were my cheerleaders and soft places to land. I can't grasp the idea that I will never hear their voices again, share in their accomplishments—or, dammit, even their defeats. Not knowing what to do with the anguish, my hands are trembling balls at my side. I stand there for several minutes, eyes going from casket to casket, wondering how I'm going to get through life without them.

My thoughts go to the phone in my coat pocket. Is it weird to want to reach out to my followers at a time like this? Probably, but I so don't care. Taking out my phone, I do a selfie among the tombstones with the grand oak tree swaying gently in the background.

"Dear Followers: I'm burying my mother today. My Grammy and Grandpa. Uncle Tyrese. They were killed by a coward dressed in body armor, who came into the church hall angry at the world. Instead of doing something useful, he took his frustrations out on the innocent—you know the drill." My body shudders. Closing my eyes, I wait for the tears to show themselves. I'd welcome the release, but they refuse to come. The grief is caught in my esophagus like a chicken bone. Just swallowing my spit literally hurts. "This fresh hell has brought me to a new low. A dark pit deeper than I thought possible. I don't know if I will ever be able to climb out." I pause in my narration to look out over the caskets in the distance, trying to find meaning in all of it, but there is none to be had. "I have nothing else to say."

Chapter 33

The weeks following the funerals go by in a daze. Professors have been understanding about my missing and late assignments. Dora at work isn't quite as understanding. She has reminded me that there are hundreds of perfectly qualified people lined up to do my job. If I miss any more days before the end of the year, she will find a replacement. In hindsight, Dora's hard-nosed attitude did me a favor. Having a purpose and interacting with people forces me to focus on something other than the massacre.

Socially, I've withdrawn from all my friends except Jerome. I hate myself for finding solace in his company. He doesn't scold me for drinking too much, sleeping too long, or slacking off on my school work. Of course, I still see Kylie a lot because we live together. I could do without her eyes of condemnation when she wakes up in the morning to discover Jerome has spent the night. If only I could make her understand how dead I am inside. The only time I feel pain or pleasure is when I'm with him.

Pastor Bianca Mouflon has made an effort to stay in contact with me. After enough of her pestering, I decide to go in and meet her for a free counseling session. I know she is going to try and talk about how God has a plan. Well, so do I. My plan is to act agreeable enough that she'll stop calling.

She welcomes me to her office and has me sit down in the pink vinyl chair across from her desk. She's wearing that same pink cardigan and crucifix she had on when I met her the first time. Apparently, she has a thing for pink and also for rabbits of every color. They're all over the wallpaper. Rabbit figurines cover the shelves. *Some Bunny Luvs You* is written on her coffee mug. A degree of divinity hangs on the rabbit-covered wall just underneath a doctorate of psychology. She seems qualified and nice enough, but talking about "it" is the last thing I want to do. After fifteen minutes of skirting around the issue at hand, with Mouflon asking innocuous questions about work and school, and me offering only monosyllabic replies, she finally forces the issue.

"How is your stepfather doing?" she asks.

"His children from the first marriage took him off the ventilator a couple of days ago. They're burying him in his hometown in Nevada."

"How does that make you feel?"

"I know I should feel sad. But honestly, I don't feel anything. I'm not even going to the funeral."

"Why not?"

"The only person who will be there that I know is Ray. And he's dead, so what will he care?" I say nothing more, wondering if my response has shocked her. Not wanting to be guilted into changing my mind about not going, I sit there tight-lipped, drumming my fingers on the arms of my chair.

After a few minutes of just sitting there, she breaks the silence, "You mentioned that Ray won't care if you go or not, because he's dead. Where do you think God fits into all of this, Gina?"

"God," I give an incredulous snort and roll my eyes.

"Are you mad at Him?"

"No," I snap a little too forcefully. "How can I be mad at someone that probably doesn't exist?" Glancing at the walls, I frown. "What is up with this decor? I'm not sure I want to be counseled by a pastor with a rabbit obsession."

"I'm sensing a lot of hostility here," Pastor Mouflon says, seeming to realize we are not getting anywhere. "If my being a Methodist minister bothers you, Gina. I can arrange for you to meet with Sister Lucia at Our Lady of Perpetual Help."

"It's nothing personal against you, Sister Lucia, or even rabbits," I assure her. "I just don't want to hear how God's ways are a mystery and any of that *Thy Will Be Done* crap from anybody right now. Okay?"

"Oh, my. There seems to have been a misunderstanding. Because the incident took place at a church, the school assumed that a counselor with a Christian background would be a good fit for you. We don't have to bring religion into any of our sessions—if that's the problem."

"Let me clear it up—I don't want to talk to a Catholic, a Methodist, an atheist, a proctologist, or a psychologist. All I want is to be left alone. Got it?"

"That's a normal reaction to a situation like yours, but if you bottle up your emotions, they will tear you apart to find a way out. It's best to let them surface in a controlled environment with a counselor."

"Unless my schooling is contingent upon me getting counseling, I respectfully decline."

"It's not a requirement per se, but I strongly advise ..."

"Thank you for your time." I stand, trying to end the discussion.

"I'll be happy to find you a different counselor."

"No, thank you."

"If you change your mind, I'm available 24/7." She follows me to the door. "Here is my card, Gina. Call me any time."

Chapter 34

During the last week of November, there is good news for a change. JustSharing has made a hefty deposit to my bank account. The silver lining comes attached to a cloud. Due to recent changes in their policies, it's half what I was expecting. Yet it's ten times what I could make in a year working full-time at Fashionable Young Things.

I stock the pantry and buy a batch of new clothes. The court date with Anne Davis Auto hasn't been set yet, but now I have the funds to pay off the truck in full. The lawyer I met with said that paying off the truck isn't going to satisfy Anne Davis Auto, but he believes he can get me out of the deal. On his advice, I haven't paid off the truck in full, but I will continue to make monthly payments until the court date. I certainly have the money now, but that's not enough to pull me out of this dark funk.

Kylie leaves to visit Miguel's family over Christmas Break. They invited me to come along, but it would just be awkward. Jerome asked me to accompany him to his family's estate as well. It's tempting, but meeting the parents is a big step. I don't want to give Jerome the idea that our relationship is more serious than it is. I politely decline. So I stay at school alone over the holidays, watching old movies, drinking spiked nog, and feeling sorry for myself.

On Christmas day my Aunt Viv calls me. She's inebriated. Crying half the time. Going on and on about how nobody understands what she is going through, being a police officer is so much bull, trying to raise the kids alone in a dying world is breaking her heart, she will never find a man who can compare to Tyrese. I can barely get a word into the hour-long conversation. Not once does she ask me how I'm doing. By the time she hangs up, I'm feeling more angry than sympathetic. What about *my* suffering and loneliness?

I spend the rest of the day seething about the phone call. It takes me a while to realize what's at the heart of my puzzling reaction. It's not really about Aunt Viv's indifference. She was drunk and not in the right state of mind. I love her and totally forgive her temporary lack of mutual concern. It's hearing her sob and go through the motions of grief like a normal person makes me wonder why I'm not. I mean, there's definitely a sense of despair, but I haven't cried or felt anything beyond numb. What's wrong with me? Am I a sociopath or just plain broken?

New Year's Eve arrives. Jerome is back in town and wants me to accompany him to a fraternity party. I'd rather have a quiet evening at home. I tell Jerome he should go out and have fun without me. So he does, which pisses me off. Why couldn't he read between the lines and realize that he was supposed to choose me over his buddies? What a lousy sort-of-boyfriend.

A week before the new semester, Jerome rides along with me when I go to pick up my new truck, fresh off the factory floor, with all the bells and whistles. I purchased it from Anne Davis Auto's biggest competitor, Tom Ryder's across the street, and vlogged the entire transaction for my JustSharing account. Afterwards, I drive through Anne Davis Auto, honk, and wave at them through the storeroom window. With Jerome egging me on, I flip them all off. How childish, but it feels like a little piece of revenge. And I like it.

We take a drive around town testing out my new wheels, feeling on top of the world. Later, we stop at Willie's Bar & Grill for steaks and beer—my treat for a change. When I drop Jerome off at his apartment, he invites me inside. We drink and mess around until we both pass out. I slink out at the break of dawn.

It isn't until I get back to the dorm room and have a couple of coffees under my belt that I begin to have cognitive dissonance over my large purchase. I had gone into the dealership planning on getting a *used* truck. Buying brand new was a spur-of-the-moment decision. And what was I thinking blowing so much money on food for me and Jerome? In one sitting, I spent the equivalent of last month's entire grocery budget.

Sure, I have a wad of money in my bank account now, but if I keep spending like this, it won't last long.

After a nap, I awake around 1 p.m. with a splitting headache. My shift at work begins in an hour. It's awesome having my own vehicle again, but I do regret having spent so much on it, when used would have been perfectly fine.

I head into the mall, obsessing about the money I wasted yesterday, not paying much attention to my surroundings. I'm almost in front of Fashionable Young Things before I notice the gate is down. The lighted name above the store is no longer there. In place of it is a cheap banner: SPACE AVAILABLE FOR LEASE. Call 555-1282 6for details.

Tell me it ain't so. Fashionable Young Things is out of business.

I've known this was probably coming, yet I'm unprepared. My insides feel like a sinking boat. Instead of crying, the absurdity brings up a bubble of laughter. Civilization was even more fragile than we imagined. All it took was a big rock to smash it to pieces. While I'm standing there in disbelief, my co-worker Doug shows up for his shift, sporting a Space Cowboy look, leather chaps and spurs included.

"Son-of-a-smelly-whore." Doug throws his ten gallon hat onto the floor. "Did you know anything about this?"

"Would I be standing here like an idiot if I did?"

"I reckon not," he drawls in a fake western accent.

"Wanna go get a beer or something?"

"Only if you're buying, ma'am."

"Drinks on me, cowboy."

"Count me in, pardner."

The grating sound of cawing crows wakes me from a stupor. My tongue is coated with vinegary ick. Slowly, I realize I'm at home on the bathroom floor lying in a puddle of my own vomit. A vague memory of Doug helping me up the stairs swims around in my head. The door creaks open. Kylie enters without knocking, holding a roll of paper towels.

"Don't you need to get ready for work?" she asks, looking down on me from above with a judgmental frown.

"FYT went out of business. I'm un—" An attack of dry heaves comes on, forcing me to hover over the bowl. "Unemployed."

She slowly closes the door to leave me in peace. I hear her leave for class. When she returns a few hours later,, I'm right where she left me.

Kylie puts the toilet seat down and uses it for a chair, saying, "We have to talk."

"If this is about Jerome being bad for me—I'll have you know I wasn't out with him last night. It was Doug from work. We were bummed about the store closing and cried together into our beers. So sue me."

"Jerome *is* bad for you, but he's not what I want to discuss. Ever since The Warning, you've been different."

"You're one to talk."

"Yes, I am different. Happier—thank God. But you've gone the other way."

"Seeing yourself damned tends to do that to a person."

"That's what I want to talk about. As long as there is breath in your lungs, there is hope for salvation. With everything that's happened to your family, open yourself to the peace only Jesus can bring."

"No," I hold up a halting hand, not wanting to hear it. "Just no."

"Somewhere deep inside, you realize your soul is empty, starving to death for lack of sustenance, so you try to satisfy it with all the wrong things."

"Like alcohol and Jerome?" I ask resentfully.

"You said it, but the only thing that can fill the emptiness within is God."

"Who in the hell do you think you are, giving *me* religious advice?"

"Oh, now the truth comes out. You think you're better than me."

"Look in the mirror, Kylie. You are so arrogant. Always going on about how smart you are and treating the rest of us like ignorant wankers. As if that wasn't irritating enough, ever since The Warning, you've been prancing around like you're spiritually superior as well."

"I don't think I'm spiritually superior," she says defensively. "And I don't prance."

"Not very long ago you had nothing good to say about God. Whenever you got on one of your rants against religious people, I was there to defend them. So why was I cast into the flames, while you were shown mercy?"

"Aha, now I get where your anger is coming from, you think I should have gone to hell."

"Damn straight. You didn't even believe in God, but I did."

"Did you really?" she inquires, sounding less than convinced.

"You know I did—do."

"You have never believed in anything except the false God you made up in your head."

"What's that supposed to mean?"

"Did you or did you not say, *The God I know wouldn't have made sex feel so good if He didn't want us to do it as often as possible. The God I know doesn't care what religion a person is, because as long as you believe in something, all paths lead to Him. As long as we don't murder anyone, purposely harm children, or steal something really expensive, our sins are of no consequence, because God always forgives.'* Oh, and let's not forget your favorite line: *The God I know would never send anyone to hell, especially not me.'*"

"You are putting words in my mouth."

"Tell me where I have misstated your position."

"Well, I have never used that exact wording. But yeah, that's basically right."

"Don't you see? You have made God into what you think He ought to be, what you want Him to be, and not what he actually IS. You don't like the real God's rules. But Jesus said, *'If you love Me, keep My commandments.'* In turn, you have said to Him, *'I don't like Your commandments. I'm going to ignore them, make my own rules, and pretend like they come from You.'* Talk about arrogant!"

My mouth hangs open as I search for a good comeback. Nothing comes to mind, so I take the low road. "I liked you better when you were an atheist." Nose in the air, I march to my room and slam the door.

Chapter 35

Time rolls on into February. Kylie and I have gotten over our spat, but our relationship hasn't been the same. She's always with Miguel anyway, so what does it matter?

This has been the warmest winter on record. The scientists on the news say we are moving out of Nuclear Winter into what they're calling the Greenhouse Effect. Say what?

First, we were told the cold was going to last for decades and eventually kill us. Now, they're saying it's the heat. I'm getting the feeling that they're just making up shit as we go along.

The Fraternity of Dionysus has decided to welcome the rising temperatures in their usual fashion—by throwing a big party. Its illustrious alumni, both men and women, will be there for the occasion, including the CEO of Balor Industries, the president of the university himself, and State Representative Sharon Pennington. There's also going to be a live band to blast our eardrums.

The night of the party, Jerome shows up at my door at a little past ten. He's dressed in blue jeans, a *Death Note* T-shirt and a black tuxedo jacket with suit tails. I'm in a slinky black dress, with black sequins and long sleeves. In anticipation of the outdoor location, I have opted to wear fashion boots instead of stiletto heels. The clutch tucked under my arm holds my phone and the gun.

"You look delicious, Gina." He playfully flickers his eyebrows. "The guys are going to be lining up to get a shot at you tonight."

"Probably." I flash him my prettiest smile. "It's a good thing I have you to keep me safe."

Thirty minutes later, Jerome and I are tucked into the front seat of his graphite blue Porsche, driving along a tree-lined route about twenty minutes south of the city. We come to a strip of road with cars parked along the edge. He slows and pulls off the road to park behind a Mercedes with Louisiana plates.

"Alumni," Jerome explains. "No matter where they go, they never leave. You'll see a lot of lifers here tonight."

He reaches in the back seat to retrieve two pairs of plastic devil horns.

"I'm not wearing those." I frown. "It will mess up my hair."

"The theme is *Hot Damn*." He slides the headband with curved white horns onto his head. "You have to make a little effort to dress for the occasion."

I snatch the matching pair out of his hands with a huff and slide them onto my head. We get out of the car and follow the line of vehicles toward the battery-powered lantern hanging from a tree. When we get to it, I see a path winding through the forest. Black and white signs with arrows, along with more strategically placed lanterns, guide us deep into the woods.

Up close and personal with nature, I see that the trees have opened their starving buds way ahead of schedule. I'm not a horticulturalist, but it seems like Mother Nature has taken a big gamble by coming out so early. This little hike through the woods is heating me up. Beads of sweat are running down my back. A thin sheen covers Jerome's face. It feels more like summer than February.

"When the alumni get involved, these parties take on a different kind of vibe," Jerome says as we're walking. "I hope you can handle it."

"With older people running the show, I figured it would be lame," I reply. "But as long as the booze is free, I'm sure we'll have a good time."

"You have the wrong idea." He laughs and shakes his head. "After tonight, those post-baseball game slosh fests we like so much are going to seem like dainty English tea parties."

I hear the music first. It has a wild jungle beat that makes me want to thrash my body with the rhythm. As we keep walking, a wall of orange flame appears behind the skeletons of the budding black forest.

"I hope that's a bonfire," I comment, worried by the size of it. "Not a forest fire."

"Don't worry. Everything is under control."

Jerome's calmness assuages my fear that we're walking into a raging hellmouth. The trail finally opens up to a circular clearing the size of a football field. A couple of police officers stand at the end of the path, checking IDs. Jerome and I show them ours and we're waved on through.

There must be a thousand people out here, many of them older, and definitely not students. Some are in full costume, so it's difficult to discern their ages, faces or even their genders. I see ghosts in white sheets. Devils, in both the sexy and the scary variety. Frankensteins, werewolves, skeletons, witches and random monsters galore.

As we make our way through the crowd, I bump into Professor Langley, who has dressed in a demon costume for the occasion. Upon seeing my demon horns, he raises his glass of beer at me in a gesture of solidarity. Never in a million years would I have pegged him as a Dio. This is going to be an interesting night.

Jerome and I get in the long line behind one of the kegs, watching the men add kindling to the bonfire. The flames are at least two stories high. In keeping with the hellish theme, big wooden crosses are arranged around the clearing, some upside down, some right-side up, and cauldrons dotted around the place bubble with dry ice. Oddly enough, there's a portable metal cage with a couple of pigs inside it.

Julie finds us. She's dressed like a slutty witch, talking loudly, slurring her words, trying to pull us out to the designated dance floor. Her boyfriend, Brad, hasn't been seen since his blow-up in class during finals week. In a way, dealing with his absence has been worse than losing a loved one from an accident or disease. The not knowing if he's suffering and in need of rescue has been torture. It's nice to see Julie finally moving on and having fun. She's with a handsome older guy dressed like a vampire. I've never seen him before tonight, but I'm guessing he's Long Distance Sam. She calls him that because he lives three or four hours away. They've been commuting back and forth to spend their weekends together. The two of them are all over each other.

"Hello." He extends a hand to Jerome. "I'm Sam Bledsoe—the Comptroller of Cleveland. Nice to meet you."

"I'm Jerome Miller, future First Baseman of the Indians."

"You've come a long way to party," I mention to Sam.

"A lot of alumni are here tonight," he replies. "Wouldn't want to miss it."

While we're waiting in line for the alcohol, Jerome pulls out his flask of whiskey and passes it around to me, Sam and Julie. By the time we get our beer, I'm already warmed by the hard liquor. Julie's large group of friends, and Sam's large group of older friends, seem to be well-acquainted already. They come dancing around us in line, eagerly waiting for us to join them on the freshly mowed dance floor.

"What are the pigs for?" I ask anyone within earshot.

"The pig roast, duh," Julie says. "People gotta eat."

"Every year the fraternity slaughters pigs as a mock sacrifice to Dionysus, the Greek god of food and wine," Sam explains.

"Isn't that kind of creepy?" I look over at the pigs. They're squealing, huddled together on the far end of the cage, like they know we don't have their best interests in mind. "Seems unnecessarily cruel to me."

"Bacon lover," Jerome coughs into his hand.

"Okay," I laugh. "You got me. I'm a hypocrite."

We finally get our turn at the tap. The woman manning it hands us an entire pitcher. I wasn't expecting that. How efficient. These Dios have partying down to a science.

As we pour and talk, talk and pour, the party grows wilder. Silhouetted by the bonfire, the people in their costumes take on the appearance of black ghouls. A Congo line begins to form, weaving in and out of the crosses like a big black serpent, slithering through the forest.

Julie grabs me by the arm to drag me into the Congo line. We've barely caught the end of the tail when the sound ends, and the snake breaks apart. A slower song begins and Jerome pulls me away to dance with him. One of the things I like about Jerome is that he is a physical person in every way. Unlike a lot of men, he loves to dance. In each other's arms we sway as one, letting the music take us over.

As one song leads to the next, two different synthesized drums beat slowly out of rhythm, gradually getting faster until they become synchronized as one, like two lovers in the throes of passion. Jerome presses himself against me, eyes full of desire. The night is still young, but he's already aroused. I hope he's not going to want to leave early. Someone taps my shoulder.

I turn around to see Sam with his hand out, offering three pink pieces of candy shaped like roses. "Take one."

My brow raises in surprise. "Is that what I think it is?" I ask, already knowing the answer. Sublime Rose, they're calling it. A newish drug in the category of Ecstasy. Only stronger.

"Something to intensify the mood," Sam explains. "Just hold it on your tongue until it melts."

"They're perfectly safe," Julie says, popping one in her mouth. "I've done roses lots of times."

"This will be my third time," Jerome says, taking one for himself. "So, relax. It will help you find happiness beyond anything you have ever known. And, in the end, isn't that everybody's goal—happiness?"

Yes, that's what I want. Happiness. That elusive thing. Between the cajoling of my friends, the suggestive music, and the alcohol swirling through my body, all systems are go. Jerome playfully places the last Sublime Rose on his tongue, holding it out, daring me to take it from him.

"Go on," Julie and Sam urge.

"I promise," Sam says. "You won't regret it."

I close my eyes and open my mouth, inviting Jerome to give it to me. He pulls me close to pass the Sublime Rose from his tongue to mine. Julie, Sam, and everyone around us cheer and whoop, making me feel like a marathon runner who has just crossed the finish line.

It isn't long before the Sublime Rose takes effect, enhancing my senses. The scent of pine mingled with sweat and earth rises up like a spicy perfume. The flames become dancers, whipping themselves into a frenzy. The thump of the music seems to have taken on the job of pumping my blood. It's as if the mass of bodies on the forest floor has become a single entity. Coiling. Intertwining. Writhing. All of us move

179

together like a beautiful beast in motion. Every touch of flesh sets my nerve endings tingling with pleasure. I've never felt so accepted. My inhibitions have evaporated.

"The devils are out thick tonight!" The DJ's voice echoes across the forest. "If you're having a good time, yell hot damn!"

The voices rise up. "Hot damn!"

"If you're losing control and just don't care, yell hot damn!"

I raise my cup with the rest of the crowd and yell, "Hot damn!"

A woman's fearful screams rise up from somewhere deep in the forest, but everything feels so fantastic, I don't want to let anything spoil the moment, so I tell myself it's nothing to worry about.

"If you want to see blood spill, feel it running down your throat, yell Hot Damn!"

"Hot damn!"

The music beats faster. The flames lick higher. My body is on fire up against the front of Jerome.

A shirtless devil with a pot belly comes up behind me. I don't know his name, but he's one of the older fellows. The starting pitcher from the baseball team comes up behind Jerome, thumping against his backside in a provocative manner. A lifetime ago I would have told them to back the hell off. Tonight, somehow, everything feels right. Bathed in pleasure, my eyes close in ecstasy.

From somewhere far away, terrified squealing rends the night. A male voice thunders, "Bow down to Dionysus. Or die, pig!"

"Kill the pig!" the crowd cheers like the characters in *Lord of the Flies,* and the dance goes on. "Kill the pig!"

The pigs are squealing frightfully somewhere nearby. For a moment, they sound like a woman screaming in pain. "Forgive them," I hear her call out, voice trembling. "They know not what they do."

My eyes pop open in concern. "Did you just hear that?" I ask those around me. "Is everyone okay?"

"Don't worry about it, sweetie," they assure me. "It's only a pig."

Not wanting to pull myself away from the embrace of this mystical creature that has come to life in the middle of the forest, and the wonderful feelings it has awakened inside me, I decide to believe them, and dance into the night.

Chapter 36

As my consciousness returns, my eyes crack open to see pale sunlight glittering through tangled black branches. I'm lying on my back in rotting mulch. The air around me is warm for a February morning, but too cold for sleeping outdoors without a blanket. It's a wonder my chattering teeth haven't crumbled. Looking to my left, I see a naked guy sleeping next to me smeared with blood. To my left is another bloody naked guy. They both appear to be breathing without any difficulty. I don't think it's their own blood. Doing a quick inventory of my own body, I am also smeared in blood. However, I'm not in any pain. Just a bit raw in alarming places. That's when I realize my dress is hiked up to my neck. My bra, panties and boots are gone. I sit up with a horrified gasp. What went on here last night?

Sliding my dress down, my eyes survey the forest in the morning light. There are people sleeping all over the place. Some are fully clothed, still in costumes, but most of them are nearly or fully naked. Bits and pieces of the previous night slowly return to me. The Fraternity of Dionysus party.

Jerome and I got so wasted, I must have passed out. I had the freakiest dream about a slaughter of pigs. Even now their frightened squeals echo through my mind. An image of a limp pink body hanging from a cross flashes in my head. Its blood drips down the wooden plank, pooling into a bucket on the ground. In the dream I dipped my hand in the bucket and smeared it on my body. Fully awake now, but feeling loopy, I see that I'm still covered in the blood.

From the corner of my eye, I catch a glimpse of small black shadows scurrying about the clearing. Like a pack of hungry rats, they sniff at the partygoers scattered across the ground, looking for an easy meal. Only when one pauses at my bare feet to look me straight in the face do I realize these are no ordinary rats. They are black, hairless, with mouths full of razor sharp teeth and gleaming crimson eyes. I cringe and let out a shriek.

The creature shrieks back at me in a raspy voice laced with malice, "We are the Fade!" Then turns to smoke and evaporates before my eyes.

I scramble to my feet and back away, trying to process what I just saw. Rats only talk in cartoons. They can't disappear into thin air. The creatures have to be the combination of booze and drugs still in my system, making me see and hear things that aren't really there.

Hugging myself, I try to blink the rats away, but they continue to rustle about the clearing. Reason tells me they don't exist. I do my best to ignore them, while going about the business of finding my missing items. While searching, I can't shake the feeling that a great evil took place here last night, but there are big holes in my memory. To my dismay, I remember some of it. Lying in a mass of pulsating flesh. Wanting those men to do unspeakable things to me. Knowing it was wrong and letting it happen anyway. Not wanting it to ever stop.

A wave of nausea sweeps over me. Pushing the disgust aside, I crawl around on my hands and knees, looking for my clutch, which contains my weapon, cell phone, and a credit card. Beneath one of the crosses, I spy a broken cross necklace wet with pig's blood. An image of a pink pig roped to the cross, nails sticking out of its head, forms in my mind.

A case of the dry heaves instantly strikes. Once it passes, I continue to look for my clutch. No sign of it, but about ten yards away, tucked between a naked blonde woman, and the pitcher from our baseball team, I find Jerome—asleep, pants down to his ankles, shirt missing. Somebody etched *Man Whore* on his forehead with a marker or something. The woman has *Insert Here* tattoo written on her abdomen with an arrow pointing down. I'm noticing that a lot of people have unflattering words written on them in various places. I'm glad to have been spared that humiliation.

As I'm the only thing moving around the clearing, the rats follow me with interest, swirling around my feet, eyes glowing red. They whisper unintelligible words amongst themselves. So far, they haven't made a move to touch me. More and more rodents join the group scurrying around my feet. *They're not real,* I tell myself. *They're drug-induced vermin.* One of them comes straight at me with a hiss, I give it a kick. My foot passes right through it like nothing is there. The rodent poofs into black smoke. All around my feet, they begin to explode like popcorn. There seems to be no end to the hallucination. A new batch of rodents scurries from the underbrush to watch my every move. Doing my best to ignore them, I moisten a finger to double-check Jerome's forehead, hoping it's just a red marker. When I try to wipe it off, it's doesn't even smear. Holy crap, it's a scabby tattoo. If that was on me, I would be livid.

His eyes flutter open at my touch. I give him a few hard shakes, but nothing seems to get him to wake completely. Digging his phone out of his jean pocket, unlocking it with his limp fingerprint, I dial my own number. Following the sound of *Requiem For A Dream,* I find it in my clutch, next to the gun, buried under the leaves. Relieved to have found my valuables, I gaze around at the passed-out drunks on the ground.

If they haven't already, some of them are going to freeze to death. I go from person to person, trying to nudge them awake. As a smattering of people rouse, they join me in waking the others. I don't see Julie or Sam among them. Hopefully, this means they have gone home. Jerome finally finds the strength to get up. He never does find his shirt. Nor I my undies or boots. His teeth are chattering like mine as we follow the signs back to the road. Taking out his flask, he sips more whiskey. Offers it to me. I hold up a halting hand. The mere idea of alcohol makes me want to puke.

Neither of us says a word. His car is still parked along the side with dozens of others. Just as I'm trying to figure out what to do about the people left stranded in the woods, a fleet of taxi buses pulls up to the scene. I should have known that a fraternity with the motto *Party On!* has had vast experience handling the sloppy leftovers.

Jerome is still too out of it to drive, so I take his keys. I haven't asked him if he knows about the *Man Whore* tattoo on his forehead. He'll notice it sooner or later. Hopefully, when I'm not around.

184

At 8:36 a.m., I drop him off in front of his off-campus apartment. Once he's safely inside, I drive his car to the visitors' lot near my building. I have to walk barefoot across a couple of acres of asphalt to get home.

When I go through the door, I'm trembling uncontrollably. Kylie's at the kitchen table eating a bowl of flakes. Her eyes widen upon seeing me. Catching a glimpse of myself in the oval mirror on the wall, it's no wonder. My hair and clothes are filled with leaves and twigs. I have raccoon eyes and a cheek is coated with dried blood. My exposed skin is blue and purple from the cold. I look down at my numb feet. They're bleeding, but I can't feel it. The universe does seem to have a sense of humor though, because through it all, the devil horns have managed to stay on.

"Gina, what on earth happened?"

Her words sound far away, like echoes across the Grand Canyon. The intensity of my emotions takes me by surprise. If I open my mouth, I'm afraid of what will come out. So I ignore her and hobble to the bathroom on numb feet. The chair legs screech as Kylie slides back from the table in a hurry to trail after me.

"Talk to me, Gina. Who did this to you?"

"God did it to me!" Great sobs erupt from my body. "Why did they have to die, Kylie? Why?" I collapse in a heap on the bathroom floor. "I should have gone to St. Michael's that day. Having nobody left who cares about me hurts worse than dying, and I don't know what to do."

"I care about you," Kylie assures me with a hug, tears running down her face. "You're my sister from a different mister, remember?"

As I softly sob, shaking uncontrollably, Kylie works on cleaning me up, telling me everything is going to be okay. She kneels down on the floor, washing the dirt from my face with a soft hand towel. She takes repeated trips to the bathroom sink a few feet away to rinse the towel with fresh warm water so she can work on me some more. Drained of all strength and will, I'm a whimpering limp rag on the floor. "I shouldn't have let those people touch me. How can something that feels so right in the heat of the night, turn out to be so bad in the light of the morning?"

While Kylie cleans up my outside, I think that all the water in the world cannot wash away the mess I've made of myself. And I have nobody to blame but myself.

I must have dosed off, because the next time I open my eyes, I'm in bed snuggled in a warm quilt. I can't even remember leaving the bathroom. Kylie is sitting on the mattress, gently brushing the twigs and leaves from my hair. I'm cleaner and calmer, but no less depressed.

"Why does God hate me?" I whisper to my only real friend. "Why, Kylie? Why?"

"God doesn't hate you. That's why He showed you where you were heading, so you could fix it." She sucks in a deep breath and holds it in a minute before continuing. "I think you should talk to Father Kramer over at St. Faustina's of the Divine Mercy. He's been counseling people who went to hell during The Warning."

"Seriously?"

"Do you think you're the only one struggling with it?"

Intrigued by the thought of a counselor who specializes in traumatic warnings, a glimmer of hope sparks to life, but I'm not sold on the idea of speaking with a priest. "He won't yell at me for being a lapsed Catholic?" I ask.

"Father Kramer is cool. Just say the word and I'll take you to meet him."

"No," I shake my head. "This is something I need to work out on my own."

"If not him, please talk to someone. What can it hurt?"

"I'm not ready to talk to a priest, but I'm not writing it off altogether because I don't want to go on like this. I probably do need help. Possibly of the spiritual variety. Are you sure Father Kramer won't bawl me out if I decide to go?"

"Positive, but if you're worried about getting bawled-out, be sure to avoid Monsignor Nikwande. I don't know if it's because he's from Africa, and there's a cultural difference, but he tends to rub people the wrong way." After a few minutes of quiet, she inquires, "So will you talk to Father Kramer?"

"I don't know yet," I sniffle and a new batch of tears works it way to the surface. "I think it will be a waste of time. I'm a horrible person, Kylie. Nobody can help me."

"You're not *that* horrible."

For some reason, her comment strikes me as funny. I laugh a little through my tears until she accidentally pulls my hair. "Ow!"

"Sorry," she quickly apologizes. "You have a knotted mess here."

"I don't know what I'd do without you, Kylie. I'm sorry to be such a burden."

"Don't worry about it."

"Even though I treat you like shit sometimes, it's only because that's what real sisters do. That's not an excuse though. I want to be a better friend. A new and improved person."

"Then be."

"What if I fail?"

"Everybody fails. All we can do is keep trying."

"Thank you for not giving up on me."

"Never. Where's the detangler?"

"Under the sink."

She leaves and comes back a minute later with the plastic spray bottle in her hand. We stay there on the bed quite a while, just talking about nothing and everything, while she works out the knots. My appreciation for Kylie grows tenfold in the space of the morning hours. Despite all my crappy comments over the last year, she has remained a loyal friend, a rare treasure beyond value. I vow to treat her better from here on out.

The day after my meltdown, I've mentally pulled myself together, but I'm sick with a bad cold. Kylie's suggestion about seeing a priest weighs heavy on my mind, but I can't handle the idea of baring my deepest longings and shortcomings to a stranger. What if he thinks I'm too far gone to help?

Outside the dorm room window, hearty daffodils and tulips are springing up out of season. It's been a long time since I've seen students walking around in shorts and tank tops. According to the news channel, plants all over the world, desperate for warmth and sunlight after nearly two years of deprivation, have opened their buds early. I crank open the window. A fresh breeze stirs the curtains as the skateboarders roll by below. Normally, I'd go out and enjoy the nice weather, but this stupid cold has zapped my energy. On top of that, I've been struggling with what happened at the party.

I'm not sure if I ever want to see Jerome again, but he sent me a text about retrieving his car keys, so I'm going to have to. There's a knock at the door. Knowing that it's probably him, my body tenses. Turning the knob is a struggle. I open it to see Jerome standing there in the hall with *Man Whore* tattooed on his forehead. What an ugly reminder of that abominable night. Instead of inviting him in, I keep the door half shut.

"Have you heard from Julie?" I ask. "I've tried calling and texting her, but she hasn't responded."

"She's still with Sam. They left the party early and took it to his hotel suite. A bunch of people are going up there tonight. Do you want to come?"

"Hell, no. I'm still trying to recover from Hot Damn."

"Oh, yeah." He rubs his forehead, giving a sheepish grin. "I can't even remember how I got this thing."

"Me, neither."

"Speaking from experience, the bigger the blast, the less you remember the next day." He grins some more, like it's all a big joke. I don't understand his casual attitude. "Wasn't it great?"

"About as great as your hideous tattoo. What if you end up with hepatitis?"

"We'll all be dead before it gets around to killing me. So who cares?"

"If that's what you think, why bother going to school?"

"I'm in it for the baseball and the parties."

"Oh." I should have known. Hugging myself as if that will keep me safe from my own stupidity, I say softly, "I can't believe we got so wasted. Why didn't you warn me about what we were in for?"

"I wanted it to be a surprise. The alumni are going to host another party next month, which will be even bigger than the last one. Now that

I've advanced to the next level, I'm automatically invited. All of our friends will be there. You'll be my date, right?"

"Are you crazy?" I ask in disbelief. "The people who put that tattoo on your forehead are not our friends."

"It's a Dio right of passage." He touches his forehead again. "I already have an appointment to get it removed."

"I hope so. You look like a fool."

"I know you have higher aspirations than managing a clothing store. No offense, Gina, but you being from a family of limited means and connections, the fraternity is a great way to schmooze with influential people." He's right about that, so my ears automatically perk up. "For someone wanting to climb the corporate ladder, it opens doors to opportunities closed off from the rest of the schmucks. The senior members really like what they saw from you at the party."

Totally grossed-out by the reminder, I re-cross my arms across my chest and make a sour face. "I'm sure they did," I humph, shaking my head. "The only good thing is that I can't remember most of it."

"Since Julie and I are both willing to recommend you for a membership, one of the senior members will contact you for an interview. It's no big deal, just a few questions about where you stand on certain issues. Getting in is a process, you know. But it's totally worth it for someone looking to build business connections."

"I'll think about it," I say, but there is no way I'm ever partying with Jerome's fraternity pals again. However, if I outright say no, he's going to stand here all morning, trying to talk me into it. "Let me get back with you when I'm feeling better."

I make to close the door, but he blocks it with his foot.

"I thought maybe we could watch a movie together."

"I'm sick and just want to rest. By myself."

"Why do I get the feeling you're blowing me off?"

"What part of *I'm sick* don't you understand?"

"Fine, fine," he says holding up his hands and backing out the doorway. "I'll call you later."

Over the days that follow, my cold gets worse. I have a deep down cough and can hardly drag myself out of bed. Friends worry I'm on the verge of pneumonia. Nevertheless, I push myself to attend my classes. It's strange how things have been different with the professors I saw at the party.

The biggest change I've noticed has been in Professor Langley. For instance, I had him last semester for Business Ethics. This semester it's Legal and Political Philosophy. Up until the party, he didn't even know my name. Now, he's going out of his way to be nice to me. On my test, he counts two answers correct that were clearly wrong. When I talk to him about it, his tone is sweet as sugar cream pie.

"The 'A' isn't based on how well you memorize the facts," he says. "It's about what you accept as the truth."

"I don't understand."

He winks and smiles, explaining no further. Wondering if he touched me that night makes my skin crawl, but I don't argue for a lower grade.

"Will I be seeing you at the next Dio event, Gina?" he asks, smiling even broader.

"I've been ill," I say, giving a cough for emphasis. "I'll have to wait to see how I'm feeling."

Avoiding eye contact, I scurry out of the classroom. Later in the evening, I receive a phone call from the human resources manager of Balor Industries. They want to interview me for a paid internship. Remembering the CEO of the company was at the party, I know it cannot be a coincidence. It's hard to say no, but I remind myself of the vow I made to be a better person. "I appreciate your interest in me," I tell human resources, "but no thank you." After I hang up, I'm seized with panic at having blown a once-in-a-life-time opportunity.

I pace back-and-forth wondering if I've made a huge mistake, but if I want to be a woman of moral substance I'm going to have to be willing to sacrifice personal gain for the sake of the greater good. Turning down the internship wasn't easy, but I conclude that it was the right thing to do.

In hindsight, one of the positive things that came out of the Hot Damn party was how it opened my eyes to the insalubrious collusion between the university and the business community at large. It's an army of the ungodly versus the believers. Has it always been this way or did the battle rise up on the cusp of the dying light?

Chapter 37

Kylie leaves with Miguel on Friday morning to attend a pre-engagement retreat for Catholic couples. I'll have the apartment to myself, but I don't have any plans. And, of course, now that I'm feeling better, the warm weather has retreated. A quick glance at the weather app on my phone tells me I have a mixture of rain and sleet to look forward to over the next ten days. With lows reaching the mid-teens, it makes me wonder what happened to the Greenhouse Effect the scientists have been warning us about.

I'm noticing that, much like religious people, scientists seem to be living in a fairytale world. The researchers believe they're receiving secret messages from the numbers and data, instead of the angels and saints. When things don't work out as expected, they blame the mysterious Unknown Variable, instead of God. The older I get, it seems the less faith I have in either of them.

Around 3:30 p.m., after my last class of the day, I head home and put my music mix on surround sound. My tastes are eclectic—a collection of old and new. I'm especially fond of movie scores, but right now an old rock song is drifting through the room. It's about a woman begging her lover to wake her frozen soul with his touch. As I'm preparing a can of soup on the stove, I turn it into a prayer, emotion pouring into my voice as I sing along. A knock on the door interrupts my heartfelt plea for Jesus to save me from the mess I've made of my life.

Since it's Friday—party night—my guess is that it's Jerome, trying to talk me into going out for the evening. I haven't figured out how to end our relationship. My hope is that, when he realizes I've sworn off alcohol, parties, and sex, he'll drift away of his own accord. If he doesn't,

I'll have to put my foot down. I trusted Jerome to look out for me at the Hot Damn party. Instead, he fed me to the wolves.

Another knock, this one more forceful, rattles the door. Steeling myself for a confrontation with my ex, I fling it open. Only it's not Jerome. There's a clean-shaven man in his thirties or so, standing behind a smiling blonde girl who looks about eight or nine. His hands rest on her shoulders.

"Can I help you?" I ask, wondering if she's selling cookies.

"Is this her, Daddy?" the girl asks.

"It is."

Before I can react, she gives me a spontaneous hug around the waist.

"Uh …" taken aback, my brow furrows in confusion. "I think you have the wrong person."

"Aren't you the lady who gave us the truck?" She says, looking up at me with adoring blue eyes. "It's because of you I'm all better. Well, you and God."

"Ashley?"

She nods and steps back to smile happily up at me.

My jaw drops. She looks like a different child—so peppy and bright-eyed. I didn't recognize her at first. Even Eric, her father, looks a far sight better than he did at the mall. His scruffy beard is gone. The greasy grunge look has been replaced with a clean blue work shirt and pressed black pants.

I ask the question that has been on my mind all this time, "Is she cured?"

"One hundred percent." His voice cracks with emotion. "The poster child of health. Even her asthma is gone."

"That's wonderful," I gush, heart pitter-pattering in excitement. However, my joy quickly evaporates into a scowl. "What took you so friggin' long to come back?"

He looks down at the ground, unable to meet my gaze. "Having a truck gave me the opportunity to start my own handyman service," he mumbles into his chest. "I kept telling myself I was only going to hold onto it for a few weeks, until I had enough money to buy my own. But time got away from me."

"Obviously," I say curtly, not intending on letting him off too easily. "You put me in a terrible position. I'm getting sued because of you."

"I'm very sorry. Hopefully, now that you have it back, everything will work out."

Eric meekly holds out his hand with the keys resting in his palm. I snatch them back, trying to hold onto my anger. Between his shame, and Ashley's healthy glow, I let it go. After all, being mad at him now wouldn't change the past. I survived and became a bit tougher because of it.

"Well, I suppose it's better late than never. What matters is your daughter has been healed. I'm curious though, what prompted you to bring it back after all this time?"

"Believe it or not, an old woman appeared to me in my dreams, telling me to return her butterfly's truck, or else. I could tell she meant business, so I didn't want to wait around to find out what the 'or else' might be." My hands shoot to my mouth. Tears well-up in my eyes. Oh, Grammy. "I never intended to keep the truck," Eric continues. "I really didn't, but the longer . . ."

I interrupt, saying, "Hold that thought." As the initial surprise wears off, I realize what a terrific opportunity this is. My followers are going to flip out when they hear about this. "I'm to fetch my camera phone."

"I really need to get back on the road before sundown." Eric glances nervously over his shoulder. "Please, don't call the police."

"I just want a video for my JustSharing channel. You owe me that much—don't you think?" Not waiting for his reply, I wave them in. "Come into the kitchen and pull up a chair. We'll eat soup while I interview you. My followers will want to hear all about how Ashley was healed and what the family has been up to." At my insistence, they step inside the room. "I'll only be a minute."

I dash off to the bedroom and toss blankets and clothes aside until I find my phone. When I return a short time later, Ashley and Eric are gone. Camera switched on, I sprint down the hall after them, vlogging about my unexpected visitors. I skip half the steps on the way down the flight to the ground floor. Out in the parking lot, I spot an orange truck with the engine running. Eric's wife, Claire, is behind the wheel. The older daughter is sitting next to her. She smiles at me, real friendly-like, not seeming to understand what's going on. Eric opens the passenger door, pushing Ashley in first. Then he climbs in, cramming the four of them into the front, yelling, "Go!" Claire peels out on his command.

"Wait!" I run after them. "I just want to interview you! Please, don't go!"

The daughters are facing backwards, watching me give chase. They wave goodbye through the windshield. I quickly give up the pursuit. Turning around, I see my old truck from Anne Davis Auto parked in front of the building. I go to stand beside it to do a selfie, focusing only on me first.

"Dear Followers: What do you get when you play country music backwards? Your job back, your wife back, and your sobriety back. I don't much care for country music, forwards or backwards, but guess what I got back today?" I widen the viewfinder so my followers can see for themselves. "My truck. And guess what else I got back. Hope. You see, little Ashley, who I had given up for dead after all these months, was healed in Rome City." I set my phone down and dance in front of the lens. "Doing the happy dance."

A group of five students, three girls and two guys, are walking past and laughing at me. Undeterred, I call over to them. "I'm celebrating a child's miraculous recovery from cancer. Come join me."

Much to my delight, they eagerly participate and turn out to be excellent dancers. A couple of them do flips and cartwheels before taking off on their merry way. I return the lens to focus on myself again. "Well, that was fun. Thank you for sharing in my joy."

I head back into the building and up to our apartment. After dinner, some light cleaning, and heavy editing of the video, I download it to my JustSharing account. Around 7:30 p.m., Kylie calls to give me a subdued squeal. "I caught your latest vlog." She's almost as excited about Ashley as I am, but she's whispering for some reason. "It's absolutely inspiring. Do you believe in The Miracle now?"

"I think I do."

"Praise the Lord. I'd love to talk more, but phones are verboten during this portion of the retreat. Gotta go before I get caught. Catcha later."

"Bye."

After she hangs up, I head to the bedroom. Taking the silver string rosary off of the bedpost, I sit on the edge of my mattress. Clutching the rosary to my chest, I immediately feel a wave of love and support. It's like Grammy is here, holding me close.

"Grammy," I say, looking up at the ceiling, "thank you for continuing to look out for me." I proceed to crawl into the covers with the rosary wrapped around my hand and fall asleep with a smile in my heart.

Lost in Dreamland, I'm trapped in an empty well with steep sides coated in slime. Try as I might to climb out, I can only manage a few feet before slipping back to the bottom. Thinking escape is impossible, I drop to my knees in despair. A woman's voice calls to me from the top. "Climb up, my daughter!" She throws a silver rope with a big knot at the end and ten equally spaced smaller knots going up.. Using the knots for handholds, I slowly make my way to the top.

Climbing over the stone ledge, the view takes my breath away. An evening garden spreads out before me in every direction, white roses growing freely in uninhibited groups, interspersed with an occasional red. The air is sweet as honey, while the velvet sky twinkles with stars. Having fallen asleep thinking of my grandmother, I expected to find her waiting at the top. I'm surprised to see a beautiful young woman with long inky black hair instead. She's dressed in a glittering white gown and a silver tiara topped with glowing white stars. Her eyes are of the deepest blue. With a smile so tender, no beating heart could resist it. She says to me, "My rope is your lifeline out of the darkness. Cling to it and be saved."

My eyes flutter open, taking me out of the perfumed garden. I dwell on the dream, wondering about the meaning of the rope, the roses, and the identity of the lady. She called me daughter, but she looked my own age. Could it have been the Virgin Mary? The idea is compelling, but it might have been just a lovely dream and nothing more. Not wanting to be the kind of person who gives into flights of fancy, I decide not to make too much of it, and let my thoughts drift to dreary reality.

My to-do list begins to roll through my head: 1) Big accounting exam on Monday—must study over the weekend. 2) Paper due in Business Operations II. 3) Figure out what to do with my extra truck. 4) Decide whether to make a clean break with Jerome or just let it die off. 5) Make more videos … As usual, the list goes on and on, refusing to stop. Even in the daytime, it's always there at the back of my mind, making me anxious. Alone in the dark, I'm to item twenty or thirty before I finally nod off to sleep again.

"Regina Magdalene Applegate!" The distinct sound of my grandmother's voice jars me out of my slumber. "Remember your promise!"

I sit up with a start, head jerking around. The room is empty, but I swear it smells just like my grandparents' house. A mix of baking bread, laundry detergent and vanilla air freshener.

"Promise—what promise?" I ask aloud.

My memory banks sift through my life with Grammy until they hit the phone conversation I had with her on the city bus. We were discussing the vlog where I turned my truck over to the homeless family so they could go to Rome City. If the little girl got a miracle, I told my followers that I would become a believer. Over the phone, Grammy had made me seal it with a formal promise. If Ashley was healed, I would return to the church.

"Okay, okay," I say, throwing my hands up in the air. "You win. I'll go to church first thing in the morning."

A few hours later, around 5:30 a.m., I drag myself out of bed to shower and dress. Based on Kylie's previous recommendation, I decide to head over to St. Faustina's of Divine Mercy to hunt down Father Kramer. According to my GPS, it's a 56 minute drive. After grabbing a bite to eat, I head out with the rosary in my coat pocket. The university is at the edge of the city, so it doesn't take long for the landscape to transition from shopping malls, and tightly spaced homes, into vast open spaces and farmland.

In less than an hour, the water tower, with its town's logo, appears in the horizon:

Welcome to Burlington
Land of a Hundred Churches

It's more like thirty or forty, but who's counting? I keep driving, noticing the overabundance of places to worship. No wonder people are confused about what to believe or not. Within the last mile, I have passed a beautiful Baptist church, a towering Pentecostal, a Jehovah's Witness temple in a storefront, an Episcopal church done in a modern style, a Jewish synagogue of light brick with a copper dome, Baker Street Second House of God, Baker Street First House of God, and a Greek Orthodox Center to rival the Holy Sepulcher in Jerusalem. If I squint hard enough, further down the road there's a mosque with a golden dome surrounded by four white towers.

If Burlington is anything like the town I grew up in, I have a good idea how the impressive structures came about. Back in the nineteen hundreds, the various denominations were competing for members. The logic seemed to be, the taller the church, the closer it would get you to God. Subsequently, the steeples got higher, the architecture fancier, with each new building surpassing all the old ones. Since the falling away from Christianity, many of these mammoth churches sit almost empty. Their sheer size makes them a burden to the small remnant of the faithful. Since the Illumination, though, there's been an upswing in attendance. I'm a little late to the party. Hopefully, they'll let me in.

I pull up to St. Faustina of the Divine Mercy, right across the street from Trinity Lutheran. St. Faustina's cornerstone says 2010. As far as church buildings go, it's relatively new, not the biggest or the fanciest, but it's still a magnificent piece of work. I'm not up on my architectural terminology, but if I had to put a label on the style, I'd call it Modern-Gothic.

At the very top is a copper cross that sits upon the fattest steeple I've ever seen. It reminds me of a pagoda, except it's made of brown brick, instead of frilly white wood. Below that is a deeply pitched roof covered in ceramic red tiles. The base of the building is a wide rectangle with a huge jutting wing that serves as the front entrance. A triple set of double doors stand invitingly atop a tall concrete stairway guarded by archangels cut from stone on either side. Above the entrance is a large, round, stained-glass window, with two slightly smaller ones flanking it. Going all around the building, at least as far as I can tell, are double layers of arched windows. The bottom windows are tall, at least three or four stories high, made of stained glass. Above them are shorter windows, also made of stained glass.

I climb the stairs, push open the center doors, and go inside to find another wall of doors. Standing in the area between them, I'm seized with uncertainty. I haven't been inside a Catholic church since high school. Even then, I was a reluctant hostage of my grandparents, who made me attend Mass whenever I stayed with them. I remember how humiliating it was during communion, to sit alone in the pew like a goober while everybody else went to receive the Bread and the Wine. I wanted to go up, but my grandparents said no. According to my grandfather, as long as my mother and I attended Ray's church, we were not in communion with the Catholics, so it wouldn't be right. That stung.

What if the priest tells me I'm not worthy? I will be embarrassed if he yells at me in front of everyone. What if he tells me I'm hopelessly damned and kicks me out of the church? Where am I to go?

From the corner of my eye, I catch a glimpse of a painting hanging on the wall opposite the stairwell. It has a stormy dark background. The focal point is a glowing image of Jesus in blue and red robes. Rays of light are pouring out of his chest. The painting is entrancing. I'm especially drawn to the comforting message at the bottom, *Jesus, I Trust In You.* Okay, I tell myself. I'm going to do exactly that. Sucking in a breath of courage, I push on through the next set of doors.

From the soaring groin-vaulted ceiling above, painted sapphire blue with constellations of golden stars, to the pastel mosaic floor, the world inside is a mesmerizing expression of reverence. Smooth creamy pillars match the wall-to-wall stairs going up to the altar. Behind the altar is a triple-arched stained-glass window of Jesus, heart exposed on his chest, with rays of red and white light coming out of it like shooting stars.

A banner with words stretches across the window: *Holy God, Holy Mighty One, Holy Immortal One*. The words at the bottom of the window say: *Have Mercy On Us, And On The Whole World*. I repeat the words over and over, committing them to memory. That way, should the priest tell me to get out because I'm too big of a sinner, I can remind him what the wall says.

Glancing around, I hope to spot Father Kramer somewhere. Kylie says he's in his mid-thirties, tall, glasses, receding hair line. I'm realizing that in my enthusiasm, I didn't plan my re-entry into the community of believers very well. Maybe I should have called ahead to make an appointment.

A young girl in a white robe and sneakers is up front, holding a metal pole with a small flame on the end. She is walking about lighting candles, prepping for Mass. Some of the pews are already full, and people are strolling in as I scan the room. Realizing I'm going to have to wait until the end of the service to catch the priest, I take a seat in the very last pew and try to remain inconspicuous.

Sitting in the back allows me to watch the people who are just arriving. The young and old alike pause at the edge of their pews to genuflect toward the golden box on the altar. From my childhood religious education, I remember the box holds communion wafers and there's a fancy name for it, but I can't think of it for the life of me.

Everyone looks so holy, like they know what they are doing. I feel so out of place. The longer I sit here, the more agitated I become. Will I have to take a written exam before they let me be Catholic again? I'm going to look really stupid if they question me on the name of the box. Glancing at the doors, I think about bolting away. The words by the entrance give me courage. *Jesus, I Trust In You*. I repeat them like a mantra. *Jesus, I Trust In You*.

When the pews are about a third of the way full, a woman at the podium tells everyone to open their Songs of Praise book to number 252, *All Are Welcome*. I do my best to sing along as a priest of African descent parades in behind two girl alter servers and a woman holding a golden Bible over her head. Oh, balls. That must be Monsignor

Nikwande, the priest from Africa Kylie warned me to avoid if I was looking for someone who wouldn't bawl me out.

He begins Mass with the sign of the cross. "In the Name of the Father, the Son, and the Holy Spirit," Monsignor Nikwande says, his rich accent readily apparent. "The grace of our Lord Jesus Christ, and the love of God, and the communion of the Holy Spirit be with you all."

The people reply, "And with your spirit."

Afraid that if I wait too long I'll talk myself out of believing my grandmother spoke to me this morning, I decide to approach the monsignor at the end of the Mass. If he's rude, I tell myself not to take it personally. After all, Kylie said he rubs a lot of people the wrong way. As soon as service concludes, I intercept the monsignor just as he's about to go into that little room where the priests keep their robes and stuff.

"Father, I … I've been away from the church for a while. I was wondering if we could talk and maybe do a confession."

He takes out his cell phone and checks the time. "I have Mass across town in one hour," he says in his thick accent. "If you've been away from church, talk will take too long. Call the secretary. She will find slot for you."

"You don't understand." I shake my head. "If I don't do this now, I might lose my nerve."

He studies me a moment, his eyes like drills to my soul. I put on my best lost little lamb expression. It's not difficult because everything I've been through over the past year has certainly taken a toll. Just as I'm about to give up, he lets out a sigh of defeat.

"Very well, young lady. Give me five minutes. Use time to examine conscience. Then I will meet you by St. Faustina to hear confession."

Monsignor Nikwande disappears into the room, leaving me to wander through the church, videoing everything with my camera phone. In my exploration, I find an alcove with a statue of a nun raised up on a stand. To the left are four closed doors to the confessional booths.

"Dear Followers," I whisper into my phone, "you're never going to believe who I heard from last night—my dead grandmother. Seriously. I'll fill you in on the details later, but she's the reason I'm here, getting ready to go to confession." I zoom in on the base of the statue, specifically the words on the engraved black plate: *Oh, St. Faustina Kowalska, Secretary of the Divine Mercy, pray for us.* "The priest told me to meet him here." There's a rack of votive candles and a box for donations to the side. I drop in a couple of dollars and video myself lighting a candle. The sound of shuffling gets my attention. I turn the camera that direction. "Here comes the priest, Monsignor Nikwande. I hear he's very old school. I don't think he would appreciate me vlogging our conversation, so I'm going to shut off the camera. I'm so nervous. Wish me luck."

Chapter 38

Monsignor Nikwande points at the doors. One says SCREEN on it. The other says FACE-TO-FACE. He tells me to take my pick. Since he has already seen me, it seems silly to go for the screen.

We enter the confessional room and sit down in wooden chairs across from each other. There's a tiny coffee table between us. There's so little space, his knees are hitting one side of it, and mine the other.

There's a laminated sheet on the table, instructing unpracticed people like me on what to say. I pick it up and hold on tight. We make the sign of the cross together. Then he says, "May God, who has enlightened every heart, help you to know your sins and trust in his mercy."

"Forgive me, Father," I say, following the instructions on the sheet, "for I have sinned. I haven't been to Confession since I was 13-years-old. My sins are …"

I begin to confess everything that I remember. From using the Lord's name in vain about a million times, to not being a regular Mass goer, to my doubts about God, my sexual failings, and my falling into Hell during The Warning, how it has left me despairing, and how angry I have been at God for taking away my loved ones. He listens quietly as I tell him about Riley dying of cancer, my father's possible suicide, and the recent massacre of my uncle, grandparents, and beloved mother. One of the most difficult things I confess is the incident at the Hot Damn party. The monsignor tells me to spare him the details, give him just enough information so that he has the gist. I gloss as much as I can, but it's still extremely awkward.

While confessing, I recall something that I had forgotten until this very moment. The woman screaming at the party. "There was true terror in that sound," I tell the monsignor, "but I was too caught up in feeding the pleasures of the flesh to give a damn—er, I mean darn. Sorry about that, Father. Should I also confess that I cussed during confession?"

"You just did." He shakes his head and glances down at his phone to check the time again. "Is there anything else?"

"I'm sure there's more. But it's all I can think of at the moment."

"You have been through much for one so young. Lean on Jesus, and the Holy Mother, they will lead you through the storm. About The Warning—let me give you quick advice. Get over it. Like a road sign warning of *Falling Rocks* or *Bridge Out Ahead,* the Illumination of Conscience was placed at side of road to warn travelers, turn around before it is too late."

"I want to believe you, Father, but it feels more like God hates me."

"Does highway department put up sign so that travelers speed up and fall off cliff? I think not. Signs are placed by highway department to keep drivers from harm. Your sign indicated *Damnation Ahead,* not because God hates you, but because He thinks you are worth saving. He was trying to convince you to turn around. Understand?"

"I think so."

"The Warning, you see, is a sign of His great love for us and His unfathomable mercy. For penance, say Joyful, Sorrowful, Luminous and Glorious—one time each."

"Uh, you mean as in the mysteries of the rosary?"

"Yes. Say all mysteries of rosary."

"For crying out loud, that's like four times around the beads. Can't you give me anything easier—like fasting or doing a good deed or something?"

"Do you think God could have done something easier than sending his Son to die on a cross?"

"Of course, God can do whatever He wants."

"But did He?"

"No, it's just that I've never said a rosary all by myself. I don't know all the words."

"You attend university—correct?"

"Well, yes."

"Then no hiding behind stupid. Google it. Now, make a good Act of Contrition."

"I can't remember how."

He clicks his tongue in condemnation, while gesturing in annoyance at a laminated card. I read the Act of Contrition from the sheet, a prayer that expresses sorrow at having sinned against God, pleads for forgiveness, and asks for help to do better in the future.

After I'm through, the monsignor hovers his hands over my head and gives me a rushed, "God, the Father of mercies, through the death and resurrection of his Son has reconciled the world to Himself and sent the Holy Spirit among us for the forgiveness of sins; through the ministry of the Church may God give you pardon and peace, and I absolve you from your sins in the name of the Father, and of the Son, and of the Holy Spirit. Amen."

"Thank you, Monsignor."

"Now, go in peace, and proclaim to the world the wonderful works of God who has brought you salvation."

"You can count on it." I clutch my phone tightly, knowing I will soon be proclaiming His wonderful works to my followers, but I want to double-check that I've understood the effects of my confession correctly. "Just so I'm clear, Monsignor. Does this mean I'm officially a Christian again?"

"Upon completion of penance, it means you are forgiven, in good standing with the church. Welcome home, daughter."

An expected wave of emotion goes through me. It takes every ounce of strength to keep from sobbing with relief. Feeling like I want to give back somehow, I remember my plan to get rid of my extra vehicle. "By the way, I have a nice truck I don't need anymore. Do you think one of your charities could use it?"

There's a long silence.

"Monsignor?"

"Definitely, yes. Call the parish office or stop by on the way out. Our financial manager will arrange everything. God bless you, child."

"Thank you, Father."

After I stop by the office to get the transfer of my truck in motion, I start off for home, feeling like my soul has been restored to factory settings. This is a fresh start with God. About forty minutes into the drive, I turn on the university's radio station. Smoky City Night, a modern piece written and performed by a local pianist, is playing at the moment. It's nice, but I can't stop thinking about the way the priest put The Warning into perspective for me. God showed me Hell because He doesn't want me to go there. That means He wants me in Heaven with Him. I guess I needed to hear the obvious conclusion from ordained lips before it sunk in. For the first time in a long while, I don't feel hopelessly damned. The words 'Welcome Home' keep ringing through my head like happy wedding bells. A sense of peace is spreading over me. Although my life is no better on the outside, I have a hopeful new outlook. As long as God and I are copacetic, everything will be okay in the end.

Dear Jesus, I say interiorly, I'm sorry that I lost my trust in You after Riley died. *From there, our relationship went on a downward spiral. At least it did on my end of things. I'm beginning to realize that even when You didn't answer the prayers as fast as I thought you ought, or in exactly in the way I had prescribed, You have had my back all along. Thank you for sending me to the monsignor today. I wasn't expecting to be let back into the church so quickly. I'm going to try live a better life. Help me not to screw up. Amen.*

As I continue to drive along, I return my attention to the truck's dashboard. The clock shows the top of the hour. A male student is going over the weather forecast—cold, cold, and more cold. Then he gets to the local news. "The body found dumped along I-70, with nail wounds in the skull, hands, and feet indicative of torture, has been identified as the university's very own Pastor Bianca Mouflon."

I slam on the brakes and pull over to a parking spot at the side of the street. The DJ moves onto another story far too quickly for my liking, so I bring up more details on my truck's computer dash. A recent photograph of the victim appears on the screen. It's definitely the Mouflon I met last fall. She has on the same pink sweater and the cross necklace she wore every time I saw her. Even though I refused her counsel, she was a nice person. Sick of the senseless violence around me,

I pound the steering wheel in frustration. My eyes go back to the cross in the photo.

It seems I've seen one like it somewhere other than around her neck. I search my brain and, instead of seeing crosses, the squealing of pigs comes to mind. *Forgive them*, a woman's voice echoes in the darkest corners of my mind, *they know not what they do.*

That awful morning I've tried to forget comes back to me. How the sunlight bled through the branches of the trees. The large wooden crosses planted around the smoldering remnant of the bonfire. Crawling around them on hands and knees in search of my clutch and coming across a bloody metal cross in the leaves.

In hindsight, it looked exactly like the one Mouflon used to wear. It's just a coincidence, I try to convince myself, but deep down I know there is more to it than that. Skimming through the article, I'm horrified to realize the pastor disappeared on the same date as the Hot Damn party. An image of a blonde woman on a cross, with nails driven into her skull, flashes before me. Wait, no. I'm sure it was a pink pig. Or was it?

Vomit rises without any warning. I manage to hold it in long enough to fling open my door and let it spew out onto the street.

Chapter 39

When I get home, the first thing I do is pull up the university website, and go to the missing persons list. Doing a little digging, I learn that at least eighteen of the thirty-two missing were dedicated Christians. There may be more, but I couldn't find the religious affiliations of everyone on the list. Less than a third of the university population indentifies themselves as having any religious affiliation at all, so the number seems significant. Maybe I'm just jumping to conclusions. The cross in the woods could have belonged to anybody, but if it didn't … Unsure who to trust with my suspicions, I decide to put off taking action until I think it through more.

Disturbing questions roll through my head. First, how much does Jerome know? What about Julie? Several professors were at the party—did they have anything to do with it? Then I remember all the powerful people who were there that night. It doesn't seem possible that they would participate in a murder. On the other hand, how far up the community ladder could this thing go? I need to tell someone of the fraternity's possible connection to Mouflon's death, but there were also police officers in attendance. Who can I trust? Only one name comes to mind. Aunt Vivian.

Since she's already a homicide detective, if anyone would know what steps to take in such a situation, it would be her. I send her a text to call me back ASAP. Feeling antsy while waiting for her to get back to me, I pace around for thirty minutes. She still hasn't called me back, so I try to focus on something productive. Seems like the perfect time to complete my penance. Sitting at my laptop, I Google info on how to pray the rosary.

It takes me the entire afternoon to get through the Joyful Mysteries. Once I get that round of the beads under my belt, the Sorrowful, Luminous, and Glorious come more easily. By evening I'm prayed-out and tired of waiting for Aunt Viv to call. Needing a respite from my problems, lest I go mad, I plop down in front of the television just before 8 p.m. A new episode of *Good Cop Gone Bad* is just about to start when someone bangs on the door.

"Who could that be?" I sigh.

I go to the door. Open it. Jerome is standing in the hall looking dashing in a pair of black jeans and an unbuttoned leather duster. The *Man Whore* tattoo is still faintly visible on his forehead, but the laser treatments seem to be working. I say hello, but refrain from inviting him in.

"Get dressed, Gina. I'm treating you to dinner at the comedy bar."

"You should have called first. I'm planning on spending a quiet evening at home alone."

"Then it looks like I came in the nick of time, saving you from boredom."

He smiles broadly, acting pleased with himself for swooping into the rescue. Glancing back at the television, I see my favorite show has started. Last week's episode ended on a cliffhanger. I'm eager to see what happens next, but that's not why I want him to leave. It's because I don't like who I am when we're together. If I want to change for the better, he can't be part of my life anymore.

"Aren't you going to invite me in?" He frowns impatiently. "Ever since the party, you act like I've turned into a blood-sucking vampire."

Not feeling up to a confrontation just yet, all I can do is shrug.

"If it's because I was with Jay and that girl at the Hot Damn party, need I mention the dozens of men who went down on you that night? Professor Langley said he couldn't get enough."

I hold my hand up like a shield, as my head begins to pound, trying to protect myself from Jerome's words.

"I have no memory of being with Professor Langley that night, yet alone dozens of men, so let's keep it that way."

"Clearly, you've won them over, but the women of Dionysus are going to be harder to impress. I suggest ..."

"Quit talking! Can't you see you make me sick?"

Jerome steps into the room, shaking his head. "I know you didn't mean that, Gina." He pulls me by the arm to his chest, stroking the back of my head. I try to pull away, but he only holds me tighter. "You took a big step that night, opening yourself up to the passions. Don't go backwards now. If you want to be with other people from time-to-time, you'll get no judgment from me, only my love and admiration. You see, Gina, as a couple we have risen above the antiquated rules of society. That's what makes us so great together."

"We are not great together, Jerome." I push him away more forcefully. "You and I are moving in different directions."

"The Stonehenge party is on for next Friday. Everyone is supposed to dress like druids. You'll need a robe with a hood—preferably in brown." I frown, realizing nothing I've said has sunk in. "And, get this, anyone who brings a Christian automatically moves up to the next level of the fraternity. I figure we can bring Kylie."

"No way am I bringing Kylie to one of your frat parties."

"C'mon, Gina. I already told them we would bring her. They'll be mad if we back out now."

"Tell them I don't want any part of their organization."

"But I've already talked to the president of Digital Genesis International about you. He's interested in hiring you for a management position in distribution, but in order for it to happen, you have to prove that you can follow orders by bringing a Christian." I pull away from Jerome, staring at him as if I'm a recovering crack addict and he's holding out a fresh pipe. A job at the wireless communications company, Digital Genesis, has always been a dream of mine. For a moment, my newfound principles fly out the window.

"A management position with D.G.I.?" I verify in disbelief. "Are you serious?"

"Of course, providing Kylie shows up to be counted. She doesn't have to stay, but who knows? Maybe she'll see how much fun we're having and decide to hang around. So, Gina, are you in?"

Suddenly, it occurs to me this might be how the fraternity lured Pastor Mouflon to her death. They had a 'friend' extend her an enticing invitation. The idea that Jerome might be lining up my best friend for the slaughter brings me to my senses and ignites my fuse.

"Do you really think I'd turn my best friend over to Christian killers just to climb the corporate ladder?" Three neighbor women from down the hall, just happen to be walking past as Jerome and I argue. They pause to gawk through the door, but I'm too angry to care. I point out into the hallway and yell at Jerome, "Get out of here, Jerome. And don't come back. We're done."

He rapidly blinks and continues to stand there with his mouth hanging open. If my neighbors weren't watching, he might try something. But the nosy threesome are watching with interest. I assist Jerome out the door with a shove, slamming it shut behind him.

Could Jerome really be part of an evil plot to murder Christians? Now that Kylie's name has come up, I cannot take any chances. I secure the locks, cursing my loose tongue. I had planned to be cautious around him. The last thing I should have done was tell him about my suspicions. If the fraternity finds out that I'm onto them, they might come after me.

"The comedy act starts in twenty minutes," I hear Jerome say through the door. "Julie, Sam, and a couple of the guys are meeting me there, so I'm going to head out now. I'll call you tomorrow after you've had a chance to cool off. Okay?"

"Go away, Jerome," I say through clenched teeth. "And don't call me anymore."

"Bye, Gina. I love you."

Shaking my head, I wonder what it's going to take to get through to him. I listen through the door until his footsteps fade away. As soon as the stairwell door at the end of the public hallway bangs shut, I text my aunt again: Call me STAT.

To my relief, my phone rings within seconds.

"What's up, Gina?" Aunt Viv asks.

"I might be mixed up in a murder conspiracy."

"Whoa." There's a pause. "Tell me what's going on."

I pour out everything that happened. By everything, I mean *everything*. She probably thinks I'm a skanky ho, but I figure the smallest clue could make a difference. I can tell by her silence that she is paying close attention. Only occasionally does she interrupt me to ask for more details.

"So, what do you think, Aunt Viv?" I ask at the end. "Have I let my imagination run amok or is there reason to think the fraternity killed Pastor Mouflon?"

"Have you mentioned your suspicions to anyone besides me?"

"I didn't mean to, but I let it slip to Jerome."

There's icy silence on the other end of the line before she speaks again, "Let me get this straight, your ex-boyfriend, Jerome Miller, is a member of the fraternity?"

"Just a junior member—not full-fledged."

A heavy sigh comes over the phone.

"Does this mean you think there's something to it, Aunt Viv?"

"Let's not jump to any conclusions, but possibly."

"What should we do?"

"It's not my jurisdiction, but let me run it by the chief. If he thinks your intel is pertinent to the case, he'll get it to the right people."

"What about the fact that police officers were there at the party—do you think you can trust the powers that be?"

"Of course not, but there are plenty of good guys left on the force. If we run into any roadblocks, the chief will know a way around. He's smart that way."

"What should I do on my end—I mean, should I file a report with the university or the police department down here?"

"I'm not comfortable with you doing that until I talk to the chief. He has access to information I'm not privy to, so sit tight for now, but be ready to leave at a moment's notice."

"Leave? I don't want to do that. With everything that happened last semester, I can't afford to miss anymore classes."

"That's why I said sit tight. I understand school is important, but your safety comes first." There's a long pause. "Gina, did you hear what I said?"

"Yes, I heard. You're totally right. Do you think it's that serious?"

"The whole time we've been talking, I've been cross-referencing the data. I'm seeing, wherever there's an active Fraternity of Dionysus in the area, the number of missing Christians is ten times anywhere else." She quiets for another thirty seconds, softly saying, *hmmm*. Then exclaims loudly into the phone, "Whoa, doggy. The chief is going to want to see this."

"See what?" I ask eagerly. "What did you find?"

"I can't explain now. Gotta go."

"But ..."

"One more thing, Gina. If anybody confronts you about this, deny everything. You weren't at the party. You didn't hear any screams. There were no bodies, pigs or otherwise, hanging from crosses. Nor did you find a necklace covered in blood or suspect anyone of murder. Got it?"

"Deny, deny, deny."

"Good girl."

"I'll have to warn Kylie that she might have been singled out as their next victim."

"Good idea, but keep it between yourselves. Hate to cut you short at a time like this, but I absolutely must go."

"Bye, Aunt Viv."

Chapter 40

Sunday morning, I head out to Mass at Our Lady of Perpetual Help down the road from the university. It's smaller than St. Faustina's, but only fifteen minutes away, making it the logical choice. Built in the 1970's, it looks more like an office building than a church. Plain gray brick inside and out. Carpeting designed to mimic flagstones. The crucifix behind the altar looks like an orange letter 'T'. There's no Jesus hanging on it. Nonetheless, an unexpected joy washes over me. It's edifying the way the people kneel, even the young children, in humble respect before the altar. Seeing them express their faith so openly bolsters mine. I'm especially moved when the priest holds up the host because this is the point of the Mass where Jesus is supposed to come down into the bread and the wine in a literal way. Grammy once told me the altar is covered with angels who bow down in adoration at this very moment. Whether true or not, it's wonderful to imagine. I can't see any angels though. Or, Jesus. His Presence during the Mass is one of those things you just have to take on faith. God knows, I'm trying hard to believe it.

A few minutes later, I follow the slow-moving line up to the altar. My grandparents always said that Holy Communion is the most powerful connection we have to heaven on earth. When it's my turn to stand in front of the priest, I cup my shaking hands and hold them up in anticipation. He raises the round white Bread before me. My mind races a mile a minute. *Is it really YOU, Jesus? Please, help my unbelief.*

"The Body of Christ," the priest proclaims.

"Amen," I reply, my heart full of hope.

On the way back to my seat, I let the Host rest on my tongue, trying to prolong my Communion with Christ as long as possible. Once in the pew, I kneel and close my eyes. There's a lot I want to say. *It's good to be back, Lord. I'm sorry to burden You, but it's really tough down here. Half of the time I'm afraid of dying. Half of the time I'm afraid of living. I need your grace to get me through …*

The priest takes his time cleaning the wine goblets and the bowls before he sits down. Everyone slides back into their pews. The priest rises. Following his lead, the congregation does the same. Then he raises his hands to bless us and tell us to go in peace. The altar servers and priest face the crucifix as the last hymn begins. After a moment or two, they turn around and then walk down the aisle to exit through the doors. The rest of us continue to sing the next verse. Finally, the people in the pews file out behind them in orderly fashion to the outdoors.

Making my way down the cement steps, I'm recollected within myself, dwelling on how my return to Holy Mother Church went better than expected. I genuflected, sat and kneeled like a pro. *Grammy, if you're watching, I hope you're happy.* I glance up to find where I parked my truck along the street. A group of tattered men and women are wandering nearby. They're shouting at the people leaving Mass.

"These souls burn with His Holy Light," says a girl of maybe sixteen or seventeen. Her face is dirty. Teeth missing. Menstrual blood stains her jeans. "Tomorrow they shall be extinguished."

"The Fade will feast on your flesh!" cackles an old woman with frizzy gray hair.

"The darkness is coming!" says a young man in an army jacket. His eyes look like black cesspools. "Hell will devour the Earth!"

I hesitate on the middle of the stairwell with a bunch of other parishioners, who don't want to walk through the loonies any more than I do. A tap on my shoulder causes me to jump. I spin around to see it's the 'dork' from school, Zachary Lombardi.

"Don't sneak up on me like that," I gasp, holding my heart. "You nearly gave me a coronary."

"Sorry, Gina."

"No big deal," I say, after the initial fright wears off. "It's not your fault I'm so jumpy. Let's start over." I take his hand and give it a warm shake. "Nice to see you, Zach. How have you been?"

"Now that you're here, couldn't be better." There's that goofy smile I like so well. "I didn't know you were Catholic."

"Neither did I," I laugh. "Well, actually I just forgot for a while. Are you a regular here?"

"Only recently."

"Does that mean you're a convert?"

"More like a revert," he explains. "I quit going to church back in high school, but came back after The Warning."

"I guess that means I'm a revert, too. But it's not The Warning that brought me back."

"Oh, then what was it?"

"My grandmother. She's a very persistent woman."

"The trumpets sound," screams the tattered man in the army jacket, "and the walls come tumbling down."

The group of tattered people begins to dance around in a circle, making groaning sounds, cackling and screeching, "Toil, boil, mortal coil." That's odd behavior even for the crazies, but I have to admit, it's rather entertaining.

Zach and I watch them for a minute or two, until I say, "My roommate thinks that as the Three Days of Darkness approaches, the crazy will get crazier. According to her, the first wave of demons has already been set loose. The junkies on the street are like a smorgasbord to them. Many are truly possessed."

"Wouldn't surprise me one bit." His voice turns from serious to cheerful in the same breath. "Hey, I just thought of something. This is coffee and donut week. Are you going?"

"How much does it cost?"

"Free."

"Seriously?"

"Yeah, down in the church basement. Would you like to join me?"

"Sure."

He offers me the crook of his arm. Paying no mind to the screeching crazies, I hook my arm through, letting him lead me to the church basement. Turns out that the basement doubles as a gymnasium and reception area. There is a serving window that peers into a commercial kitchen. A long countertop offers a bowl of punch and vats of coffee. An artist easel holds a poster board with a message written in a rainbow of colors:

> Our donut vendor has closed shop.
> We are currently looking for a new supplier.
> Sorry for the inconvenience.
> Please pray for our farmers and the hungry.
> ★ OLPH Parish ★

"Well, that sucks," Zach says.

We fill up on the free coffee and powdered creamer. In place of the donuts, there's a tray of graham crackers with canned pink icing on the side for the spreading. A hand-written note is propped up against the sign: One Per Person, Please.

A frosted graham cracker is better than nothing. I slop one together and then head over to a round table in the corner with Zach. He helps me take off my coat and drapes it over an extra chair. When he takes off his own coat, it looks as if he was dressed by a blind man. A diagonally striped tie is paired with a plaid dress shirt. The huge brass belt buckle, shaped like a galloping horse, sticks out like two dozen sore thumbs. Not that long ago, one look at a fashion nightmare like Zach would have sent me fleeing out the door. Instead of being repulsed, I find it adorable.

"I haven't seen you around school lately, Zach," I say between nibbles of cracker and sips of coffee. "I was worried you decided not to come back."

"I've been around." His voice is so deep it reminds me of a foghorn. It's so sexy, I forget about the mismatched outfit. "I guess our classes haven't intersected."

"Last spring you mentioned something about taking off a semester to help with the family business. How did that go?"

"Slower than expected, but expanding our hydroponics division was a great opportunity to put my Ag-Tech degree to use. I took a semester off to complete it. There's still a few kinks to workout, so I spend a lot of weekends up on the farm."

"You already have a degree, then?"

"Just an associate's. I'm still working on my bachelor's in agribusiness, but I'm sure you'd be bored hearing about plants and fertilizer. What about you—does your family live around here?"

I feel my esophagus constrict. My eyes begin to well-up. Afraid if I speak too quickly I'll turn into a blubbering mess, I look away. He seems to sense my shift in mood and grimaces.

"Oh, geez. I sound like a stalker, prying into your personal life."

"No, it's not that." Having regained control over my emotions, I try to reassure him everything is okay. "You didn't say anything wrong, Zach. It's just that I lost five family members last year."

"Aw, geez. I'm so sorry," he says. "I didn't know."

"I guess you don't watch my JustSharing channel."

"Sorry, no," he mumbles into his coffee cup. After a long and awkward pause, he says in a low voice, "Five in one year. That must have been rough."

"It was like having my heart ripped out of my chest and stomped on." He fidgets across from me. I try to turn the conversation around before I alienate him completely. "My closest relative lives in Valparaiso. She is a homicide detective."

"That's an interesting career choice," he says, his brow raising in interest.

"Have you ever watched *Good Cop Gone Bad*?" I ask.

"Huge fan."

"Really?" I smile widely, using the connection as an excuse to reach out to touch his hand. "Me, too."

His ears instantly turn red. Suppressing a smile, I dive right into the most recent episode. Our discussion turns into a critique of the detective show, the colorful characters, who is sleeping with who, and the unexpected plot twists. As we are talking, I decide that Zach is not drop dead gorgeous like Jerome, nor is he a snazzy dresser, but I like his company. A lot. It's refreshing to be able to connect with a man over something other than booze, sex and baseball.

All too soon, the basement clears out. Zach and I are the last ones left, so he walks me to my truck. We chat about little things like my JustSharing channel and his dislike of chemical herbicides, but I'm secretly hoping he will ask me out for dinner, or at least ask for my number. When he opens the door for me, I think I'm about to get my wish.

"It was really nice talking with you, Gina," he says as I belt myself in. "I hope I'll see you again next Sunday."

"Yeah," I say, trying my best to hide my disappointment. "Same."

Maybe he's gay, I think as he closes the door for me, but no matter what way his gate swings, I can see us becoming great friends. As I drive off, I get a glimpse of him waving goodbye in the review mirror like a big dweeb. Zach is so unconcerned with acting cool, it makes me like him all the more.

On the way home from church, I stop at my favorite grocery store. A sign on the front window says:

Temporarily Closed Due to Low Inventory
Check Back on Monday

Concerned that this marks the beginning of starvation time, I drive over to my second favorite grocery store a few blocks away. The parking lot is packed. When I go through the automatic doors, I'm hit with a blast of frenzied activity. People are yelling. Carts are slamming into things. Shoppers are fighting for the little that's left on the shelves. I hesitate to go in, but I think about my bare shelves at home and decide to enter the arena.

Upon walking inside, a primitive survival-of-the-fittest mentality washes over me. I'm a lioness on the prowl, stepping into a pack of hyenas, ready to fight for my share of the kill. Pushing a cart with a wobbly wheel, I hunt through the store for food. I quickly realize that there's not much left to fight for. No milk, no cereal, no fresh produce, except a couple of bags of potatoes covered with nasty eyes and a few mangled onions. The potato bag is marked $84.99. Crap a coot, that can't be right. A single onion is $14.99. When someone snatches the second-to-last bag of potatoes from under my nose, I feel a sense of panic. No matter the cost, I must get whatever I can. Caught up in the frenzy, I grab the last bag and hurry off to the next section. When I get to the meat department, it's almost empty. The stock boy is filling a shelf with sausage links. The price is $149.99 a pack. That's nuts, but I just gotta have 'em. Pushing my way to the front of the line, I grab an armful. Other shoppers claw at them, so I emerge with just four.

Using my cart like a battering ram, I cut through the aisle of canned goods. There are no soups left except plain vegetable broth. No fruits. Only a few cans of gross stuff like Spotted Dick Sponge Pudding, Pork Brains in Milk Gravy, McLeod Haggis and Hanover Chopped Beets. They're like $50.00 each. As barfy as they sound, I scoop them up.

A couple of police officers are monitoring the checkout lines. When it's finally my turn, I ask the cashier, "What's the deal with the bare shelves? Is there a shipping problem?"

"Yeah, there is," replies the surly clerk. "As in, there is no fucking food to ship."

Swallowing hard, I hope he's mistaken.

Out in the lot, shady-looking people are eyeing the customers coming out of the grocery store with bags of food. Sensing trouble, I hold onto the cart and charge on ahead. Nobody stops me, I figure because there's slower targets to choose from. Sweat is dripping down my face by the time I get to my truck. I throw the groceries in the front seat as fast as I can, then drive away with my hard-fought spoils of war, feeling victorious.

Chapter 41

By midnight, the feeling of victory is long gone. I'm still lying awake in bed worried about food shortages. The government has assured the public that, through the careful management of resources, we have enough to get us through at least another three years. Some parts of the country still produce crops. Even here, there are plants that manage to do okay in the diminished light. But for the most part, the country has been surviving on the stockpile. Everybody knows it isn't a matter of IF we run out of food, but WHEN. If I had a choice between dying of cancer, starvation, or being eaten by cannibals—which would I choose?

My morbid thoughts are interrupted by the sound of a key turning in the front door. I hear the familiar sound of Kylie's squeaky suitcase on wheels roll into the living room. Miguel says something unintelligible, followed by Kylie's stifled laughter.

"Quit it," she giggles. "We'll wake up Gina."

"She's probably out partying with Mr. Baseball," Miguel says knowingly.

"You saw her last vlog," Kylie said. "Things might be different now."

"Let's hope she's nicer. I don't know why you put up with her snark."

"Because up until The Warning, I was the one giving the snark, and she was the one taking it. Gina is family to me, so you better get used to having her around."

"For you, anything." It hurts to hear him complain about how I treat Kylie. Regrettably, he's right. I can be a real jerk at times. "Hey," he continues. "Do you wanna mess around?"

"I can't believe you would ask me that after a retreat on the beauty of abstinence."

"Sorry. I had a momentary lapse. It's just hard being near you without wanting to get even closer. But you're worth the wait."

"Of course I am. And, so are you. It would be so easy to slip back into my old ways, Miguel. Try not to tempt me like that again."

"Forgive me," he replies. "But in my defense, you are very hard to resist."

"I know."

"Maybe we should call it a night, beautiful."

"That's probably wise."

They're really taking this Christian thing seriously. Good for them. Well, at least good for Kylie. Miguel is clearly a horn dog. When it starts to get quiet in there, I drag myself out of bed to flip on the kitchen light. I find them locked in a goodbye embrace.

"Hey, Gina," Miguel says, not sounding happy to see me.

"Hey, Miguel," I reply. "Don't leave yet, I have something to tell both of you."

"I'm really tired," Kylie says, fanning a yawn. "And Miguel was just heading out. Can it wait until morning?"

"No," I reply. "This is really important."

"Uh-oh," Miguel jokes. "We're in trouble."

"That's exactly it," I say without cracking the slightest smile. "You're in trouble. Have a seat."

They exchange curious glances. Gesturing for both of them to join me at the bistro table, the three of us squeeze around it. Despite my Aunt Viv's warning not to talk about my suspicions with anyone other than Kylie, I know Miguel has her best interests at heart. The problem is Miguel already has a negative opinion of me. If I go straight to the part about Kylie being a target of the fraternity, he might think I'm playing a cruel prank. I need to build my case first.

"I don't know how to say this without sounding like a nutter, but I have come to believe that there's a conspiracy against Christians on the campus."

"Tell me something I don't know," Miguel says. "I've endured more than my fair share of rude students and professors."

"I'm afraid that it goes deeper than rudeness. Did you hear that Pastor Mouflon was murdered?"

"Yes," Kylie says. "It was on the campus news. Are you saying she was killed for being a Christian?"

"Not only am I saying that, I think she was murdered by the Fraternity of Dionysus."

"That's ridiculous," Miguel says, rolling his eyes at me. "The Dio boys and girls are just a bunch of party animals, looking to have a good time. Harmless. I can't see them taking things to that level."

"After attending one of their alumni parties, I can. Which brings me to the reason I wanted to talk to you both." Abandoning my plan to lay out my case first, I simply throw it out there. "Kylie might be one of their targets." They both frown, looking cheesed off at the mere suggestion. "Hear me out," I press on through the scoffing. "Jerome asked me to bring a Kylie to the Stonehenge party on Friday."

"Maybe he was just being nice," Miguel reasons.

"When I said no, he got pushy about it because, get this, the alumni are making him bring a Christian as part of his initiation. Isn't that odd?"

"That is odd," Miguel says, sounding more concerned than he was a second ago. "Did Jerome explain why?"

"Not really, but if he gets a Christian to come, he'll be promoted to the next level in the organization." I can practically see the wheels turning in their heads as they consider my accusations, but they're not convinced. "Kylie, do you remember the morning I came home from the fraternity party stoned half out of my mind?"

"How could I forget?"

"Let me tell you more about what happened that night—well, at least the parts I can remember. Then you can decide for yourselves if there's anything to worry about." I go on to spill the entire story. The two of them listen with rapt attention as I describe the depravity. If Miguel thought I was bad before, he probably thinks I'm ten times worse after hearing my story, but I don't hold back. "And get this," I continue. "Pastor Mouflon disappeared on the same day as the Hot Damn party.

It's all conjecture at this point, but my Aunt Viv thinks the fraternity might be connected to murders all across the country."

"Your Aunt Viv," Kylie's voice goes up a nervous notch. "Isn't she a homicide detective?"

"Yes, and she's brought her police chief into the matter. That's how serious it is."

"I always knew Jerome was bad news," Kylie says. "But I never pegged him as a murderer."

"Wait a second." I hold up a palm. "We don't know how involved he is in any of this. He was even more wasted than I was at the party. If Mouflon was killed in the woods that night, he had nothing to do with it. The fraternity's alumni are powerful people. I'm sure it's run like a big business. Underlings rarely know the company's darkest secrets. My ex isn't even a full-fledged member."

"I don't think we should take any chances," Miguel cuts in. "If Mr. Baseball even comes near Kylie again, I'll kill him myself."

"Don't talk that way," she says. "You're a Christian. Don't make yourself a bigger target than you already are."

"Pack your things, ladies," Miguel is so agitated about the situation, he doesn't seem to be thinking in logical steps. "We're leaving right now."

"Leaving for where?" Kylie asks.

"St. Faustina's will help us out," Miguel says.

"How is the church going to help?" I interject. "We need real protection, but I'm not sure if we can trust the police. Do you know how to handle a gun, Miguel?"

"I do, but the three of us wouldn't have a chance against the entire fraternity. However, there is another option. " He looks over at Kylie. "Should we tell her?"

She nods.

"What I'm about to say doesn't leave the room, " Miguel whispers, as if the walls are bugged.

"You have my word."

"Okay, Gina," he takes a breath and then continues. "My volunteer activities at St. Faustina's go beyond fixing leaky roofs and drywall. I work with an underground coalition that aids Christian immigrants from Neuist countries."

"But ... but the United States hasn't let in immigrants since World War III." My eyes widen in concern. "Are you telling me you're helping them enter the country illegally?"

"Yes," Miguel says. "They have nowhere else to go."

"If you get caught, you're looking at fifty-to-life."

"I've been helping, too," Kylie informs me. "I use my computer skills to help them forge new identities."

"Do you know how incredibly dangerous that is?"

"We know the risks," Miguel says. "So we are very selective about who we let in. I hope we didn't make a mistake in telling you."

"I'm just blown away," I say, shaking my head. "That's all. It's a worthy cause. I would never turn you in for saving people's lives."

"I'm so glad you feel that way," Kylie says, letting out a sigh of relief. "I've been dying to tell you, but Miguel doesn't—*didn't* trust you."

"A man can't be too careful," he says. "Things are different now. If the fraternity has truly targeted Kylie, none of us are safe. We need to fall off of the grid for awhile. There are good people at St. Faustina's who can help us do exactly that. Let's pack our things and go."

"Not so fast, Miguel." Kylie beats me to the punch. I shut my mouth and the lovebirds hash thing out. "I have a big project due on Thursday that I've been working on for months. If we really are in danger, nothing bad is going to happen until the party on Friday night. So let's calm down and not do anything rash."

"Where's the logic in that? What if they decide to kidnap you early?"

"If they were planning on doing that, they wouldn't have extended a party invitation."

"Need I point out that the Stonehenge party is being thrown on Good Friday?" Miguel says. "That can't be a coincidence. Those Dio s.o.b.'s are planning on crucifying Christians."

"I understand your concern," Kylie replies. "But if we flee, what's going to stop the fraternity from filling my empty cross with some other unsuspecting person?"

"That's where my Aunt Viv comes in. If the police department here gets a heads up about the party from Valparaiso's chief of police, they can't just ignore it. They'll have to intervene whether they want to or not."

"Maybe," Miguel says. "Maybe not."

The discussion turns into an argument. In the end, it's Kylie and I against Miguel. No matter what he says, we're not leaving. He storms off in a huff, telling us to call him at the first sign of trouble. After his departure, we discuss how he's playing the part of the over-protective alpha male. However, in his absence, it doesn't take long for the paranoia to get the best of us.

After we slide the loveseat in front of the door, whe retires to her room with the switchblade on her nightstand, and. I crawl back into my own bed. The irony of praying for peace with a loaded gun under my pillow isn't lost on me, but there is nothing wrong with arming both the body and soul.

Chapter 42

It's two in the morning, but I'm too restless to sleep. It doesn't take me long to notice Kylie's silhouette hesitating in my doorway. "I'm awake," I say without turning over. "What's up?"

Kylie scurries over to my bed. In the eerie green glow of the clock, I notice the worried look on her face. "You still have your gun, right?" she asks.

"Yup." I pat my pillow. "Right here. Got your switchblade?"

She holds it up in the dim light. I roll to my side and flip open my blanket in invitation, I say, "Get in."

I don't have to ask twice. She dives into the bed beside me, and we curl up together like scared children.

Come morning, after we wake to find ourselves perfectly fine, we share a laugh over having acted like wimps last night. Half an hour later, we head out the door into our separate Monday routines. Although I put on a brave face, the worry still lingers in my thoughts as I move about campus. My video of my return to the church is hardly my most popular, but it has already gotten a hundred thousand views. Maybe it was a bad idea to go public.

Between classes, I catch myself anxiously glancing over my shoulder. It's as if every unfamiliar face is accusing me of being Christian, as if that's a bad thing. Real or imagined, I feel the hatred cut into me like razor blades. The slightest noise makes me jump. If strangers walk a little too close for my comfort, I veer to the opposite side of the hallway or sidewalk.

That evening, feeling there's safety in numbers, Kylie and I sleep together again and go our separate ways come Tuesday. As I travel around the campus for classes, I experience more of the same paranoia. I head over to the cafeteria for lunch, where my mood changes to exasperation. My stomach is growling, but the doors are locked. There is an official-looking red piece of paper taped at eye-level:

CLOSED

DUE TO COCKROACH INFESTATION

This food facility has been ordered temporarily closed by the Department of Health until the violations are corrected.   Reference No: 9785-NR98-MA999-R12

Under normal circumstances an infestation would be no more than a disgusting inconvenience. Due to the shortages at the grocery store, I question whether there is more to it than that. By the worried comments of the students gathering at the doors, it's clear that I'm not the only one who is thinking along the same lines. Students get a big discount for using the cafeteria's ticket system. They pay for three square meals a day for the entire semester in one lump sum. Probably half the students rely on their tickets as their sole source of sustenance. What are they supposed to do now?

As the crowd grows more agitated about the closure, and speculate out loud that this could be a permanent situation, a man in coveralls with "Acer Extermination" printed across his back comes into the area with a metal spray canister. Seeing him seems to put everyone more at ease.

"Aw, man," a male student complains. "How long is it going to take to spray?"

"It's a two or three hour process," the man says. "And another 24-hours for the chemicals to settle. Then the Board of Health has to do its inspection, so you're looking at anywhere from two to four days."

"It better not take four days," another student snaps back. "I'll starve to death by then."

"All I do is spray," says the exterminator. "How fast it opens up again depends on the Board of Health. Until then, I heard you guys will be served right off the food trucks."

"When and where?" I ask.

"Beats me. I'm just the exterminator."

The crowd groans, but his reply seems to quell their fears that the school has run out of food. People begin to peacefully disperse. I watch the exterminator squeeze through the doors to do his thing, still not one hundred percent convinced there's a cockroach infestation. As I'm standing there, being my usual cynical self, I get a text from Jerome:

We need to talk, Gina.

About what?

Are you a Christian now?

Not your concern. BTW, the cafeteria has shut down for a few days. Eat on the road if you can.

I heard. You need to take down the JustSharing vlog of you at the church.

Why would I want to do that? It's getting a lot of views. Cha-ching.

For once in your life, just listen to me. It's for your own good.

Are you worried your frat pals won't like it?

My game is starting. We will talk about this when I get back tonight.

I have other plans. Bye.

I end the conversation and stomp away from the cafeteria. Despite our break-up, Jerome is still telling me what to do. As soon as my temper recedes, I realize that he's just trying to look out for me. In light of recent events, the video does indeed pose a danger. Even before Jerome's text, I was debating about taking it down, but pretending I'm not a Christian feels like cowardice. However, that's not what has me so riled. It's the

229

thought that, if my newfound lease on life has Jerome worried for my safety, does this mean that he's aware of what the fraternity is doing to believers? If only I could see what's going on inside that head of his.

Logging into my account via the phone, I take Jerome's advice and remove the videos of my return to the faith. I mean, they're still there, but inaccessible to the public. I can make them viewable again in three clicks whenever I feel like it.

Back at the dorm, I fry up sausage and boil a couple of potatoes. There's no butter or sour cream to slather on. Salt and dried chives will have to do. Once everything is cooked, I wrap up a portion for Kylie to eat when she returns from class.

Plopping down on the loveseat, I'm getting ready to stream an episode of *Good Cop Gone Bad,* when a text from Aunt Viv comes in:

> The chief and I were pulled into a meeting today with Homeland Security. The case is bigger than we imagined. That's all I can say for now. Will update you soon.

Homeland Security is involved. Whoa. I don't know whether to be relieved or more afraid than ever.

Later in the evening, Jerome shows up at my door. When I don't open it all the way, he barges in to look around the place like a Brahma bull guarding his territory.

"Where is he?"

"Where is who?"

"Don't lie to me, Gina." He goes from room to room, opening closet doors, even peering out the window as if he's going to catch someone clinging to the ledge. "I know you're seeing someone else."

"We're not dating anymore, so who I'm seeing is none of your business."

"Who could possibly treat you better than me? I want to meet this clown."

"Don't make me call campus security. Please, you need to go."

"Does he go to this school?"

"What I can I say to convince you that I didn't leave you for some other guy?"

"Tell me the truth. Did you meet him at church?"

"If you must know, yes."

"I knew you were lying, Gina," he says, nostrils flaring. "What's this poser's name?"

"Uh," I reply. "Jesus Christ."

Jerome's eyes bore into me as if he's searching for any sign of deception. By my serious expression, he knows I'm telling the truth.

"Leaving me for Jesus is worse than 'some other guy'." He sighs and slumps onto the sofa, holding his head in his hands. "How am I supposed to compete with a god?"

"Our relationship was in trouble long before I found Jesus, so don't go blaming Him."

"Don't you realize this is a bad time to get religion?"

"You couldn't be more wrong. In fact, I've recently come to understand that the opposite is true. This is a bad time *not* to get religion."

"You've been religious for five seconds, and now you've become a preacher."

"St. Paul went from persecuting Christians to becoming one in the time it takes to fall off a horse, so I'll count myself in good company. But back to what I was saying. You need to get straight with God while there's still time."

"I can't believe this. You're starting to sound like all of the superstitious weirdoes we used to make fun of."

"In the woods after the party, I saw the darkness with my own eyes, scurrying over the godless people passed out on the ground. On the streets, I've heard it in the voices of the tattered men and women." Jerome unscrews his flask, while I'm talking. I don't let up as he takes a deep swig. "Now that I've opened myself to the truth, I'm beginning to see things more clearly. That is how I know that, when the darkness comes, Jesus will be our only hope."

"Look around you," his voice raises. "God has left the building. It's just you and me trapped in the here and now. We might as well suck the marrow out of life before everything dries up."

Instead of getting angry, all I can feel towards Jerome is pity. He regularly mistakes enemies for friends, accepts outright lies for indisputable truth, and the worldly pleasures that hold him captive for freedom. Attacked by forces he's ill-equipped to understand, he doesn't recognize the danger. A surge of protectiveness goes through me. I need to make him see that we're in the middle of a raging battle and he should fight back.

"Jerome, listen to me. There is so much more to you than flesh and bone. God cares about you. He gave you an immortal soul more valuable than gold. I beg of you, guard it with care. Don't trade it away for passing pleasures."

I sit down on the sofa beside him to take his hand between mine. His expression is unreadable, but he doesn't pull away. I hope that's a good sign.

"If what I saw during The Warning was my immortal soul, I got the shaft," he replies with resentment, as if someone else is responsible for its sorry condition. "The thing is an ugly piece of garbage. If God cares about me, He has a funny way of showing it."

"Your soul wasn't garbage when He gave it to you. It's sin, the bad choices you've made, that turned it ugly. I'm sure all it needs is a good washing." He raises in incredulous eyebrow. Realizing I'm over my head here, and rambling like an ignoramus, I'm quick to refer him to a professional. "There's a priest who specializes in helping people who fell into Hell during The Warning. I think he could do you some good."

"I'm not talking to some pedophile priest."

"You know it's unfair to lump all priests together like that. The one I talked to helped me a lot. He said what we saw during The Warning isn't written in stone. It was God putting up a yellow warning sign, Bridge Out Ahead, giving us a chance to turn around before we fall off the edge."

"You sound like one of those Christian zealots."

"How nice of you to say so." Knowing he meant it as an insult, I smile instead and take it as compliment just to annoy him. "Thank you."

"If you're too foolish to be embarrassed, at least be prudent about who you tell. I know people who will hurt you if they find out you've become a Christian." His eyes are full of concern, making it difficult to get angry. "For your own safety, please don't attach the label to yourself. Zealot or not, I love you, Gina."

"Then do as I ask," I plead for his own good. "Get down on your knees and ask God to open your eyes."

"It's not in my nature to kneel before men or gods."

"The world has brainwashed you to think that way. Please, Jerome. Open your heart and mind to the truth."

"And what truth is that, Gina?"

"That you were made for God and your soul will never be at peace until it rests in Him."

"I didn't come here to be sermonized by a girl I used to bang."

The remark earns him a withering scowl. He rises from the sofa to storm out, slamming the door behind him and leaving me discouraged. Even though nothing I say to Jerome ever seems to get through his thick head, I will always care about him, but if he doesn't want to save himself, what more can I do?

By the next morning, there is a rumor going around that the government has cut off federal funding, the school is living on air and will be forced to shut its doors at the end of the semester. The students and staff are on edge throughout the day. Even the crows seem agitated. They've been circling the area all afternoon. As I'm hurrying across campus from my last class of the day, dozens of them are fighting among the trees and on the sidewalk, shredding the weaker members of the flock. Black feathers are floating down as I walk. I've never been fond of crows, but their behavior is detestable even for them. Come evening, I'm glad to get home and crawl beneath my covers. Wrapping Grammy's rosary around my hand, I drift off to sleep.

Just before dawn, I wake to Kylie shaking me by the shoulder. She got a text that the entire campus is on lockdown and we are not to leave our rooms. I shoot out of bed to join Kylie at the computer and television, but the reason for the lockdown remains a mystery.

Trying to figure out what's going on, we peek through the edges of our blinds at the parking lot below. There are no police cars, ambulances, fire trucks, or soldiers. Maybe it's just a drill. The rising sun is creating a halo of pale beige at the base of muddy colored skies, but not much is happening on the ground. The thermometer suction cupped to our window has already reached 48 Fahrenheit. Looks like it's going to be warm for a post-Yomogi April day. As I'm gazing out the window, I see a young woman in a pink hoodie and a man in a brown leather jacket weaving through the cars in the lot below. She's holding a handgun. The man has a baseball bat. They appear to be together. Perhaps they have something to do with the lockdown. My eyes roam over to seven or eight people in hooded brown robes, closing in around the man and woman.

"Monks?" Kylie's voice goes up in confusion. "That's weird."

"Jerome said everybody was supposed to dress like druids for the Stonehenge party on Friday. Maybe they decided to start a day early."

As the druids pursue the man and woman, a few of their hoods come down.

"Hey," Kylie exclaims. "That girl with the toy Uzi is in my electric circuits class."

"I'm not so sure it's a toy," I reply.

The druids yell something to the man and woman. The pair stop and put down their bat and gun. I think the confrontation is over, but the girl with the Uzi and the rest of the druid gang, begin shooting. My brain can't process what it's seeing, as the man and woman fall over each other onto the ground, blood pooling onto the pavement.

"They shot them," Kylie gasps. "The druids shot them."

A male druid with a machete starts to hack away at the couple. I'm beyond stunned, but can't pull myself away from the horror show. A volley of gunfire comes from the west. Puffs of pavement come up around the druids' feet where the bullets miss their marks. By the trajectory, I think someone is shooting them from up high, like on the roof, or maybe a third or fourth floor window. The druids flee across the parking lot, but in less than thirty seconds all eight of them are dead or too injured to move. I can't believe the scene below me. It's like something I'd see on TV, except this is real life. The dead bodies aren't actors and everything won't disappear when I change the channel.

An eerie hush falls over the campus.

Kylie and I get busy, responding to texts and sending out our own inquiries as to the safety of our friends. It's strange how most of the television and radio stations are off of the air, yet the internet and phones still seem to be working. Jets scream overhead like they're going somewhere in a hurry. The last time I heard so many planes go over at the same time was when the government scrambled them right before Yomogi hit the planet.

Glancing up at the ceiling, I say, "Some serious shit is going down."

"For sure," Kylie replies, the worry in her voice reflecting my own.

It's only natural when people get scared, trapped in their rooms with nothing to do, that they reach out to each other however they can. Kylie and I get busy on our phones, but I can't keep up with all the incoming messages. My friends across the campus are speculating that the violence is related to the cafeteria shutting down. They're remarking on the increase in sky traffic. Planes and helicopters are buzzing back and forth every few minutes.

Friends off campus are saying that the entire city is on lockdown, as are all the major metropolitan areas across the nation. When Kylie and I try to confirm it, the few stations left on the air aren't addressing the food shortages or the lockdowns. Oddly enough, they're running human interest stories and reporting on the weather.

The day wears on and we go to bed none the wiser. At night, Kylie and I hunker down together under the blanket again, jumping at every sound. At the break of dawn on Friday, we awake to the screeching of crows feasting on the carrion scattered across the parking lot. Sky traffic has returned to nearly normal levels. According to the newest messages in my inbox, nothing bad happened overnight on the campus. There is laughter coming from down the hallway. It sounds out of place after yesterday's slaughter, but the Generation of Fading Light is used to random violence. Give it a few more hours, and the incident will be a blip in our collective memories. At least, that's what I'm expecting.

As I continue to sift through the deluge of messages, I notice that I missed a call from an unknown number that came in late last night. Normally, I'd hit delete, but it's a Valparaiso area code. It could be Aunt Viv with an update on the Mouflon case. I hit play and put it on speaker for Kylie's benefit.

The tension coming through the message is loud and clear. I can hear my Aunt Viv huffing away through the speaker like she's in the middle of running a foot race. My innards clench, knowing something is wrong. Kylie and I lean over my phone, bracing for whatever she's about to say:

> The case we were digging into unearthed something bigger than we expected. Bigger than any fraternity, bigger than the university, bigger than the whole damn state. There's a coup against the government happening under our noses. There are traitors among us, waiting for the right moment to take over key positions at every level. The chief and his family were murdered last night. Everyone who touched the case in my precinct has fled. I'm on the road with the kids right now. We're going to lay low for a while. Get out of the city while you still can. Trust no one. Shoot to kill.

Our eyes widen as we exchange grim expressions.

"Holy crap, Gina," Kylie says. "I can't believe this is happening."

"What are we going to do?"

"We're still on lockdown," she points out. "If those druids are still running around, we might be better off in here than out there."

"It's weird how there's still nothing useful on the news. Last I checked, the local channel was running a story about the warning signs of leukemia."

"Three heads are better than two. I'll call Miguel."

As she's dialing, a call comes in from Jerome. The display indicates that he is using Face2Face. Heading to my bedroom, I click on the app so we can see one another as we converse. I take his call and hold the lens up to eye level. Always looking for an excuse to show off his nice six-pack, Jerome has angled the phone to display himself from the waist up. He's sitting shirtless on his leather sofa with a half empty bottle of JD between his legs.

"Hi Jerome," I say, making it obvious that I'm not thrilled to talk to him. "How are you holding up?"

"I hate being trapped like this." His speech is slow and slurred. "I miss you, babe."

"Have you heard how far the food shortage extends?"

"All across America." He pauses to take a swig from the bottle. "The National Guard is here—sort of."

"If what you're saying is correct about it happening all across the country, why haven't we heard anything?"

"The news stations were shut down hours ago. You're probably getting outdated information."

"I don't understand. Rioters aren't usually this organized."

"The dumbasses set the supermarket down the street on fire. When the fire fighters came to put it out, people shot at them just for the fun of it." He turns his finger into a gun and aims it at his temple. "Pop, pop, pop. So now the whole block is blazing out of control. If the wind changes direction, I'm going to have to evacuate. Between the fire, the shootings, and the looters, all the stores have closed, and I'm down to my last bottle of whiskey. What am I going to do?"

"I don't know, Jerome. It's hard to imagine you getting through life without a drink in your hand."

He turns around to open the curtains behind the sofa, aiming his phone out the window. "Take a look, babe. It's a war out there." His camera lens lands on a tank parked in the street. He does a sweep, showing two more tanks. Trails of black smoke billow past in the wind. "They rolled through here about two hours ago and stopped for no reason. The soldiers got out and just walked away." He begins to sing a throaty tune I don't recognize. *"Their boots were made for going AWOL. And that's just what they did."* He stops singing to take another swig of JD and then resumes the conversation. "Wesley said it's the same thing where he is in Little Rock—soldiers abandoning their posts, police joining the looters, people shooting anything that moves."

"God help us all," I gasp. "The government has collapsed."

237

"It wasn't supposed to be like this," Jerome slurs and lets the curtain fall shut again. "They promised a peaceful transition."

"Who are *they*?" I ask suspiciously.

"Shhh," he holds an index finger over his lips. "I'm not supposed to tell."

"Are you a Neuist sympathizer, Jerome?"

"Nope," he says, casually tracing his finger along a geometric design on the sofa. "I'm a plain old Neuist."

"I thought so." At this point, his confession isn't a shocking revelation. "Is the whole fraternity made up of Neuists?"

"At the top levels, yeah. But the newbies take awhile to adopt the party's way of thinking. Usually a professor sees they have Neuist leanings in a research paper, or they make some pro-Neuist comment in front of a Dio, and that's how it begins."

"When you realized the fraternity was a front for the Neuists, why did you stay?"

"Their philosophy started to make sense."

"And what philosophy would that be?"

"If humanity is to survive, we need a strong central government that's not afraid to weed out the weak. Survival of the fittest, you know. Plus, their All-You-Can-Eat-Drink-Smoke-and-Fuck buffet is to die for." He takes another swig of JD and holds up a fist. "Party on, dudes!"

Jerome laughs at himself like he's the funniest guy in the world. How could I have ever thought that grin of his was charming? Since he's drunker than usual, this might be a good time to pump him for information.

"Tell me, Jerome. Did you have anything to do with the death of Pastor Mouflon?"

"I swear to God, I don't know anything about that."

"Neuists are all atheists—right? What good is a swear to God coming from you?"

"Touché."

"What I don't understand is, if they don't believe in a higher power, why did they sacrifice her to Dionysus?"

"They don't really worship Dionysus. The sacrifice of the pigs is all in fun."

"Mouflon's blood was real blood. Her pain was real pain. How can you call murdering an innocent woman fun?"

"I don't know what you're talking about." He shrugs and burps. "As far as I know, nobody got hurt that night. Except the pigs, of course. About me being a Neuist—I hope that doesn't change anything between us. As far as I'm concerned you could hail Hitler, worship Bill Cipher, and sacrifice kittens to the moon, and I'd love you just the same."

"You have to be kidding. How can we be together if you're with a group that's trying to wipe out Christianity?"

"I can protect you. As long as you're with me, nothing bad can happen."

"That is so NOT reassuring."

"You wait and see, Gina," Jerome says, jabbing the bottle of JD at the camera in sloppy drunken fashion. "When the roundup begins, you'll be spared."

"Roundup?" Just when Jerome has me convinced that his hands are clean of innocent blood, he says something to incriminate himself once again. "I don't like the sound of that at all, Jerome. Tell me what they're planning."

"Oops," he belches again. "I'm not supposed to talk about that outside the organization."

"I'll be 'spared' from what, Jerome?"

"Forget I said it," he mutters.

"I'm not going to forget it. I need you to explain …"

"Gotta go, babe. Bye."

I look down at my phone to see that he has ended the call. My mind flits back to the previous conversation I had with Kylie, how we didn't know if we would be better off staying here or going elsewhere. After talking to Jerome, my gut is telling me we need to get out fast.

Chapter 43

After my call with Jerome ends, I return to the kitchen to find Kylie at the bistro table, dressed in a white winter coat, pounding away on her laptop.

"Did you reach Miguel?" She nods, but seems more engrossed in the computer than the conversation. I impatiently inquire further. "What did he say?"

"He's braving the lockdown to come get us. Be ready to go as soon as he texts me."

"Good," I reply. "Because Jerome was saying something disturbing about a roundup and ..."

"Hold that thought, please." She doesn't bother to look up from the keyboard. "I'm in the middle of something."

Glancing over her shoulder, I see a picture of the White House on the screen. Not the White House from my childhood, of course. That one was leveled by a bomb. The president's base of operation has been rebuilt further inland. The new White House, the one I'm looking at right now, is located just outside of Boise. It was designed to mimic the old building, but it's not a perfect replica. A wide cement staircase leads up to the pillared portico, where the president frequently addresses the nation.

"What are you doing?" I ask.

"Originally, I was looking for news about the food shortages. In trying to get it straight from the top, one trail forked into another, and here is where it led." She waves her hand toward the screen, leaning back in her chair to let me take a good look. "I wasn't even trying to break into the thing. It's like some hacker program took over my computer and threw me onto the president's doorstep. We're looking through the lens of a security camera."

Sure enough, there's the familiar classical white building on the screen. Soldiers are marching onto the lawn. I get only a five second glimpse before the computer freezes up. A digital gray bar appears. I think it's buffering or something. Kylie cusses and rapidly clicks through various windows on her computer.

"How are you getting past the firewall?" I say, trying to sound more knowledgeable about computers than I am. "Don't you need a special password?"

"I'm not a computer geek for nothing. But honestly, I wasn't trying to hack into the system. It's as if the homeowner purposely unlocked the door in the hopes someone would turn the knob and find it opened. Anyone who visits the website is redirected here."

"The nation is collapsing," I say aloud, which somehow makes the disconcerting revelation more real. My stomach begins to churn as I talk. "Maybe the government's security system has crashed."

"It's only a glitch," Kylie says dismissively. "I'm sure I'll be kicked off in a minute."

"You don't get it—nobody is minding the store."

She's too busy fiddling with the computer controls to seriously consider what I'm saying. A second later a live image of the White House surrounded by tanks and soldiers reappears on the screen. A strange new flag hangs down from the portico. Not the red, white, and blue of Old Glory. This one is red, white, and black with a dot of green. Minus the wording, it's just like the poster above Julie's bed.

"That's the flag of the American Neuist party," I gasp. "They're taking over the country."

Kylie's hands go over her face, but she continues to peek through her fingers as the president of the United States is brought out in front of the White House with his hands cuffed behind him. A man in a military uniform covered with medals stands over the president. Five stars line the brim of the man's helmet. The Neuist flag is sewn onto his right sleeve. His lips are moving and his eyes keep sweeping back and forth across those gathered in front of him, but there's no audio, so we can't hear what anyone is saying.

241

Soldiers wearing Neuist armbands lead blindfolded men and women in business suits onto the patio in front of the White House. They're cuffed like the president. The soldiers push their captives ahead, causing them to stumble clumsily about.

"This is bad. Very bad," Kylie says, voice trembling as she points to a woman in handcuffs and a blindfold. "That's the vice president." I squint closer. Kylie's correct. Her fingers move across the screen to tap on a man centimeters down the line of hostages, bouncing from person to person. "He's the Minority Whip. She's a senator from Texas."

"He seems to be in charge." I press a finger over the man with five stars on his helmet. "Who is he?"

"A military general, I presume. He looks familiar, but I don't know his name."

"Does this scene remind you of anything?"

"Yeah," she replies. "The beheading of the pope and the cardinals by the Neuists."

"That's what I was thinking."

"Oh, no." She's pointing frantically at the computer screen. "They're going to kill them. Now I get it why my computer was directed here. An insider, maybe the president himself, or one of the people in the blindfolds, wanted eye-witnesses to this terrible crime."

Holding my hand over my mouth, I watch in horror as the president, vice president, and at least a dozen other men and women are lined along the front of the building to face a firing squad. The audio still isn't working, but we can see the soldiers raise their guns on command. I cringe as the bodies of our leaders gyrate and fall while being filled with bullets. My mind struggles to makes sense of it, while my heart is ahead of the game. Hot tears run down my face. Those Neuist bastards have murdered more than our leaders. They've destroyed the last vestige of liberty. Beset with grief and outrage, not knowing what else to do, I make a fist and punch the fridge. Dumb idea. My hand is throbbing now, but it's a small thing compared to what's happening on the White House lawn.

A few minutes of stunned silence follow.

Kylie speaks first. Anger lines furrow across her brow, but her voice is amazingly calm. "I recorded the massacre. I'm going to send it to everyone I know, plus every subscriber list I can get my hands on. The world needs to see exactly what happened, before the Neuists can edit it and add their spin. Is it okay with you if I send it out to your JustSharing subscribers?"

"Please do. Should I add some commentary first?"

"That's a good idea, but keep it around twenty seconds."

She slides out from the keyboard and motions for me to take her place.

"Dear Followers: The Neuists have murdered the president of the United States and several of our top leaders in cold blood. The Christians are next on their list of targets but, be it known, they've been murdering them *just for fun* for quite a while, including Pastor Mouflon from my own campus. Mark my words, if nobody steps up to stop these evil bastards, you and your loved ones are next."

"That's good," Kylie says, cutting me off as she slides back in front of the laptop and presses a couple of keys. "Sent." She glances at her phone. "Miguel will be here any minute. Be ready to make a dash for it."

The sound of gunfire grabs our attention. Out the window, there are hundreds of people marching across campus in hooded brown robes. I pull out my phone to record, unsure if I'll ever have the opportunity to share it online. They're carrying guns, metal pipes, sledgehammers, knives, boards, and there are even a few swords. Recalling the Stonehenge party is scheduled to take place tomorrow, it doesn't take a brainiac to figure out who's underneath the cowls.

"The fraternity is here," I say. "We can't wait for Miguel."

Somebody from inside the building lets out a chilling scream. The sound of boots pounding up the stairwell follow. I run into my bedroom and put on my captain's jacket. Then I loop my travel backpack across my shoulders. At the last second, my eyes fall on the blanket slung over the back of my desk chair. Mary's mantle. Even if it has no real value, I can't bear the thought of leaving Grammy's treasure behind. I fold it lengthwise and drape it around my neck like an extra long scarf. My loaded gun is still under my pillow. Men's voices are yelling in the hallway. I'm still recording as I toss my pillow aside to grip my trusty Ruger LC9.

"Room 215 is on the list," he says. "Pentecostal—is that a Christian thing?"

"I think it's a Jew branch," another man responds. "But it doesn't matter. If they're any religion at all, they're part of the roundup."

Looking to escape, Kylie and I glance at the window. We're only two stories up, but it's a very high two stories. Men and women in the parking lot are being herded into the center by the druids. An older man with gray hair steps in front of a druid. I can't hear what he is saying, but I can tell the words are heated. Two young men beat him down with the butt of their rifles. A third aims a gun at the back of his head.

"Oh, Jesus. Help him." The druid pulls the trigger. The older man goes down. My whole body shudders. Despite the shock of the brutal act, I manage to narrate for the benefit of my followers. "This is terrible. Absolutely, terrible. How could this have happened here in America? It's a classic textbook Neuist takeover. I know, because I did a research paper on it my freshman year.

"First, they spend decades quietly building their numbers and planting their people in the media, businesses, government, military, and throughout the schools. In Europe, before the uprising, the universities were Neuist hotspots. It's where they recruited and brainwashed the next generation of movers and shakers. I thought it couldn't happen in my own country. To think it was going on at this university ..." I stop talking a moment to listen to my surroundings. Down the hall I hear men yelling. A woman yells back. Her voice is cut off in mid-shout. Another woman is crying, *'Stop it, you're killing her!'"* I pause, bottom lip trembling as I look in the direction of the sound, then resume my narration. "It took the Neuists less than a week to take over the UK. On the first days, they concentrated their efforts in the big cities. Once those fell under their power, the smaller cities and towns didn't have a prayer. Is that what's happening outside my door this morning?" My head jerks at what sounds like bodies being slammed around. A woman is begging for her life. "Oh, balls! I think my neighbors are being dragged away by the Neuists. God help us all."

My eyes go anxiously to the door. The situation is beyond my control, but I still have the power of my voice. "Dear Followers: Civilization as we know it is drawing to a close. Nobody knows what we will find on the other side of tomorrow. There are Neuists with guns storming the building. This might be the last video I ever make." Feeling like I'm about to breakdown into sobs, I pause to recollect myself. Breathing deeply to calm my nerves, I find the strength to continue. "Sharing my life with you has been a privilege. God willing, we'll survive these days of darkness and meet again somewhere under the rainbow." A man's painful scream in the apartment above us ends abruptly. I pause to look up. A loud thump, what I imagine to be a man falling onto the floor, causes the pictures to vibrate on the wall. Swallowing hard I look back to the camera. "Good luck, my friends. This is Gina Applegate, signing off."

My fingers dance across the phone, taking only a few seconds to upload the latest video and send it out to a million followers.

"Put that stupid camera away and help me figure out what to do," Kylie lashes out.

"Some people drink to cope with stress. I vlog, so deal with it."

A muffled conversation between two men out in the hallway drifts through our door. "Room 218 is next on the list—two Catholics. They've been marked for the full treatment, so try not to kill them."

"What's the full treatment?" the other man asks.

"They'll be scourged, crowned, and crucified during the ritual tonight."

Kylie and I exchange fearful glances. They're pounding on our door now, trying to kick it in. My heart thumps wildly as I fumble for the gun in my coat pocket. *Shoot to kill.* Aunt Viv's words thunder in my head. Kylie steps out of my line of fire, holding her switchblade at the ready, and gives me a nod.

My hands grow surprisingly steady as I aim at the door. It bursts open. Time seems to move in slow motion as I fire into the chest of the first druid to enter our apartment. The force sends him backwards. The other druid seems confused, standing there dumbly as his cohort crumples to the floor at his feet, while I take aim a second time. As soon as druid number two realizes the danger, he holds up his hands. "Wait, no … don't!"

The bullet goes through the second druid's right cheek, splattering the hallway wall with red and gray gunk.

"I killed them." My voice sounds far away. I continue to aim my gun, though nobody is left standing. "I shot them both dead."

"They gave us no choice." Kylie sidles up to me and places a hand over the gun, gently lowering it. "Keep it together, Gina. You did the right thing, I have an idea to get us out of here." She yanks Grammy's blanket from around my neck. "It's close to the color of their robes. Wear it and you'll blend in."

"What about you?" I ask.

"You'll be Han Solo. I'll be the wookie."

I have no idea what she's talking about and return a blank expression. She looks at me like I'm the dumbest person in the world and snaps the blanket open. Following her instructions, I drape it over my head. The bottom edges reach just a few inches below my knees, but a lot of the druids have ill-fitting robes. Using a brown hair clip, she closes it together at the neck, arranging it around my face to look like a cowl.

"Hold onto my arm like I'm your prisoner," Kylie orders me. "And hold your weapon out in the open like the rest of the druids."

"This is crazy." I'm so afraid, my skin has turned into gooseflesh. "This is never going to work."

"Have faith," she says confidently. "You could almost pass for Allanon."

"What's Allanon?"

"The druid in the Shannara books."

"Doesn't ring a bell."

"You really need to brush up on your classic fantasy and science fiction."

"Just so I can understand obscure nerd references? I don't think so."

"Han is not obscure. He's a legend in this quadrant of the galaxy."

The frivolous bickering, so familiar and comforting, helps soothe my rising anxiety. Just a tad, but I'll take whatever I can get. Trying to add an even deeper level of comfort, I decide to tell her about the blanket.

"Do you want in on a little secret, Kylie?"

"Sure."

"This blanket adorned the Virgin Mary's head during The Warning until she gifted it to my grandmother."

"Cool," Kylie replies so casually, it's obvious she thinks my claim is part of our playful banter. And, maybe it is, because I really don't believe it myself. She straightens my cowl, then tugs on the material at my waist. "You're good to go. Let's do this."

Kylie and I pause at the doorway, sharing a long look that says, *Courage. We're going to get through this together.* Straightening my spine, I steel myself to face the chaos.

Stepping over the two dead bodies in front of our door, I'm relieved to find the hallway empty. We hurry twenty or thirty feet to the stairwell, listening through the metal door for any signs of life. Everything is quiet. Upon opening the stairwell door, we have the misfortune of running into three armed druids coming down from the third floor. My breath catchs in my throat. Kylie lets out a whimper. We both freeze in our tracks.

They have strung together four students by a length of rope—three young women in short sleeves, certainly not dressed for the outdoors, and a man in an orange Dragon Ball Z jacket. I know the auburn-haired woman in the middle from one of my accounting courses—Danica. We're not best friends, but we always say hi when we see each other outside of class. There's a deep gash under her left eye. The man in the orange jacket is her boyfriend. I've only met him a couple of times. I think his name is Ed. He is in worse shape than his girlfriend, wearing a black eye, bloody nose, and swollen lip.

Seeing Danica, Ed, and the other two women, battered and trembling, fills me with anger. I manage to hold it in to plaster on an impassive expression. However, Kylie isn't able to control her emotions and lets loose.

"Why are you doing this to us?" she yells at the druids. "No matter how you try to justify hurting people, deep down inside you have to know it's wrong."

One of the guys lifts his rifle as if he's going to smash her in the face with it. I immediately step between them and hold up a palm.

"This one gets the special treatment," I growl. "You'd do well to remember we're saving the Catholics for tonight's ritual."

The druids try to peer into my makeshift cowl. I don't know what they see, but the men recoil as if I'm a terrible beast. Their fear emboldens me. Holding out my hand and flicking my fingers impatiently for the rope, I order them in no uncertain terms, "Hand me the rope."

To my amazement, they do as I ask. Without saying a word, the three druids back away and then rush down the steps as if they can't leave fast enough. The four hostages on the rope look at me with apprehension, as if they're not sure whether they've gone from the frying pan into the fire, while Kylie takes a wad of Grammy's blanket to examine it with sudden interest.

"Don't worry, I'm not one of them," I say, removing my cowl. "I'm on your side."

"Gina," Danica gives a sigh of relief. "I'm so glad it's you."

As I put my cowl back up, Kylie caresses the material in awe. "Could it really be *her* mantle?"

"I don't understand why these people are dressed like monks," one of the women says, blubbering at the same time. "What do they want? Where are the police? Why isn't anybody trying to stop them?"

"Stick with Gina," Kylie says confidently, still rubbing the fabric on my arm. "The Holy Mother is on her side. She will lead us to safety."

They turn to me, eyes question marks.

"My truck is close by," I explain. "If you want our help, just pretend like you're my hostages until we get on the road."

"Will do," Ed replies, gesturing with his hand for me to go first down the stairwell. "Lead on, Han Solo."

His comment causes me to glance back at Kylie. A smirk breaks through her grim expression for a moment, but then it's back to the serious business of outwitting our enemies.

Chapter 44

Once the others understand the plan, I take the rope and lead them outside like they're my own personal chain gang. We make it down the stairs and out to the sidewalk overlooking the parking lot without getting stopped. So far, so good. However, robed Neuists are spread out all over the place, escorting those who have already given up and beating the rest. Fortunately for us, the other druids are too busy with their own groups to pay any attention to mine.

My truck is parked in the second row closest to the building, so I take the group in its direction. When I get to the spot, I'm dismayed to discover it has been raised up on blocks. Tires are gone. Windows are smashed out. *Die, Christian Pig* is written in white paint across the driver's side. My insides sink at the sight of it.

"That's like your third vehicle in less than a year," Kylie whispers. "Remind me never to let you borrow my car."

"Speaking of ... even though yours is only a two-seater, we're all going to have to find a way to squeeze in."

"I'm sorry," Kylie says with a gulp, "I left my keys on the kitchen counter."

Her words send one of the women on the rope to the ground like a trembling bowl of gelatin.

"It's all right," Ed says, helping her back to her feet. "The keys to my van are in my left pocket. It's parked over by the library."

All heads swivel in the direction of the square building in the distance. It's a white cement structure, six stories high, and full of iridescent windows. On foot, the library is about ten minutes away. The sidewalk leading to it is thick with activity. Apparently out of options, I take the rope and head that way. I've only made it about ten feet when a group of six druids steps into the path. They're not bothering my group, though. They have stopped another couple of druids escorting a string of prisoners along the sidewalk.

This group of six seems to have authority over the other druids. The leader is a young woman with slick dark hair pulled back tightly in a bun. She stops in front of an unusually tall male student. It takes me a second to realize it's Evan Moore, the university's star basketball player. His hands are bound in front of him with plastic ties. That night after The Warning, I remember being surprised to hear him debate on the side that it had come from God. Up until then he had been known for his wild lifestyle.

"Who do you believe in, Evan?" a druid man among the six shouts up in his face.

"Jesus Christ is my Lord and Savior," Evan replies.

"Wrong answer." The woman with the slick black hair shoots him in the kneecap, making everyone in my group recoil. As he's writhing on the ground, she poses the question again: "Who do you believe in?"

"Jesus Christ is my Lord and Savior," Evan repeats, even more firmly than the first time.

"Some people only learn the hard way." She shoots him in the other knee. "One more time, who do you believe in?"

Helpless to intervene, all I can do is hold my breath and await his reply.

"Are you deaf, woman?" Evan refuses to relent. "I believe in Jesus Christ and there's nothing you can do to change that."

"Such a shame," she says, clicking her tongue like a teacher, giving a child a scolding. "All that ability wasted on a fool." A frown of matronly disappointment appears on her face as she shoots him in the forehead.

Ed lunges on the rope toward the druids who killed Evan. It takes all of the women on my rope to hold him back.

"Who's next?" the female executioner says politely, as if she's serving sandwiches behind a deli counter. Her little squad of druids brings her a barefoot young woman in a pajama shirt printed with coffee cups. The poor thing's teeth are chattering uncontrollably.

"Who do you believe in?" the executioner demands to know.

"Nobody," Coffee Cup says meekly.

"So far, so good," says the woman executioner. "Do you renounce God, under all His names, and under every creed?"

"I do," Coffee Cup says, tears flowing freely. "I renounce them all."

The others in line give the same response and they're ushered away off the lot. When the druids stop me and my hostages, it takes every ounce of willpower not to drop the rope and run away, leaving the others to fend for themselves. However, I could never live with that on my soul.

"Have these hostages been through phase two of the interrogation process?"

Feigning complete confidence in my authority, I toss my nose in the air and act miffed.

"How many times am I going to be stopped and asked the same damn question?" My lips tighten into a thin line of annoyance. "I have never seen such disorganization. Tell me, what are your names and who is your chapter leader?"

"Sorry, ma'am," says the druid. "Move along."

Still holding the rope, I force myself to lead my chain gangt at a casual pace, though what I really want to do is sprint to the library. The clock is ticking in my head, warning me time is running out. The longer we linger, the more likely it is that someone will see through our ruse. We get away from the main group of druids, but any one of them could call us back at any second.

We are about to cross a wide strip of grass when Miguel's red truck, with its open bed full of frantic-looking people, screeches to a stop in front of us. Druid heads are turning around to see the commotion. The passenger-side door opens. The interior is already jam packed with bodies. In the front seat, Miguel is behind the wheel, his hair damp with sweat.

"Get in!" he hollers.

"There's not enough room," Kylie hollers back, as we both glance back to see the druids moving in on us from all directions.

"We'll make room."

Kylie uncurls herself from the rope, gets out her switchblade, and starts to saw the others free. Danica is loosened first, then Ed. The other two women are still tied together, but that doesn't stop them from climbing into the back of the truck, while dozens of hands reach out to help haul them in. Ed urges Danica over the side of the truck bed, ignoring the complaints from the others that they're out of room.

"Don't let them get away!" a druid in the distance calls out to his buddies. "Stop that red truck!"

Chapter 45

Bullets ring out. Kylie falls forward, catching herself on the running board. A stain of blood is growing on the back of her white coat over her left shoulder blade.

"She's hit," I scream. "Oh, God. No!"

"Help her inside," Miguel yells. "Hurry!"

Ed and I lift her into the front seat, setting her across the laps of the other passengers. The woman in the middle is trying to stop the blood with a disposable diaper. Surveying the interior of the truck, I see a man cradling an infant in the backseat and quickly realize there is not an inch of room to spare.

"Go," I tell Miguel. "Get them out of here."

"I can't just leave you."

"Ed has wheels," I say, putting on a brave face to hide the wave of panic rising up within. "We'll catch up with you later."

Ed and I step back. Miguel doesn't waste any time, peeling out of the lot. A jeep and a blue sedan come roaring out of the dorm parking lot after them. Miguel floors it through a volley of gunfire. The back window shatters. I don't know who has been hit specifically, but even from here I can see the blood splatter. Forced to go into the grass, Miguel drives over the curb. A couple of passengers bounce out of the truck bed to be run over by the jeep. In the focus to stop the truck, the Neuist druids don't pay attention to the two of us on foot.

Grabbing hold of Ed's arm for show like he's my prisoner again, the two of us slink off in the direction of the library. We've made it about a hundred yards, when a cheery female voice makes me jump out of my skin.

"Gina." I spin around to see my friend Julie in a druid costume. "There you are—finally."

Unsure whether she is friend or foe, I halt warily in my tracks. Blood is smudged across her right cheek. She's wearing brass knuckles on her right hand. I'm not surprised to see a gun belt strapped around her waist. Banking that our friendship must count for something, I decide to stick around.

"Jerome and I have been worried sick about you," she says breathlessly as she dials her phone. Pointing to Ed with her head, she asks, "Who's this?"

"He's with me. What are you doing out here, Julie?"

"Looking for you." She says, seeming to not notice the condemnation in my voice. Speaking into her phone, she says, "I found her, Jerome. She's okay for now, but we need to get out of here fast if we want to keep it that way. Meet us over by the soccer field."

"Come on," she says, all smiles, like nothing has changed between us, and the morning is coming up daisies. "Let's blow this joint."

"Thanks, but Ed has a ride waiting for us at the library."

"Not a good idea." Julie informs, shaking her head, "That's Neuist headquarters."

"Julie." Her name tastes like milk that has gone sour. "I don't understand your part in all of this. If you're a Neuist, why are you helping a Christian?"

"If you're a Christian, why are you dressed like a Neuist?" she snaps back.

"It's a matter of survival, obviously. What's your excuse?"

"I'm a Neuist—true. But I am also your friend. After Brad disappeared, you were there for me and I want to return the favor, but we're running out of time. Are you coming or not?"

Torn between the affection I feel towards Julie, and the abhorrence over her affiliation with the enemy, my tongue ties itself into a knot.

"We're coming," Ed answers in the space of my hesitation. "Definitely."

She nods and motions for us to follow. We jog after her across another lot and over the soccer field, constantly looking over our shoulders. Now that we are in an open space, with no buildings to obscure the city in the distance, I can see that the pale morning skyline is dancing with flames. A helicopter is flying over the skyscrapers with its tail trailing black smoke. Orange flashes light up the city streets from grenades going off. A group of women runs past us in just their underwear, bloodied and screaming in terror.

Up ahead, a graphite blue Porsche is mowing through the grass to meet us. It rolls to a stop, giving me a clear view of Jerome behind the wheel. Julie yanks open the passenger door and slides the seat forward, ushering Ed and me into the back. She takes the front. My knees are squished against the seat in front of me. Poor Ed is even more scrunched than I am. He can't straighten his head because the car roof is in the way, but neither of us are complaining. We're just relieved to be on our way.

Jerome drives over the grass, then bottoms out on a curb to pull out onto the highway, music coming out of his car speakers. He turns it up, singing along to the lyrics as if we're just out to have a good time. Having spent the morning with Jack Daniels, he's swerving all over the road. Fortunately, there is very little traffic during the lockdown. While the young Neuist army is busy policing the town, everyone else is hunkered down in confusion.

"I love this song," he says, glancing back to smile at me, not seeming to notice that he has drifted into the other lane.

The radio display on the dash reads: Across the Line, by Linkin Park.

"How appropriate," I say scornfully. "Where are you taking us?"

"I'll explain when we get out of town."

"Why can't you tell me now?"

"Because I'm half-drunk and it's taking every bit of effort to stay between the dotted lines. So shut up and let me drive."

"Typical." I fold my arms and lean back with a grunt. "You can't even stay sober for your own revolution."

Julie turns around to grin, but I can't tell whether its from my comment or the situation in general. Either way the sight of someone acting happy with everything that's going on makes me sick to my stomach. Kylie was shot. I can't get the pain on her face out of my head. The sight of those people, falling out of the bed of the truck and getting run over will haunt me the rest of my days. Not to mention all the other violence I witnessed this morning and I doubt we have seen the worst of it. I just hope that Julie and Jerome will get us through.

The dash compass indicates we are moving west in the direction of Burlington. Good, but I'm sure Jerome's goal isn't St. Faustina of Divine Mercy Church. However, it's mine. Of course, I can't tell Jerome or Julie that. Who knows what they would do to the Christians hiding out there? The smudge of blood on Julie's cheek, clearly not her own, is a big clue.

After another ten minutes on the road, we come to a roadblock made of dump trucks. Men and women in military fatigues and red berets are patrolling the area. My thoughts go to Miguel. Did he get past the roadblock? He grew up in the area and is well-connected with the local Christian underground. If anyone could steer around it, I believe it would be him. But right now, I'm worried about me and the others in the car.

"Is that the old army or the new?" I ask from the backseat, voice trembling.

"The new," Jerome says. "I'm sure."

Feeling like a trapped animal in the cramped back seat, a whimper escapes my lips.

"Relax," Julie says. "You're with us."

Trying to conceal my face as much as possible, I readjust the cowl around my head. Ed and I clutch each other's hands for support. His palms are sweating profusely, but his face remains passive. Jerome rolls his Porsche to a stop. The soldiers approach both sides of the vehicle, big guns strapped over their shoulders.

"Good morning," the soldier says through Jerome's window. I notice his uniform sports the disturbing Neuist flag instead of the beautiful American one. The mere sight of it fills me with outrage, but my good sense, along with healthy amounts of fear, douses any desire to express it. "State your business." The soldier addresses Jerome, but Julie is the one who answers.

"The roundup at the university is nearly complete. We've been ordered to help at the Community College over in Cridersville."

"Let me see some IDs," the soldier says.

Jerome fumbles through his wallet, but Julie already has her card out. I can see it well enough to note that her photo is on it and it's not a state driver's license. The Neuist flag is embossed on the back. Seeing the identification cards already made and distributed, I wonder how long the Neuists have been preparing for this day. The soldier slides the edge of Julie's card through a portable scanner. Ten seconds later, he returns it.

"Thank you, ma'am."

They do the same with Jerome's card after he finds it. What am I going to do when they ask for mine? My throat is so tight, I can't even swallow. The soldier leans into the window to survey the back seat.

"ID, please."

"I'm sorry, sir," Ed replies. "It was in my robe. Those damn Christians tore it off me in a fight, and I didn't get it back."

The soldier studies Ed carefully. The swollen eye and dried blood adds credibility to his story.

"You should have seen the other guy," Julie says. "Ed's a true soldier for the cause."

I'm sweating buckets, waiting for my turn. But the soldier never makes eye contact. His gaze seems to glide right over me as he gives Ed one last glance and then a nod.

The soldiers step away from the vehicle and motion the car through the barricade. Stroking the fabric of the blanket, I'm beginning to think it really is Mary's mantle.

We hit three more roadblocks on the way out of the city. Each time, it's a repeat of the first stop. Soldiers scan Jerome and Julie's IDs, Ed explains his was lost in a fight, but nobody questions me or acknowledges my existence. By the third stop, Jerome and the others are grateful, but thoroughly puzzled by the way the soldiers continuously overlook me.

"How do you keep slipping under their radar?" Ed asks.

"If you must know," I say with a grin because there's no doubt my reply will irritate the snot out of them, "the Virgin Mary has turned me invisible."

"I can still see you," Jerome says dryly.

"And so can I," Ed agrees.

257

"She's yanking your chains," Julie chuckles and glances back at me. "Gina, you are so hilarious."

I smile back. If only she understood how serious I am, she wouldn't be laughing.

The road is relatively deserted, but not completely. Along the way, we go by an overturned semi-truck on the side of the road. As we drive along, we see cars and trucks stopped here and there along the highway, headlights on, doors wide open, but the occupants are gone. Three or four cars pass us by at wild speeds, like they're chasing each other. A parade of military vehicles rolls around us. We breathe a collective sigh of relief after they're gone.

About forty minutes out of the city, we pass the sign: Burlington: 10 mi. Where I normally veer to the left to get to St. Faustina's, Jerome veers to the right. My panic alarm goes off inside of my head. *Wrong way! Wrong way!* Leaning my body between the bucket seats, I ask Jerome, "Talk, mister. Where are you taking us?"

"My parents have a cabin up at Bear Lake."

"Why there?"

"It's isolated. Runs on a generator. There used to be good fishing up there before the comet strike, and maybe there still is."

"I don't know how to fish," I point out.

"I do," says Ed. "I'm an excellent fly fisherman."

"Was anyone talking to you?" Jerome says to Ed. "The only reason you're here is because …" He pauses to look at Julie. "Who is this asshole anyway?"

"I don't know—ask Gina."

"A friend," I reply.

"In strictly a platonic sense," Ed quickly adds as if he senses the Jerome's territorial feelings towards me. "I have a serious girlfriend."

"Good for you," Jerome says. He pauses to take a sip of whiskey. "The cabin is great, Gina. My father used to go up there whenever he got pissed off at my mother. In other words, he practically lived up there. You can stay until things settle down. I'll come visit you as often as I can and bring you supplies."

"You actually expect me to live alone in a log cabin?"

"Well, yeah."

"Where are *you* going to be while I'm growing old all alone in the woods like a hermit?"

"His country needs him here on the front lines," Julie says.

"And what country would that be?" I ask.

"The better one built upon the foundation of Neuist ideology."

"By better, you mean built upon the corpses of our president and anyone else who gets in the way of the Neuists," I say, not trying to hide my loathing. "Correct?"

"In the beginning, sacrifices will need to be made. As a Christian you well know that anything good always comes at the price of blood." Julie is so enamored with the righteousness of the cause, there's a glow about her as she speaks. "Fifty years from now," she goes on dreamily, "when the words *homeless, hungry* and *war* are just footnotes in history, our grandchildren will thank us. History is going to remember us as the founders of the greatest nation the world has ever known. It's a great honor to be a part of it."

"Is your ass jealous of the amount of shit coming out of your mouth?" I retort.

This time it's Jerome who turns back to grin at me.

"Ha, ha—very funny," Julie replies with an eye roll. "If only you could understand how religion creates division. Eliminating its expression is an essential step on the way to becoming a utopia."

"To know oneself is to disbelieve utopia," Ed adds his two cents. "That's a quote from the novelist, Michael Novak."

A flash of blue light engulfs the vehicle, followed by a boom like a thousand jets breaking the sound barrier. The car skids sideways, making me clutch the seat in front of me for dear life, as everyone screams.

Chapter 46

The Porsche slides into the grass and comes to a stop before we finish screaming. A tension-filled silence falls over us as the boom continues to rumble and reverberate through our bodies. Unsure whether it's thunder or a big bomb going off, I strain my ears to the wind until Ed breaks the moment.

"That wasn't normal lightning," he says to nobody in particular. "Did anybody else notice it was blue?"

"You stupid drunken idiot!" Julie yells and punches Jerome on the arm. "Why did you slam on the brakes like that?"

"I didn't," He yells back, holding the spot where Julie slugged him. "They locked up on their own for no reason." Eyes narrowing to slits, he adds, "And don't ever hit me like that again, bitch. Girl or not, I'll smash your face in."

"Oops." She glances down at the brass knuckles on her hand. "I forgot I was still wearing these. Sorry, dude."

There's another flash of blue light, followed by a crash of thunder that makes everyone jump. A moment later, the sky returns to the usual dusty beige color. Julie points to the east, saying, "Look over there."

Black clouds are rolling in, hugging the horizon like mountains of liquid asphalt hot out of the mixer, obscuring the bottom half of the rising sun.

"I've never seen clouds like those before," Ed comments. "They're so low and dark."

"Maybe it's fog," I suggest. "Except I thought fog was white."

"Haven't you ever heard of the phrase *lost in a gray fog*?" Julie says, shaking her head. "Duh."

"Everybody shut up for a second," Jerome barks. "My car stalled out. I can't hear the engine turn over while you're running your fat mouths." We all settle down as he tries the ignition again. Not even a click. He pounds on the steering wheel. "Dammit."

While Jerome is busy swearing at his Porshe, I'm secretly celebrating the fact that his car has stopped within walking distance of St. Faustina's. I mean, it's a very long walk, but well within my physical capabilities. Now to find an excuse to extricate myself from present company.

Giving up on starting the car, Jerome turns to Julie. "What do we do now, Miss Know-It-All?"

"I'll call Sam to send us a vehicle."

"But what about these two?" Jerome points at me and Ed in the backseat. "How are we going to explain them?"

"Leverage. If Sam turns in Gina, I'll turn in his brother," Julie says, smacking her cell phone. "Shit. It's not working. I bet that little skank on floor three broke my phone when she knocked me down the steps. I thought Christians were supposed to be all peaceable and meek and shit."

"I know a little bit about cars," Ed pipes-up beside me. "It could just be a loose connection. Pop the hood. I'll take a look."

"Okay, but if you fuck up anything," Jerome says, pulling on the hood release, "I'll line you up in front of the firing squad myself."

Everyone piles out of the car. The taint of ash is in the air. Could it be from all the fires burning in the city? The temperature feels like it has dropped twenty or thirty degrees since we got in the car at the university.

"Brrrr," Julie says, hugging herself, and stamping her feet to keep warm. "The weatherman said it was supposed get up into the fifties and stay there all week. It's freezing out here."

Pulling my robe closer for warmth, I survey the deep ditches that line both sides of the road. A tall chain link fence with a string of barbed wire across the top runs along the opposite bank. A plowed field stretches out beyond, but it hasn't sprouted anything except hearty weeds. Further out in the landscape are farm houses, a scattering of metal sheds, wooden barns, and neglected silos. It's going to be impossible to make a run for it without my companions noticing.

The wind is beginning to pick up, making it feel even colder as I consider my options. Ed sticks his head under the hood of the Porsche, while Jerome hovers over his shoulder. Taking out my phone, I hope to find an update from Kylie or Miguel. However, it seems to have gone dead. That's odd. It was fully charged when I woke up this morning.

"We need a jump or a new battery." Ed says, pulling himself out from under the hood. "Not even the tiniest spark. It's completely drained."

"That battery is only a year old," Jerome says. "Are you sure you know what you're doing?"

"I'm an electrical engineer—well, I will be soon. Trust me."

"Crap," Julie says, rubbing her hands rapidly together. "Is it my imagination or is it getting colder by the second?"

A jagged flash of red lightning tears across the horizon. The air turns scarlet for a moment, followed by a tremendous crash of thunder. A gust of strong wind stirs up the dust in the field, pelting us all with little shards of sand.

"Let's get back in the car," Jerome says.

"We're not going to last long at these temperatures," Ed says, while zipping his orange jacket higher. "Maybe we should head to one of those houses over there."

Another streak of lightning zigzags across the sky, followed by a deep rumble. The wind begins to howl.

"I agree with Ed," I holler over the wind. "With all the stuff going on, it might be a while before we get a jump. We could freeze to death before someone comes along to help."

In the distance, the black fog begins to unfurl like a sail across the field.

"That's weird behavior for clouds," Jerome says, a quiver creeping into his voice.

"Could it be smoke from a brush fire?" Ed suggests, furrowing his brow in puzzlement.

"There's barely any brush to burn, dumbass," Jerome quips.

"You're a dickhead," Ed says. Now that Jerome no longer has wheels and is useless to us, I guess Ed no longer cares about pissing him off. "Keep running your mouth like that and you'll quickly discover that real men don't need a firing squad to settle the score."

Jerome steps forward, trying to intimidate him with a fierce stare, an aggressive thrust of the shoulders. Instead of backing down, Ed takes a step forward as well, fists curled at his side.

As the two begin posturing, something about all of the strange occurrences gets my mind racing. A list forms in my head: 1) Lightning. 2) Thunder. 3) Sudden drop in temperature. 4) Loss of electricity. 5) Blackness to rival the angel of death passing across Egypt.

Fear blooms in my chest as I make the connection. These are the signs Kylie has talked about nonstop since The Illumination of Conscience. The dreaded darkness the prophets have spoke of from across the ages. And, wouldn't you know it, I'm trapped out in the open with a group of bickering morons. Ed and Jerome look like they are about to come to blows. Knowing that the gates of Hell are about to open wide, and time is running out for anyone caught outdoors, I step in between them.

"There will be none of that," I say, trying in vain to hold my voice steady. "The Three Days of Darkness are upon us. We need to find shelter fast."

"C'mon, Gina," Jerome says. "You can't honestly believe in that Three Days of Darkness bullshit."

"Look around," I say, waving my hand toward the approaching black. "Do you doubt your own eyes?"

"I'm not denying something strange is going on, but it has nothing to do with your lame Christian prophecies."

"Blessed are those who believe without seeing," Ed says. "And stupid are those who see and still don't believe."

"Stupid and dead," I add.

"Oh, I see how it is," Jerome snorts. "You always take every side except mine, Gina."

"It's not about taking sides," I reply in earnest. "The prophets said that anyone caught outside during the Three Days of Darkness, both the good and the bad, will die. Even if you don't believe me, the cold should be enough to convince you to go indoors. Let's start walking."

Julie opens her mouth to argue, but I don't wait around to listen. I take off toward the ditch in the opposite direction of the approaching fog, the mantle flapping around me. Afraid it will blow away, I hold a wad of fabric against my chest.

I'm the first of the four of us to slide down the side of the ditch. The wind is lighter down here. There's only a trickle of water at the bottom, so I'm able to leap over it with ease. Using the dead grass along the sides as handles, I pull myself up the steep bank to the other side.

The lightning is coming more frequently now, sending thunder crashing over the earth, as the others join me. Behind us the fog looks like a slow moving river of molasses, overflowing its banks. A thin layer drifts over my feet, sending a wave of cold malevolence up my ankles, stopping where it reaches the hem of Mary's mantle.

The four of us gather behind the barbed-wire-topped fence. At six feet tall, it seems even more insurmountable up close. A foreboding sound builds behind us like the approach of a thousand freight trains rolling down the tracks. Julie begins to lose it. Clutching at her ears, she screams.

Jerome suddenly rips Mary's mantle off of me and drapes it over the top of the fence. Fear explodes in my heart. Cold instantly penetrates my bones. Is this the terror the others are feeling without the mantle? He urges me over first. I climb and drop down to the other side. The others follow behind me. Jerome takes my hand, trying to whisk me across the field. I won't leave without Mary's mantle. I tug on it, but the fabric is hooked on the barbed wire. The fog is now billowing up to our knees. My companion's eyes widen and their breath quickens as the fog clings to our skin, awakening our sense of the supernatural.

"Forget about the stupid blanket," Jerome yells.

"No." I pull and tug, trying to fight off Jerome at the same time. I feel something slither across my feet and let out a yelp. "It's the only chance we have."

Behind us, a black stovepipe tornado appears. It breaks off into two, then three, then four different funnels, continuing until it grows into a forest of spinning vortices. Some are moving east, others west, spinning in every direction until the horizon is full of more than I can count.

"Oh, God," Julie cries out. "We're not going to make it!"

"There's something moving beneath the fog," Jerome hollers. "Holy, shit! Something bit me!"

"Beetles!" Ed cries out. He's frantically jumping around, looking fearfully down into the fog, trying to avoid something at his feet. "Millions of them!"

The others are beginning to panic. They're clawing at their own arms and legs, while I climb partway up the fence to free the mantle from the barbed wire. To my relief, it finally lets go. Dropping to the ground, I can't get it around me fast enough. As soon as I'm covered, the overwhelming sense of doom leaves. Naturally, I'm still scared, yet at the same time I feel motherly arms going around me in a protective embrace.

"Get them out of me," Julie screeches. "They're burrowing into my ears."

"Worms. So many worms!" Jerome is spinning in a circle, tearing the skin off of his face with his fingernails. "Wriggling into my brain!"

"Everybody," I yell over the tempest. "Get under the mantle. Hurry."

They ignore my frantic gesturing for them to join me. Instead, they take off running in three different directions.

"Listen to me,," I plead, dashing after Jerome. "This blanket was a gift from the Virgin Mary. She has promised to protect anyone who seeks refuge under her mantle."

He doesn't slow, but I keep following the best I can. "Wait up, Jerome." My heart quickens as he pulls farther and farther away, but then I realize why he's going so fast. A twenty-foot snake, which seems to be made of the fog itself, is skimming across the surface of the billowing blackness in pursuit of Jerome. As I try to catch up, it coils up his torso. Right before I get there, the snake divides in half to jam itself up into Jerome's nostrils. His eyes go wide and then flare with orange flames. He flails around in agony, holding his head, not seeming to find any relief. He gropes blindly at me, but I cringe away in horror.

Taking a moment to gather my courage, I move toward him to help. Up close, I see that his eyes have become as black as the fog. They look right through me. Nonetheless, I try to wrap him in the mantle, but that

265

makes him scream like I've poured acid on him. His skin smokes where the fabric touched it. He pushes me away, causing me to fall hard to the ground and let go of the mantle. Caught in the wind, it begins to tumble across the field. Scrambling to my feet, I stomp it down with one boot.

As I'm exposed to the blackness, I see a hairless white creature the size of a pony, with the head of a dragon. Long yellow claws protrude from its tapered paws. Membranous white wings are folded against its side. Its hellish orange eyes regard me with sudden interest and intelligence. I quickly gather up the mantle with trembling hands, cloaking myself under the blanket. The creature seems confused a moment, then turns its attention to something in the distance. It bounds across the field, spreads out its wings, and takes off into the air with a screech. Turning around, I see that Jerome and the others are gone, leaving me to face the growing darkness alone.

Chapter 47

As the fog envelops me, the sun is snuffed out like a flame. Terrifying sounds fill the air: banshees shrieking, chains clanking, and groans so hateful I'm sure an army of the damned has risen to seek revenge upon the living. It's as if the rusty gates of Hell have opened, spewing evil across the land. The lightning continues, but instead of giving my eyes a reprieve from the scourge, it serves to illuminates the monstrosities all around me in shades of wicked red.

Twisted animals scuttle around, ranging from the size of rats to larger than a house. Some look like dragons. Others primates. Many are a strange combination of different creatures. Broken lengths of chains attached to their limbs clatter along behind them as they pass me by. Their horrible screeching threatens to shred the little courage I have left. Not knowing what else to do, I begin to weave my way through them in the hopes of finding shelter.

The prophets said anyone who looks outside during the darkness will fall dead on the spot. I'm an anomaly walking among the damned, but even with the mantle's special protection, my breaths are growing shallow. A heart can't continue to pump at this rate without ripping itself apart. Kylie told me several times over that demons cannot enter a building where the faithful have lit a blessed candle. The candle will burn for as long as the darkness lasts and not even the wind can extinguish it. Knowing I can't survive out here much longer, my goal is the first place with a lit candle. However, a distressing thought occurs to me. The prophets instructed the faithful to not open the door for anyone because the demons will imitate the voices of loved ones in order to trick you into letting them inside.

I am so screwed.

Yet, I have to believe that Mary gave me her mantle for a reason. The thought helps me to keep pushing forward, but I have lost all sense of direction. Looking down during a lightning flash, I appear to be on a gravel road. A brown squirrel, of all things, scurries in front of me with a hickory nut in its mouth. It looks happy enough, as squirrels go. How odd that the demons don't seem to notice it. The next flash reveals a dozen tornadoes spinning on the horizon. If they get too close, I will surely die. All goes dark again, but I dare to press onward. When the gravel ceases to crunch beneath my boots, I realize that I've lost the road.

A few minutes later, the next strike reveals a meadow of dry weeds and grasses. All is dark again. Something huge is lumbering in my direction. Although I cannot see it, I know it's there because its every step sends vibrations through the soles of my feet. I hurry to get out of its way, moving blindly across the land, not knowing if I'm going to fall into a pond, or a ravine, or run into a devil.

My foot hits something big and soft, kicking my already rapidly beating heart into overdrive. Lightning flashes at the same time. When I see only a human body, its back snapped in half with spine protruding, I don't know whether to be relieved or to throw up. It takes me a moment to recognize the orange Dragon Ball Z jacket. It's undeniably Ed. *Please, no.* His eyes are not burned out the way Jerome's were. Nor is his skin burned. He's clutching a small prayer book. For me, this is enough reason to hope his soul escaped the torments of hell.

"You!" An accusing voice from behind makes me gasp and spin around. My eyes fall upon a man with his skin torn off who is crawling commando style through the dry grass. The rippling muscles of his torso are exposed along with shards of bones in his feet and hands. Black veins run over him like spider webs, but the most gruesome part is his head. It's a bare skull. The hollowed-out eye sockets burn red with pinpoints of white light for pupils. Suppressing a gag, I pick up the pace. When I look back, it's following me on all fours. None of the other beings have noticed me—why this one?

"Gina!" It calls my name in an all too familiar voice. "I saved you once, babe. Now it's your turn to save me."

I walk backwards, warily watching the skinless man draw nearer. "Stay away from me." This hideous thing cannot possibly be my handsome Jerome. "Don't you come any closer."

"Have you already forgotten me? I'm in so much pain. Please take off your mantle and help me."

The longer he talks, with all the familiar inflections, the more I'm convinced it's truly my ex-boyfriend. Moved with pity, I try to figure out how I might help. Against my better judgment, I allow the tormented man to approach. Streaks of fire fall from the sky like rain as his fingers slowly wrap around my ankle where the blanket doesn't reach. "Why did you forsake me?" he wails with anguish so deep it chips away at my sanity. "You knew the fate of those who reject God, but you didn't try to warn me. Don't you know that I loved you with every inch of my flesh? I would have poured out my last drop of blood for you. But you repaid me with indifference."

"I'm sorry this has happened," I cry, trying to shake him off of my ankle. "But I did try to save you—don't you remember that conversation we had back in my dorm room?"

"One conversation for a priceless soul? Woe upon my selfish lover!" He lets out a wail, digging his boney digits into my flesh. "If only I could be unborn!"

"Let go of me, Jerome," I plead through hot guilty tears. "Please, you're hurting me."

"You don't know the meaning of hurt until everything good is torn out of your soul." Suddenly, he tightens his grip around my ankle and yanks me toward him. I fall onto my back, the breath knocked out of me. "You whore, I'll tear you apart!" He tries to rip the mantle away. I clutch onto it with all my might. As soon as his fingers touch it, he begins to sizzle and smoke all over. A howl of agony escapes his mouth. Seeing my chance, I break free to scramble to my feet and sprint away. His maddening screams follow me through the darkness.

"I hate you, Gina Applegate!" Jerome calls after me. "Damn you to the deepest pit of Hell, with the devil and his angels, where the worm dies not!"

Pulling the mantle tightly around me, I stagger on ahead, regretting my many failings, especially where Jerome was concerned. After I had found the light again, I avoided my ex-boyfriend because it was easier that way. If only I had tried harder to convince him about God maybe he could have been saved. After awhile his screams fade away and my thoughts turn to other people I care about. Did Aunt Viv and my cousins find shelter in time? Then there's my dearest friend, Kylie. To suffer the darkness with a bullet in your back, her chances are slim. What about my former coworkers and Eric's family? I don't even want to think about Julie.

When the lightning flashes, I see the line of tornadoes is still there. I keep waiting to be swept away, but the funnels never seem to get any closer. Part of me wishes they would finally come and do me in. I'm mentally and physically exhausted. My hands and feet are numb from the biting cold. It's only a matter of time before I lose my grip on the mantle. I'd rather be taken by the wind than devoured by demons. Feeling death is inevitable, I'm seriously considering giving up when the playful barking of a dog grabs my attention. How can such an ordinary sound bring so much consolation? I strain to figure out where it's coming from. A moment later, a black and white pit bull terrier trots up to me, wagging its tail like everything is normal. A name is embroidered on his collar: Rigby. The demons don't seem to notice the dog, nor the dog the demons. It's as if Rigby cannot see the hell laid out in front of him. Could it be possible that animals, who are devoid of sin and immortal souls, would be unaffected by everything going on?

"It's a good day to be a dog," I tell Rigby, leaning down to pat his head. *Oh, goodness.* He is so warm and soft. The mere act of touching him is like a balm to my soul. I get down on one knee to hug him to my chest. He seems to be enjoying the attention until a rabbit hops across the path. The excited dog rips himself out of my arms to shoot after it. Come back, Rigby!" I cry, as he is swallowed up in the black. "Please don't leave me!"

Even though the dog doesn't return, meeting him has bolstered my spirits. The brief encounter has reminded me that the darkness isn't going to win. For three days the world will be blind, but then the light will return. A question hits me from out of nowhere. What's the world going to be like on the fourth day? I have no idea, but my curiosity has awakened. Clutching the mantle tighter, I continue on my way.

The land transitions into a scraggly forest. The lightning is almost constant. Fierce winds batter me with leaves and twigs. I have come to accept a million unthinkable horrors in these days of darkness, but when the land breaks into a clearing I cannot believe my eyes. A black humanoid creature taller than the trees is standing in the meadow, fanning its enormous wings. Its arms are powerful. Its chest broad. The face is like a man's, but unnaturally angular, as if cut from rock. Twenty or more protruding yellow horns encircle its skull like a crown. Curling a great fist to the heavens, it speaks in a guttural language, each word a crash of thunder.

Thinking it might be Lucifer himself, my blood pools in my feet, making me feel faint. He's crying out in different languages, most of which I don't recognize. However, I catch pieces of Latin, Spanish and Mandarin. When he gets around to using English, I realize it's a cry of prideful disobedience. "I will not bow down to flesh, Man-God!" The malice in his voice causes me to fall down into the fetal position, completely covering myself with Mary's mantle. I sense all manner of creatures passing by, because their hatred is a penetrating stench like sulfur and brimstone. Some of the demons are so large that the ground shakes with their every step. Others are small like buzzing flies.

I don't know if the demon parade has gone on for minutes or hours, time passes by differently amid the fury. However, I do know my body has reached the limit. No matter how afraid I am, it needs to sleep. Afraid of letting go of the mantle and having it blow away, I fight the urge to succumb. Daring a peek, I see with relief that the huge demon is gone, but my plight is far from over. More devils than ever are gathered in the area. They're cackling and howling, biting and clawing each other, fighting over the bodies of the dead. One of the damaged corpses is female with long legs and silky blonde hair. Realizing it could be Julie, my eyes well and I stifle a sob, while the demons cackle all around me. They seem to take great pleasure in tearing apart human flesh and gnawing the bones. I watch them play tug-o-war with the body of an old man until his head comes off. They scamper around, fighting over it like a prize. Unable to take it any longer, I lower the mantle.

If they find me, they'll torture me for sure. Oh, my Jesus. I am so afraid. Have mercy on me and the whole world. Finding the string rosary in my pocket, I pray to ward off the madness. *Holy Mary, Mother of God, pray for us sinners, now and at the hour of our death.* I go around the beads several times, but it's not enough to drown out the sounds of hell coming through the fabric. Just when my last thread of sanity is about to unravel, an unexpected flutter of gold and white catches the corner of my eye.

It's a beautiful winged creature no bigger than my hand, a glowing butterfly. I marvel that it has found its way beneath the mantle and instantly know it's something special. Holding out my hand, it lights on my index finger. Wherever its dainty feet touch, warmth seeps into me, pushing away the gloom in my soul. The scent of baking bread, vanilla and laundry soap accompany its arrival. If hatred can take demonic form, why not love on a set of butterfly wings? I believe with all my heart that Grammy's prayers have sent down an angel to lead me to safety.

Reverting to using the mantle as a traveling cape, I rise to my feet. The delicate butterfly flutters with grace and strength. The gusts of wind that threaten to knock me off my feet seem to have no bearing on its flight plan. I follow the glowing butterfly for what feels like a mile or two, ignoring the shadows constantly crossing over our path. In the onyx fog, my steps are surer with Grammy's butterfly prayers to guide me.

After what seems a short time, the lightning flashes over a long street, casting the mammoth buildings on either side in a blood-red glow. We're here, I realize to my great relief, in Burlington, on the street of churches where St. Faustina of the Divine Mercy stands in magnificent splendor.

As we pass the different denominations along the road, their steeples look longer and sharper than I remember. The windows are darker and more uninviting. The storm rattles them, while the trees along the sidewalks bend deeply, their bare branches sweeping the ground. My original plan was to take shelter in the first building I found. However, the butterfly keeps going. It has guided me true thus far, so I decide to continue to follow. We pass the Baptist church, a Pentecostal church, a

272

Jehovah's Witness temple, an Episcopal church, a Jewish synagogue, Baker Street Second House of God, Baker Street First House of God, and a Greek Orthodox. There's the Lutheran church, right across the street from St. Faustina of the Divine Mercy. Finally.

In the howling winds, the butterfly guides me to the handrail and up the steps to the center set of double doors at the front entrance. I pound on them until my voice grows hoarse. "Let me in! It's Gina Applegate! Kylie, are you in there? Miguel? Seriously, it's me! I'm not a demon! Please, help me!"

Even if they can hear over the roar of the wind, and all of the annoying moaning coming from the damned, nobody is going to open the doors after the prophets have warned them not to. Can't say that I blame them.

The butterfly hovers around my dejected head. I talk to it, saying, "Surely, you didn't bring me all this way to let me die on the doorstep. Show me what to do."

The butterfly lights on the set of doors to my right. I pull the metal handle. To my shock, it gives. I open it a little way, then the wind gusts extra hard. The door flings open to repeatedly bang against the wall. Worried about letting demons into the church, I grab for the door to get it under control. In my efforts, I fail to hold onto the mantle, and the wind tears it off of my body. It's as if the darkness itself suddenly sees me and a hateful roar rises up over the wind. Just when I thought the world couldn't get any scarier, a nebulous blob of smoky tentacles rushes at me from the street. The mantle flaps in front of the blob, holding it at bay just long enough for me to grab the door handle. I hurry inside and slam it shut. Whoa, that was close! Leaning against the door, I try to catch my breath, feeling like a soldier who dropped her shield in the middle of a great battle. I can't believe I lost the mantle. What a tragedy. Nonetheless, I feel victorious for having made it to the church in one piece.

It's so much quieter here, like a different world. For the first time since the darkness descended, I am breathing a little easier. Lingering against the door inside the vestibule, that narrow empty space between the exterior and interior doors, I take inventory of the situation. I didn't realize how parched I've become until now. Swallowing is difficult and painful. As I glance around for a water fountain, my eyes land on the fat candle burning on a stand. Despite the gust of wind when I entered, the flame is still burning strong. *It must be blessed,* I think in wonder. If it wasn't so hot and melty, I'd kiss it.

Remembering the butterfly, I glance around, hoping it is still with me. No sign of it. I'm disappointed, but what I really need now is a drink. I strain to push through the interior doors into the main area of the building. They seem to be stuck, so I grunt and strain until one of them opens with a loud bang that echoes through the cavernous church. Candles are burning along the edges of the vast interior, barely illuminating the place, but compared to outside it's a sunny day in Disneyland. The shadowy pews appear to be empty.

"*Kyrie eleison.*" A male voice shouts in my ear, making me jump. "God, our Lord, King of ages, All-powerful and All-mighty, we beseech You to make powerless, banish, and drive out every diabolic power, presence, and machination."

Dozens of human-shaped silhouettes begin to slink around me in a half-circle. Afraid that the church is already infested with demons, I back up against the door, crying out, "Jesus, deliver me!"

Chapter 48

The silhouettes appear to be holding crosses. Before I can process what I'm seeing, a blast of wetness douses me in the face.

"Burn, monster," someone yells. "Burn!"

Before I can catch my breath, the shadows lunge and pummel me with their crosses.

"Ow!" I wildly fling my fists, hitting flesh and bone. A lantern is brought into the area, giving me a better look at my attackers. I quickly realize they're humans, not demons. "What are you doing? Stop it!"

"Take that, spawn of Satan!"

"For the love of God," I manage to yank a cross out of the hands of a teenage girl before she strikes me in the head. "I'm human. Quit hitting me!"

"Step back," a man's voice comes from the dark. "Give it some space."

"I don't think it's a demon," a woman says. "The holy water didn't faze it."

"Devils are deceivers," a male says. "They can take any form they want, so don't be fooled. Push the thing back outside before it can do any damage."

"It called on Jesus," a woman argues. "I don't think a devil would do that."

"What do you know about it, Caroline?" a man retorts.

"Look," Caroline says, pointing at my wrist. "She's clutching a rosary."

"You're telling me someone survived out there for two whole days?" a different woman says incredulously. "Impossible."

"I swear to God, I'm not a demon." My legs feel so weak, I slide down the door to sit on the floor. "My name is Gina Applegate. I'm just a regular person. Please, don't hurt me. I've been caught out there in the black for far too long. I beg you, give me shelter."

The people are shifting uncomfortably, muttering amongst themselves.

"Oh, dear," says an elderly woman, "I think we've made a terrible mistake."

"But it cried out in pain when we hit it with the crosses," says a young man standing near my head. "It's a she-devil, I tell you."

I clunk him across the knee with the cross in my hands.

"Ouch," he grunts. "That hurt!"

"I know," I reply in aggravation, hoping I've made my point. "So knock it off, you gimp."

A couple of gray-haired guys begin to chuckle. I take it as a good sign that they're starting to believe me. "Water," I say, as I finally give into the exhaustion I've been fighting off for hours or possibly days. "Please, I haven't had a drop since this whole thing started."

"Here comes Dr. Castor," the gimp says, stepping aside with the others. "If you don't have a heartbeat, you'll be really sorry."

Too tired to make a witty comeback or rise to my feet, I'm feeling woozier by the second. I can barely hold my head up as the crowd gathers around.

The doctor kneels next to me to check my vitals. In less than a minute he announces, "Definitely human—badly dehydrated and going into shock. Don't just stand there being useless, folks. Somebody bring a drip from my stash and a blanket."

Now that the doctor is on my side and I know that I'll be safe for awhile, my muscles go limp and every thought slips away.

When I come to again, the last thing I remember is being beaten to the floor with crosses. The storm is still raging, but the interior of St. Faustina's is peaceful, filled with the sound of chanting.

"Death to humanity," a band of demons to the north screeches from outside. "Fade, the sons of Lucifer, shall rule forevermore."

"No!" cries a group of demons from the opposite side of the building. "Legion! Legion!"

Furious roars rise up as if the demons are now battling each other. Thanks to the protective walls of the church, I am somewhat able to ignore the noise and concentrate on better things. I'm in a small room with dozens of chairs facing a wall made of glass, looking out into the main area of the church. A knee-high ledge runs along the bottom. Six lit candles in glass cylinders are set along its surface. Short pews line the side walls. This is the cry room, I realize. It's a place for parents to take unruly children so they don't disturb the Mass. I'm lying on one of the miniature pews with a tube duct-taped to my hand. Following the tube with my eyes, I see it's connected to an I.V. bag hung on a metal coat rack.

Some thoughtful person has slid thick woolen socks onto my feet to keep them warm. My boots are on the floor next to the pew. Grammy's rosary is around my neck. I reach for it automatically and hold onto it like a lifeline. Thunder repeatedly rattles the building. It takes me all this time to notice that the pillow under my head is Kylie's lap. She looks down at me with that wry smile I've come to appreciate.

Sitting up with a start, I throw my arms around my friend, only to have her flinch away. In my exuberance, I failed to notice that her left arm is in a sling.. "I'm so sorry," I say, ashamed that for a second I had forgotten about her getting shot.. "Are you okay?"

"Sore," she says. "But beyond thrilled you're alive. We are truly family, you know."

"Without a doubt," I reply with tears of gratitude welling in my eyes. "If you were a blood sister, I couldn't love you anymore than I already do."

We grip each other's hands for a moment and the subject quickly shifts to what happened after we parted ways during the Neuist takeover. She tells me Miguel got them to safety by taking a bunch of back roads. Even then, they were forced to blow through a roadblock. In the process, three passengers were killed. Miguel was shot in the left shoulder—same as her, which proves they're soul mates, according to Kylie.

When I inquire about Danica, I'm relieved to find out that she made it to the church as well. Kylie tells me our auburn-haired classmate came into the cry room a dozen times while I was sleeping, hungry for news about Ed. The mention of his name makes my throat ache. I lower my head, while my hands clamp over my eyes in a futile attempt to block out the memory of his broken body.

"The demons got him, Kylie," I wail, head shaking vigorously from side-to-side. "I can't tell her that. I just can't. I can't. I can't. I can't."

"Calm down, Gina." Kylie takes my chin in hand, forcing my head to still. "Look at me." I slowly open my eyes. "You don't have to be the one to tell her. We can have someone else break the news. If that's what you want."

"Yes. Someone else. Not me. I can't."

Kylie moves onto another topic. She informs me that there are 508 people taking shelter here in St. Faustina's. We have two doctors and a dozen nurses among us. The same doctor who helped me is the one who took the bullet out of her shoulder. The injury was not life-threatening, but nobody will be out of harm's way until the storm passes.

The horde outside is getting louder and angrier. Mostly, the demons speak in strange tongues. Occasionally, however, they cry out blasphemies against Jesus, the Virgin Mary, and humankind in recognizable languages. Inside of the church, the people continue to chant and pray. The sound of the rosary is constantly going up from one side of the church. *Oh my Jesus, forgive us our sins, lead all souls to heaven, especially those in most need of thy mercy* … On the other end of the church, people are singing, *For the sake of His sorrowful Passion, have Mercy on us, and on the whole world.*

"Everyone is taking shifts so that the air will be filled with around-the-clock petition and praise," Kylie informs me. "The faithful are creating a force field of prayer to keep the evil at bay."

"Are these the same 'faithful' who tried to beat me to death with crosses?"

"Understand, your arrival created quite the panic. They thought a demon had found its way inside."

Two priests in black and white collars knock on the open door to the cry room. The one on the left looks old enough to poof into dust at any second. His beard is gray and wispy, but his eyes are golden brown and intelligent, reminding me of a wolf's. Come to think of it, I've seen him somewhere before. Oh, yeah—television. The local channels have interviewed him many times. It's Bishop Crowley, the man in charge of the entire diocese. The younger priest is well over six feet tall. Wide at the shoulders. Trim at the waist. Brown hair cut close to the scalp. Behind wire rimmed glasses, his inquisitive dark eyes study me with intensity. I can't decide if he looks more like a scholar or a linebacker.

Kylie waves them both into the room. "Come meet Gina." Her voice is upbeat as she arcs a hand toward the older of the two. "This is Bishop Crowley." Then she points to the younger man. "And, this is Father Kramer. You've probably heard me talk about him at home."

"Yes," I nod. "You're the priest in charge of the Shelter Me program."

"That's me," he says with a grin while turning a couple of chairs around to face me. "It's nice to meet you, Gina."

The bishop lowers himself into the chair on the left. He leans back, arms crossed over his chest with a scowl on his lined face. Father Kramer sits down in the chair to his right and reaches out to take my hand. He shakes it warmly, while Kylie excuses herself to let me talk to them alone.

"Everyone is eager to know your story," says Father Kramer. "Myself included."

Bishop Crowley joins in. "Your survival goes against every prophecy. For the folks who believe you were hiding out in the basement all along and only pretended to come through the doors, what do you have to say?"

"Nothing."

"You aren't going to try to defend yourself?"

"Convincing fools to think logically takes more energy than I care to spare. So, no."

Father Kramer chuckles. The Bishop grunts at him in irritation, causing the younger man to turn off his laughter. Bishop Crowley wastes no time and starts tossing out questions.

"If you were outside in the poisoned atmosphere as you claim, why didn't it kill you like everyone else?"

I proceed to tell them about Mary's mantle. How it was given to my beloved grandmother straight from Our Lady's hands during The Warning. "Mary's mantle shielded me from the Neuists," I explain. "And, later, the powers of hell itself."

He presses me for more information about my journey through the demon-infested darkness. However, the wounds are too fresh. Staying engaged in the conversation will force me to revisit the nightmare and I'm not ready to do that. My eyes dart from the bishop, to the priest, and then to the window overlooking the main part of the church where dozens of teenagers have been walking past, back and forth, the entire time. The youths are trying to be subtle, but it's obvious their goal is to catch a glimpse of me. I make eye contact with a girl on the other side and refuse to look away. She yelps and runs off like I'm the boogeyman, which I find extremely annoying.

"They act as if I'm a tiger in a cage."

"Kids will be kids," Father Kramer says apologetically, motioning for the teens to go away. "They want to meet the woman who walked through the fires of hell and lived. Your arrival has become a welcome distraction."

Due to the priest's gestures, waving the teens away from the cry room, and the deepening frown of the bishop, which he has directed through the window, the foot traffic begins to disperse. Now that things are more private again, I go on to tell them about the angelic butterfly that led me to the safety of the church. Throughout my story, Bishop Crowley's arms remain crossed over his chest, giving me the sense that he's rejecting every word I say. In contrast, Father Kramer is on the edge the seat, apparently enraptured by my tale of woe.

I wrap up the horror story with my entrance into the front doors of the Church of Divine Mercy. Am I naive to hope that the bishop will follow up with comforting words or advice on how to cope? Yes, I am.

Because all he offers is a judgmental glare and a roll of the eyes. So I turn to the parish priest instead. "Do you believe me, Father Kramer?"

"Absolutely." He pauses to wipe his glasses on his shirttails and speaks in an unrushed fashion while doing so, as if every word is a carefully thought-out choice. "The protective power of Mary's mantle is well-known. It's a tradition that goes all the way back to the early church, symbolic of Mary's motherly embrace. Today it has been brought to the literal level."

"I promise you, every word I said was true."

"You survived the darkness," Father Kramer says. "That's proof enough for me."

"She's lying!" Bishop Crowley explodes. "Demons aren't real-life characters. They're archetypes of rebellion. Mere symbols."

Father Kramer's jaw drops open, but he makes a quick recovery. "With all due respect, Your Excellency," he says. "Do you not have eyes? Do you not have ears? If not demons, who do you think it is outside of these walls, seeking to destroy us?"

A heated debate breaks out between the religious on the existence of evil, stirring up fresh memories I'd rather forget. I close my eyes tight, trying in vain to blot out images that are going to haunt me forever. Grasping my head in hands, I rock back and forth, mumbling the Hail Mary at a hundred-miles-per-hour. My sudden breakdown surprises even me, but I can't seem to stop.

Kylie returns in the nick of time with a bottle of sports water and a granola bar. Her shocked expression at all of our behaviors quickly morphs into anger directed at the clergymen. "Enough!" she raises her voice over their argument. "Look at what you're doing to Gina!"

The debate instantly dies. Seeing a friendly face restores my grip on reality. She sits beside me and wraps an arm around my shoulders. The rocking stops, but my muscles continue to quiver. The men stand up, explaining they need to prepare for the Easter Vigil Mass.

I'm relieved when they finally leave. Kylie rubs my back, telling me to trust in the Lord. This trial will soon pass and everything will be okay in the end. Feeling a little better, I inquire about the whereabouts of the monsignor from Africa who heard my confession awhile back. She tells me he was called home last week for a family emergency. Realizing how much I owe him for getting me right with God faster than I had planned, I say a prayer for his safety. Kylie and I sit quietly together for a few minutes until she asks if I feel up to helping with food preparations. "There's going to be a meal in the church basement after the Easter Vigil," she explains. "The cooks could use an extra hand."

My feet are blistered from all the walking, but I want to be around other people. "Food," I reply. "Count me in." After I slip into my boots, the two of us head out of the cry room and through the church, down a narrow staircase off to the side of the sanctuary.

The basement is full of candles, so the lighting is pretty good considering the circumstances. Four men are playing Euchre at a card table. A couple of old ladies are teaching a group of teenagers how to play Five Card Stud. Young kids are chasing each other around. Kylie leads me through a large scattering of musical instrument cases, explaining that two busloads of public high school kids were on the way to an orchestra performance when the uprising began. Since they couldn't return home during the lockdown, Father Kramer offered them the church basement, and that's where they were when the darkness arrived. Now I understand why there's an overabundance of young people on the premises.

I follow Kylie through a door into a back room full of supplies: giant boxes of pretzels, chips, cereal, powdered milk, canned goods, plastic bags of unconsecrated communion wafers, and a storage locker full of wine. It looks like a lot, but she informs me it's only enough to keep everyone fed for a couple of weeks. Therefore, we have to keep the Easter celebration simple. She sends me out to a group of middle-aged women who are preparing the meal. My job is to keep stirring a big pot of canned baked beans. It sits on a rack above a dozen presumably blessed candles. Over to my left, a couple of women are trying to steam stale dinner rolls they found in a cupboard. While I stir, my eyes go over to the big boxes marked potato chips. I hope they open them tonight.

Across the basement, people are setting up tables. Kylie and Michael, both of them with their left arms in slings, are working together to spread white linens over tabletops. Watching them struggle to do everything one-handed is kind of amusing.

While working and chatting with the ladies, I learn that, in addition to the high school orchestra, numerous random families and individuals who just happened to be near Burlington at the time, ended up taking shelter at the church. Many of them aren't Catholic, so they have kindly volunteered to tend to the food and finish the preparations while the rest of us head up for Mass.

Upstairs in the main church, the number of candles has tripled, giving me a better view of the life-sized bronze statues of St. Joseph and Our Lady, flanking the huge crucifix on the wall behind the altar. They're both standing in prayerful poses with their hands folded. I can't help wondering about the real St. Joseph and Virgin Mary. Are they sad for us or do they think humanity is finally getting what it deserves?

Letting Miguel take the lead, and then Kylie, I file into a pew with them at the middle of the church. Kneeling down, I pray for the Lord's continued protection, and then slide back into the seat. People continue to straggle up from the basement and elsewhere. The church still feels empty when the entrance hymn begins to bellow from the pipes in the choir loft above. Not expecting any music beyond our voices today, I startle at the intrusive sound. It must be an old style organ to not need any electricity.

Three altar servers in white robes walk in first, one in the middle with a cross on a pole, the other two holding candles, followed by the lector with a golden Bible hefted above her head. Behind her walks Father Kramer in white vestments, followed by the bishop. I'm surprised he's wearing a robe the color of merlot, trimmed in gold, with a shepherd's staff in his hand. When I used to go to church with my family, priests normally wore white or gold on Easter.

As the Mass begins, the storm seems to increase in fury. Having taken comfort in the rosary while I was out in the darkness, I realize it has replaced the gun as my weapon of choice. I wrap it around my hand, ready to defend myself with the beads as if they were bullets. The bishop steps up to deliver his sermon. He has to yell to be heard over all the wind and thunder. Expecting a heartfelt talk about everything that's going on, I'm disappointed when his homily is a generic speech about not judging our neighbors. Red flashes of lightning are happening every few seconds. I don't want to leave, but my bladder won't hold out much longer. Whispering in Kylie's ear, I let her know that I have to step away.

By the time I return, Bishop Crowley is holding the chalice above the altar. I hesitate at the back, waiting for a less profound part of the service to return to my seat. When Bishop Crowley lowers the chalice, I hurry up the aisle to rejoin Kylie and Miguel. I'm halfway there when I notice the statues of Mary and Joseph. Their arms are lifted to the heavens as if they've given up on this sinful world and are imploring God to end it once and for all. Squinting at the statues, I could swear that their hands were folded in prayer when I first laid eyes on them. The frightened gasping and pointing coming from the congregation tells me that they have noticed the changing poses as well. As I'm frozen in the aisle, trying to make sense of it, the ground beneath my feet begins to shake.

Unsure what to do, everyone turns to our religious leader for direction. The terrified look on Bishop Crowley's face isn't reassuring. Huge cracks begin to form in the ceiling. The bishop responds by hefting up his robes and taking off down the center aisle. When I try to block his escape route, he shoulders me out of the way. I stumble, but manage to stay on my feet.

"You're the shepherd of this flock," I call after him in desperation, as the shaking of the building grows in intensity. "Please, don't abandon us."

Paying me no mind, the bishop runs away, continuing through both sets of doors to the outside, exposing the faithful to the maelstrom. Pieces of plaster and brick begin to rain down on top of the altar and pews, crushing people beneath them. The storm has come in, flooding the church with demonic shrieks and darkness. The entire roof collapses.

Chapter 49

Expecting to wake up on the other side of the veil, I find myself in the quiet dark with a kink in my neck. Sharp and bumpy objects are poking along every inch of my body. Grammy's rosary remains wound around my wrist. I'm in a moderate amount of pain, not enough for me to think I'm in hell, but I feel lousy enough to know I haven't landed in heaven, either. Stings cover my skin. Every movement takes effort because my muscles are stiff and uncooperative. Biting back the discomfort, I worm my way through a mountain of rubble as it shifts and groans. After all I've been through, it would be just my rotten luck to die from getting bonked in the head with a stray brick.

Streaks of light begin to show through the debris, giving me hope. As soon as I break free, I'm hit with what surely must be a spotlight. Throwing my arms up to shield my eyes, I lose my balance and tumble down a slope of broken concrete to land on my back with an *oompf.* My vision quickly adjusts to the intense light. Rolling to my feet, I cautiously stand to take in my surroundings.

The darkness is gone and, to my astonishment, so is the dust that's been hanging in the atmosphere for years. The sun is rising in a fantasy skyline of turquoise swept with wispy pink and golden clouds. The marvelous sight makes me forget how to breathe for a second. However, the church will never be the same. The walls are twisted metal girders. Mounds of brick, wood, metal, and glass are scattered all over the place. All that's left is its foundation.

Worse than the destruction of the building is the sight of arms, legs, and faces protruding from the rubble. Unable to bear the thought that Kylie and Miguel are among the dead, I turn my head away with a sob.

After the initial shock subsides a little, I find my voice to call out their names. The reply is deafening silence.

Dazed and confused, covered in powder from the pulverized building, I wander out of what's left of the church. When I step onto the lawn, I note that the grass has turned from brittle brown straw, into a lush green groundcover. Branches litter the ground, but other than that the trees appear to be okay. In fact, they are bursting with healthy buds. Along the sidewalk, a hedgerow of weeping white spirea are in full bloom. Yellow dandelions have popped up overnight as if to say, *Hello, Springtime!* The temperature feels perfect—like soothing bathwater. The scent of honeysuckle and lilacs drifts to my nose. My senses go from one beauty to another, while my mind tries to make sense of it all.

In contrast, as far as the street and manmade structures go, it's an endless scene of destruction. Except for two or three homes in the distance, the entire town seems to have been leveled.

Other survivors are beginning to emerge. Young and old, they are quietly wandering around, gathering together into small groups. Our awareness of one another is somehow heightened. It's as if we know each other's thoughts without having to say a word. And we simply understand that the storm was not confined to our area. It was worldwide. Every city has been laid to waste. The few of us that remain will spend our lives picking up the pieces.

A dust-covered boy, maybe eight or nine years old, tugs on my shirt and points to the east behind me. His eyes are shining with awe. I turn around to see what has captured his attention. As I gaze into the horizon, my heart skips a beat. Jesus Christ, in all His luminous glory, is hovering in the sky. Bigger than the mountains. Wearing billowing red and blue robes. Rays of red and white light radiate from His chest, hands, and feet, washing me clean, giving the world new life.

At this moment, I no longer envision Jesus Christ as the hippie god invented by my own imagination. For the first time, I see Him as the The Holy of Holies. The Mighty King of Kings. The Immortal and Everlasting God. However, unlike during The Warning, I am not afraid, and my heart is expanding with joy beyond anything I've ever known.

I feel the Creator's love transfuse me, the undeserving creature, and happiness is finally mine. His Divine Will has set my soul aflame. Reverential awe drops me to my knees. The spirit leaps inside me in thanksgiving. I feel myself plunged into an infinite well of forgiveness. It's so wonderful, more than this frail body can contain. Should it go on much longer, my heart shall burst and die of Love.

In mix of relief and disappointment, the experience begins to ebb. A sobering thought comes to mind. *The world should have ended, but didn't. Why?* My connection with the people around me is still there, so I'm aware that they are wondering the same thing.

In answer to our question, a gigantic brown rosary materializes around Jesus like an oval frame, with the attached cross suspended below his feet. An understanding beyond words passes through me. The world was spared because the prayer of the saints drew down His Unfathomable Mercy. As the vision of Jesus begins to fade away, He infuses me, and all of the survivors, with the task of rebuilding civilization, based on what we have witnessed here today. Going forward all shall be for the glory of God. Subsequently, we will not go down in history as the Generation of Fading Light. Our children's children will remember us as the Peacemakers.

Chapter 50

The vision of Jesus Christ, the Divine Mercy, eventually dissolves from sight, but His love remains in our hearts, infusing all of creation with a heavenly light. A new era has begun, but what does that mean exactly?

There are maybe a hundred of us left standing around, talking in hushed tones, considering how to proceed. Glancing down the road to the north, there's a group of thirty or so people, some of them little children, walking down the street toward St. Faustina's. From the south there's another group of about the same size. For the most part, they look just like us—covered in dust, shell-shocked, and bedazzled all at the same time. A distinguished-looking man with salt-and-pepper hair approaches from the group on the left. He can't seem to pull his gaze away from the rosary clutched in my hand. Several of the men from the group on the right are wearing brown beanies—kippahs, I think. They stop in front of me, pointing at my rosary, and seem to be having some kind of debate amongst themselves.

"I'm Reverend Arthur Percell," the man with the salt-and-pepper hair speaks first and offers me his hand, "from the Episcopal church down the road. Is one of your priests available?"

"I haven't seen either one of them since the cave-in."

"They could still be alive," Reverend Percell suggests. "Should we try to search for them?"

"Are you offering to help us?" I ask.

"Of course. One question though before we begin. Those around me witnessed the vision of Jesus and saw the importance He placed on the rosary. We don't have anyone to explain what it means. Will you teach us?"

"I'll do my best."

As we're talking, more and more people are coming from all corners of the compass, including women in hijabs, congregating on St. Faustina's lawn. Everyone must have seen the same vision. They're looking at me for direction because I'm holding what they are after in my hands—the rosary. The realization that others might have survived drives me to action. I start by addressing everyone within earshot.

"Do we have any firemen, police officers, or experienced search and rescue people here?" No hands go up. Oh, boy. Looks like I'm going to have to wing this. Sucking in a deep breath, I begin to formulate the game plan. "The first thing we need to do is sift through the wreckage for survivors. Who here knows about big machinery or whether there is any in the area we can use to speed up our efforts?" Four hands go up. I send them on their way. "The rest of us will organize into groups, going from building to building, searching the rubble."

People shift into action mode, looking to me for direction throughout the day, making me wonder how I got to be in charge. Running a clothing store is one thing. Making life and death decisions for the community is entirely another. The responsibility is incredibly draining. I hope we find Father Kramer soon because, even though I'm management material, I'm certainly not qualified to organize a fledgling civilization.

We work late into the night, some resting early in the evening so they can get up later and dig until morning. I take one of the later shifts, catch a power nap, and then it's back to a full day's worth of supervising and heavy lifting when needed. There is still a long way to go. Our teams have pulled more than fifty people from the wreckage around town, but there is no sign of Kylie, Miguel, or Father Kramer. I've set up a salvage area for important items found in the wreckage. There's a pile for tents, generators, food, water, blankets, medicine, tools, garden implements, tarps, and even clothing. The exhausted workers sleep right out on the lawn, atop broken pews and on mattresses pulled from destroyed homes.

By the next day, the doctors and nurses have set up a large triage area in the middle of town. I've sent them every generator and tent that we have found so they can take care of the injured. Their organizational abilities under such rustic conditions are impressive, but St. Faustina's ruins remain the town's unofficial headquarters.

Later in the afternoon, I get word that Danica has been found. She's banged up, but awake and talking, over in the triage area. Bishop Crowley wasn't as lucky. His body was discovered in the middle of a field about two miles from the church. At least, they're pretty sure it's him. The head and limbs have been torn off, but the merlot colored robe on the torso and priestly collar are a match. The survivors have placed the decision on me as how to handle his burial. Should a bishop be given a special spot? Or, do we lower him into one of the mass graves being filled on the outskirts of town? Feeling stressed by the zillions of decisions I have had to make today, I plop down onto a damp wingback chair and run my fingers through my hair, as if taming my disheveled strands will do the same for my frazzled nerves.

Taking a breather, I sip from a bottle of water, watching the front loader remove large piles of broken bricks from the foundation. The people have been working for hours to unearth the entrance to the basement. It's been slow going, because we don't want to run over any survivors who may still be trapped beneath. The last bit of hope I have at finding my friends resides in that basement.

As I'm sitting on the chair, Mr. Hurley, a hunched old man who probably weighs ninety pounds wet, comes up to me all agog. Late last night he introduced himself to me with shovel in hand as 'an eighty-six-years young servant of the Lord, here to dig out the injured.' Meeting him has been a bright spot amid the cleanup efforts. Instead of having Mr. Hurley dig through rubble, though, I put him in charge of the Rosary Brigade. Since the vision in the sky, dozens upon dozens of people, some who are coming to Christianity for the very first time, have shown up with all kinds of questions about the rosary, and Catholicism in general. Mr. Hurley's very important mission is to put together a band of teachers to instruct anyone who wants to learn.

"Ma'am, we've rounded up twenty sets of beads," he informs me, "but we got over 300 students. What should we do?"

"Are you good with your hands, Mr. Hurley?"

"Rebuilt seven classic cars from the ground up, so I reckon yes."

"Perfect." I hand him my grandmother's twine rosary. "Do you think you could duplicate this, if we find some string?"

"It looks simple enough." He runs his fingers over the knotted beads, bringing them up to his eyeball for closer examination. "I think me and the missus can figure it out."

"I know you can."

"We found the entrance!" a man on the rescue team hollers. Men and women begin to stream onto the foundation to pull chunks of concrete out of the stairwell by hand. Mr. Hurley and I join them, passing chunks on down the line. It takes us about twenty minutes to create a dark opening.

"Hello," one of the rescuers calls into the darkness. "Is there anybody down there?"

"Glory be," a male voice, sounding like Father Kramer, calls from down in the basement. "What took you so long?"

Cheers rise up from the rescuers. Encouraged, we begin to work even faster, clearing the rest of the path within minutes. Miguel's familiar face appears out of the stairwell. He's helping Father hobble up the stairs.

"My leg is broken," the priest says, seeming in good spirits. "But, overall I'm doing quite well."

"Miguel!" I'd hug him, but he's holding up Father Kramer.

"Gina!" he calls back, face lighting up at the sight of me. "Praise Jesus Christ, you made it. Kylie is going to be ecstatic."

"She's okay then?" I ask breathlessly.

"Perfectly fine." He uses his head to point backwards. "And on her way up."

More beautiful words have rarely been spoken. My heart does happy flip-flops in my chest. The line of smiling people coming up the stairs can't move fast enough for my liking. Watching them emerge one by one, I feel like a kid sifting through a cereal box, eagerly trying to get to the toy prize. *Where is she?*

Meanwhile, as the people come up from the basement to see the drastically altered landscape for the first time, their smiles fade into shock and sorrow. Everything goes quiet as the rest of us give them space to absorb this new reality.

Finally, my best friend comes up out of the darkness. She's carrying a stack of folded white table linens in her good arm. It feels like she's been gone for years, off fighting a bloody war, and today she has come home. Upon seeing me waiting for her, she drops her linens, lets out a joyful shriek, and flings herself into my open arms.

"You're alive!" she exlaims.

"You, too!" I squeak, hugging her close, while trying to avoid her injured shoulder.

"Back up a little," she suddenly says, taking a step back. "We're mucking up my wedding dress."

"Huh?" I look down to notice we're standing on the table linens. "Wedding dress?"

"You heard me." She gives an elfish grin. "Two days buried alive with no guarantee of rescue gives a couple time to think. Life is short and unpredictable, so Miguel and I swore to each other that if we ever got out of that hole, we would get married as soon as possible."

"That's awesome," I say, helping her pick up the linens. "Congratulations."

Kylie's gaze goes from the destruction to the most gorgeous sunset our generation has ever laid eyes on. Free of haze, the sky is painted in serene blues, tropical corals, and magical pinks.

"We have entered the thousand years of peace," she whispers. "I am sure of it."

"A thousand years of peace." I savor the words, liking the sound of them, but I'm not sure what they mean. "Can you please translate from prophet-speak into plain English?"

"In Scripture, a thousand years doesn't stand for a literal number. It's simply means 'a very long time'. In other words, Satan has been bound.

The world, united under one Church, is about to enjoy an extended period of peace."

"What about the Antichrist and the Final Judgment—where do they fit into all of this?"

"They're still coming. Men continue to have free will and the capacity to sin, so the peace won't last forever. Nothing on Earth ever does."

"I guess I'll just have to take life one day at a time."

"Hey, everybody. I got some good news," a woman shouts happily from somewhere in the distance. "A couple of crazy kids have decided to tie the knot!"

I can't help but laugh. News sure travels fast in our budding new community.

"Woohoo!" a man yells. "Let's celebrate!"

"Where is our bride-to-be?" a chubby middle-aged woman asks as she scans the crowd. When she spots Kylie, she waves enthusiastically. "There you are, sweetie pie!"

The woman and a herd of other motherly types quickly surround Kylie, whisking her away so fast that I'm left following after them with my eyes. Surely, Kylie didn't mean they were getting married this instant. Then again, maybe I should hurry after them … A tap on the shoulder pulls me out of my thoughts.

Thinking yet another person wants something from me, I turn around with a tired sigh. I look up to see a towering young man with jet black hair. It's Zachary Lombardi. I blink in surprise. He's offering me his metal thermos.

"Well, hello there, Gina. Fancy meeting you here." He grins in that wonderful dorky way. I want to throw my arms around him, but I follow his lead and act like it's just another ordinary day. "Would you like a cup of hot cocoa?"

"That's very generous of you … Robert," I tease with a coy smile. "But is there really hot cocoa in that thermos?"

"It was hot when I poured it three days ago."

Bypassing the thermos, I reach around to hug him close. My head fits under his chin like a puzzle piece. He holds on to me a little longer and a little tighter than I expected. But I like it. When we let go, there's tears in his eyes.

"Thanks to your last vlog, I realized what was going on and fled the campus before the Neuists made it to my building. You're the reason I was safely hunkered down in a friend's basement when the darkness came." His normally booming voice lowers to barely a whisper. "The university is gone, Gina. There is nothing left in the city." His voice wavers. Clearing his throat, he tries again. "The roads are impassable on four wheels, so I traded down to two." He points out a motorcycle parked in the grass. I didn't hear the roar of the engine over the noise of the big machinery. "It took me eight hours to travel what normally only takes one. Along the way, I saw apple trees in blossom, fields full of spinach, and strawberries ready for the picking. It's beautiful out there among the destruction."

"All of nature was dead or dying a few days ago—how can that be?"

"God is good," Zach says, matter-of-fact.

"Yes, He is," I say, truly believing it. "What brings you to Burlington?"

"My family's farm is twenty miles north of here. I was riding up to see if they made it through the storm, but then I spotted a good-looking brunette on the side of the road and decided to stop to ask her a question. Pathetically, I lost my nerve and started talking about cocoa."

"If you hadn't lost your nerve, what would you have asked her?"

"Would you like to explore the new world with me?"

A huge smile breaks across my face, but not wanting to spoil our playful exchange, I reply, "Too bad you lost your nerve because I'm pretty sure she would have said yes. That is, if you were willing to help search for her missing aunt and cousins after you checked up on your family."

"Do you really believe that's what she would have said?"

"Probably. But first she would have wanted some cocoa."

"You know, I would do anything for that girl, given the chance."

We stand there, both beaming at each other, while the work crews clear away the last bit of debris on the church floor. A squad of ladies follows behind to sweep it clean. From the corner of my eye, I notice a group of high school students wheeling a fully intact piano up the cement handicap ramp. Elementary-aged children are running around, passing out hymn books salvaged from the leveled Lutheran church across the way. I take the one offered to me, watching as three high school boys begin to erect poles made of broken lumber around the marble altar, which is cracked but still standing upright. The girls have found boxes of white Christmas tree lights and are stringing them along the poles.

One of their mothers is showing them how to hook up the strands to a car battery. When the twinkly lights come on, a smattering of applause breaks out. My gaze goes from the artificial lights to the night sky above, traveling deeper into the universe than ever before. The stars have never shined so bright. I look over to see that the high school orchestra has gathered together with its instruments at the ready. Despite his broken leg, Father Kramer has somehow made it up to the altar. He's struggling to remain upright on a homemade crutch, with two altar servers are holding candles on either side of him.

Caught up in Zach's company, I hadn't noticed people of every creed, gathering around for the wedding, or Kylie standing there in a dress and a veil made of white table linens. She's holding a bouquet of purple clover in her hands. Miguel is beside her in a tie and black suit jacket that looks a little too tight.

"Holy Matrimony," I marvel aloud. "They're really going to do it."

Two warbling elderly voices sound from behind us: "Your presence is requested." Glancing back, I see Mr. and Mrs. Hurley pushing at us from behind, urging us toward the front of the church. "We need a Maid of Honor and a Best Man. The bride asked us to come find you."

"But, but ..." Zach tries to protest. "I hardly know them."

The Hurleys are not listening. Before we know it, Zach and I are standing under the twinkly lights, on either side of the happy couple.

"Page 267, everybody," Reverend Percell calls out from a podium made of crates. The high school musicians raise their instruments. I quickly turn to the proper page, *The Strife Is O'er,* holding it up so Zach and I can share. At the Reverend's prompting, the orchestra begins. The remnant of the Baptist choir leads the vocals and we all join in.

Alleluia, alleluia, alleluia!
The strife is o'er, the battle done,
the victory of life is won;
the song of triumph has begun.
Alleluia!

Alleluia, alleluia, alleluia!
The three sad days are quickly sped,
He rises glorious from the dead:
all glory to our risen Head!
Alleluia!

Alleluia, alleluia, alleluia!
He closed the yawning gates of Hell,
the bars from heaven's high portals fell;
let hymns of praise His triumphs tell!
Alleluia!

The lyrics sink deep, carrying my soul to new heights. Everyone must be feeling the same, because there is not a dry eye under the stars tonight. Since waking up on Easter, I have felt a closeness with God that I've never enjoyed before. What amazes me is that through Him, I'm in communion with those around me, both the living and the dead in Christ. This is the way it was always meant to be, I realize. Like Kylie and Miguel, the survivors have come together in hopeful anticipation. The ancient rite has become new again. Together, we will rebuild the church. It will be simpler, holier, and good. It's a wonder I don't faint away from the intensity of the bliss.

After the ceremony concludes, the celebration moves off to the church lawn, underneath the trees where the school girls and boys have hung homemade Chinese lanterns. The piano plays a peppy tune. The little kids bop around to the beat. The pretzels and the chips are opened. Wine is poured into plastic cups. The crowd urges the Maid of Honor, that's me, to make a toast.

I raise my Solo cup into the air and begin, "Dear Followers … of Jesus Christ: I am Gina Applegate, the Bride's *sister from a different mister*, as we used to say. During the fading of the light, I put my hope in all the wrong things. I was sure that science, education, politics, and money, working together, were going to save the world. Only in hindsight do I understand that the pursuit of these things made us lose sight of our true purpose. This blindness is what brought the modern era to a violent end. Because the only way to achieve real peace is through Him.

"And in Him, we are one family. Like newlyweds, we will start a new life together, based on the Truth that Jesus Christ is Lord. The task won't be easy, but nothing worth doing ever is." I pause, realizing I'm not philosophizing for my vlog. This is a wedding. "What I'm trying to say, my dear brothers and sisters, the rebuilding of society begins with people, so God bless you Kylie and Miguel, and get busy making little ones for the Kingdom of God."

Miguel and Kylie laugh and raise their glasses to give them a clink. The guests do the same and shout, "Here, here!"

The music changes to a more romantic tune, like something you might hear on a gondola in Venice. Miguel leads the bride onto the grassy area designated as the dance floor. They gaze at the future in each other's eyes as they sway to the music. After one song fades into the next, I slip my fingers into Zach's. He escorts me to the dance floor. For a big guy, he moves like a dream. A glowing butterfly flutters around us while we waltz. *Thank you, Grammy,* I whisper as it wings its way back up to the heavens.

Dear Awesome Reader:

As a struggling independent author, I rely on the goodwill of my readers to get the word out. If you enjoyed *Comet Dust* please tell your friends and consider leaving a review at your favorite book place. Thank you so much.

Sincerely,

C. D. Verhoff

A note from the author . . .

This book was written because of an intense dream I had when I was around Gina's age. I shared the experience with those who were closest to me and went on with my life. Several years later, I stumbled upon the image of the Divine Mercy for the very first time and couldn't get over how much it looked like the vision of Jesus from my dream. Sometime after that I came across a description about a strange event called the *Illumination of Conscience*. It had so many similarities to that old dream, I had to learn more. Thus my interest in eschatology was born. Inevitably, some of that dream has interspersed itself into the novel, but I do not claim personal mystical knowledge of the future. When I wrote the dream down by hand, it wasn't even a full two pages long. Most of my inspiration came from the prophecies of the saints and scripture. While I find the tribulation a fascinating subject, I don't spend a lot of time worrying about the apocalypse or trying to discern dates. That's not the point of prophecy. It serves as a warning to repent before it's too late, because no matter where we fall on the cosmic timeline, the world is going to end for every single one of us. And, that's a certainty. Knowing I'm a sinner, in desperate need of forgiveness, I'm drawn to the Divine Mercy. Jesus, I trust in You.

A heartfelt thank you to my multi-talented critique buddy and first line of defense, James Vernon, author of the popular *Bound to the Abyss* series; to Eric Postma of Gingerman Editorial for his helpful advice at every level; to my trustworthy proofreader Lisa Nicholas of Mitey Editing for expertly pruning away the weeds; to my beta reader, a hospice nurse full of heart and wisdom, Kathy Kalina, author of *Midwife for Souls: Spiritual Care for the Dying* and *Wisdom for Living the Final Season*; to Padraig Caughey, author of *On Meeting Mary and Learning to Pray*, for calling me a 'seanachie' and lending me his insights; to my amazing family for their prayers and support; to Our Lady of Consolation, Saint Pope John Paul II, and my parents for their intercession. Last, but certainly not least, thank you to Jesus Christ—for everything.

Holy God, Holy Mighty One, Holy Immortal One,

Have mercy on us and on the whole world.

PROPHECIES FOR YOUR DISCERNMENT

Prophecies coming from sources other than Scripture and Sacred Tradition fall under the heading of 'private revelation'. No matter how holy the saint, even if he or she claims it came from the mouth of Our Lord, belief in private revelation is never binding upon the faithful. Use caution in approaching this material.

For your convenience, the prophecies have been divided into separate sections: *The Future, Illumination of Conscience (The Warning), The Miracle, Three Days of Darkness,* and *The Era of Peace.*

SECTION 1: The Future
(Politics, Religion, Morality and Ecology)

Luke 21: 25-26: And there shall be signs in the sun, and in the moon, and in the stars; and upon the earth distress of nations, with perplexity; the sea and the waves roaring; Men's hearts failing them for fear, and for looking after those things which are coming on the earth: for the powers of heaven shall be shaken.

Our Lady of Akita, Message To Sister Agnes Sasagawa (1973): As I told you, if men do not repent and better themselves, the Father will inflict a terrible punishment on all humanity. It will be a punishment greater than the deluge, such as one will never have seen before. Fire will fall from the sky and will wipe out a great part of humanity, the good as well as the bad, sparing neither priests nor faithful. The survivors will find themselves so desolate that they will envy the dead. The only arms which will remain for you will be the Rosary and the Sign left by My Son. Each day recite the prayers of the Rosary. With the Rosary, pray for the Pope, the bishops and priests.

The work of the devil will infiltrate even into the Church in such a way that one will see cardinals opposing cardinals, bishops against bishops. The priests who venerate me will be scorned and opposed by their confreres ... churches and altars sacked; the Church will be full of those who accept compromises and the demon will press many priests and consecrated souls to leave the service of the Lord. The demon will be especially implacable against souls consecrated to God. The thought

302

of the loss of so many souls is the cause of my sadness. If sins increase in number and gravity, there will be no longer pardon for them.

Sister Elena Aiello (1895 - 1961): Oh, what a horrible vision I see! A great revolution is going on in Rome! They are entering the Vatican. The Pope is all alone; he is praying. They are holding the Pope. They take him by force. They knock him down to the floor. They are tying him. Oh. God! Oh, God! They are kicking him. What a horrible scene! How dreadful!

~

Russia will march upon all the nations of Europe, particularly Italy, and will raise her flag over the dome of St. Peter's. Italy will be severely tried by a great revolution, and Rome will be purified in blood for its many sins, especially those of impurity. The flock is about to be dispersed and the Pope will suffer greatly.

Sister Lucia (January 3, 1944): *I felt my spirit flooded by a light-filled mystery, which is God, and in Him I saw and heard*: the point of a lance like a flame that is detached, touches the axis of the Earth and it trembles. Mountains, cities, towns and villages with their inhabitants are buried. The sea, the rivers, the clouds exceed their boundaries, inundating and dragging with them in a vortex houses and people in a number that cannot be counted. It is the purification of the world from the sin in which it is immersed.

Note: This vision, which seems to describe a comet hurling toward Earth and its aftermath, allegedly occurred while Lucia was praying before the tabernacle at her convent. She wrote it down in her diary, but it wasn't made public until recently. It's authenticity hasn't been confirmed (or denied) by her convent, so use extra discernment.

Pope Pius IX (1792 - 1846): The present wickedness of the world is only the beginning of the sorrows which must take place before the end of the world.

Pope St. Pius X (1835-1914): "What I have seen is terrifying! Will I be the one, or will it be a successor? What is certain is that the Pope will leave Rome and, in leaving the Vatican, he will have to pass over the dead bodies of his priests!" He then cautioned the witnesses, "Do not tell anyone this while I am alive.

~

Just before his death, Pius had another vision. "I have seen one of my successors, of the same name, who was fleeing over the bodies of his brethren. He will take refuge in some hiding place; but after a brief

303

respite, he will die a cruel death. Respect for God has disappeared from human hearts. They wish to efface even God's memory. This perversity is nothing less than the beginning of the last days of the world.

Hellen Wallraff (19th century): Someday a Pope will flee from Rome in the company of only four Cardinals...

The Ecstatic of Tours (19th Century): Before the war breaks out again, food will be scarce and expensive. There will be little work for the workers, and fathers will hear their children crying for food. There will be earthquakes and signs in the sun. Toward the end, darkness will cover the Earth. When everyone believes that peace is ensured, when everyone least expects it, the great happening will begin. Revolution will break out in Italy almost at the same time as in France. For some time the Church will be without a Pope.

Blessed Rembordt (18th Century): God will punish the world when men have devised marvelous inventions that will lead them to forgetting God. They will fly like birds and have horseless carriages. But they will laugh at God thinking they are very clever. There will be signs in the heavens but men in their pride will laugh them off. Men will indulge in voluptuousness and lewd fashion will be seen everywhere.

Venerable Bartholomew Holzhauser (17th Century): The fifth period of the Church, which began circa 1520, will end with the arrival of the holy Pope and of the powerful Monarch who is called "Help From God" because he will restore everything. The fifth period is one of affliction, desolation, humiliation, and poverty for the Church. Jesus Christ will purify His people through cruel wars, famines, plagues, epidemics, and other horrible calamities. He will also afflict and weaken the Latin Church with many heresies. It is a period of defections, calamities and exterminations. Those Christians who survive the sword, plague and famines, will be few on Earth.

During this period, many men will abuse of the freedom of conscience conceded to them. It is of such men that Jude the Apostle spoke when he said, "These men blaspheme whatever they do not understand; and they corrupt whatever they know naturally as irrational animals do." They will ridicule Christian simplicity; they will call it folly and nonsense, but they will have the highest regard for advanced knowledge, and for the skill by which the axioms of law, the precepts of morality, the Holy Canons and religious dogmas are clouded by senseless questions and elaborate arguments.

These are the evil times, a century full of dangers and calamities. Heresy is everywhere, and the followers of heresy are in power almost everywhere. but God will permit a great evil against His Church: Heretics and tyrants will come suddenly and unexpectedly; they will break into the Church. They will enter Italy and lay Rome waste; they will burn down churches and destroy everything.

Maria Laach Monastery (16th Century): The twentieth century will bring death and destruction, apostasy from the Church, discord in families, cities and governments; it will be the century of three great wars with intervals of a few decades. They will become ever more devastating and bloody and will lay in ruins not only Germany, but finally all countries of East and West. After a terrible defeat of Germany will follow the next great war. There will be no bread for people anymore and no fodder for animals. Poisonous clouds, manufactured by human hands, will sink down and exterminate everything. The human mind will be seized by insanity.

Mother Shipton (16th Century): The great chastisement will come when carriages go without horses. It will come when thoughts will fly around the world in an instant. When the many taxes are funded to levy wars.

John of the Cleft Rock (14th Century): Towards the end of the world, tyrants and hostile mobs will rob the Church and the clergy of all their possessions and will afflict and martyr them. Those who heap the most abuse upon them will be held in high esteem. At that time, the Pope with his cardinals will have to flee Rome in tragic circumstances to a place where they will be unknown. The Pope will die a cruel death in his exile. The sufferings of the Church will be much greater than at any previous time in her history. But God will raise a holy Pope, and the Angels will rejoice. Enlightened by God, this man will rebuild almost the whole world through his holiness. He will lead everyone to the true Faith.

Johannes Friede (13th Century): When the great time will come, in which mankind will face its last, hard trial, it will be foreshadowed by striking changes in nature. The alteration between cold and heat will become more intensive, storms will have more catastrophic effects, earthquakes will destroy great regions, and the seas will overflow many lowlands. Not all of it will be the result of natural causes, but mankind will penetrate into the bowels of the earth and will reach into the clouds, gambling with its own existence. Before the powers of destruction will succeed in their design, the universe will be thrown into disorder, and the age of iron will plunge into nothingness.

When nights will be filled with more intensive cold and days with heat, a new life will begin in nature. The heat means radiation from the earth, the cold the waning light of the sun. Only a few years more and you will become aware that sunlight has grown perceptibly weaker. When even your artificial light will cease to give service, the great event in the heavens will be near.

Saint Hildegard (12th Century): The time is coming when princes and peoples will reject the authority of the Pope. Some countries will prefer their own Church rulers to the Pope. The German Empire will be divided.

Before the comet comes, many nations, the good excepted, will be scourged by want and famine. The great nation in the ocean that is inhabited by people of different tribes and descent will be devastated by earthquake, storm, and tidal wave. It will be divided and, in great part, submerged. That nation will also have many misfortunes at sea and lose its colonies.

[After the] great Comet, the great nation will be devastated by earthquakes, storms, and great waves of water, causing much want and plagues. The ocean will also flood many other countries, so that all coastal cities will live in fear, with many destroyed.

All sea coast cities will be fearful, and many of them will be destroyed by tidal waves, and most living creatures will be killed, and even those who escape will die from a horrible disease. For in none of those cities does a person live according to the Laws of God.

A powerful wind will rise in the North, carrying heavy fog and the densest dust, and it will fill their throats and eyes so that they will cease their butchery and be stricken with a great fear.

Premol (5th century): Everywhere there is war! Peoples and nations are pitted against each other...but mercy, mercy for Rome! But Thou hearest not my entreaties, and Rome also collapses in tumult. And I see the King of Rome with his Cross and his Tiara, shaking the dust off his shoes, and hastening in his flight to other shores. Thy Church, O Lord, is torn apart by her own children. One camp is faithful to the fleeing Pontiff; the other is object to the new government of Rome which has broken the Tiara. But Almighty God will, in His mercy, put an end to this confusion and a new age will begin. Then, said the Spirit, this is the beginning of the End of Time.

St. Anthony the Great (3rd Century): A time is coming when men will go mad, and when they see someone who is not mad, they will attack him, saying, "You are mad; you are not like us."

SECTION 2: The Warning
(Also known as The Illumination of Conscience)

Revelation 6:12-17: And I beheld when he had opened the sixth seal, and, lo, there was a great earthquake; and the sun became black as sackcloth of hair, and the moon became as blood; And the stars of heaven fell unto the earth, even as a fig tree casteth her untimely figs, when she is shaken of a mighty wind. And the heaven departed as a scroll when it is rolled together; and every mountain and island were moved out of their places. And the kings of the earth, and the great men, and the rich men, and the chief captains, and the mighty men, and every bondman, and every free man, hid themselves in the dens and in the rocks of the mountains; And said to the mountains and rocks, Fall on us, and hide us from the face of him that sitteth on the throne, and from the wrath of the Lamb: For the great day of his wrath is come; and who shall be able to stand?

Maria Esperanza (1928-2004): The consciences of this beloved people must be violently shaken so that they may "put their house in order." A great moment is approaching, a great day of light... it is the hour of decision for mankind.

St. Faustina Kowalska (1905 – 1938): Jesus said to St. Faustina: Before I come as the just Judge, I am coming first as the King of Mercy. Before the day of justice arrives, there will be given to people a sign in the heavens of this sort: All light in the heavens will be extinguished, and there will be great darkness over the whole earth. Then the sign of the cross will be seen in the sky, and from the openings where the hands and the feet of the Savior were nailed will come forth great lights which will light up the earth for a period of time. This will take place shortly before the last day.

St. Faustina explains her experience: Once I was summoned to the judgment (seat) of God. I stood alone before the Lord. Jesus appeared such as we know Him during His Passion. After a moment, His wounds disappeared, except for five, those in His hands, His feet, and His side. Suddenly I saw the complete condition of my soul as God sees it. I could clearly see all that is displeasing to God. I did not know that even the smallest transgressions will have to be accounted for. What a moment! Who can describe it? To stand before the Thrice-Holy-God!

Jesus said: I am prolonging the time of mercy for the sake of sinners. But woe to them if they do not recognize this time of My visitation.

Marie-Julie Jahenny (1850 - 1941): There will come three days of complete darkness. Only blessed candles made of wax will give some light during this horrible darkness. One candle will last for three days, but they will not give light in the houses of the Godless. Lightening will penetrate your houses, but it will not put out the blessed candles. Neither wind, nor storm, nor earthquake will put out the blessed candles.

Blessed Anna Maria Taigi (18th Century): A great purification will come upon the world preceded by an "Illumination of Conscience" in which everyone will see themselves as God sees them.

St. Edmond Campion (16th Century): I pronounce a great day, not wherein any temporal potentate should minister, but wherein the Terrible Judge should reveal all men's consciences and try every man of each kind of religion. This is the day of change.

Thomas à Kempis (15th Century): This sign of the cross will be in the heavens when the Lord comes to judge. Then all the servants of the cross, who during life made themselves one with the Crucified, will draw near with great trust to Christ, the judge.

SECTION 3: The Miracle

In *Comet Dust* a miraculous vision of light akin to the burning bush or Ezekiel's wheels, accompanied by physical healings, are occurring in places like Fatima, Guadalupe, Lourdes and Rome City. I chose these places because in real life, genuine apparitions of Jesus and Mary have already occurred.

However, the messages given to visionaries of Garabandal (1960s), concerning the upcoming "Miracle," makes no mention of The Miracle happening anywhere other than Garabandal. In fact, the seers are under the impression that on that day only those who happen to be at Garabandal will be healed. Additionally, a mysterious Permanent Sign will be left there for all the world to see.

Fast forward a few decades to a different set of apparitions in Medjugorje (1980s to the present). The six visionaries from this location also mention a Miraculous Permanent Sign. They make no reference to the one in Garabandal, but in my mind they seem to have been promised a very similar thing. Extrapolating from this material, and taking a bold poetic liberty, in my fictional account I decided to spread the Miracle out to all genuine apparition sites across the globe, giving more people access to its healing graces, including the main character who travels to Rome City, Indiana to witness it for herself.

By the way, I didn't make up the *Our Lady of America* apparition mentioned in the story. In real life the apparition is tied to Rome City because Our Lady appeared there to Sister Mildred Neuzil (also known as Sister Mary Ephrem) in 1956.

Note that both Garabandal and Medjugorje are controversial apparitions. They do not have church approval at this time. Including a mention of them in the book is in no way a personal endorsement of the authenticity of either message.

Medjugorje (1981 to Present)*: In 1981, Mary, Mother of Jesus, allegedly visited six young teenagers, two boys and four girls, at Medjugorje, Bosnia Herzgovina, and announced ten secrets, future events that are going to unfold in the future.

"It is a Warning. It has to be seen…this has to shake us up so the world will start thinking…but to prove there is a God…the first Warning will be self-explanatory."

Two of the Seers Were Interviewed
About the Alleged Miracle in 2008

Mirjana: Yes, Our Lady will leave a sign at the Hill of Apparitions, and everybody will see that she was truly present there and that it's something from God. And the sign will be something that when you see it, it will be clear that it could not have been created by human hands. But you won't see it from America, you'll have to come there to see it. Pilgrims from the United States often ask me if we will be able to see it from home or will we have to go there to see it … The third secret will be a visible sign at Medjugorje – permanent, indestructible, and beautiful.

Vicka: The sign will remain on Podbrdo, and one will have to come here to see it. This sign will be indestructible and will remain in that place forever. I want to say about those people who will see it and not believe, the Madonna leaves everyone free to believe or not, but those are ones whose hearts are too closed. It's the same thing as the Madonna said to us, "If one wants to go to Heaven, he will go to Heaven. If one wants to go to Hell, he will go to Hell." Those people who are far away from God and do not want to believe, they will not believe in the sign. For those who do not know God, but have good intentions and a desire to love, they will be benefited by the sign. But I think that those who do everything against God, they will run away from the sign. They will not believe.

*This apparition is ongoing, still under investigation, and highly controversial. The Church has not approved it, so approach with great caution.

Garabandal Apparitions (1961 – 1965)*: *Four young schoolgirls in the rural village of San Sebastián de Garabandal in Northern Spain allegedly received messages from Saint Michael the Archangel and the Virgin Mary over numerous visits.*

Conchita (1965): The Blessed Virgin told me that *a warning* would be given before *the miracle*. The warning is a thing that comes directly from God. No one can escape it. It will be visible all over the world. We will feel it bodily and interiorly. The warning is like a chastisement, a terrifying thing for the good as well as for the wicked. It will be like a revelation of our sins. We shall see the consequences of the sins we have committed. God will send the warning to purify us, so that we may better appreciate the miracle by which He clearly proves His love for us and hence His desire that we fulfill the message. The warning will draw the good closer to God and it will warn the wicked that the end of time is coming.

Interview with Conchita (1973)

Q. What is going to happen on that day (of the Miracle)?

A. I will tell you all that I can, just as the Virgin told it to me. She told me that God was going to perform a great Miracle, and that there would be no doubt about the fact that it was a miracle. It will come directly from God with no human intervention. A day will come–and she told me the day, the month, and the year so I know the exact date.

Q. When is that day?

A. It is coming soon, but I can't reveal it until eight days before the date.

Q. What exactly is going to happen on that day?

A. I am not permitted to say exactly what is going to happen. What I can reveal is that the Virgin said that everyone who would be there (in Garabandal) on that day would see it. The sick who are there will be cured, no matter what their disease or religion. However, they have to be there.

Q. On the day of the Miracle, did you say that those present would be converted?

A. The Virgin said that everyone present would believe. They would see that this was coming directly from God. All sinners present would be converted. She also said that you would be able to take pictures and televise it. Also, from that moment on there would be a permanent sign at the pines that everyone will be able to see and touch but not feel. I can't explain it.

An even later Interview with Conchita (Originally published in a 1990 Special Edition by *The Workers of Our Lady of Mt. Carmel*):

Q. On the day of the Miracle there will be an extraordinary sign not made by human hands?

A. Yes. And this sign will remain until the end of time.

Q. Did you say that this sign could be televised and photographed but not felt by touching?

A. It will be like smoke. You can touch it but not feel it.

*This apparition has been investigated by the church and NOT approved, which incidentally, was exactly what Mary said would happen. Approach with extreme caution. I'm including it because I drew on it for the 'Miracle in Rome City' portion of the book.

Pope St. Pius X (1835-1914): Since the whole world is against God and His Church, it is evident that He has reserved the victory over His enemies to Himself. This will be more obvious when it is considered that the root of all our present evils is to be found in the fact that those with talents and vigor crave earthly pleasures, and not only desert God but repudiate Him altogether. Thus it appears they cannot be brought back in any other way except through an act that cannot be ascribed to any secondary agency, and thus all will be forced to look to the supernatural.

There will come a great wonder, which will fill the world with astonishment. This wonder will be preceded by the triumph of revolution. The church will suffer exceedingly. Her servants and her chieftain will be mocked, scourged, and martyred.

~

There will come a great prodigy, which will fill the world with awe. But this prodigy will be preceded by the triumph of a revolution during which the Church will go through ordeals that are beyond description.

Marie-Julie Jahenny (1850-1941): All the works approved by the infallible Church will cease to exist as they are today for a time. In this sorrowful annihilation, brilliant signs will be manifested on earth. If, because of the wickedness of men, Holy Church will be in darkness, the Lord will also send darkness that will stop the wicked in their search of wickedness.

SECTION 4: The Three Days of Darkness

Revelation 9:13-19: And the sixth angel sounded, and I heard a voice from the four horns of the golden altar which is before God, Saying to the sixth angel which had the trumpet, Loose the four angels which are bound in the great river Euphrates. And the four angels were loosed, which were prepared for an hour, and a day, and a month, and a year, for to slay the third part of men. And the number of the army of the horsemen was twice ten thousand times ten thousand: and I heard the number of them. And thus I saw the horses in the vision, and them that sat on them, having breastplates of fire, and of jacinth, and brimstone: and the heads of the horses were as the heads of lions; and out of their mouths issued fire and smoke and brimstone. By these three was the third part of men killed, by the fire, and by the smoke, and by the brimstone, which issued out of their mouths.

Akita, Japan Apparitions (1973): *Mary to Sister Agnes Sasagawa:* In order that the world might know His anger, the Heavenly Father is preparing to inflict a great chastisement on all mankind. As I told you, if men do not repent and better themselves, the Father will inflict a terrible punishment on all humanity. It will be a punishment greater than the deluge, such as one will never have seen before. Fire will fall from the sky and will wipe out a great part of humanity, the good as well as the bad, sparing neither priests nor faithful. The survivors will find themselves so desolate that they will envy the dead. The only arms which will remain for you will be the Rosary and the Sign left by My Son. Each day recite the prayers of the Rosary. With the Rosary, pray for the Pope, the bishops and priests.

Marie-Julie Jahenny (1850 - 1941): *Jesus to Marie-Julie:* I forewarn you that a day will be found, and it is already appointed, when there will be little sun, few stars, and no light to take a step outside of your homes, the refuges of My people. The days will be beginning to increase. It will not be at the height of summer nor during the longer days of the year, but when the days are still short. It will not be at the end of the year, but during the first months that I shall give My clear warnings. That day of darkness and lightning will be the first that I shall send to convert the impious, and to see if a great number will return to Me, before the Great Storm which will closely follow. The darkness and lightning of that day will not cover all of France, but a part of Brittany will be tried by it. On the side on which is found the land of the mother of My Immaculate Mother will not be covered by darkness to come, up to your place. All the rest will be in the most terrible fright. From one night to the next, one complete day, the thunder will not cease to rumble. The fire from the lightnings will do a lot of damage, even in the closed homes where someone will be living in sin. My children, that first day will not take away anything from the three others already pointed out and described.

~

The crisis will explode suddenly; the punishments will be shared by all and will succeed one another without interruption.

~

The three days of darkness will be on a Thursday, Friday and Saturday. Days of the Most Holy Sacrament, of the Cross and Our Lady—three days less one night.

~

Our Lady to Marie-Julie: The earth will be covered in darkness, And Hell will be loosed on earth. Thunder and lightning will cause those who have no faith or trust in My Power to die of fear. During these three days of terrifying darkness, no windows must be opened, because no one will be able to see the earth and the terrible colour it will have in those days of punishment without dying at once.

~

The sky will be on fire, the earth will split. During these three days of darkness let the blessed candle be lighted everywhere, no other light will shine ... no one outside a shelter will survive. The earth will shake as at the judgment, and fear will be great. Yes, We will listen to the prayers of your friends; not one will perish. We will need them to publish the glory of the Cross.

~

Our Lady to Marie-Julie: The candles of blessed wax alone will give light during this horrible darkness. One candle alone will be enough for the duration of this night of Hell. In the homes of the wicked and blasphemers, these candles will give no light. Everything will shake except the piece of furniture on which the blessed candle is burning. This will not shake. You will all gather around with the crucifix and my blessed picture. This is what will keep away this terror. During this darkness the devils and the wicked will take on the most hideous shapes. Red clouds like blood will move across the sky. The crash of the thunder will shake the earth and sinister lightning will streak the heavens out of season. The earth will be shaken to its foundations. The sea will rise, its roaring waves will spread over the continent. The earth will become like a vast cemetery. The bodies of the wicked and the just will cover the ground. Three-quarters of the population of the globe will disappear. Half the population of France will be destroyed.

Blessed Gaspar Del Bufalo (19th Century): The death of the impenitent persecutors of the Church will take place during the three days of darkness. He who outlives the darkness and the fear of those three days will think that he is alone on Earth because the whole world will be covered in carcasses.

Prophecy of Mayence (1854): Three days the sun shall rise upwards on the heads of the combatants without being seen through the clouds of smoke.

St. Anna Maria Taigi (1769 - 1837): There shall come over all the earth an intense darkness lasting three days and three nights. Nothing will be visible and the earth will be laden with pestilence, which will claim principally, but not exclusively, the enemies of religion. During this darkness, artificial light will be impossible. Only blessed candles can be lighted and will afford illumination. He who out of curiosity opens his window to look out or leaves his house will fall dead on the spot. During these three days the people should remain in their homes, pray the Rosary, and beg God for mercy.

On this terrible occasion so many of these wicked men, enemies of His Church and of God, shall be killed by this divine scourge, that their corpses round Rome will be as numerous as the fish, which a recent inundation of the Tiber had carried into the city. All the enemies of the Church, secret as well as known, will perish over the earth during that universal darkness, with the exception of a few, whom God will soon convert. The air shall be infected by demons, who will appear under all sorts of visible forms.

~

Three-quarters of the human race will be exterminated, more men than women. No one will escape the terror of these days.

SECTION 5: Era of Peace

In *Comet Dust*, I tried to make it clear that the survivors are not going to enjoy a literal thousand years of peace. Nor did Jesus Christ physically come down to walk among them as He did two thousand years ago. During the Era of Peace, Jesus will reign in their hearts as King of Kings, but His throne remains in heaven.

Revelation, Chapter 20:1-6: And I saw an angel come down from heaven, having the key of the bottomless pit and a great chain in his hand. And he laid hold on the dragon, that old serpent, which is the Devil, and Satan, and bound him a thousand years, And cast him into the bottomless pit, and shut him up, and set a seal upon him, that he should deceive the nations no more, till the thousand years should be fulfilled: and after that he must be loosed a little season. And I saw thrones, and they sat upon them, and judgment was given unto them: and I saw the souls of them that were beheaded for the witness of Jesus, and for the word of God, and which had not worshipped the beast, neither his image, neither had received his mark upon their foreheads, or in their hands; and they lived and reigned with Christ a thousand years. But the rest of the dead lived not again until the thousand years were finished. This is the first resurrection. Blessed and holy is he that hath part in the first resurrection: on such the second death hath no power, but they shall be priests of God and of Christ, and shall reign with him a thousand years.

Cardinal Joseph Ratzinger/Pope Benedict XVI (1927 – ?): The Church will be reduced in its dimensions, it will be necessary to start again. However, from this test a Church would emerge that will have been strengthened by the process of simplification it experienced, by its renewed capacity to look within itself … the Church will be numerically reduced. – *God and the World, 2001; Interview with Peter Seewald*

St. Pope John Paul II (1920 – 2005): This is our great hope and invocation, "Your kingdom come!"—a kingdom of peace, justice and serenity, which will re-establish the original harmony of creation. – *Zenit, General Audience, November 16, 2002*

Cardinal Mario Luigi Ciappi, personal theologian to five different popes (1909 – 1996): Yes, a miracle was promised at Fatima, the greatest miracle in the history of the world, second only to the Resurrection. And that miracle will be an era of peace which has never really been granted before to the world. I believe that this peace will begin in the domestic church, the family, and go out to the parishes and into the diocese, the country, and the world. – *Letter of October 9, 1994 to Jerry and Gwen Coniker of Apostolate for Family Consecration*

Ralph Martin (1975), *significant because prophesied in the presence of Pope Paul VI at St Peter's Basilica:* Because I love you I want to show you what I am doing in the world today. I want to prepare you for what is to come. Days of darkness are coming on the world, days of tribulation. Buildings that are now standing will not be standing. Supports that are there for my people will not be there. I want you to be prepared, My people, to know only Me and to cleave to Me and to have Me in a way deeper than ever before. I will lead you into the desert. I will strip you of everything that you are depending on now, so you depend just on Me. A time of darkness is coming on the world, but a time of glory is coming for My church, a time of glory is coming for My people. I will pour out on you all the gifts of My Spirit. I will prepare you for spiritual combat; I will prepare you for a time of evangelism that the world has never seen. And when you have nothing but Me, you will have everything: land, fields, homes and brothers and sisters and love and joy and peace more than ever before. Be ready, My people, I want to prepare you.

St. Faustina Kowalska (1905 – 1938): Today I saw the glory of God which flows from the image [of the Divine Mercy]. Many souls are receiving graces, although they do not speak of it openly. Even though it has met up with all sorts of vicissitudes, God is receiving glory because of it; and the efforts of Satan and of evil men are shattered and come to naught. In spite of Satan's anger, the Divine Mercy will triumph over the whole world and will be worshiped by all souls. *~Diary: Divine Mercy in My Soul, 1789*

Maria Steiner (19th century): I see the Lord as He will be scourging the world and chastising it in a fearful manner so that few men and women will remain. The monks will have to leave their monasteries, and the nuns will be driven from their convents especially in Italy. The holy Church will be persecuted and Rome will be without a shepherd (brief period). But the Lord showed me how beautiful the world will be after the punishments.

Father Bernard Maria Clausi (19th Century): Before the triumph of the Church comes, God will first take vengeance on the wicked, especially against the godless. It will be a new judgment; the like has never been seen before, and it will be universal. It will be so terrible that those who outlive it will imagine that they are the only ones spared. All people will then be good and contrite. The judgment will come suddenly and be of short duration. Then comes the triumph of the Church and the reign of brotherly love. Happy indeed they who live to see those blessed days. However, before that, evil will have made such progress that it will look like all the devils of Hell were let loose on Earth, so terrible will be the persecution of the wicked against the just, who will have to suffer true martyrdom.

Mother Alphonse Eppinger (19th Century): After God has purified the world, faith and peace will return. Whole nations will adhere to the teachings of the Catholic Church.

Ven. Elizabeth Canori-Mora (1774 - 1825): [T]he sky was covered with clouds so dense and dismal that it was *impossible* to look at them without dismay ... the avenging arm of God will strike the wicked, and in his mighty power He will punish their pride and presumption. God will employ the powers of Hell for the extermination of these impious and heretical persons who desire to overthrow the Church and destroy its foundation ... *Innumerable* legions of demons shall overrun the earth and shall execute the orders of Divine Justice.... Nothing on the earth shall be spared. After this frightful punishment I saw the heavens opening, and St. Peter coming down again upon earth; he was vested in his pontifical robes, and surrounded by a great number of angels, who were chanting hymns in his honor, and they proclaimed him as sovereign of the earth. I saw also St. Paul descending upon the earth. By God's command, he traversed the earth and chained the demons, whom he brought before St. Peter, who commanded them to return into Hell, whence they had come.

Then a great light appeared upon the earth which was the sign of the reconciliation of God with man. The angels conducted before the throne of the prince of the Apostles the small flock that had remained faithful to Jesus Christ. These good and zealous Christians testified to him the most profound respect, praising God and thanking the Apostles for having delivered them from the common destruction, and for having protected the Church of Jesus Christ by *not* permitting her to be infected with the false maxims of the world. St. Peter then chose the new pope. The Church was again organized …

Blessed Mary of Agreda (17th Century): It was revealed to me that through the intercession of Our Mother all heresies will disappear. The victory over heresies has been reserved by Christ for our Blessed Mother.… In the latter days the Lord will in a special manner make Mary known in renowned way. An unusual chastisement of the human race shall take place towards the end.

St Nicholas of Fluh (15th Century): The Church will be punished because the vast majority of its members are perverted (both in deed and doctrine). It shall sink deeper and deeper until she will at last seem to be extinguished, but then she will be victoriously exalted before all.

Abbot Werdin D'Orante (12th Century): The great monarch and the great Pope will precede Antichrist. The nations will be at war for four years and a great part of the world will be destroyed. The Pope will go over the sea carrying the sign of Redemption on his forehead. The great Monarch will come to restore peace and the Pope will share in the victory.

St. John Vianney (1786 – 1859): They will imprison very many persons, and will be guilty of more massacres. They will attempt to kill all priests and all the religious. But this shall not last long. People will imagine that all is lost; but the good God shall save all. It will be like a sign of the last judgment… Religion shall flourish again better than ever before. ~*The Christian Trumpet*

St. Augustine (5th Century): Those who, on the strength of this passage [Revelation 20:1-6], have suspected that the first resurrection is future and bodily, have been moved, among other things, specially by the number of a thousand years, as if it were a fit thing that the saints should thus enjoy a kind of Sabbath rest during that period, a holy leisure after the labors of six thousand years since man was created … (and) there

318

should follow on the completion of six thousand years, as if of six days a kind of seventh-day Sabbath in the succeeding thousand years; and that it is for this purpose the saints rise, viz., to celebrate the Sabbath. And this opinion would not be objectionable, if it were believed that the joys of the saints in that Sabbath shall be spiritual, and consequent on the presence of God.

Lactantius (240 – 320 A.D.): Therefore, the Son of the most high and mighty God ... shall have destroyed unrighteousness, and executed His great judgment, and shall have recalled to life the righteous, who ... will be engaged among men a thousand years, and will rule them with most just command ... Also the prince of devils, who is the contriver of all evils, shall be bound with chains, and shall be imprisoned during the thousand years of the heavenly rule ... Before the end of the thousand years the devil shall be loosed afresh and shall assemble all the pagan nations to make war against the holy city ... then the last anger of God shall come upon the nations, and shall utterly destroy them, and the world shall go down in great conflagration. ~ *"The Divine Institutes", The ante-Nicene Fathers, Vol. 7, p. 211*

Epistle of Barnabas (70-79 A.D.): [W]hen His Son will come and destroy the time of the lawless one and judge the godless, and change the sun and the moon and the stars—then He shall indeed rest on the seventh day ... after giving rest to all things, I will make the beginning of the eighth day, that is, the beginning of another world.

Other Novels By C. D. Verhoff

Resist the Machine (Avant Nation, Book 1). When the nanny state controls your life down to the cellular level, resistance is futile. Or, is it? Clara was genetically engineered to do a specific job, but she wants to forge her own path. A cautionary tale set in a futuristic North America where human beings are treated as commodities and their dignity is violated down to the cellular level.

Escape the Machine (Avant Nation, Book 2). When the government controls the gene pool, what could go wrong? Quite a lot, Clara has learned and the worst is yet to come. Mind-blowing suspense with implications for today.

Kill the Machine (Avant Nation, Book 3). Arriving soon!

The Wish Thief. Modern fantasy with holiday spirit that stays with you long after the last page. A teenage spelunker battles mystical forces in her search for the mother lode.

Red, The First (Prequel, Galatia Series) An alien pandemic has left the people of earth with amazing new abilities, but former used car salesman, Red Wakeland, must rely on the good old-fashioned power of persuasion to prepare them for the battle of their lives. The fate of humanity rides on one man's sales pitch, but can Red close the deal?

Emerge (The Galatia Series, Book 1). After living in a posh underground shelter their entire lives, the last survivors of the human race are plunged into a mind-blowing adventure on the surface of the Earth.

Seeker (The Galatia Series, Book 2). The hunt for the Blood Map is on. Follow the last survivors of the human race as their adventures on a radically altered earth continue.

Printed in Great Britain
by Amazon